THE
BINDING
OF ISAAC

JEFFREY SALLOWAY

Winter Goose
PUBLISHING
where words take flight
wintergoosepublishing.com

Winter Goose Publishing
45 Lafayette Road #114
North Hampton, NH 03862

wintergoosepublishing.com
Contact Information: info@wintergoosepublishing.com

The Binding of Isaac

COPYRIGHT © 2019 by Jeffrey Salloway

First Edition: 2019

Cover Art by Jennifer Beard
Cover Design and Formatting by Winter Goose Publishing

ISBN: 978-1-941058-93-0

Published in the United States of America

For all the children of all the Isaacs

CHAPTER 1

The squat, frame-built houses of Southmoor hunkered close to the earth like ground-gripping birds shielding themselves from the pre-winter chill. The harvest moon was a hole in the cloudless sky that sucked the day's warmth from the soil. Every summer the sun gave its heat to the fields of Midwestern corn and every fall the sky reclaimed the gift by night.

Every Southmoor home was guarded by a black lamppost, lit hours earlier, by a solar switch standing sentinel on the lawn. Each picture window shed second-hand light on a driveway. And each drive poured out black asphalt from the mouth of a thrust-front garage. The back yards leaked darkness into the spaces between the houses. Each street lay north-south or east-west, confused at their corners. And every street culminated ultimately in a cul-de-sac, a dead-end to the monotony.

This night a short figure patrolled the street. Clad in a leather jacket that gently reflected the cold moonlight, he rounded the corner of Linden onto Beech leaning slightly into the turn. On his head set a Persian lamb cap, cocked askew. The hat and the man ambled, a Cossack deprived of his horse, hurrying along, intent on motion without destination. He was not silent. There was babble.

Mumbling, hands exiting from his jacket pockets, he gestured aggressively to no one. He was in conversation, in logical disputation, in animated argument. He was alone. His voice rose and fell, mumbled and mused more and more as words came faster and louder and hands jabbed and poked at no one in particular. He was audible. He was vocal. He was not to be idly dismissed. He spoke to no one visible.

The black and white squad car moved lightless and all-but silent past the corner of Linden and Beech. The two-man patrol didn't wish to frighten the prey. The car slid quietly up to the raised ridge of the asphalt that substituted for a curb. More gliding silently than rolling, it stalked the small man still so involved in his one-sided dialogue he never heard the motor.

The audible click of the blue bubble-gum machines on the light bar alerted him. He stopped in the midst of a critical hand stab of logic and stood for a brief instant in the night without turning to face this intrusion in his argument.

The squad car stopped, the lights did not. The spotlight from the driver's side swept the small man's face as he turned and riveted squinted black eyes. Wired bifocals reflected the evil light while his forehead shone the color of the moon. Fine lines dug deep by the light went flat and featureless. Emotion drained from his face.

The passenger door opened, and a young patrolman unfolded from within. He kept the car door between him and the man, a shield to the unexpected. His partner, small and indistinct in the spotlight's glare, slipped from the driver's side and with a microphone in his hand reported:

"Interception at 129 Beech."

The tall officer addressed the dismounted Cossack, "Sir, we'd like to talk to you for a minute."

The Cossack stood transfixed, a deer before night hunters. "Yes?" he whispered and croaked. He was at once frightened and annoyed. His business had been interrupted. "What do you want?"

"Would you please take your hands out of your pockets slowly and step over to the rear of the car." There was no question mark at the end of the request. It was an order.

"What for?"

"Just step over here, please; just a routine check."

"My routine checks go to the bank! What do you want?"

"There's no need to get excited. We'd just like to talk to you." His spoken words mixed soothing tones and firm orders, his partner held the microphone close to his mouth and said, "Back-up request at 129 Beech."

"Please remove your hands from your pockets slowly and step to the rear of the car. This is just a routine check. There's no need to get excited."

Comforting, yet firm, he stepped out from behind the door of the car and, keeping a distance from the man that left him room to strike, he pressed a cushion of authority against the small figure, moving him toward the trunk lid of the black and white.

As the man stepped toward the car, resigned to this indignity, the young officer followed him, re-assembling the pair in the red glare of the taillights. As they did, a second black and white slipped around the corner of Linden and Beech and slid to a halt behind them, its lights intent on the scene. Two more officers, more than could be conveniently catalogued and remembered, exited their leather seats out to the street to complement the single patrolman who had already surrounded the hapless man.

The small, leather-jacketed man now stood, slightly frightened, somewhat angered, dancing a step here and there to keep his distance from three officers who towered over him. They stabbed him with flashlights and bled him with questions.

"Who are you please?"

"What're you doing here?"

"Can I see some identification, please?"

The man stood, arms slightly upraised, high enough to sign helplessness, not so high as to sign surrender.

"I'm Isaac Abrams. I'm out for a walk. I live near here. I don't have my wallet with me. I've done nothing wrong."

As he spoke, his w's turned to v's, his "am" turned to "em", his "don't" turned to "duhn't", and he slowly transformed from a man to a refugee.

An audience assembled in opera boxes framed by picture windows. Front doors cracked ajar and paired eyes watched the hounds around the deer, grateful for their protection, fearful for attack. They dared not onto their identical porches but peered through windows that didn't open or past doors that could be closed. They were silent.

"We've had some reports of disturbances, someone on the streets, making a lot of noise. We've had a couple of complaints in the neighborhood. Where do you live? What're you doing out at this hour? We heard you yelling. Who were you yelling to?"

"I was taking a walk. I was having a discussion with myself. I didn't do anything wrong."

"What did you say your name was?"

"Isaac Abrams. I live at 96 Crosscut Drive about a half mile away."

"Do you have any identification?"

"No, I told you already, I left my wallet at home. I was out for a walk. I'm not a burglar."

"Isaac," said the first officer, "would you please get in the back of the car, so we can take down some information from you."

Again, the "please" and the question were perfunctory. This was an order, not a request.

"No! I haven't done anything and I'm not getting into your car!"

The stand-off remained a petrified scene, as a figure of a man turned the corner of Linden onto Beech. Barely taller than the Cossack, he was flanked by two huge Newfoundland dogs, each blacker than the late fall night. At the sight of the bubbling blue lights and the assemblage between them, the two dogs halted, leaving their companion no choice but to halt as well. Each bellowed a belligerent greeting to the odd scene, their bark bouncing off the squads. The dog-walker, his hands filled with leashes and a dangling plastic bag, was paralyzed by the sheer inertia of it all. Re-assembling his feet, he leaned first to the left and then to right, gently coaxing his canines to approach the successful hunt.

The focus of the officers was broken by the bark of the dogs. They withdrew a significant six inches from their prey and watched as the dogs approached, leading their human caretaker. The dog-walker was so helplessly in charge of his pack that he engendered involuntary smiles and childlike questions.

"Damn! Those're the biggest dogs, I ever seen."

"What the Hell are those?

"How much do those suckers eat?"

"You gotta have one hell of a big back yard, mister."

The dog-walker stepped closer, his charges sniffing at the legs of the officers, who were now less interested in Isaac Abrams. Both dogs wore elegantly from their mouths long silver strings of spit, dog-slobber translucent as pearls in the night. Each shook its head, flapped its ears and catapulted its string of pearls. One stuck with adhesive tenacity to a midnight blue pant leg.

"Oh, I'm sorry, officer," said the dog-walker, "Here, I have a tissue, let me wipe that off for you . . ."

As he curled into his own jacket pocket in search of a tissue, he turned and found in the glare of the headlights a familiar face.

"Well, Rabbi Abrams!" he exclaimed, "I'm sorry, I didn't notice you. Are you leading a police prayer service here?"

One of the officers, deprived of his focus by the dog spit that clung to his trousers, had exited the arrest. The remaining two stood still in the street, one at the rear of the black and white and the other at the driver's door, both immersed in proper procedure. The Cossack grasped visually at the dog-walker as a way back to civility.

"Ah, ah, ah . . . not really . . . " he stumbled.

The intercepting officer turned from his suspect toward this new situation. For the first time it was not only the suspect who was in an uncomfortable situation. His partner and colleagues seemed less than serious about his mastery of this threat to the community. He addressed the dog-walker in formal tones.

"Do you know this gentleman?"

"Of course. He's Rabbi Abrams -- Isaac Abrams. He lives around the corner from me on Crosscut. He's not being drunk and disorderly, is he?"

The dog-walker grinned the grin of a man who is purposefully foolish. It was a time of foolishness for neither the officer nor Isaac Abrams, however.

"Is that a positive identification, Sir? And do you have any identification yourself?"

"Well, let's see . . . Yes, that's positively Isaac Abrams; I'm sure of it. He's the rabbi at the temple out on Diana Road. I don't know him real well, but I do know him. And no, I haven't got my wallet with me. Uhh, I'm Jack Israel and I'm just walking my dogs. But, just a second -- the dogs have IDs. You could check them. They each have a tag that gives their address and my name -- and a license and rabies tag. You can check their tags and they'll identify me. But I'm not sure that they can identify the rabbi. You know, neither one of them is Jewish!"

The two late arriving policemen were by now smiling the silly smile of the dog-walker as they retreated to their squad. The driver of the original pursuit vehicle slid quietly back behind the wheel to wait out the embarrassment.

The officer squared his shoulders to the rabbi and salvaged what he could of the situation. "We've had some calls about a disturbance in the neighborhood, Rabbi. We had complaints about a man walking down the street yelling. I s'pose that you're no felon, but if you gotta talk to yourself out loud, I suggest you do it at home." With that pronouncement he remounted the sidewalk signaling that the confrontation was over.

"Yes, of course," was all that Isaac could muster.

"I'm sorry for the inconvenience, Rabbi. Good night." And with that he reached manfully for the door of the car, got in and ended the episode.

The Rabbi made a curious, confused motion as if to spit on the ground as the cruiser departed, but he did not spit. In a series of wasted moves he re-assembled his identity. A turn, a half-lifting of the arms, a re-pocketing of hands, an attempt to re-establish the stable disequilibrium of his interrupted argument. Only he was now not alone.

Jack Israel stood at his back with two lounging dogs and an insidious-looking plastic bag. He seemed still foolish, yet deliberately so. He still smiled, but not the silly smile of the foolish child. It was the smile of the jester, who has amused his audience and himself and caused all thoughtful pause. Curtains were drawn across the opera windows and the two men walked awkwardly along a few steps, encumbered by the dogs.

"You OK, Rabbi?" said Jack with a sympathetic tone.

"Yes, it's nice to see you, Jack. Thank you for the identification. I hope it didn't trouble you."

"No, I always go around fingering rabbis for the cops," he replied.

"Look," the Rabbi implored, "Could you please move both of these dogs to the other side, so they don't walk next to me? I don't like dogs."

"It's not that easy, Rabbi," Jack pleaded, "One's trained to walk on my left and one's trained to walk on my right. We can all walk together if you just give them a little space and a little patience."

"It doesn't make any sense to have dogs like this. What do you have in that bag?"

"Oh, Rabbi, we don't have to talk about that. It's a personal matter. If we find a garbage can, I'll get rid of it."

"I know what's in the bag. What the hell kind of meshugginah walks around with animals like this and a bag of . . . a bag of . . . Achh! I don't understand."

The two men had made precious progress along Beech Street. Isaac was being unceremoniously shouldered onto lawns by the presence of the dog nearest him while the other dog was forced onto the parkway by the sheer width of the crowd. Jack shifted nervously trying to create space where there was none. At the next corner a wide paved drive ran to the left up to the Holston Elementary School. The quartet automatically set out along the drive as the only route that accommodated them all.

Their pace quickened as the jostling eased. Heading into the clearing that was the unpaved schoolyard, the trees ceased to shield the earth from the moon. Four dark gray moonshadows accompanied them as they set out on a circuit of the field. The wind picked up its head. Unbroken by the stand of trees, it bit mischievously at sleeves and cheeks, singing a song of winter to come. The men hid their faces in the fresh breeze while the dogs joyfully turned their noses to the wind catching scents denied them until now. They began the circuit of the playing field and the awkward conversation resumed.

The rabbi took deliberate control. "I think I met you at Kol Nidre services," he asserted, in an ever so slightly accusatory tone. "I haven't seen you since. Where are you keeping yourself?"

"Well, I'm really not much for going to temple, you know. And we've only been here for a few months and boy, it's busy. I'm trying to get started at work and we've got a lot of work to do on the house. And our kids really keep us busy."

"How many kids do you have?"

"Three."

"How old?"

"Well, Simmy's ten and Lee's eight and Dinah's almost five. And we've got one more on the way."

"And what's your wife's name again?"

"Rae. I'm surprised you don't remember. Frankly, I'm amazed you remembered me. We only talked for a minute after services."

"One of the tests for becoming a rabbi is the ability to remember names and faces -- especially of people who have money. You work at the university, no?"

"Uh-huh. Doesn't everybody?"

"Not everybody. What do you do for them?"

"I'm a social psychologist. I have a joint appointment at the medical school and in psychology."

"Ah, everybody needs a psychologist! The whole damned world is crazy; you guys must be making a fortune."

"I'm not that kind of psychologist, thank you. And by the way the craziest of the crazies become psychologists, so be careful what you say."

As he spoke, Jack spotted a dumpster behind the school and dashed with dogs through the moonlight to deposit his precious plastic bag. The resounding slam of the dumpster lid rang off the brick wall of the school and reverberated as he returned with dogs to the rabbi's side.

"Why do you subject yourself to these animals?" Isaac barked dogmatically.

"They keep me in touch with reality," was the practiced reply.

"So, are you going to get active in the temple?" the rabbi asked.

"Nope! I don't belong to the temple and I don't expect to join."

"Why not? You're a Jew; you have children; your community needs you. You need it. Why not?"

"Because, I'm Jewish, but my wife isn't and therefore rabbis such as yourself tell me that my kids aren't Jewish and because I just don't want to belong, that's why not?"

"Hmph! That's good news and bad news."

"What's good and bad about it?"

"Bad is that every Jew has an obligation to support the temple. Bad is that it's my job to remind you of that obligation. Bad is that your children aren't getting any sense of their spiritual identity. Bad is that you and your wife don't have a common religious life. Bad is that you're one more Jew that doesn't want to kick in a dime to support a temple, but you came on the High Holy Days so that you can go there to pray. That's what's bad."

"That's an impressive list of bad. I can't wait to hear the good."

"Good is that you're one less person whose opinions I have to worry about."

Jack halted in his steps drawing the leashes tight to face his antagonist. The two dogs sank slowly with sighs to the earth, first to a seated position and then prone. He ceremoniously placed a leg on a bench at the edge of the playground for support as one would assume a lecturer's pose.

"You know, Rabbi, for someone that I just rescued from the police line-up, you're pretty testy! Did you go to rabbi school when you flunked Dale Carnegie?"

"Seeing as you don't belong to the congregation, you don't have to call me 'rabbi.' My name is Isaac, not rabbi. I thanked you for the rescue already -- and I'm sorry for being a grouch. I don't like policemen."

Relaxing, Jack asked, "What'd they want you for?"

"I don't know. I was walking along, and they said that I was making noise and they thought I was a burglar."

"Were you making noise?"

"Of course not. I was having a discussion."

"By yourself?"

"For your purposes, yes, by myself."

With a light jerk on the lead Jack collected the dogs and the rabbi. The now silent quartet resumed their march. They completed their circle of the schoolyard and re-invaded Beech Street, headed back to the eastern reaches of Southmoor, the cluster of homes which shared what had been cornfields only a half-decade before.

They had, by now, abandoned the sidewalks as insufficient for their communal mass and walked in the roadway. Traffic was light enough that they were a bother only to one another. They mumbled in common key and harmony the inanities of life in Bloomington, their cold concern for the coming winter, the fate of Jews in a university town, the small talk of men escaping from the confined cabins of their families.

As they approached the cul-de-sac of Tamarack Court, Jack shifted his position in the street perceptibly, the first sign of his impending departure. The dogs quickened slightly in anticipation of arrival. It would have been an easy parting but for Isaac's rapid grasp of Jack's sleeve before he could bring the conversation politely to a closing "good night."

"Jack," Isaac said, half collegially, half plaintively, "I go for walks every night. Would you like to keep me company?"

"Well, I walk the dogs every night, so that would be fine."

"No, I don't want to walk with dogs, but I wouldn't mind a little human company."

"Well, I don't know, Rabbi, I gotta walk the dogs anyway and I really can't do two walks a night, you know. I just get too tired."

"Jack," he replied, "don't call me rabbi. Come with me sometimes. I'll make it worth your while."

"Worth my while? Do you pay for walking companions?"

"Better than that, I'll tell you stories."

CHAPTER 2

The bus wheezed out of the driveway as Merrill the paperboy strode up Tamarack Court. Jack waved and smiled through the windshield. He always tried to be friendly to Merrill who was one of the few black kids living in Southmoor. It wasn't that Bloomington had no black families. It was just that they didn't live in Southmoor. That was for aspiring white families and there were only two black families who wanted to live among aspiring whites. Jack wasn't so sure he wanted to either.

Carmen and Jade Clifford, the only black family other than Merrill's, lived in the house on the corner of Tamarack and Crosscut. They were nice people. He was a foreman at the Beatrice Foods subsidiary on the north side of town and she worked at the university. They had moved from the north side, which was primarily black, into this nice little tract. Jack was about the only person on the cul-de-sac who made an effort to talk to Carmen. The next-door neighbor, Charlie Poston, a well-meaning geriatric case, kept telling Jack what a nice "boy" Carmen was and how he didn't mind having a boy like him living across the street. Jack shuddered when he spotted Charlie's aged, cigar-chomping bulk headed his way.

Merrill's father was the principal of the junior high school. He had been there two years, imported from somewhere or other to fill an ecological niche at this new school to which north-side black kids were now being bussed. Merrill seemed quiet, but always a little antsy. Jack smiled lots of smiles at him, tipped him well and offered volumes of unanswered pleasantries. Merrill had a nice way of saying, "Honky" silently as he handed him the morning paper.

Rae had grown up in Milwaukee, on the south side, the segregated side. It wasn't so much that she buried prejudice in her heart. It was more that she lived with lack of experience. Merrill pressed experience upon her.

"He makes me nervous," she offered. "He doesn't just throw the paper on the porch. He comes up on the porch. He opens the screen door and puts the paper inside. Occasionally, he knocks on the door and asks if he can use the bathroom. He just makes me nervous."

Jack came from somewhere else. "He's just a kid. He's probably overwhelmed with gratitude at the generous tips he gets from me. We're probably the only house he delivers to whose bathroom he feels comfortable in."

In his mind he questioned if such suspicions were the sequelae of a long pregnancy or perhaps the fears of a middle-aged woman with three children in a new neighborhood.

Jack parked the Volkswagen bus in the lot behind the Labor Institute in his stealth parking spot. When all the lots were full and lesser souls had failed in the hunt for spaces, Jack called upon his primitive instincts as a stalker of game. He knew each almost-legal spot at the university and could procure a space when others had given up hours earlier. The VW engine ground to a halt. He jerked on the parking brake, popped the door and took a half step down to the pavement. He slammed the door behind him listening for the familiar light-metal "pingggg" that was engineered in at Wolfsburg.

Hands deep in pockets, he marched toward work. It didn't rain. It didn't have to. The dampness of the Midwest winter penetrated everywhere and made cold what was warm. Jack ducked into the back door of the Newman Center, the Catholic student organization on campus. There was a door on the other side of the building and the corridor was warm and dark on a cold day. Exiting the opposite end of the building he faced McCormick Hall.

McCormick housed psychology, sociology, anthropology, political science and history. The remainder of the university's behavioral and social science colleagues—social work, economics, geography—were distributed elsewhere on campus and were given specific notice through their locations as to their status in the Chancellor's office. Social work lived in a converted home at the fringe of campus. Geography had a few meager offices in the Natural History Museum. Economics occupied the second story of the new Wentworth School of Management. It was an ascending scale of power and prestige in the university.

McCormick was an old building. It had classic grace, broad halls with fifteen-foot ceilings, elegant staircases, large windows. It was also thoroughly uncomfortable for a modern academic department. It had been built with money donated by Silas McCormick, the grim reaper of the Great Plains. He envisioned a classic Greek revival building that would support classical learning. It was a vision that did not stand well the test of time or the drive of the university to modernize.

Psychology occupied the top two floors of one wing. That still wasn't enough space. The offices were large—too large, and so faculty shared space. This was guaranteed to keep faculty out of their offices. With no privacy, professors who gave themselves to numb mumbling stayed at home to work and kept mandatory office hours for the few foolish undergraduates who sought them out. Graduate students knew better and confined their contact with faculty to bars and labs. Faculty who didn't drink or have labs didn't have graduate students. The labs were in the basement – converted coal bins and storage spaces which once domiciled only ignorant mice. Now they housed graduate students and educated mice who could be relied upon to train successive generations of scientists in the intricacies of maze behavior. Had Silas McCormick, Greek revivalist, foreseen modern academia he would have built Greek revival taverns instead of universities.

Though only an assistant professor, a novice, a neophyte, employed on a six-year long probation by the university, Jack had ample office space. He had brought with him to

Bloomington a large grant which funded a private secretary-assistant, a project director, and two research assistants. This substantial project commanded respect and jealousy among his colleagues. The respect came from the intimation that this young man had won recognition for his talent in the competitive reviews of funding agencies. If they were willing to give him money to do his work, he must be good. The jealousy came from his having grant budgets for modern equipment, scholarly travel to academic meetings to present papers, and his own staff. He wasn't beholden to the department for money and that was the height of insolence. Having research assistants meant that he had graduate students – without necessitating labs or taverns. The tenured faculty waited patiently to see what this young man would do with the six years they would give him. Few were allowed to stay.

Worse yet, he had been afflicted with an additional office. He was jointly appointed in psychology and the medical school. Bud Blumberg, Dean of the medical school, had assigned him an office in his brand-new building. It was a small cubicle on the third floor, which he never used. His colleagues who shared offices in psychology would have been thrilled at a private space in a new building. Jack needed no part of it, but Dean Blumberg had given it to him with the admonition that he had "real responsibilities to our medical students" and would want his own space. This surfeit of space was an added burden of proof to his less fortunate academic colleagues.

He climbed the stairs to his third-floor office. His was the largest office in the department and it was subdivided to provide a cubicle for Ilene Mariko-Dunphy, secretary-assistant and part-time philosopher. She had come to him as half of a package along with Patrick Bernard Dunphy. Dunphy had been a graduate student in the Department of Psychology at the university in Milwaukee. When the grant was awarded, Jack had arranged to have it transferred, along with himself, to Bloomington. He was in need of a project director who could manage the grant somewhat independent of him. Dunphy was a good candidate for the job and preferable to some stranger handed to him by his new department. He didn't come cheap. He insisted that he needed a job for his wife, Ilene, and so the deal was struck. Dunphy got admitted to the department at Bloomington, a real step up for a student with no particular talent. He got a job. Ilene got a job. And Jack had two people to talk to.

"Good morning," he said rushing through the door.

"Hi, boss," smiled Ilene.

"Don't call me that. I never wanted to be anybody's boss," he replied, accustomed to the taunt. "Any action?"

"Yes. Two good bits. A woman from political science was in here looking for you. No message, no name. Said she'd be back. From the look of her, she's got an agenda. No idea what it is. Second item: Dr. Morton called from the Regional Medical Program. We owe him a quarterly report on the project and he wants to know how things are going."

"Oops! Quarterly report, eh? Do you happen to know the whereabouts of Senor P.B. Dunphy? He and I need to talk quarterly report, pronto. Comprende?"

"The last time I saw Monsieur Dunphy, he was naked in the shower and it was a disgusting sight. I left to come to work, preferring to look at dust-balls in the corner, thank you."

Ilene was polyglot America writ small. She was half Japanese and wore her mixed heritage with special charm. At just under five feet, perhaps ninety pounds, she was petite, even delicate. Her medium-brown hair was long, tied in back, and her dark eyes smiled all the time, even when her face did not. She had been an English major in Milwaukee and could be found sneaking into a Jane Austen novel whenever there was not enough work to keep her attention – which was most of the time.

Dunphy, as he was known, was a particularly inappropriate mate for her. At five-ten, and one hundred eighty-five pounds or so, he was already showing the signs of too much beer across his center. Next to Ilene's darkened, ballet-like form, he was all Wisconsin dairy-farmer, big, brash, open-mouthed and friendly to a fault. He sported Irish blue eyes behind rimmed spectacles, blond hair, rosy cheeks, and the faint aroma of lager. Hidden behind his good nature was a remarkable intensity whose origins were unclear.

Jack passed into the larger half of the office that served as his workspace. His chair was surrounded by a desk and two tables forming a horseshoe that permitted him to enter and exit in only one direction. Every piece of furniture in view was piled to a depth of fourteen inches with papers, books, journals, computer print-out, large brown envelopes, old pink telephone messages, unopened second-class mail, and half-finished manuscripts carefully organized in managed chaos.

There were scientific principles behind this. The first principle was that piles over fourteen inches high eventually de-stabilized and fell over onto other piles, thus negating principle two. The second principle was that the keen academic mind could look over an item, place it in a pile of fourteen inches or less, and remember with remarkable precision the exact location of the item and its pile. A destabilizing pile in excess of fourteen inches was an obvious threat to this principle as it randomly re-arranged items to places where they had not been catalogued by the professorial mind.

Unfortunately, there was a third principle. The piles could not ever be totally cleaned up or their constituent elements totally discarded. Every item had worth. Only some could be dispensed with and then only with great pain. But most could not. There was a pressure to create piles greater than fourteen inches, thus violating principle one. There was an obvious solution, of course: An ever-increasing number of flat surfaces on which to pile and an ever-increasing office space in which to keep ever increasing surfaces on which to create piles. The need for ever increasing space was easy to satisfy. By writing more grants and hiring more people, an enterprising scientist could demand more space and expand his empire continuously. It was a kind of academic entropy, an ever-expanding volume of waste energy in an expanding universe. Jack loved academia.

Hanging his coat on the rack in the corner behind the intersection of two tables, he settled into the metal armchair and shuffled through his pink message slips. One read: "Dr. Morton - quarterly report." A second read "Mysterious woman from political science. She'll be back. Tell wife - no danger here (ed.)."

Peace was short lived. A large, blond, bespectacled figure loomed in the door to the office and inclined itself over Ilene's desk as she tried to ignore it.

"Hey, Cutie, yer lookin' pretty good! Can I take yah out for a beer tonight?"

Without raising her head from imaginary work, she replied, "If you can't do better than a beer, not only do you get no date, but you can sleep with the dog tonight."

"Nice try, Sweet Stuff, but we ain't got no dog, so there!"

"No dog! Then who was licking my face all night? Yuk!"

Jack couldn't resist the conversation. He rose from the chair and ambled into the ante-cubicle. Leaning against a bookcase he opined, "My dissertation studies of interactional congruity and incongruity in diverse cognitive styles predicts that you two have a very low probability of getting married."

"Wrong again, boss," sneered the dairy farmer, "Been at it three years and I'm happier than a pig in . . ."

"You use that phrase again and the best part of you gets ground into bratwurst!" snapped Ms. Mariko-Dunphy.

"Now, now, my little flower. I was only singing the praises of our connubial union to this disbeliever."

"How on earth did you two ever get married?"

"It was easy, Professor. You see, I spied this young lovely at a very high-class keg bust in Milwaukee and I determined to make her acquaintance. Being adept at conversation, I sidled up to her and said something like, 'With all the dogs here, you could do worse than me, ya know?' And she said something like, 'Uh-huh, and you look kind of like an Irish setter yourself.' Well the music was on the loud side, somebody banging their guitar on an anvil or something and I thought she said, 'You look like an Irish settler.' And I said, 'Well, I oughta, 'cause my dad's one and so was my mom.' And she said, 'Of all the sons of bitches I've ever met, you're the first one to admit it.' And that's when the romance began. I took her home that week-end to meet my dad out on the farm in Dodgeville and it was love at first sight."

"She fell in love with you?"

"No, she fell in love with him and he fell in love with her. Unfortunately, he was too old to do anything about it and she had no better prospects. I married her and made them both very, very happy."

Ilene stood up from her desk and announced, "I'm sure you two have a great deal to accomplish and my being an object of obsession is only preventing you from feats of excellence. If you don't mind, I have a class in modern French drama that needs me, so the instructor won't be lecturing to an empty room. I'll be back in an hour."

"T.T.F.N.," cooed Dunphy, "Ta ta for now."

As she exited, the two men crawled through the debris into the inner sanctum. Jack re-assumed his desk chair leaving the armchair for his florid friend.

"Morton called. He wants a quarterly report. Got any word from Jewish Hospital about this community-based hypertension screening?"

"Nope".

"Dammit, the Regional Medical Program funded them to do it, they funded us to base our data collection on it and we've been hanging around since August waiting for them to get started. If they don't do it soon, we're gonna be dead."

"Sorry, Kimosabe. Man, in white coat speak with forked stethoscope. I keep calling Fredericks and he no answer. I've had our questionnaire up for three months now. It's ready to go to printing. The two slaves you bought me are trained in giving it and have set up a coding and data entry system. We've even got the first round of data analysis blocked out. All we need is a large number of persons of Negro persuasion on the South Side of Chicago to line up with their sleeves rolled up and we can begin interrogating them. It ain't my fault, Boss. You have to talk to the Fred-man yourself."

"Oh, shit! Why did I ever believe that he would do this?"

"Because he told you he would, because Morton funded him too, and Morton believed that he would. And because Morton bought him a Data-Tec PDP 1100 mini-main-frame to do his piece of the data. And because these docs have wonderful intentions to help the poor, black, and ignorant become more like white people, and when they refuse, the docs get bored and forget their wonderful intentions. I'm telling you, boss, raising beef cattle is much easier and the shit is no deeper."

"I really don't know why she married you, Dunphy. One of you is a very lucky person and the other has hopelessly bad taste and frankly, buddy, I think it's you that's lucky."

"Boss don't say that. It makes me feel vulnerable. Besides, I'm good to her. I take her home to see my dad and the cows and I keep beer in the fridge, and I drive her around in a canary yellow Camaro with wide tires and that's a very class ride, boss . . . Now, you gonna call the divine Dr. Fredericks?"

"I guess so. OK, I'll let you know how it turns out. Meanwhile, could you draft a quarterly report for Morton that outlines the questionnaire development and coding and training and so on?"

"Yes, sir, Commander, sir." And with that he rose, delivered a smart salute and headed for the door. As he graced the exit, he turned and asked, "Hey, boss. The racquetball courts at the gym are getting dusty. Can I mop the floors with you about eleven thirty this morning?"

"Sure, come get me on your way over and we can do lunch afterwards. That is, if the quarterly report to Morton is done . . . "

"No problem," and he was gone.

Jack flipped the Rolodex and picked up the phone. Unlike most of his colleagues, he had direct long-distance dial privileges, paid for on his grant. Four clicks and five rings later he got "Nephrology Department, Hypertension Clinic. May I help you?"

"Yes, this is Dr. Jack Israel calling for Dr. Fredericks."

Jack had learned early in his career in medical schools that secretaries could not differentiate between MDs and PhDs. MDs always got through. A simple "mister" or even "professor" was a guarantee of no access and probably no call-back. But a "Dr." always made the secretaries think that there might be a referral involved and therefore intercession with the "real doctor" was justified.

"Just one moment, Doctor. I believe that he's in his office . . . ".

"Jack! Bernie Fredericks here. How can I help?"

Bernie was a disgusting human being on whom Jack was totally dependent. Though he never indicated his personal background, except for his stellar academic credentials, Jack was convinced that he was Jewish and had changed his name from something like Friedman. He was the world's expert on paradigms to manage hypertension and had dozens of articles to his name. Worse still, he insisted on being charming and facilitative. He never said, "What do you want?" or "What can I do for you?" That would not have been sufficiently affirming to weaker egos. Instead he always said, "How can I help you?" leaving unsaid, "because you clearly cannot manage your meager life without my help."

"Bernie, I have a problem. Morton at Regional wants a quarterly report from me. My grant application was funded with the supposition that you were going to do a community-wide hypertension screening on the South Side in late August.

Bernie, it's November. It's too cold to do screenings at outdoor shopping centers. My research staff has been waiting around for three months for the go-ahead from you. Are you ever going to do this thing?"

"Jack, Jack. I understand your feelings of concern on this, believe me. No one's more concerned about this little delay than I am. But I've got a problem on this end too."

Jack could feel it coming. He listened bravely but his mind sold out to images of doctors with stethoscopes wading knee deep in cattle manure in rural Wisconsin assuring one another that this was no deeper than at the hospital in Chicago. Dunphy was right.

"We're supposed to screen upwards of fifty-thousand people on the South Side, Jack. Now you know the epidemiology as well as I do. At least twenty-five per cent of those people are undiagnosed hypertensives, Jack. That's twelve thousand five hundred undiagnosed hypertensives. And if we give each of those twelve thousand five hundred hypertensives a referral to Jewish Hospital for a hypertension work-up, a quarter of them are going to come in. Now that's over three thousand hypertensives, Jack, who are going to make appointments at my clinic in a span of maybe sixty days. And not only can't we deal with that kind of volume at all, old buddy, but at least half of those new appointments are going to be either Medicaid cases or totally unreimbursed. Now we simply can't dump that kind of patient load, much less an uncompensated care load, on this hospital, Jack. If we did, how would we take care of our regular patient load? Do you see what I'm saying, Jack."

"No, I don't see it but I hear it, Bernie. This may come as a surprise to you, but if you don't identify those undiagnosed hypertensives, they'll simply go on their merry way and have heart attacks and strokes or get kidney disease. Now this may sound naive on my part, but doesn't it still seem to you to be a better idea to treat them as hypertensives than as cardiac cases or strokes or dialysis patients?"

"Jack! Jack! Jack! I hear you. I hear you. I understand where you're coming from and of course I agree with you. But you know a lot of these people will wind up getting care elsewhere anyway. And don't worry about the study. I know what you need for data and I can help you get it."

"Where am I supposed to get it, Bernie?"

"It's simple. It's simple. You can have access to my out-patient hypertension clinic here at Jewish and I'll get you into the clinic at Cook County. Look, they treat more hypertension there in a day that we get in three weeks. I know the director there and I'll get you in. That's what I'm here for."

"Great, Bernie, great. I hear you and I understand. I'll have Pat Dunphy, my project director get in touch with you so we can get something set up to gather some data. I'll handle things at my end. Yeah, I understand your situation and we can manage to work this out."

"Listen, Jack, have her call Imogene Ulrich who runs the clinic for me and she'll get you clinic dates. You'll sit in my waiting room and get your interviews. And then, I'll have Imogene call Harry Lannon over at Cook County and he'll set you something up over there. Harry's a crazy South African, but you'll like him and besides, he owes me a big favor. I helped him get that job and he owes me. OK, Jack?"

"Sure, Bernie. Thanks. I'll see you in Chicago."

"Great! And when you come up with your crew, we'll get you all lunch at Uno's Pizza. You'll love it. I'll put it on the grant."

"Bye, Bernie."

Ilene slipped into the office silently. Instead of ducking for the cover of her desk as she usually did, she presented herself in front of Jack with a half-smile. "She's ten steps behind me with hunting outfit on."

"Who's ten steps behind you?"

"Ummm. Excuse me," a deepened female voice intruded, "Jack Israel?"

Ilene melted into the background. Her work as a first line of defense against unwanted interruption was beneath acceptable levels. He would mark that on her evaluatio if he ever got up the nerve to evaluate her.

"Yes, I'm Jack Israel."

"Hello, I'm Rhonda Dorfman, Phil Dorfman's wife. Shalom. We met when you first came to town. At Bud Blumberg's house. I'm sorry it's taken so long for me come over to say hello again."

She was a large woman of somewhat angular features. Her dark hair was cut in a short curl that one best described as "easy to maintain". Medium brown eyes looked over the tops of large, dark-rimmed glasses perched halfway down her nose, far enough down to look precarious, not far enough to demand being pushed back up. She wore a gray wool dress that seemed to fade against the navy gray of the office walls and furniture. It gave the appearance of a talking head, suspended in air, an imagined face from one's past come back to instill guilt.

"Of course. Please forgive me for not recognizing you. There were so many people there at Bud's that night. But, yes, I know Phil from the medical school faculty, and I do remember you."

"Well, I thought seeing as we're in the same building, I should come over to extend greetings."

"What do you do here?"

"I'm the undergraduate curriculum coordinator for political science and history. I do all the undergraduate advising, schedule the courses and the classrooms and things like that. It's part-time, but I love it."

Jack had failed his training in inane pleasantries. It just wasn't a skill that he had. Though he listened well, he had little patience for mindless conversation and his boredom turned to awkward silences. He needn't have worried.

"I saw you at services at temple and thought how nice to have a new young Jewish family in town. Are you a member of the temple yet?"

"Uh, no, but, uh, I, uh, have been talking to the rabbi."

"Oh, isn't he a dear? He is such a sweet man; I just adore him. Phil's active at the temple. He does a lot of the singing. He loves to do it. We were in Israel for two years. Phil had a sabbatical and we loved it so much that we took a year's leave to stay on. And Phil came back and got very active in the temple. You'll love the temple."

"Well . . . I'm sure . . . ."

"Your wife looks like a dear and there's an active sisterhood, so I'm sure I'll get to spend some more time with her."

"Well . . . Yes, of course."

"I can't chat for very long because I have advisees coming along, but I did want to drop by to welcome you to the community."

Ambushed by a true believer, Jack barely made it out of the chair to offer the traditional pleasantries that end a conversation. Rhonda Dorfman smiled and swept out of the office with all the grace that had marked her entry. He winced visibly and worried that this move to Bloomington might be more than just a new job.

"Pretty nice, Boss," Ilene observed, "Looks like these folks really want you as part of their community."

"Ahh, Mrs. Dunphy, you fail to understand the social psychology of voluntary organizations. You see, I represent the unaffiliated potential member. As long as I'm out there in the world and eligible to join and choose not to join, I'm an example to all those who might prefer not to belong."

"Boss, is this going to be a long lecture?"

"No. You see I'm not only necessary to the completion of the organization, whereby every eligible person seeks to belong, but I'm in addition a potential source of dues and free labor to keep the organization afloat. They want not me but my substantial resources."

"Wrong again, Boss. This lady came here because she's genuinely nice. And this bunch of temple people are really glad that you're here. You ought to feel very nice about this and you don't. Dunphy and I get no such welcome."

"Oh, Ilene, if you happened by any denomination in town and let them know that you were a potential member, the membership committee would be beating at your door before the sun set. It's in the nature of the religious beast."

"No need to argue, Boss, but I think you have this one wrong—and over-psychologized. Sometimes there's just a nice bunch of people out there and they just welcome you in. Wish I could get some of that!'

CHAPTER 3

Jack banged back into the little house on Tamarack Court after his dog walk. The aluminum storm door slapped its frame behind him and let out a hiss from the closer. The wooden cross-buck door completed the movement with a solid thud against its jamb and a metallic kiss to the latch. The dogs jangled their chain slip collars as he unsnapped the leather leads to hang on the wall hook. Each lumbered off to a corner of the small living room and located an exposed wooden area off the carpet to deposit its belly against the cool floor.

"Brrr!" he buzzed, "Winter's on its way," he muttered to no one special.

"Hey, Professor," Rae called from the kitchen, "You had a call."

"Yeah? Who?" he asked.

"Your friendly rabbi around the corner," Rae replied.

"Here's his number."

"Hmphh. I wonder what's on his mind?"

"Maybe he needs bail this time," Rae smiled past her blue-green eyes.

"Well, let me call him and find out what his current troubles are."

Jack stepped into the kitchen and plucked the wall phone off its perch. He carefully memorized the phone number off the slip of paper, transcribing it to the pearl-like dots of the phone. Sticking it to his ear, he waited for a slightly accented greeting.

"Hello . . ."

"Hello, Rabbi—I mean Isaac, this is Jack calling. Rae said that you called."

"Yes, Jack, would you like to go for a walk."

"Ahh, thanks, but I just got in from walking the dogs and I've had enough for the
evening."

"Good! I figured that you would be done walking them. I'll be over in a few minutes."

Jack slumped into the kitchen chair and drummed the fingers of one hand on the oak table while the other caressed his brow. His parka was still draped across the couch by the front closet where he had left if after walking the dogs. The dogs themselves were complacently chuffing off their exercise, expecting that their day was over. All that was left of their duties was a night patrol of the children's rooms, a draft of cool water from the bucket in the kitchen, and sleep.

The brass rap of the door knocker caused the two dogs to rise from their repose like servants in black tuxedos. Each trotted to the door and waited for Jack to raise himself from his kitchen station to admit the next guest. Eagerly, almost hungrily, they stood at the door while he opened it to find a smiling Isaac peering through the storm door.

"Step in, Rabbi," Jack said resignedly.

"No thanks, Jack. I can live without your dogs. Let's go."

"Rabbi," Jack started, cracking open the storm door to talk while trying to keep the dogs in.

"Call me Isaac," the man in the Persian lamb hat insisted through the narrow opening in the storm door. At that point Cady, having lay in wait, attacked the storm door, bludgeoning it with her hefty black shoulder. The aluminum frame of the door gave way with the snap of cracking metal. The rabbi dodged deftly aside, and the dog was out and gone.

"Oh, SHIT!" Jack jumped back from the door. He took two giant steps to the couch by the closet and grabbed his parka. With two retrieving steps he bounded back to the door, grabbed a leash off the hook on the wall, and slipped into the parka. He passed the bent door in one fluid motion and was in pursuit. Isaac politely closed the wooden door behind him and trotted after.

The dog was apparently delighted at being out again for a walk, especially without a leather leash connecting her to one hundred sixty pounds of human impediment. She loped across the lawn gracefully, her full fantail raised in greeting to the breeze. The street awaited. The cornfield at the corner awaited. The pond across the subdivision sang its siren song. And the dog was gone.

"Dammit! Let's go, let's go. We've got to follow her. She'll either get killed on the road or get into the pond and I don't know which is worse. Come on; come on!"

Isaac grabbed Jack's jacket. "Jack, relax. It's only a dog. We'll walk around and we'll look for it. When he gets hungry, he'll come home."

Jack spun, prepared to offer the rabbi a generous portion of his anger and frustration. As he turned, his temples pounding, his hands in a paralyzing grip on the leash, he found a small, large-headed man in a leather jacket and a hat cocked askew. His wire-rimmed bifocals reflected an even line of lights on lawns. A genuinely sweet and understanding smile was on his face, a rabbinic smile.

Jack stood mired in moral dilemma. He was tired. His evening had ended once already. There was no need for this intrusion into his peace: But she was, after all, a dog and she was pursuing the habits of dogs. And Isaac was an unimportant amusement in the course of days and nights in which there were few unimportant amusements.

"You know, I hate that dog," he said, loosening his death grip on the leash. "She's stupid. She's dirty. She serves no useful function. And she runs away every chance she gets."

"Why don't you give her away to a good home?"

"You don't understand," he replied, knowing that indeed Isaac did not understand. "She's an animal and I bought her. I took responsibility for her and, dammit, I'll fulfill that responsibility if it kills me."

"It might."

They began walking in the general direction that the dog had gone. Their walking pace was faster, perhaps more purposive, than that of last night. It may have been the dog; it may have been the oppressed anger; it may have been the November night chill, but it was faster.

Jack was silent as he peered into back yards and across fences. His attention was clearly divided between the lost dog and his companion. They hiked down Crosscut, past Laurel and on to Pinecrest, the last street in Southmoor before the cornfields resumed their endless march across the landscape.

Once this had been only cornfields. But as grain prices dropped and the university grew, the land became more valuable for growing families than for growing corn and beans. The family farms had been dominoes in a fast-real estate game. The ones closest to campus had been sold off first for campus development. Then the next tier had been sold for supermarkets and mini malls. Then apartment complexes. Now the fertile fringes of Bloomington were being scraped clean of topsoil and subdivisions were growing like crops - one per season.

Isaac ambled his rolling, pendulum walk. He was uncommonly short, but not small. His head was large enough to complement a man six inches taller and his shoulders were rather square. But his hands and feet were small and his arms short. He virtually lolled from side to side as he strode, perhaps unbalanced by his head, or perhaps balanced by it. One could never be sure.

"In the old country," he began, a trace of Eastern Europe returning subtly to his tongue, "we never had pets who were pets. If you had a cat, it was to catch mice. If you had a dog, it was to protect the farm. You never had an animal just to have an animal. It was too hard to feed your family let alone an animal that had no useful function."

"Where was that?" Jack asked matter-of-factly.

"Achh! Eastern Poland it was then. But you never really knew, and you never really cared. Sometimes it was Lithuania, sometimes it was Poland, occasionally it was Byelorussia. The border shifted back and forth, and nobody really took much notice of it. The townspeople didn't change. The local - the local - I guess you would call it a magistrate in English - didn't change, so it didn't really matter. We lived in our own community. All that changed when the border shifted was the army that you got drafted into. Did you ever read Isaac Babel? You should."

"Where abouts in eastern Poland was this?"

"A little stehtl — a little village — you understand any Yiddish? named Liddah. It was outside of Vilna. The Lithuanians call it Vilnius now."

"My grandmother spoke Yiddish. I studied German. I catch some of it now and then. So you grew up there?"

"Yeah, yeah. My father was a baker. He was a Hassid. You know from Hassidim?"

"An orthodox sect. Long black coats; curls hanging down in front of their ears; absolute fanatics."

"Oi, poor shnook! Fanatics, yes, but about what?"

"I don't know."

"They were fanatical believers that you didn't have to be an intellectual to be a Jew. You didn't have to be a Talmudic scholar to love God and to love Torah and to be a passionate Jew. Yes, fanatics. Fanatically committed to a Jewish way of life in a non-Jewish world."

"So?"

"So, I was descended from a long line of Hassidim."

"Great scholars and rabbis no doubt."

"You missed the point; you missed the point! My father was a bagel baker, Yankel the bagel baker, not a scholar. The Hassidim are not scholars in your hyper-intellectual sense of people burdened by books. They're passionate Jews, lifted up by their love of Judaism."

Jack's eyes continued to move back and forth from the last line of yards on his right to the cornfield across the road on the left in search of the errant dog. With half a mind he listened to Isaac, with the other half he contemplated the whereabouts of a lost dog he wasn't sure he wanted to find. By now she had been down in the culvert. She was wet and smelly and pleased with herself on both counts. At the end of Pinecrest was Bill Rothwell's house. Bill also taught at the medical school. He had a big male golden retriever named Sandy for whom Cady had a passing passion.

Cady had lost her femininity in one of Rae's quiet rages. Rae survived only one of Cady's heat cycles. The dog had turned from a fuzzy female puppy into a raging whore. The front porch had been littered with self-selected studs, not one of whom lived close by. They must have come to town on Greyhound busses drawn by rumors of a fatally attractive black bitch who couldn't be satisfied. Rae was not impressed with Cady's following. The next time Cady approached heat Rae had quietly checked her in at the vet's for urgent surgery. Though that ended Cady's cycles, it didn't erase her memory. She loved male dogs like an aging barmaid loves college jocks. She might not be able to play, but the smells still excited her. Sandy was her kind of dog.

As they approached the Rothwell house Isaac was still in Eastern Europe and Jack was still preparing mentally to intercept Cady. Bill had built a dog run of cyclone fence out back of the house to keep Sandy in. The raccoons that frequented the cornfields when the ears were ripe had bettered Sandy too often and Bill had conceded that both dog and raccoons needed a little security.

Jack left the sidewalk and walked around to the back of the house, shadowed from the moon. The lack of a warning bark was certain tip-off that Sandy was too pre-occupied to take notice of a mere intruder on the family turf. All any prowler needed to invade a house in Southmoor was a comely bitch. The legions of golden retrievers, standard poodles, and black labs that were preserved as pets and served no other useful function were suckers for sex. When hormones raged, months of obedience school lessons were erased from memory.

There stood Cady, dripping wet, nose to nose with Sandy through the cyclone fence. The two dogs were so delighted at their unexpected liaison that neither took notice of the prowler with the leash in his hand. Jack snapped the leash onto the collar without a word and simply dragged Cady away from the fence. As he applied force, she leaned heavily against his leg, soaking his pants with mud dredged from the culvert. He was sure that it was a purposeful act.

Isaac had followed silently and observed with disdain. "Another watch dog!" he mocked.

Jack sighed the long sigh of a patient man and returned to the sidewalk. Cady had now guaranteed herself a long enough walk to begin the process of drying. The night air was just above freezing, and her thick fur coat kept her warm anyway. Jack's damp pants gently caressed his leg, dropping the skin temperature noticeably. It would take at least half an hour for her to drip. That was half an hour longer than Jack had intended to be out, but the choice was not his. Damp dog, wet leg - neither were welcome at home for the moment.

Isaac positioned himself at Jack's side, opposite Cady. He seemed comfortable with that much distance. The three approached the end of Pinecrest, where it met the end of Beech. They had arrived at the exact southwest corner of Southmoor. Looking across the field of corn stubble, they could see the next major intersection of farm roads, nearly a mile away. At that intersection stood a large, low building, Temple Beth Jacob, on Diana Road.

They stopped for a long moment. Cady dropped to the ground in fatigue and complacency. The security light over the parking lot of the temple competed with the moon to illumine that small section of earth. As they stood, the distance from Southmoor to the temple was evident.

"That's a long way to the temple, Isaac," said Jack. "Then again, it's a far longer way from a village in eastern Poland to the middle of Bloomington."

Isaac stood still for a moment, as one who makes it from day to day without thinking about the things that pain. Now he was provoked to think those thoughts in the chill night. He looked across the fields for a long moment.

"There's another advantage to being a Hassid, you know," he went on without waiting for a polite response, "you stop trying to second-guess God. You realize that you can never comprehend why God sends you here or there, why He gives you this to do and not that, why he gives you pain that you can't bear or pleasure that you don't deserve. You just can't understand the plan. All you can do is what you're supposed to do and pray that He gives you the strength to see it through. Sometimes in retrospect, you understand, but never in prospect. All these intellectuals trying to figure out God. The Hassid says, 'How could I possibly understand God? I'm just a, a mere human being, how could I know?'"

Isaac was suddenly old. He looked at the ground and kicked easily at nothing, slightly unbalancing himself and repeating to no one, "How could I know?"

Jack reached across to Isaac's shoulder perhaps more tenderly than he himself expected. He touched the leather jacket tentatively but deliberately.

"When did you get out of Europe?"

"1952."

"Were you in the camps?"

"Oh, yes."

"Did any of your family survive?"

"No. Just me. They never even made it to the camps. They were shot outside the village and buried in a mass grave. You know, in a perverted way, I'm lucky. I know exactly the day it happened. Most Jews who lost their families don't know the day. You're supposed to say Kaddish - you know, the prayer of remembrance, on the anniversary of the death. So I have a date that I can say Kaddish. Most people don't even have that. Can you imagine? Not even to know when . . ."

"Isaac, I'm sorry." It was odd. Jack had done some counseling in the past. He had pride in his professional control. He was an apostate Jew with no real links to the Holocaust. This man was strange to him and an annoyance. Yet, he felt his eyes moisten and his voice crack, "Isaac, I'm so sorry".

Isaac re-composed himself without further comment and headed back down Beech, slower now. Jack called Cady to heel position and followed, a half step behind.

"Isaac, how did you survive?"

"Oh . . . it's a long story."

"We have time."

"Jack, it's a long story."

"You promised me stories."

"All right. When I got to the camp, I was twelve years old. They whispered to me in the lines, 'Hassid, when they ask if you have any skills, tell them you're an apprentice. If you can't work for them, you'll die.' I asked them what I should tell the guards and they said, 'They need shoemakers.' That was all they said. I was in a long line. I had no family, I had nothing. They came to me and asked me if I could work. I told them that I was a shoemaker's apprentice. More than that, I told them in impeccable German. We had people come to the bakery who were ethnic Germans living on the Lithuanian-Russian border, so I had learned to speak German. They dragged me out of the line and sent me off to a truck with a bunch of other people. So, I spent the war being a shoemaker. That's how I survived."

"What did you do?"

"What did I do? I was in a camp called Birkenau. I made boots for the guards. I made an occasional purse for an SS wife when we got an especially nice piece of leather. And I repaired gloves - thousands and thousands of gloves for the workers who cleaned the ashes out of the ovens."

"How long?"

"How long? Oh, four years or so. The dates disappear."

"That's a long time to survive."

I was young. I was strong. I was clever. And I always addressed the officers in my best German. They thought I was very polite for a yid, for one more little Jew."

"Is this hard for you to talk about?"

There was no audible reply. Isaac simply walked his ambling walk, lost in thought. He might have been contemplating a sermon or a vacation in the Azores. He was not lost, nor was he present. He simply walked.

They moved along Beech, repeated their circuit of the Holston Elementary School, and headed down Chestnut. The pace quickened as the discomfort of a wet pant leg transformed into genuine irritation and chill. Cady tried to linger over each lascivious smell dabbed on mailbox posts and bushes. Jack tugged insistently at the leash in the same way the dropped conversation tugged insistently at his thoughts.

"How did people bear it? How did they survive psychically?"

"Not everybody did. Lots died because they died psychologically long before they died naturally. They died when they gave up fighting for potato skins to eat. They died when they realized that their children wouldn't survive. They died when they knew that the only thing they had left to do was to die. You know, there were even people that were killed because they refused to die."

"Let me tell you a story," he went on. "One day I got sent out to the quarry to deliver a message to an SS officer. He had paid off the German shoemaker who was the Uberhaupt in the leather shop to make him a new pair of riding boots. He was a horseman and riding boots couldn't be had. For a little graft, he had us make him a pair of boots. I was sent to tell him that his boots were ready. In the quarry you saw all kinds of people. Most of the time the Jews were segregated with the Jews and the others were kept together by themselves. In the quarry they put people to work breaking rocks. It didn't matter who you were. It was a rock pile. First you broke the rocks and slowly the rocks broke you. They all died eventually, most of the time in a matter of weeks and everyone knew it. The guards were vicious. I think they were Ukrainians, but it doesn't really matter. They had a couple of Gypsies breaking rocks."

"You know, they're interesting people, the Gypsies. No politics, no guns, no interest in world conquest. They just wanted to be left alone. The SS rounded them up, they persecuted them, they drove them as hard as they drove the Jews or anyone else for that matter, but the Gypsies didn't break."

"There were these two Gypsies breaking rocks and they suddenly stopped. The guard yelled at them to get back to work. And then, one of them took out a cigarette. God knows where he got a cigarette, and the other lit it for him with a match like he was the emperor of the camp. They stood there as though they had nothing more on their mind than a break from the work. The guard started yelling at them to get back to work and they just stood there and passed that one cigarette between them. The guard started screaming louder and he took his gun off his shoulder and motioned that they should get back to work. And these two guys laughed at him. He cocked the gun and pointed it at one of them, the one holding the cigarette, and that poor bastard made a dirty gesture with the cigarette. The guard shot him dead on the spot. The other guy looked, and he just laughed and spit at the guard and he shot him dead too. I stood there looking at those two dead men. I couldn't believe it. They knew they were going to die and that he was willing to kill them. And they did it anyway. I didn't dare look at the guard. I was terrified that he would shoot me next."

"So, Mr. Professor, now you have the psychological game at its best. And who, I pray you, do you think won the game, the Gypsies or the guard? The Gypsies were going to die on the rocks anyway. They were going to starve or they were going to get too weak to work and get sent to the ovens or they were going to get shot one way or the other. But they died strong and they told that guard that he was a pig. So they died. But they died with a sneer on their faces."

"Now for the guard. That guard is probably still alive somewhere in the Ukraine or wherever - it doesn't matter - and he has the faces of those two Gypsies burning in his head. And they haunt him with every breath he takes. So who won the game? Tell me, 'cause I don't know."

"How did the Jews survive?"

"No answer, eh?"

"How did they survive? The Jews."

Isaac shifted noticeably in his posture. He dipped his head and withdrew his hands from his pockets. He watched the darkened ground and slowly told, "Really, only two kinds of Jews survived psychologically: The orthodox and the communists. The orthodox Jews survived and they survived in a number of ways and for a number of reasons. First of all, they had a lot to do. They had to daven - you understand? - to pray, morning, afternoon and evening. They prayed and prayed and prayed and prayed. Second they had umpteen little holidays to observe every month. And then, they had their ironclad, devout belief that they would ultimately be delivered, that the Messiah would come. Then, when they finally realized that this was no mere interruption in their pious lives but that they were going to be killed, they performed the ultimate act of initiative - they put God on trial for crimes against His Chosen People and found him guilty as charged for violating His own Covenant and His own principles of justice and mercy. You hear? They found God guilty in their august tribunal, their Bet Din, their Jewish court of law. With all that piety and all that Talmudic work to do, they were so busy that they never had time to contemplate their . . . their . . . their inadequacy, their ineffectualness, the . . . the uselessness of their damned rituals, the . . . the meaningless and futility of their learned arguments, the . . . the sheer human waste of their lives . . . the stupidity . . . the . . . the . . . sacrifice they had made of their children.".

His voice had spiraled in on itself winding tighter and tighter. His hands were out of his pockets stabbing, delivering pokes and punches, gesturing. Jack was a temporary irrelevance as Isaac fought with the night, alone. It was like watching a grand mal seizure or a full-blown psychotic enmeshed in, even enjoying, his own hallucination. For a while it was too entrancing, too entertaining to violate. It was all the complexity of the human psyche pouring out in a rage that had total meaning and no meaning at all. It begged interpretation - interpersonal analysis, socio-political analysis, psychoanalysis, historical analysis. And as it intensified, finally, it frightened.

Jack grabbed him by his name, "Isaac, Isaac, Isaac . . . what about the communists? Tell me about the communists. How did they survive?"

The rabbi caught his breath deeply for a moment and it was over. "Ah, yes, the communists," he sighed. "They understood. They had a means for comprehending what was happening to them. This was the final fight between the left and the right, you see. It was the ultimate confrontation between communism and capitalism at its worst. They were pawns in the great class struggle that the left would ultimately win. They had their Messiah and his name was Joseph Stalin. The Russians would overpower the Axis, the international working class would develop consciousness in Germany and Italy and Austria. The soldiers would lay down their arms and they would be liberated by a victorious working class. They had an ideology that made it all seem rational, expected, even desirable. They would die for the working class. They went to the ovens singing the Internationale."

"Which category were you in?"

"Which category was I in? I was twelve years old! You get a category when you're forty maybe. We were talking about people who survived psychologically. I'm alive. I survived. I never told you that I survived psychologically - I just survived, that's all."

Chestnut Street ended at Crosscut, half a mile from the intersection of Tamarack and Crosscut. At the pace that they had set by this time, they would part in ten minutes. Cady sensed the turn toward home and shuffled a little faster. Jack set one more hook on his line to snag a nibble of conversation, "Tell me more."

The rabbi didn't bite. "When was the last time you were in temple?"

"Kol Nidre, the High Holidays."

"Oh, yes, I remember. Listen, there's a bunch at the temple that are trying to get a regular Saturday morning service going. If we need a tenth man to make a minyan, to complete the congregation so that we have a quorum, will you come?"

"Why do you need a Saturday service? I thought you had your service on Friday night?"

"We have a service on Friday night, but some people want a more traditional service on Saturday morning. If we need somebody to make a tenth, will you come?"

"Why do they need ten?"

"That's a long story; will you come?"

"Saturday is a good day to get chores done. Sometimes Rae works at the hospital on Saturdays and I have to watch the kids. I can't really say."

"So, at least we can call you and find out if you can come? Come on, if there's nine Jews and we can't pray without a tenth you won't come?"

"All right, you can call, but I can't promise. It depends. If I can make it, I will."

"That's good, I figured I could count on you."

"Rabbi, you can't count on me. I said you could call. I said that it depends. I have a lot to do."

"All right, so we'll call."

CHAPTER 4

The phone rang throughout the house - in the kitchen, in the bedroom, in the family room. Jack had bought the phones at a yard sale and installed them himself to save the telephone company the trouble and himself the tariff. It was a ragged cacophony of bells and buzzers.

Rae loved it in the day when it broke up the monotony of captivity with children and hated it at night when it woke her captors with their incessant demands. In the day it often disappointed. No one called but Jack or telephone salespeople. At night the calls were more interesting, but they were either for Jack or they were from family far away. And to those far away whom she loved, to whom she so wished to tell tales of sweetness and success, there was little to say. And she listened.

Dinah was long asleep in the little bedroom that was hers alone. Simmy and Lee were in the last stages of struggle with the day - in their bunk beds, sleepy, but not yet willing to relinquish their grasp on wakefulness. Rae was with them, her hand administering the final tuck when the phone recalled them from drowsiness. The ring was an evil imposition on Rae's day. She leaped for the phone in the bedroom, hopeful that it was her mother or sister, annoyed that it might wake her three persecutors. She hit the hallway on a dead run only to trip over a sleeping dog. With something between an apology and a curse she lunged past the door into the bedroom and grabbed the phone off the nightstand.

"Hello . . ."

"Hello, Rae?" It was an unfamiliar male voice, at once friendly and proper. "Rae, this is Phil Dorfman calling. You met me and my wife, Rhonda, at Bud Blumberg's house."

"Oh, yes, of course. How are you?"

"Just fine, thank you. Rhonda was over to see Jack yesterday and she tells me you guys are settled in and getting used to life in Bloomington."

"Oh, yes. It's been busy getting the kids acclimated and the house ready. How's Rhonda?"

"Rhonda's fine. She said something about inviting your whole family over to dinner. We'll be away for Thanksgiving and then I have the end of semester stuff to get done and then I have to be away for about a week just as the vacation gets started. But after that, maybe we can get together."

"Well, thank you, that would be lovely."

"Rae, is Jack around?"

"Certainly, I'll get him. Just a minute."

She replaced the phone on the table and set out in search of Jack. The single-story ranch house effectively isolated the bedrooms from the living areas. One could not be expected to spend wakeful time in areas designated for sleep. She trekked down the hall, dancing over not one but two sleeping dogs, nestled together like littermates. Through the living room and into the kitchen, she arrived at last in the family room. Jack sat, reading the Bloomington Courier.

"Didn't you hear the phone ring?"

"Oh, yeah, but I figured it was your mother or your sister."

"Guess again. It's for you."

"Who is it?"

"Ummmm. Remember that couple we met at your dean's social about six weeks ago? The ones with the east coast accent where the guy was professionally charming, and it was obvious that his wife wasn't charmed. And they were definitely Jewish?"

"Phil and Rhonda Dorfman?"

"That's them! It's him on the phone. He wants to invite us to dinner, but only after he's run out of excuses."

"Thanks. I think his wife's hot for me, and he's probably called to threaten me. I wonder what else he could want."

Jack folded the Courier neatly, replacing the pages so that the paper looked like it had not yet been read. Half turning, he reached over to the stand next to him and picked up the phone.

"Hi, Phil, how are you?"

"Wonderful, Jack. How're things going for you this semester?"

"Oh, fine. It's tough to get started and I can't wait for the semester to end, but it's really been good."

"I'm so glad to hear that. You know, I've been a little concerned about you. I know how hard it is to come to a new university in a strange place to get started."

"Well, thanks for the concern, Phil. Rhonda was in yesterday and was very supportive as well."

"Look, Jack, I called to ask a little favor. There's a bunch of us that are trying to get a Saturday morning service started at the temple. We've got about six guys who are willing to come maybe one Saturday a month and the rabbi says if we can guarantee him ten for a minyan, he'll show up. We really need a couple more guys. Any chance that you can make it on Saturday? We'd be really grateful".

"Phil, I'm not much of a temple-goer".

"It'd only be for about an hour and a half, Jack, nine-thirty to eleven. And it'll be a nice experience for you".

"I don't know, Phil."

"Look, tell you what. You come just this once and see how it feels. If you don't like it, that's fine."

"Well, I'll see."

"Look, Jack, we really need you to get this thing started. Without you we might not have ten and if we don't, the rabbi's not going to let us read from the Torah and it will all be a waste. I've put a lot of effort into this. It took a year of haggling just to get him this far and I don't want to lose it now. Can I count on you or not?"

"Phil, uhhh . . ."

"It's a nice way for you to get to know some of the people in town, and frankly, that's important for you."

"Well, perhaps."

"Great! Great! I knew I could count on you. Listen, I have a couple more phone calls to make, so I have to go, but I'll see you on Saturday, right?"

"Well, maybe. Good night, Phil".

Jack put the phone down and screwed his mouth noticeably. He braced himself for the lift off of the couch, rose, snapped the switch on the light cord and let the dimness seep into his head. It was ten-thirty and the fatigue of the day was palpable. He walked through the kitchen and snapped off yet another switch, leaving the living areas to the dogs.

Rae was in the bedroom cornered between a full-length mirror and a pile of laundry. She was small and square, blond and blue-eyed and the second blush of maternity was on her belly. Jack stepped up behind her, placed his hands on the shoulders that hid under her flannel nightgown. He rubbed with firm pressure.

"Easy," she said, "not too hard."

"Sorry. How're you feeling? Nauseous?"

"No, that's pretty much gone. But I'm still tired all the time. And I have this nagging headache. No matter what I take I get this throbbing headache. So, what'd that guy want?"

"Phil Dorfman? They're trying to get a Saturday service started at the temple and they need ten men in order to have a legal service. He's the cowboy trying to round up the stray steers and get them back into the corral. Maybe 'shepherd' is a more apt term."

"I never thought of you as sheep, much less beef."

"Oh, I'll help them out this once."

"I don't like him. He's greasy. Just a little too slick. You know what I mean?"

"Ah, Rae, come on. He's a nice guy. You're just not used to New York Jews. They're a little bit aggressive."

"Oh, yeah, I'll give you that. Since when have you become religious?"

"You know me. I pray once a year whether I need to or not."

"Remember, I have to work on Saturday".

The brass rapper on the front door exploded the conversation. The dogs jumped like spiders and bolted for the door.

"Oh, no," moaned Jack. "Rae, you grab Sasha and I'll grab Cady. The minute I open that door, she'll be off like a shot."

"Who's at the door at ten-thirty at night?"

"It's probably the rabbi."

"Jack, why are you being persecuted by the Jews?"

Jack snapped yet another light switch as he headed to the door. The dogs were milling in anticipation. Already they had started to slobber, a regular prelude to meeting new people. It was clear that dogs could laugh, if only with their eyes. Rae grabbed a robe and followed.

While Jack laid hard hands on Cady's chain collar, Rae bent softly over Sasha and cooed comfort into her dangling ear. Her tail flopped from side to side. Warily, Jack braced himself and cracked open the door.

"Jack! Hello! Want to take a little walk?" It was Isaac.

"No! No!," Jack spat back. "We've been out already and I'm going to call it a day. Please don't stand there, I can't hold the dog. Just step in."

With one hand he opened the bent storm door and the small man in the leather jacket and Persian lamb hat slid into the living room.

"I'm sorry, I didn't mean to disturb you. I was just out walking and thought that you needed some exercise."

Jack closed the door securely behind Isaac, imprisoning him between the wall and the dogs. He spoke to Jack and Rae with his lips but kept his eyes on the dogs. They laughed in return.

"Are they OK with strangers in the house?" he asked.

"They haven't eaten a rabbi in months," Rae chuckled.

Isaac caught the soft lob and tossed back, "Do they keep kosher?"

"Better than that," she smiled, "they're strictly vegetarian."

"Now that I know they won't eat me; can I also be sure they won't romance me?"

"That I can't guarantee. If not you, they'll certainly love your hat. Does it respond to being licked?"

"Who of us doesn't?" Isaac turned back to Jack. "I can't talk you into a little walk. Too bad, I was looking for some company. My boys are both studying and non-communicative. I can't even get them to watch television with me."

"Would you like a cup of tea, Rabbi?" Rae offered.

"Thank you, that would be very nice."

Jack was dumbfounded. As object of the visit, he found himself left out of the invitation.

"Jack, why don't you put Sasha and Cady in the garage, and I'll put some hot water on."

"Because they'll eat the tires off my car. Other than that, it's a fine idea."

"Don't worry about the car, I'll throw them your manuscript to chew on instead."

She gently kissed Sasha on the top of her head and tugged her off toward the garage. Cady, the puppy of the household, followed her older sibling in unquestioned obedience. Isaac relaxed noticeably as the dogs trotted off behind Rae toward the general area of the kitchen.

"Can I take your jacket, Isaac?"

"No, thanks, I'll just keep it on. This is a nice little house."

"Thanks. It's only half the size that we need and twice the size that we can afford. And it gives me such delight. Mow the lawn, paint the outside. Fix the leak in the plumbing. Exterminate the field mice. Trim the bushes. Exactly what I'd planned for a career. What every kid growing up in a tenement dreams of."

Rae returned to the conversation and filled the tea kettle. "Don't believe him, Rabbi, it keeps him sane. And besides, the only time he stops complaining is when he's sick and then he just groans instead."

"Call me Isaac."

"I didn't realize that you had a family."

"Yes, I have two boys, Sage and Lev. They're in the high school."

"How old are they?"

"Sage is sixteen. He's a senior and Lev is fourteen. He's a freshman."

"How long have you been in Bloomington?"

"Three years."

"Where were you before that?"

"I was an assistant rabbi in Minneapolis."

"Is that what rabbis do; move from being an assistant to being a full rabbi? Kind of like being a full professor?"

"Not really. When you get out of the seminary, you do one of two things. Either you go to a very small congregation where no one in their right mind wants to go or you go off somewhere where any right-minded person might want to go but to a job that no one in his right mind would want to take." He took a breath. "I was a lot older than my classmates when I graduated so I got to do both. I was a handmaiden to an egotistical old bag of wind in Minneapolis for four years and then I got to come to this place."

"What kind of rabbi are you?"

"Reform. I trained at the reform seminary in Cincinnati."

"Is the temple here a strictly reform temple - or is there no such thing as 'strictly reform'?"

"That's a good question. It's a . . . uh . . . an eclectic bunch. It's a . . . we're working that out . . . but tell me, you're a Christian?"

"I'm a recovering Catholic, Rabbi."

"Call me Isaac. You know something about Jews . . .?"

"My father was once Jewish. Simon Podolsky; Jack named Simmy after him. He used to joke that the Polacks of Milwaukee wouldn't discriminate against a Jew with a "sky" on the end of his name. He married Maryjane Woczniak, my mother. But my sister and I were raised as Catholics."

"And you're recovering?"

"Yeah. It's my sister's word for what she was, but she says she's now fully recovered. My sister and I both had the poor judgement to take my mother's advice. She said that Jews made good husbands. I got Jack and she got a chemical salesman named Rosenbaum. She converted, but she says I'm still recovering."

"Exactly what are you recovering from?"

"Catholic grade school. It's a slow recovery."

By now the tea kettle was singing and the dogs were barking a distant accompaniment in the garage. Jack set out the cups for tea. Rae poured liquid steam over gasping tea bags. The trio assembled around the oak table in the kitchen. A Tiffany-style lamp, hanging slightly off-center above the oversized table shed a close light in the darkened kitchen. Rae wore a pink terry robe that split open over her expanding motherhood just beneath the waist. She set out the sugar and some milk. Her hands were reddened, her fingernails trimmed. Her face was lit softly and warmly in the kitchen light, but shadows slept under her eyes and the sweet skin under her chin sagged some.

Isaac spread elbows on the table as he carefully spooned one, two, three spoons of sugar into his tea. Jack watched each spoonful, counting silently to himself. Isaac caught him watching.

"I like my tea sweet."

"Oh," said Rae, "ignore him. He's been in medical schools too long. He smoked once, got drunk once, and once put sugar in his tea. Decided that none of them were good for him and quit on the spot."

Isaac cast a sly eye toward Jack and snorted, "Hmph! You're lucky to have more than one child," and returned his eyes to Rae. "Is Rae your whole name?"

"No, it's Rachel, but nobody ever called me that, and I don't want anyone to start now."

"What's your sister's name?"

"Leyla . . . Leyla Rosenbaum."

"Rachel and Leah. It's a wonder you don't have a brother named Laban?"

"What's that? "

"Oh, I assume that your father named you."

"I don't know."

"You've been here only a few months. Where did you come here from?"

It was Rae's conversation. "Milwaukee. Jack had a joint appointment in the medical school and the psychology department. We were there six years. Before that we were in Boston. What about you? That's not a Midwestern accent."

"No? I thought everybody talked this way. I come from Poland originally, but I travelled around a lot before I wound up in Cincinnati. You must be hearing my Cincinnati accent."

"And you picked up two boys along the way?"

"Yes, yes. Two wonderful boys."

"Are you divorced, widowed, or did you have them illegitimately?"

Jack winced but said nothing. Isaac laughed and added a warm smile to his laugh for Rae.

"I'm divorced. The boys' mother lives in Costa Rica. Why, do you have any prospects for me? Any more sisters?"

"No, sorry, but I'll keep my eyes open for you. Does she have to be Jewish?"

"No, of course not. It's funny, what your mother told you about Jewish men, my mother told me about non-Jewish women."

He looked over at Jack with the kind of smile that is a gift to a nervous friend. Jack returned with a nervous smile that was a gift to no one.

Isaac barely touched his tea, but announced, "Well, this is nice, but if I don't go, I'll never get my walk in. And then the Bloomington police would have nothing to put in their reports. After they've rounded up the stray pigs, they spy on the rabbi."

He got up. Rae rose to meet him and gently extended her hand. Isaac bowed slightly, an elegant continental bow. He reached out for Rae's hand with his, turned it softly palm down and covered it with his left hand. Holding her hand between his two palms for a long instant, he said, "Good night, my dear and thank you for the tea," and walked to the door. Rae bloomed.

"Uh, Isaac," spat Jack, "Maybe I will walk with you for a little while."

CHAPTER 5

"I thought you didn't need a walk," Isaac reprimanded.

"Don't bother me with logic." Jack answered, "I remembered there are some things I need to talk to you about."

Rae placed the teacups gingerly in the dishwasher as Jack pursued the rabbi past the front door. He grabbed his parka from the closet, absent-mindedly fumbled for a leash off the hook at the door, and then, remembering that this walking companion needed less restraint, managed to make it outdoors.

The storm door bounced off the frame and rattled badly, failing to find closure. The rabbi was fast disappearing down the block, not bothered by Jack's lack of dexterity. Jack fumbled along zipping zippers, snapping snaps, and pulling the hooded parka over his head to ward off the winter demons that now invaded the prairie each night. He remained a half-step behind the little man who was rocking along, his pocketed arms a pendulum, setting a tick-tock pace through the night.

"I got a call from that guy in bio-physics - Phil Dorfman. He wants me to come to services on Saturday morning. He says that if they can't get ten men together, you'll give them grief and that he's been haggling with you for a year over this. What's the deal?"

"It's simple." Isaac never hesitated in his stride. "If you don't have ten Jews together to pray there are prayers that you can't say, and you can't read from the Torah. If you can't say those prayers and you can't read from the Torah, then you don't need a rabbi to read for you. It's not complicated. If the community wants a Saturday morning service, they'll find ten people. If they can't, then they have no right to ask the rabbi to show up for a service that they could conduct by themselves."

"I thought you had a service on Friday night."

"We have a service. If we're lucky, we get two dozen people to mumble prayers in unison."

"Then why do you need a Saturday service too?"

Isaac stopped. He turned toward Jack and took a painfully deep breath, exhaling a blast of chilled fog at his inquisitor.

"Have you ever heard the story of the Jew who was marooned on a desert island?" he began.

"No."

Isaac assumed a pedagogical pose and began with great seriousness.

"Well, let me tell you. A Jew was marooned on a desert island. When he arrived, it was covered with woods. No one came to rescue him for twenty years. Finally, a boat came, and the captain came ashore. The island had no more trees but had a whole lot of wooden buildings. The captain introduced himself to the Jew and commented that he had certainly done a lot of building in the time that he had been marooned. The Jew was pleased that he noticed, and he offered to show him around. He took him on the grand tour, 'This is my dining room and kitchen,' he says 'it has seating for twelve; this is my library, it has a collection of one hundred volumes hand written on wood pulp paper; this is my sleeping cottage; this is my food warehouse,' and so on. Then the captain noticed two buildings; each one had a Star of David on top. So, he asked, 'What are those?' and the Jew said, 'Oh, those are synagogues. This one is Temple B'nai Moshe and that one is Temple Anshe Emet.' The captain says to him, 'How come you have one dining room and one sleeping room and one library and one warehouse, but you have two synagogues?' And the Jew tells him, 'This is the one that I pray in and the other one is the one that I wouldn't be caught dead in.'"

"Oh."

"You don't understand, do you?"

"Oh, I guess so."

Isaac gently took Jack by the coat sleeve and led him back into the walk. As he walked, he removed his hands from his pockets and began to conduct his own subtle symphony of words. His hands moved up and down in rhythm with his voice and his steps. Imperceptibly, he touched Jack's elbow and guided him around the corner, as one guides a frail elder or a child. Onto Crosscut, down the block past the pond, now dark, brooding over the coming freeze that would soon divorce it from the breeze. They walked smoothly, into the old section of Southmoor where the trees no longer relied on wire ties to gird them in the wind.

"Look. You have here a community in the middle of nowhere. A hundred years ago German-Jewish peddlers from Chicago and St. Louis came here and opened a small business. They sold dry goods to the farmers and paper to the university. For them, Reform Judaism made a lot of sense. They couldn't keep kosher - there weren't enough of them to justify a kosher slaughtering business; they couldn't take off Shabbos, they were retailers and the farmers came to town on Saturday. But they managed to start a little reform shul, a little temple. They went to their Friday night services and hung on to their identity as Jews. Now keep in mind, there were no Jewish professors and only a few Jewish students." Isaac sang as he spoke. His voice rose and fell in European melody, coaxing logic from his language.

"Thirty years ago," he went on, "they were invaded. Jews came from Eastern Europe in the early part of the century and they settled in the big cities. These were not German Jews with their intellectual pretensions. They were small town Jews who came to this country and struggled to survive. And when they made a living their children started coming to school here - in the late 50's a trickle and in the 60's a flood. Now these kids weren't German Reform Jews. Their grandparents were orthodox, and their parents were maybe conservative. This town got invaded by conservative Jews."

"The next thing you know there's a Jewish student group on campus, Hillel House, and some conservative Jewish faculty and they hold services on campus. And they have nothing to do with the little reform shul and the little reform shul has nothing to do with the conservative Jews. In short, you have two shuls in town - one that you pray in and one that you wouldn't be caught dead in. And from this everybody's happy. You understand?"

"You're trying to tell me this is a desert island."

"That, you already know. Then comes the third invasion."

"Another invasion? Who now? The Hare Krishnas?"

Isaac was silent for a long moment, assessing whether he was being taken seriously. Slowly, pedantically, he began, giving his words cadencing for emphasis, - as a patient teacher addresses a recalcitrant student, "There was a third invasion: German Reform Jews first and then Eastern European conservatives. That left two groups in town. But in the last couple of years another invasion. This time, the orthodox. They used to send their kids to places like Yeshiva University or to the orthodox seminary. Then they started sending them to the state universities."

"Why?"

"Why? Well, I suppose like everybody else they found out that it was cheaper. And they have the same problems with their kids that we have with ours. They get independent. They want freedom. They decide where they want to go to school and their parents lose control. And they do the same kind of sales job on their parents that we get from ours only instead of a year in Paris or a semester in Hawaii, they want to go to Bloomington."

"So?"

"So they come to Bloomington. But here they need not only a daily minyan, but they need a kosher kitchen and they need orthodox services on Shabbos and on holidays. And you know how they get all that? They conduct a guerilla war - at which the orthodox are very talented and they take over the

Hillel. They insist that there needs to be a kosher kitchen on campus, and they set up a kitchen. Then they insist on an orthodox service and they run their own services. And more than that they hang around. They hang around and they hang around. And the net result is that they drive out the conservative Jews."

"Why do they drive them out?'

"They drive them out because they're true believers. Have you read Eric Hoffer? They're orthodox. They don't make compromises. And the very basis of conservative Judaism is compromise. The conservative faculty hung around Hillel for years using it like their own little conservative shul - and paying no dues for it. Now they've got a bunch of orthodox who want a kosher kitchen and a full service and an orthodox ritual that makes the conservative Jews nervous. There's this little shul over on Diana Road and the conservatives want to come and use it. But it's a reform shul. They join for a while and then they begin demanding that it be more conservative to suit their tastes. Everyone should wear a yarmulke; there should be a Saturday morning service; the rabbi should conduct holiday services on two days instead of one. And on and on and on. They don't want one shul, they want two shuls - one to pray in and one that they wouldn't be caught dead in. But on this desert island there's one synagogue and one rabbi."

"You don't have to do it. Tell them it's a reform synagogue. If they want a conservative synagogue, let them build their own. Then both of you will have the luxury of a temple that you wouldn't be caught dead in!" Jack was obviously pleased with his logic.

"Don't do it? Look, they've paid dues. They're elected to the board. They have the power to make demands, and decisions."

"If you fight them, can they fire you?"

The question hung for a long moment. Isaac went away. He left the conversation. His eyes turned out, away from Jack, away from Bloomington, somewhere else. His pace slackened, like a runner whose reserves are low and he began, slowly, "Jack, you're a lucky man. You have a lovely wife and kids and a nice career. You're spending your life running to. You never run from. You know what I mean, 'running to?'"

"Not exactly."

"You probably ran from home to college. It was a nice step up for you. From college you ran to graduate school. Another nice step, no? From graduate school to a nice job in a medical school. From job to job and now to a nice job here. All your life, you've run to something. You've never had to run from. For thousands of years Jews have run from. Run from Israel; run from Spain; run from Eastern Europe. All the time being chased by . . . by . . . by, I don't know what. You American Jews know about running to, but you really don't know about running from. I've had to run from. I don't want to run from. If I get forced out here, I'm running from. I'm so damned tired of running from. I'm so tired . . ." his voice trailed.

As fathers one day lean on their sons, Isaac leaned.

"I see what you mean. I guess you've done a lot of running from in your life. Was there ever a time when you didn't feel like you were running from?" Jack softened his voice.

"Oh sure. I had a wonderful time as a kid. Then one night the Gestapo came to the door. That's when I learned about running from. You can't imagine how quickly, how instantly even a twelve-year-old kid can learn to run from!"

"Want to talk about it?"

"Acchh! No. It's such a long story, such a long story."

"Isaac, have you ever talked to anybody about all of this?"

"Have I ever talked to a shrink, you mean?"

"Oh, not even that. Have you even just told anybody what it was like?"

"Not in any systematic way. You know there are things that you just don't dredge up again. Better to let them lie. You understand?"

"But then, it's a recurring memory that you run from. Sometimes, just sometimes, if you talk about it to someone, you can stop running from the memory."

There was a long silence. They walked. It was blocks of walking. Jack rocked the pendulum walk of his friend, arms pocketed, head bent, rhythmically recounting the steps they trod together.

"Running from a memory . . .," he began. "Strangely enough, we knew they were coming; my father had been quietly warned. He refused to believe it, or maybe he didn't understand it, or maybe it was just that he didn't choose to run from. He was just incapable of acting. He thought everything would be all right. He had German customers still. He spoke some German. They came in the night - the Gestapo. They banged and he, the poor fool, he opened the door. But the jackasses botched the arrest. They were trying to roust all the Jews in the neighborhood, and they didn't have enough Gestapo to cover all the exits. They relied on the local police to fill out their ranks and they were incompetent boobs. They hadn't yet surrounded the house and I got out the back."

"Where did you go?"

"I ran. There was an alley in the back of the house and I had a friend, my age, who lived right across - Lev. We used to go into each other's houses by the back window all the time. I jumped into his back window. His family was well connected. They knew people. The local police would protect them as long as they could and at least leave them for last. I told them that the Gestapo was at our door and Lev's father told us to run and hide in the forest outside Liddah. If we had to, we could go to non-Jewish business connections of theirs in Vilna. He gave us a bundle of food and so we ran and hid in the woods. I wanted to go back to Liddah to find my family, but Lev wouldn't go. I don't remember now if he was just a savvier kid than I was or if he was more scared. But he wouldn't go. A couple of days later we snuck into Vilna at night and found their friends. They hid us for nearly a year."

"And then?"

"They were Pentecostals. They were in the dye business. They dyed fabrics and sold them to Lev's family. The father was a part-time minister. In the short term, they were useful to the Germans. They could provide fabric for uniforms. But their religion got in the way of selling fabric to the Nazis. After a while, the Nazis sent them a manager and then the next thing the business was taken over and when they protested - well, you understand. It was only a matter of time 'til the Gestapo came for them too."

"They had a son, Petr, Petr Bremski. He was maybe thirteen, fourteen at the time, a couple of years older than me. He used to come to the shed in back of the dying vats where we hid and talk to me and Lev. We told him that the Gestapo would come one day and that his only hope was to run while he could. He told his family, but they didn't believe that Christians would murder Christians. Finally, one night they came for them too. Petr came to warn us, and we grabbed him dragged him with us back into the woods."

"How long did you stay in the woods?"

"A couple of weeks maybe. We lived by our wits. We stole from the local farms. Finally, we got caught by a German patrol. Lev ran. He got maybe twenty feet. They shot him. Twelve years old. They shot him."

"Funny, you know, I was so busy surviving in those days that I never had the time to think about what was happening to my family. But when I saw Lev go down in the leaves and not get up, I came apart. Really for the first time, I just wept. I stopped running from - because I wanted to die. I just wanted to die . . . "

"They dragged us back to town, to a barracks for questioning. I managed to whisper to Petr to tell them that he didn't know we were Jewish, that he was just off on an adventure for a day with us. He did and they believed him. He was blond and blue-eyed and looked like an Aryan. He had no identity papers, but he was young enough that it wasn't so unusual. So they let him go."

"And you."

"I looked like a Yid, you know. I tried my high German on them, but my looks gave me away. They shipped me out on the next train. And I wound up in a long line claiming to be a shoemaker."

"Was that the last time you saw Petr?"

"Hmph!," Isaac let out something between a laugh and a snort. "You know, it's getting chilly out here. And I'm a little tired. Let's turn back." He stopped and turned with a curious military precision to head back.

"Isaac, let's go a little further. We can hit Matthews Road and walk back down around the other side of the pond to Pinecrest and come in that way."

"Sure, it's probably no further. Tell me, next week is Thanksgiving. You're going away?"

"No, Rae's sister and her family are coming down."

"Do they have kids?"

"No, Leyla and Mike have been married for about five years and no kids. They've had a hard time of it."

"How's that?"

"Well, Mike got Hodgkins disease - it's a form of cancer, and it's been really rough. We nearly lost him. He went from a hundred and eighty-five pounds down to a hundred and ten. And they zapped him with all the chemotherapy and radiation therapy that he could take. I think he's sterile. They've been trying to have kids but no luck. He's a nice guy."

"He's got cancer?"

"Well, it's a form of cancer of the lymphatic system."

"What does he do?"

"He's a chemical salesman. I swear that's how he got sick. He's constantly around toxic stuff. He even keeps old chemicals in the garage."

"Where do they live?"

"Outside of Chicago. First suburb west, Oak Park it's called. They've done really well financially, but his getting sick has put an awful strain on the two of them. The shame is that he worships Leyla and would do anything for her, but she's pretty burnt out."

"Why is that?"

"Oh," Jack breathed deeply, "she's a wonderful person, but she's not made of spring steel the way that Rae is. They lived with the cancer for two and half years and Leyla's just tired. And I know she wants kids desperately."

"They could adopt."

"Isaac, her sister Rae has three beautiful kids and is pregnant with a fourth. I'm a medical school professor. Leyla has no kids and her husband is a salesman. He loves her, but love just ain't enough for Leyla. Adopting a kid wouldn't do it for her. And neither would a sperm donor. She wants to be a mother and Mike can't give her that and it eats away at her like Mike's cancer ate away at him. He'll probably survive, but I'm not sure that their marriage will."

"That's a sad story."

"Kind of a night for sad stories isn't it?"

They marched in tandem to the corner of Brook and Matthews. The moon gave them languid looks through clouds that gathered from the northwest. As they walked in silence now the low moan of a plains freighter clacking on the tracks across the landscape accompanied them. The weather dampened and each man dropped chin to chest, tucked in elbows and hurried the pace for home. They passed the pond on their right, walking south. The sidewalk ended and they trod the crumbling asphalt in the night without the reassurance of a curb. Little traffic came down what was once a farm road. Even the growth of Southmoor had not coaxed cars onto this road that broke up every spring.

"Your sister-in-law . . ."

"Yes?"

"She converted?"

"Yes, when she and Mike got married."

"She observes?"

"More or less."

"Tell her to stop running from and to learn to run to."

"I don't think it's that easy, Isaac."

"I know. I know."

They rounded the corner onto Pinecrest past the twin mounds of earth that bracketed the entrance to the subdivision. The wooden sign that announced "Southmoor" to the few who entered off the farm road, swung on hinges, already starting to rust. The road was asphalt now, not yet broken by the frost. A blown coat of dirt covered the surface of the street, the finest of the topsoil from off the adjacent farm, slowly accumulating in the gutter. The wind wandered across the pond. With nothing to slow its attack it bit at skin. Isaac rolled down into his leather coat like a turtle into its shell. He was quiet.

"Give me a call tomorrow night and I'll go for a walk with you," Jack prodded.

"Tomorrow night is Shabbos. No walk."

"Why not?"

"Shabbos is different. Walking is work for me. No work on Shabbos."

"You work every Friday night. You're a rabbi. That's work for you."

"You know what, my apostate friend? You're right. I work on Shabbos. But you're not a rabbi. So you can take off from work."

"Enough! No lecture, please. The lights are on upstairs in your house. It looks like your boys are burning the midnight oil."

"Yeah. The oil they'd like to burn is in the crankcase. They're good kids. They work hard. I sometimes wonder if they're getting all they need."

"Where's their mother?"

"Central America."

"Do they ever get to see her?"

"Sometimes."

"How come you got divorced?"

"Ahhh! Jack, look I'm home. I'm tired. Our time is up for tonight. You go home and we'll go for a walk another night - we'll talk."

"Isaac, would you and the boys like to come to have Thanksgiving dinner with us?"

"No, thank you. Actually, the boys have been invited off on a trip with the family of

some friends of theirs and I'm going to be with a friend in Chicago. But thank you."

"A friend?"

"A friend! A lady friend invited me to spend the weekend in Chicago."

"A romantic lady friend?"

"Don't be a noodnick. A friend."

"Someone to run to?"

"Or to run from. I haven't decided yet." Isaac started up the driveway to the house without a parting word.

"Isaac, one more thing." Isaac half turned. Sensing Jack's need, he completed the turn and stepped back down the drive, skirting the large black car parked there.

"Nu?"

"I'll try to come on Saturday, but I won't be much use to you."

"Why not?"

"I really don't know how to pray."

Isaac laughed. He took two full steps down the driveway and positioned himself strategically across the sidewalk blocking Jack's path toward home.

"You know, that's your problem. You really are trapped in your own intellectual prison, aren't you?"

Jack backed up six critical inches. "You know, Isaac," he began, "you have this nice way of telling a man who's just admitted that he's an ignoramus that not only is he an ignoramus, but he's a horse's ass as well. You don't win any prizes for sensitivity, you know that?"

"Jack, Jack, Jack! Listen to me. You told me that you don't know how to pray, right?"

"Yes, I told you that."

"But what you meant was that maybe you don't know how to read Hebrew. Or maybe you can read Hebrew, but you don't know when to stand up or to sit down. Or maybe you know when to stand up or to sit down, but you don't how to recite the blessing over the Torah. Or maybe you meant that you're a total klutz and you don't know anything about what's expected of you in a shul. That I understand and that I believe. But you, you poor noodnick, happen to be a professor. You figure, 'Aha. If I haven't had Synagogue Skills 101, and Intermediate Synagogue Behavior 406, and Advanced Methods of Hebrew Discourse 922, and a master's degree all over, then I don't know how to pray!' Maybe you're right. Maybe you are a horse's ass!" His voice was getting loud. It grew in intensity but without the cues of anger, disdain, or humor. It was just loud.

"You want to know how to pray?" he went on, "Then pray. But you damned professors have got to have a Ph.D. before you can even go to the bathroom. You need coursework; you need degrees and certificates and matriculation and graduation and if you haven't got your damned credentials then you can't so much as walk into a shul without a footnote on your ability to pray. You need to pray? So pray!"

"Stop yelling at me!" Jack yelled. "I don't know what to do in a synagogue."

"Listen, I once had a member of my congregation who had too much money and not enough training. You hear? I said training. That was all right, because he had wisdom. The congregation elected him vice-president, which meant that occasionally he had to come up on the bimah, the pulpit, to help officiate. He came to me and told me he didn't know what to do. To come to the rabbi and to say 'I don't know what to do' takes wisdom and he had wisdom. I gave him his own prayer book and in the prayer book I wrote all kinds of instructions: 'Here you stand up. Here you sit down. Here you turn towards the ark. Here you bow slightly. Here you follow the rabbi around the sanctuary.' My vice president knew what to do. Not only that, he was smart enough to read what was written in the book and to stand up or sit down just an instant before everyone else in the congregation. It took no time until everyone in the congregation watched the vice president in order to know what to do and when to do it. And they all figured about him, 'Oy, what a learned man!' You want to know what to do in a shul? I'll write in a book for you. You want to know how to pray? Put your book down and pray, for God's sake!"

"I'll feel funny."

"After a while, you won't feel funny. I'll see you on Saturday."

Without a look back he walked past the black Chrysler coupe in the driveway and into the front door. Jack stood watching him retreat. The outside light went out and Jack stood for just a moment and then hustled along the sidewalk toward Tamarack. Striding up the drive he saw that the light in the bedroom was off. The house was nearly dark and felt somehow distant and uninviting. The storm door let out yet another death rattle as he slid past, through the wooden door and into the dim living room. He dropped his coat on the couch. In the corridor to the bedrooms, he heard the dull thump, thump of two large tails slapping the floor in greeting.

Deftly stepping past the dogs, he entered the bedroom and slipped off his shoes and socks, uttering an audible sigh. He tore off his shirt and dropped his pants into a heap on the floor before the closet. Softly, carefully, delicately he slid into bed next to Rae. "Honey," he said, "are you there?"

"No, I'm somewhere else. But you can leave a message for me."

"Can we get a sitter for a couple of hours on Saturday morning?"

"Oh, Jesus, Jack, the cult's invaded your brain."

CHAPTER 6

Rae was the first one out of the house when she worked at St. Mary's Hospital. The sun crept just past the crack in the blind when Jack heard the sound of marbles rolling around a tin can punctuated with exhaust pops, the Volkswagen bus starting in the garage. Simultaneously, the garage door ground open, its electric mechanism grieving at its task, and the mustard-colored bus whined out of the drive.

Jack rolled over to face the world, believing that he had at least fifteen minutes more to prepare for his day of ordeal. He had just rolled passed the vertical to snatch a moment's more repose on the other side of the bed when a cold, wet nose stabbed his eye and a tongue lashed out in love to cover his mouth. He knew instinctively the proper response: Don't open your eyes; don't scream; keep all orifices tight or they will be invaded by dog spit. He yanked the sheet over his head and rolled back defensively only to find that Cady, in tandem with her friend, had launched a flank attack and now stood over him where a half-hour before Rae had slept.

"Aarrgh! I've been French-kissed by a dog!" he moaned and slithered off the bed onto his knees on the floor. In a trice, Sasha, the old bitch, was at him, licking and snorting her satisfaction at his apparent willingness to greet her on her own level. Cady bounded off the bed and playfully mounted Jack's backside in an act of passion.

"Oh, get the hell out of here!" he cried and looked up to find Simmy, Lee, and little Dinah staring at him in the door.

"Dad, can we watch cartoons?" they asked, virtually in unison.

"Yes. Go watch cartoons. Go watch cartoons."

He picked his posterior up off of the floor and dashed for the bath with his romantic coterie in pursuit. An attempt to close them out of his life for a brief but peaceful purge was only half successful. Cady forced her way through the door before it latched and deposited herself belly flat on the cool tile floor taking up only two thirds of the bath. Sasha lay just outside the door whimpering at her rebuff. Jack stared in the mirror and debated the merits of a shave. Reluctantly, he determined to scrape his face with surgically sharp steel as a fitting prelude to the day.

His features were one degree too large for the face that contained them. The stubble that shaded his cheeks and chin was noticeable after twenty-four hours and it was only on an off day that he could go without scraping. Today was not an off day. His short stature made him lean over the sink to get a good view in the mirror and he felt his softening stomach press hard against the sink. After navigating his flesh with a razor for a few minutes, he stepped into the shower, emerging with a new sense of self and a fine layer of dog-hair deposited as an aerosol by the bathroom fan.

Dodging the dog on the floor, he draped a towel around himself, pried the door open, stepped manfully over Sasha and retreated to the bedroom to dress. Moments later he emerged, hair combed, long-sleeved sport shirt showing past a gray sweater at the cuffs and neck and corduroy pants just breaking over his black loafers.

He dashed into the kitchen and called to the children cast casually on the floor in front of cartoons, "Guys! I have to walk the dogs. Simmy! Will you get some bagels out of the freezer and pop them in the oven on low heat 'til I get back?" No response.

Jack next extracted four bagels from the freezer and placed them in the oven on low heat, grabbed his parka off the couch, two leashes off the hook by the door and exited with his friends.

Fifteen minutes later he was back in the house, the senior representative of a refreshed trio. The dogs sniffed the burning bagels in the oven and headed for the assemblage by the TV without critical comment on the cuisine. Jack snatched the bagels back from carbon, liberated the cream cheese and orange juice from the fridge and commenced to prepare what would substitute for breakfast.

Rae made real breakfasts for the kids. They dined on hot Farina cereal with brown sugar or cheese omelets with toast, blueberry pancakes with real maple syrup or fresh apple-cinnamon muffins. Jack typically watched them ingest their starches, fats, and simple carbohydrates while he crunched granola and skim milk and drank herbal tea. He tried to get the kids to eat granola, but they insisted that it tasted like dirt and went back to their early morning hedonism. On the weekends, however, he threw caution to the winds and spread real cream cheese on bagels and made real decaffeinated coffee. He even drank orange juice in place of his normal low-sodium V-8. In his own way, he made Saturday special.

He carefully laid out four paper cups filled with orange juice and four paper plates on which he placed four sliced cinnamon-raisin bagels with cream cheese. "OK, you guys, breakfast is served. Come and get it."

Five bodies got up from the floor and headed for the kitchen and warm bagels. "Uh, uh. Not so fast. Dogs eat dogfood, not bagels. Kids, watch out for these thieves – they'd steal a bagel from their own grandbitches."

"Dad," Simmy began, seemingly innocent, "why do you walk the dogs?" His face barely turned toward his father as he asked casually. "Other people don't have to walk their dogs."

"They have to be exercised and they have to piddle and poop."

"Why don't you just let them out in the back yard. They could do it there."

"For several reasons. First of all, it might make the grass grow and that would be a terrible thing. Second, it would definitely make the back yard a mine field of dog poop and that would be a terrible thing. It would stink and our dear neighbors, the Bascoms, whom I despise, might feel the need to move, thus lowering our property values."

"Do you let them poop on other people's lawns?"

"No, dear, that would be irresponsible and unkind to our neighbors. I pick up after them with a plastic bag."

"Then what do you do with it?"

"I put it into some unsuspecting neighbor's trash can."

"Can we eat breakfast while we're watching cartoons?"

The three soldiers and their canine patrol about-faced and trooped single file back to the family room, rations in hand. The officer in charge followed, paper plate held aloft to join his legion.

"Team," he began, a note of oratory in his voice, "I will be going to temple this morning for a little while. Anyone want to come with me?" The crunch of crusted bagel drowned out any response that might have been. He tried again. "What do you say? Anyone want to come to temple with me?"

"Can we stay home and watch cartoons?"

"I'd rather not. We couldn't get a babysitter and I'd feel happier if you came with me."

"Is there anything to do there?"

"You can bring some books or toys."

"I'd rather stay here."

"What about you Lee?"

"I want to watch cartoons."

"O.K., that's easy, then. Simmy, you and Lee can stay here and watch cartoons. I'll take Dinah with me. We'll only be gone about an hour and a half. The rules are simple: No cooking, no water games, no going out, don't answer the door or the telephone and try to keep the destruction to a minimum, please."

"When's Mom coming home?"

"Your mother is at this moment ministering to the ill and will be home about four o'clock this afternoon. However, she'll be tired and will probably want a nap. A nap is a fine thing to have and I hope you will each do likewise. Dinah, you and I are going to temple together."

Dinah smiled and said, "No!"

After a bagel and half an hour of systematic child-abuse, Jack had succeeded in getting Dinah out of her flannel nightgown and into a bright green turtleneck jersey, blue overalls, white socks and running shoes. She fought the process like a tiger, but without reinforcements from her brothers or the dogs, she never had a chance. The boys were too involved in the pathos of Road Runner cartoons to care about their sister's fate and the dogs were well along in their morning repose.

"OK, guys! It's nine-thirty. Dinah and I will be back around eleven-fifteen. I want to come home and find you all dressed, and your room picked up. Is that clear?"

Neither face turned in response. A muttered duet of "Yeah" was all.

"OK, see you later." Jack hauled Dinah to the living room where he wrestled her little arms into a pink hooded jacket. He donned his own parka, picked Dinah up and exited past the flapping storm door.

Parked in the drive waited the aging Chevrolet three-quarter ton pick-up. It had been one of the first Chevies with an extended cab and a little bench seat in the back for diminutive passengers. Fastened over the pick-up bed was a high cap with windows that made this a rolling mini habitat. Built into the cap were cabinets for storage. This had been Jack's rational calculus for providing his growing family exotic vacations on a limited budget. Humans were welcome in the cab of the truck: Jack, Rae and Dinah in the front bench seat with the rear bench reserved for the boys. The dogs rode in the bed of the truck, leaving behind a musky aroma that made sleeping in the truck distasteful. On the back bumper was a tow hitch which connected this contraption to a pop-up camping trailer. Thus equipped, Jack could simply load people in the front, dogs in the back and haul bed and baggage behind to explore all the natural and scenic wonders of the Midwest.

He opened the passenger door, deposited Dinah on the front seat and lovingly belted her in place. That done, he walked to the driver's side, opened the door, grabbed the door jamb and hoisted himself behind the wheel. Stabbing the key into the ignition, he lit the engine only to hear the vicious whine of a starting motor that was divorcing itself from the engine. After a moment's hesitation he tried again and this time the big V-8 cranked and started. It rumbled some and shook the truck, but it kept on going. With renewed faith, Jack eased the big rig onto Tamarack, right onto Crosscut, left on Pinecrest, and out onto Matthews toward Diana Road and Saturday morning services.

It would have been hard to predict that a service was in progress from the number of cars and a single bicycle in the parking lot at Temple Beth Jacob. Jack backed the truck into a space, unleashed Dinah and stood for a moment surveying the best approach. Though the door to the classrooms seemed closest to the lot, he decided on a frontal assault through the main door. The parking lot was graded on an incline up toward the door. The temple itself was built in the form of a minor elevation, sloping gently from the lot up toward a peak to the east. The eastern wall that swept vertically some forty feet was largely glass, admitting the morning sun. The walls that faced the lot were of fieldstone and mortar with gun-slit windows framed in aluminum. The main door crackled with the colors of stained glass, lit from within.

Jack opened the door and stepped inside. There was no one to be seen. He stopped at the coat rack just to the right and hung his parka. In a rematch of his earlier bout, he wrestled Dinah out of her jacket and hung it inside his own. Taking her firmly in hand, he walked deeper into the temple, at last hearing murmurings from within what had to be the main sanctuary. Dinah protested with an insistent whine, but Jack ignored her.

Peering through the thin vertical window in the door to the sanctuary he could see a small number of men scattered about. Each stood, head bent, seemingly silent, swaying slightly. A tallit, the fringed ritual prayer shawl, was draped over every pair of shoulders and a yarmulke or skull cap was on each head. Isaac stood on the bimah or pulpit in similar stance, facing the ark and the gaping windows beyond.

As silent as he might, Jack opened the door and entered with Dinah in tow. The door swung shut with a barely audible "thud."

The man nearest the door swung his bowed head deftly and identified this newcomer. A broad smile crossed his face. He set down his book on the seat and scurried to meet the stranger. Jack didn't know this man by name. He recognized his bald head and gapped-tooth smile as someone that he had seen before, perhaps at a service on the High Holy Days, perhaps somewhere in town, but he didn't know him by name.

"Hello and Shabbat Shalom," the man said, extending a hand in excited greeting. "We're so glad you came. And hello to you too, young lady," he said to Dinah who immediately retreated behind her father's right leg. "We only had nine here. You're the tenth man! That's a mitzvah! Oh, I'm sorry, I'm Marty Feldman."

"Hi. I'm Jack Israel."

"Jack, welcome! There's a tallit rack over in the corner and yarmulkes. Help yourself. I'll get you a prayer book." With that he scooted off to a pile of prayer books.

Jack meandered over to the rack and plucked a tallit, the ritual prayer shawl. He had no need to worry about Dinah. She stayed glued to his right leg. He slid the tallit over his shoulders and picked up a light gray yarmulke from a multi-colored pile to put on his head. Inside the yarmulke was stenciled in silver letters "Daniel Liberman's Bar Mitzvah, October 27, 1973". Putting it on his head, he turned to find Marty Feldman extending a prayer book to him.

"We're just finishing the Amidah," he said helpfully. Page 386. Sit anywhere."

Jack ushered Dinah to seats at the very back of the sanctuary. Though everyone was standing, he sat with Dinah. She fairly hid behind the seat in front of her. Jack surveyed the sanctuary to find that, indeed, there were nine other men present. He recognized Phil Dorfman from the rear. And Bud Blumberg, the dean of the medical school. In a corner at the left was Myron Tabanov, a local psychiatrist whom Jack had invited to class to speak to his students. No others looked familiar. Off to the left, by himself stood a younger man, clearly alone.

Isaac turned around to survey his flock and spotted Jack in the back. Jack waved slightly, but Isaac gave no hint of recognition. Instead, he retreated to the back of the bimah and sat until each figure had individually and separately sat down. He then rose again and announced in his slightly accented speaking voice, "Well, we now have enough to start the service for taking out the Torah." He then announced a page number, to which Jack dutifully turned, and began a series of chants in Hebrew which stirred no recollection in Jack's mind.

After a few minutes of chanting and "Please rise" and "Please be seated" and "Please rise", Phil Dorfman ascended the bimah to the ark, which he opened. Within the ark were four Torahs. Each scroll was covered in a velvet cloak. On top of each scroll was a silver crown and in front of each cover was a silver breastplate. The ark itself was lined in yellow silk cloth. Lights shone down from above the Torahs. Behind them, the soaring glass windows let in the late November morning sun. Each of the congregants seemed oblivious to the drama, immersed in his own thoughts.

Phil approached the ark and took from it one of the Torahs. Lifting it to his right shoulder, he turned toward the congregation and began a soulful chant. The congregation repeated his chant. Then, as Isaac closed the doors to the ark, Phil stepped down off the bimah and began a circuit of the seating area. Each man took the fringes of his tallit and touched it first to the Torah as Phil passed and then to his own lips. As Phil approached Jack he whispered, "Shabbat Shalom. You're the tenth man!" and smiled. Jack grasped a fringe and followed the custom he had seen the others perform - touching the Torah and then pressing the fringe to his lips.

Dinah watched all this with shy fascination. She planted a thumb foursquare in her mouth, climbed onto the padded maroon seat next to her father and assumed a fetal position. Whether this was fatigue, fear, or simple boredom, her father could not guess. For the moment, he was grateful for her quiet.

Phil completed his travels around the sanctuary and returned to the bimah with his burden. He lifted it off his shoulder slightly and Isaac removed the silver crown, the breastplate, and the velvet covering. The two men then lay the scroll itself on a table-like platform in the center of the bimah and untied some kind of sash which bound it. They unrolled the scroll slightly and pored over it, pointing here and there and talking to one another in animated conversation. At last, Isaac pointed to a particular spot, Phil nodded agreement and the two stood upright having accomplished some small success.

Isaac next attacked a book lying on the reading table, thumbing furiously through its pages. He announced, "The reading for today is Chaye Sarah and begins on page 169." Jack caught only the page number to which he dutifully turned, only to find that it was the middle of the prayer for mourners, which made no sense to him at all. Phil then called to Bud Blumberg to come up on the bimah, which he did with obvious relish. Bud positioned himself between Phil and Isaac. He took a corner of his tallit and touched it to the parchment scroll of the Torah at a place which Isaac directed. He then kissed the fringes of the garment and began to mumble some kind of prayer with obvious difficulty. He was reading it in halting Hebrew with prompts from both the left and right. The congregation, meaning seven disassociated souls in the seats, mumbled some kind of response in turn.

As Bud finished, Isaac muscled him aside and leaned over the parchment scroll. Using a small silver pointer, he began reading the text in a sing-song Hebrew that went on and on in oriental rhythms. His body swayed, his head bobbed, his hand traced the text; he was at home.

After a few minutes he finished. Bud re-enacted the hand ballet with the fringes of the tallit and the kiss to the Torah and recited another prayer in the same halting Hebrew. The trio on the bimah were obviously pleased with themselves as they passed around enough handshakes for a small political convention.

Isaac called another man up from the remainder of the congregation. Jack had no idea what they were reading, but he could count. There were ten men in the sanctuary. Two were on the bimah. There were seven men beside Jack in the seats. One by one each of the other seven was called up to recite a prayer after which Isaac read. There was only one man left who had not been called up and the inevitable was apparent. As Isaac finished reading and the seventh man said the prayer, Marty Feldman came down the aisle on tiptoe and whispered, "What is your Hebrew name?"

"I'm sorry, I'd rather not . . ."

"It's okay. What's your Hebrew name?"

"I'm sorry, I don't know . . ."

"Look, Jack, is your real name Jacob?"

"Yes."

"Okay, you're Yaacov. Now, what's your father's name in Hebrew?"

"I don't know and he's dead, so I don't dare ask."

"O.K, what was his name in English?"

"Joseph. Listen, I don't want to go up. I don't know the prayers or anything."

"So, your father was probably Yosef. You don't have to say any prayers. We just want you to lift the Torah."

"I don't know how."

"We'll guide you through it. Don't worry." And Marty slipped away and scurried to the bimah where he whispered to Isaac. Isaac nodded, stood erect, recited something in Hebrew followed by "Yaacov ben Yoseph" and motioned to Jack to come up.

Jack cast a furtive glance at Dinah who slept peacefully in the pew. With no defense he slid out of the seat and walked with hesitant steps up to the bimah. As he approached Isaac, he hissed, "I don't know how to do this."

Isaac hissed in response, "You have the perfect credentials to lift the Torah, a strong back and a weak mind. Now listen. You grab the handles at the bottom and slide the Torah halfway down on the table. Then bend your knees and tilt the Torah toward you and it will lift straight up. I'll back you up. If you're sufficiently righteous, the Torah will rise by itself. You'll have to hang on to the handles or it'll fly all the way up to Heaven."

"You're hallucinating! What do I do with it after I lift it?"

"You go where I tell you and you'll be fine."

With that, Jack approached the scroll. He took one wooden handle in each hand and slid the Torah halfway down off the table. Bending his knees, he got under the weight and lifted straight up. The Torah rose in an easy vertical line. People sang behind him. Phil and Isaac stood on either side and gently turned Jack around so that his back faced the congregation. They guided him to a chair at the back of the bimah, turned him once again and sat him down. Quickly, Phil rolled the scrolls together, tied the sash around them, placed the velvet cover over it, followed by the breastplate, the pointer, and the crowns on the top of the scroll. He then lifted the Torah from Jack, placing it deftly on a stand at the side of the ark. It was all over in less time than it takes a medical technician to draw three vials of blood from a trembling arm and it was no less pleasant for Jack.

Phil motioned him off the bimah. As Jack made his graceless exit, every person he passed pumped his hand and wished him something in Hebrew that he couldn't interpret. As he reached his seat and re-joined the sleeping Dinah, sweat beaded his brow and confusion knit his soul.

Isaac rose to the front of the bimah and indicated his intention to speak.

"I'll tell you a little story," he began in a voice suited to a sanctuary full of people. Phil Dorfman rolled his eyes heavenward in a gesture that was not religious. Isaac went on, "Once upon a time there was a man who approached the great rabbi on Saturday night. He said, 'Rabbi, I want to have a son so badly." And the rabbi said, 'So, pray to God.' But the man replied, 'Rabbi, I don't know how to pray to God. I need you to pray for me.' The rabbi said, 'Let me tell you a story.' And this was his story:

"Once upon a time there lived a very righteous man - a tzaddik, a holy man. He was such a righteous man that he was able to speak to God face-to-face as only the greatest of our forefathers were able to speak to God. He even knew the secret name by which God was addressed. He was known as the Bal Shem Tov, the Master of the Good Name."

As he spoke, Isaac's voice changed. He spoke in melodies. He spoke in subtle Eastern European accents. His hands, so silent in his Torah reading, now swept softly through the air before him. He conducted; he choreographed; he danced with his eyes. He smiled a sweet and bitter smile as he spoke, and he spoke to no one in particular.

"This Bal Shem Tov wasn't a king or a high priest. In fact, he was a simple wood cutter who went in and out of the forest. But he had learned how to speak to God. And this is what he had to know in order to speak to God."

"First, he had to know where to go. He had to know where the Gates of Heaven were located. This was a secret place in the forest where there was path that led right up to Heaven. And only the Bal Shem Tov knew where it was."

"Then, he had to know how to prepare a sacred fire at the entrance to the Gates of Heaven. What was this fire? It was the fire that the High Priest knew how to make on the altar of sacrifice at the Temple in Jerusalem. And the very specific way that the fire was laid out was a secret that was passed down from High Priest to High Priest. but the Bal Shem Tov knew how to do it."

"Then, once he had gone to the entrance to the Gates of Heaven, and he laid out the sacrificial fire, he had to know the secret name of God in order to address Him. And this secret name of God was uttered only at the Gates of Heaven after the sacred fire had been laid out. That secret name of God was passed down from High Priest to High Priest. But the Bal Shem Tov knew it."

"Finally, the Bal Shem Tov knew how to open his heart in prayer to God. And when he prayed, the Master of the Universe heard his prayers because, after all, he had entered the Gates of Heaven, laid out the sacred fire, and used the secret name of God. And with his heartfelt prayers, the Bal Shem Tov was able to plead for miracles - the kinds of miracles that he used to heal the world from hurt. For the sake of his prayers, God made miracles."

"But nobody lives forever. Not even the Bal Shem Tov. And if miracles to heal the world from hurt were to happen after he left this world, the Bal Shem Tov would have to pass on his wisdom about how to approach God. So he carefully instructed his most dedicated disciple with the place in the woods where he could find the Gates of Heaven, and the way to lay out the sacrificial fire, and the secret name of God so that he could bring his heartfelt prayers to God for the kinds of miracles that would heal the world from hurt.

"But when the Bal Shem Tov died, his disciple forgot the secret name of God. And in terrible fear that God wouldn't hear his pleas, he went to the secret place in the woods that was the Gates of Heaven and he laid out the sacrificial fire and, without the secret name of God, he prayed. And for the sake of the Bal Shem Tov and for the sake of the Gates of Heaven and for the sake of the sacrificial fire, God heard his heartfelt prayers. For the sake of his prayers, God made miracles."

"But nobody lives forever. Not even the chief disciple of the Bal Shem Tov. So, his disciple carefully passed on to his own disciple the place in the forest where he could find the Gates of Heaven and the way to lay out the sacrificial fire so that he could enter his prayers before God. And when the first disciple died, the next disciple forgot how to lay out the sacrificial fire. And in terrible fear he went to the place in the forest where he could find the Gates of Heaven and without the sacred fire and without the secret name of God, he prayed. And for the sake of the Bal Shem Tov and for the sake of his first disciple at the Gates of Heaven, God heard his heartfelt prayers. For the sake of his prayers, God made miracles."

"But nobody lives forever. Not even the disciple of the first disciple of the Bal Shem Tov. So, the disciple of the disciple passed on to his own disciple the place in the forest where he could find the Gates of Heaven. And when he died, his disciple forgot the location in the forest of the Gates of Heaven. And in terrible fear he threw himself into prayer and he opened his heart and he begged God that for the sake of the Bal Shem Tov and the Gates of Heaven and the sacrificial fire and the secret name, that He should hear his prayer. And He did. For the sake of his prayers, God made miracles."

"So then," Isaac's voice returned subtly to more calculated English, "the great rabbi turned to the man who wanted a son, and gave him a piece of challah and said, 'So pray to God for a son.'"

Isaac stopped for a punctuating moment and adjusted his glasses. He next announced that the reading of the - Jack didn't catch the word - would begin on page 196 and began to chant. Jack thumbed through the blue prayer book at his hand and couldn't find a page that matched and looked believable. Then he noticed that there was a larger blue book in the holder at each seat. He grasped the larger book, turned to page 196 and understood that the service was now derived from this larger book. He thumbed the pages absent-mindedly and without reading.

Dinah stirred. A whine slipped from her lips. As she turned, her legs dangled off the seat and she slid ingloriously onto the floor with a muffled cry. Jack picked her up from the floor gently and shouldered her, much as he had shouldered the Torah. His daughter was softer, more yielding than the sacred scrolls, and less of a burden for now.

He carried her into the hall and held her there for a while. The display at the little gift shop entertained for a time, as did the books in the small library and the pictures in the classrooms. But Jack wanted to go back to the sanctuary. When Dinah balked, he helped her select some books to look at in the library and walked back to the congregation.

All stood. They faced the ark, the soaring windows, the late morning sun. Silently they swayed in rhythm, heads bobbing now and again, mouths mumbling off and on. One by one they trailed off and sat. Isaac led them in a Hebrew hymn or two and then he asked, "Does anyone have to say Kaddish? Does anyone have yahrzeit?" Two hands went up. He said, "All right. We have ten for a minyan. We can say Kaddish."

This Jack understood. When Joseph Israel had died seven years earlier, the local rabbi, who knew him not at all and who knew Jack only slightly better, led his grieving family for the first time through the Kaddish, the ancient praise of God said for the dead. He had told Jack, "This you say every day for eleven months and then on the anniversary of his death. It is not a prayer for the dead. It is an affirmation of your faith in God."

For some reason, Gertrude Israel, who played contract bridge on Friday nights, did laundry on Saturdays and had a vicious recipe for stuffed pork roast, expected her son Jack to attend services and to say Kaddish. Jack had gone to temple for a few days after the requisite period of mourning at home to say the Kaddish for his father and then stopped. He had never noted the anniversary of Joseph Israel's death, but after all these years he sat and heard again the words of the prayer with two fellow Jews who faithfully remembered.

Isaac ended the Kaddish. They sang a final hymn. "Now, there is a small kiddush in the social hall. Everybody has to come and have some wine and a piece of cake," Isaac demanded. All moved from their seats. Marty Feldman greeted Bud Blumberg. Phil Dorfman came down from the bimah and shook hands with Marty and Bud. That threesome headed down the aisle, leaving Isaac to walk slowly by himself. They approached Jack who was immobilized by his ambivalence for Phil, his awe of his dean, and his need to rescue Dinah. His immobility made him prey and his peers captured him. They struck him with firm handshakes and beat him about the ears with, "Shabbat shalom! Shabbat shalom! Shabbat shalom!"

Phil pummeled him with, "Jack, thank you for coming. I knew I could depend on you. You'll stay for kiddush, of course!"

Bud Blumberg hit him the hardest with, "Jack, good shabbos! I'm so glad to see you here. We really needed you today. What a pretty little girl you have."

They were assassins. Jack was trapped, cornered. He smiled and nodded. There was no escape. Phil grasped Jack's hand and elbow in a political handshake, "You know this wouldn't have worked without you. You were the tenth man. Without you there would have been no minyan."

Jack smiled weakly. From his right he saw Myron Tabanov entering the aisle. As he approached alone, Jack sensed an escape from his assailants. He begged a handshake from Myron, "Myron, nice to see you." The others drifted off down the aisle at Myron's approach. Phil and Bud turned noticeably away, into their own conversation with a, "We'll see you in the social hall," leaving Jack at Myron's mercy.

The psychiatrist gave a stylized wince at the offered hand. He grasped it and instead of shaking, examined it as a manicurist or fortune teller might. "Jack, you've been biting your nails again. Things that bad?" He laughed. It was the peculiar laugh of someone who has told a joke which was not entirely a joke.

"Myron, I'm surprised to see you here." Jack attempted to retrieve the conversation to normalcy as the two walked slowly down the aisle.

"Oh, in my business you have to do these things."

"You do? Why is that?"

"This is marketing, Jack, marketing. I have to be visible so that people feel that I'm approachable. That way when their problems become acute, they can come to me for help and I can charge them exorbitant sums to get them to say things they already know but don't want to hear."

"Oh," Jack puzzled.

"Now, look at these fine people here today. They're here because they're working out their relationships with their fathers or because they're repenting for their sins. Now, which are you here for?"

"I'm here because Phil Dorfman arm-wrestled me into coming."

"Now, now. It's okay. You can tell me the truth. I'm a doctor. Is it your father or your sins?"

"Myron, have you been spending too much time with your patients?"

"Hmmm. I wonder what he meant by that?" And the psychiatrist chortled a little laugh and walked down the aisle by himself, making it very apparent by his pace that he was alone. And still he chortled.

Isaac stepped up behind Jack at the end of the aisle and gently placed a flat palm between his shoulders. The subtle pressure was warm and comforting.

"Jack, it's nice to see you. Come have kiddush with us. What did you do with your daughter?"

"She's in the library. I can only stay for a few minutes."

"I'll stay for less than that, thank you," Isaac replied.

The two walked into the social hall. The hall was large and carpeted in a plush maroon. Windows as large as those of the sanctuary looked off to the west. Off in a corner was a small, lost table that bore a bottle of sweet wine and some meager cakes and cookies. Around it stood a handful of men in animated chat, obviously pleased with themselves for the success of their Saturday service. To the side, clearly alone, was the younger man whom Jack had noticed earlier.

Isaac approached and the clattering chat subsided. His eyes made no motion to grasp the eyes of others. He walked to the table, poured a small paper cup with wine and raised it above his head with words of Hebrew. All followed. The sip was done when next he selected an innocuous cake over which to say yet another blessing. Again, all followed suit.

The men re-gathered themselves in conversational knots as soon as the ritual was over. As no one watched, Isaac quietly slid along the wall to the door and left. The young man left. Myron Tabanov stood off by himself, a smile on his face. Bud Blumberg remained cornered by Phil Dorfman. Marty Feldman hung on to that duo by the thread of the conversation. Others drifted to the doors.

Jack made a feint to the left to emulate Isaac's exit, but Phil caught him with a glance that held him captive while he sauntered over. "Well, thank you for coming, Jack. I hope you enjoyed the service."

"Oh, yes. Yes. I didn't understand a lot of it, but I was really impressed with your command of the language and the chanting."

"Thank you, thank you. It comes easy to me. My father was a cantor in a little shul in New York before he went into professional singing and I guess I have a natural thing for it."

"And I loved the sermon."

"Oh, Jack," Phil winced, "Give me a break. That wasn't a sermon. That was one of Isaac's little tales from the old country. It had nothing to do with the Torah reading, with serious issues of Judaism or with anything that is anything."

"I enjoyed it."

"Well, I'm glad you enjoyed it. Isaac does that all the time and it really annoys me. He dredges up some old story from his childhood and gets melancholy up there. He doesn't make it relevant; he doesn't relate it to anything; he doesn't draw any conclusions - he tells stories."

"He's the rabbi. That's his choice, I suppose."

"No, it's not his choice. He's got a congregation here that's crying out for real meat and he's tossing off breadcrumbs. We need some serious adult education here and some genuine discussion about Torah and Jewish law. We need a Hebrew school with a tight curriculum where the kids can sink their teeth into some serious Jewish learning. And what do we get? Stories from the old country, complete with Yiddish accent! He's a real disappointment, Jack, and we deserve better."

"You know, Phil, I'm not a member of the congregation and I really did enjoy the story. But right now, I left my daughter in the library and I have to go get her. Please excuse me."

"Of course, of course. I'm sorry, I didn't mean to involve you in my pet peeves. Please say hello to your wife for me. It was really nice to chat with her the other night. Oh, and Rhonda says she'll be calling to invite you folks to dinner."

"Thanks, Phil. See you later." And Jack slid along the wall to the left and drifted toward the library and Dinah. Dinah's face was still red from pouting as Jack carried her through the tortured storm door. They were greeted by effervescent dogs but no bubbling children. The screech of the TV, its volume knob twisted toward infinity, blasted from the family room. Jack dodged the dogs, parked Dinah and his dress coat on the couch and peered around the door of the kitchen into the family room. Simmy and Lee sat close enough to the TV to deposit nose smudges on the screen. Images of race cars paced past their eyes and their heads made small swiveling motions as the roar of engines and the voice of Chris Economaki, Mr.

Auto Racing, drilled in their ears. Both boys wore the pajamas in which they had waved good-bye over two hours ago.

"Turn that thing off before your brains turn to broccoli!"

Simmy turned slowly, blinked hard, fixed an apathetic face on his father and said wanly, "Hi, Dad." Lee turned, said nothing, and reverted to the hypnotizing voice of Mr. Auto Racing. From his rear, Jack heard Dinah resume her plaint. He turned to relieve her of yet another sorrow and found the two behemoths staring into his eyes, slathering spit from their mouths and shifting nervously from paw to paw to paw to paw in eager anticipation of their own moment with the leader of the pack. Jack backed up a step and forged bravely through the crowd to Dinah. He took off her jacket and carried her into the family room where he ordered, "Guys, you watch Dinah for a few minutes while I walk the dogs."

They replied, "Dad, what's for lunch?"

Jack was back through the door in five minutes. The dogs found comfort in their corners. The kids were still disassembled in the family room - the boys watching the TV side-by-side and separately, Dinah on the couch, sucking her thumb disconsolately.

Jack removed the phone from its place on the wall and thumbed through the directory parked on the edge of the kitchen counter. He dialed the number for St. Mary's Hospital and asked the operator for "Five-East, please." After fully ten rings, the phone on Five-East released its stubbornness with a voice.

"Five-East. Can I help you?"

"Is Rae Israel there, please?"

"Yeah, I think she's lying down in the call room. Just a minute and I'll see."

"Lying down in the call room?" he thought, "That's odd."

"Uhhh, hello?"

"Rae, is that you? Are you all right?"

"Oh, yeah. I was feeling this really bad headache and then I got real dizzy and I had to lie down for a minute."

"What happened?"

"I don't know. I was in the med room pouring meds and all of a sudden it was the dizziness and then nausea and then I don't know what happened."

"Did you pass out or something?"

"Not exactly. I just sort of slid to the floor. I think I'm fine now."

"Do you want me to come get you? Do you want to come home?"

"No, I'm okay. The kids okay.?"

"Oh yeah. Sure. Everything's fine here. No problem with them this morning."

"Did you get to services?"

"Yeah, that went fine too. I'll tell you about it later. Say, would you mind if we invited the rabbi and his two boys to dinner one night?"

"I suppose. Some special reason?"

"Oh, I don't know. I just think it would be a nice thing to do."

"Well, OK, you can set it up."

"Good. Thanks. Look, I have to make these kids something for lunch before they dine on one another. Are you sure you're all right?"

"Oh, I'm all right. I have a little headache and some slight nausea."

"Look, why don't I come get you? "

"Uh. No. You can't leave the kids. I'll be all right"

Out of the corner of his eye, Jack saw a yellow Camaro pull into the driveway.

CHAPTER 7

Rae rested her folded arms comfortably on her expanding belly. One elbow propped her body on the kitchen counter. As she leaned to leeward a large hoop earring dangled out to the side. Behind her in the family room the three children sat in front of the television, none of them watching, each at play, isolated from one another.

"You know, I hate when you cook."

"Thank you, my love," Jack replied, "You really know how to use positive reinforcement to keep a man in the kitchen."

"You make more mess than any normal human being ever has to make. And you don't measure anything. You just toss stuff in. And you spatter your fat and don't wipe it up."

"My spattered fat is my own business, young lady," he replied. He was wrist deep in melting butter on the stove. About him was a colorful array of bowls mismatched for size, shape, material of construction, and state of petrified encrustation. In each bowl was a spoon, spatula or fork in similar state of crud. "Remember, when we made this little agreement that he (or she) who cooketh, and cleaneth not, we made no subjunctive clauses about how many dishes it took to prepare the meal. So there!"

"What do you call this mess again?"

"Kasha mit varnishkes. Brown buckwheat groats with pasta bows. An old Jewish favorite known to followers of the faith around the world, a dish famed for its high vegetable protein content, low fat, high fiber, and best of all, ability to fill an empty belly so completely that it will last a full day's fast. Not bad for an ethnic group that all but invented diabetes and heart disease, eh?"

"Your mother used to serve this? What does it taste like?"

"Like everything my mother made - bland, hard to chew, and colorless." Jack smiled the vile smile of a parent feeding a child some awful food with the admonition, "But this is good for you."

"I never got clear why you invited them for dinner tonight. Not that Thursday night isn't a fine time for dinner, I mean. And not that a week after Thanksgiving isn't a great time for entertaining. And not that we haven't had enough company with my sister and Michael here for four days. And not that the kids have to go to bed and be up for school tomorrow or anything. I just thought that there might be some very, very special reason that you just had to have the rabbi and his kids over to dinner this very night."

"Well, last week was shot with the holiday and your sister and brother-in-law. Isaac was out of town, his gang of delinquents was out of town; Fridays he works, Saturdays he plays and this was really the earliest I could arrange for us to get together. I'm sorry if it's inconvenient. I am doing the cooking and trying not to lay everything on you."

"That's true. You are doing the cooking. All I had to do was to clean the house after you tidied, set the table, do the shopping - and then, because of your he-or-she-who-cooketh rule, I have to clean up. Jack, you are truly a model husband. You know what a model is, don't you?"

"I guess I'm supposed to ask what a model is."

"That's a small representation of the real thing."

"I sense that a joke just flew over my head."

"Hardly."

"Speaking of head . . . How're you feeling?"

"It comes and goes. Sometimes it's just this pounding in my right forehead and I get dizzy and think I'm going to faint again. Sometimes I'm just fine."

"Think it's anything serious?"

"No. I've got another appointment with Dr. Acosta next week and I'll ask her about it again. At this very moment the only thing that's bothering me is what kind of insult I'll make to the rabbi without even knowing it."

"Fear not, mon petite matzoh ball. I have it all covered. We serve a totally vegetarian meal and we cannot possibly offend. Keep the conversation light and off religion and we'll all have a good time."

"How are we doing on time?"

"Great. The bows are ready. The kasha goes in next and simmers for a while. The salad is done. The garlic bread is done. The gefilte fish appetizer is on the table. Ah, my mother would be proud."

"Ah, Jack, you would have made a fine daughter for her."

"No, love, I was supposed to marry someone who would be the daughter she never had."

"Let her down again, didn't you?"

"Now, come on. She loves you like a daughter."

"And I love her like a . . . like a . . . like a . . . Jack, you're so good with words. Think of something."

"You love her like a . . . like a . . . like a . . . is that the doorbell we could be saved by?"

The rap on the storm door filled the house with the echoes of loose aluminum. The sudden noise started a small stampede to the door. Two self-appointed herd-dogs and their human hosts headed for the door on a dead run, as much to prevent a recurrence of the rap as to welcome the guests. Jack reached the heavy wooden door a half-step after Cady and Sasha who stared with wide blood-shot eyes in anticipation of diversion. Rae stood dutifully to the rear of the crowd, gently massaging the two black butts and one white one that stood in line ahead of her.

Jack swung open the door to find three faces smiling at him in the yellow of the porch light. Each face was graced with glasses, each body wore a leather jacket, and each stood in the cold November evening with hands pocketed and head bobbing in greeting. Cady made for the door, but Jack grabbed her and halted her assault. All three guests back tracked a tandem step in anticipation of attack. Jack laughed and invited them in, past the wrath of tormented aluminum which used to be the storm door.

"Come in, Gentlemen. Come in."

"It's all right, boys, Mrs. Israel assures me that the dogs are vegetarians," barked the rabbi.

As each entered, the storm door rattled the sound of rifle fire - once, twice, thrice, followed by the soft artillery thud of the wooden door and the snap of the metal catch. Isaac entered first and the boys fell into formation in a neat line just inside the door. Without missing a beat, he announced, "Sage, Lev, this is Mrs. Israel and Dr. Israel." He took Rae's right hand gently between his own and oozed, "Thank you so much for having us over." Rae smiled. Each boy took her hand in turn, looked directly into her eyes and repeated, "Thank you for having us over." They then turned to Jack and dutifully shook hands.

"Hi, I'm Sage."

"Hi, I'm Lev."

"Hey, great to meet you, guys. Your Dad has told me nice things about you."

Both boys looked at Isaac with accusing glances. Isaac shrugged in response.

"And these are the Baskerville twins that we've heard so much about," laughed Sage. "They're not as small as I imagined. Dad occasionally, just occasionally, embellishes on his descriptions of things and I assumed that he had done a little overestimating on the size of these things. But now I'm not so sure. I know there's a Puppy Chow and a Dog Chow. Is there a Cow Chow that you feed these guys?"

Rae dropped to one knee and placed a loving arm around each canine neck and protested, "But they're just baaaabeees!"

Lev followed with, "Baby bison? Are these the original inhabitants of the Great Plains?"

All chuckled, having made the obligatory jokes about the size of the dogs. When this ritual greeting had ended, Jack took their coats and ushered them into the kitchen.

"Come in. Come in. Dinner is just about ready and you must be hungry."

The three guests walked in a troop. They were an unlikely platoon. Sage stood a full head over his father and Lev a half-head. They were broad shouldered and slender-waisted and though they lacked Isaac's heft, they mimicked his rocking walk. Each had skin deep in olive tones and a head of jet-black hair that shone even in the light of the living room. Their facial features were full, their eyes black. They had a handsomeness that had never graced their father. And yet they were so clearly his sons in gait and courtly manner.

The kitchen was small and there was no dining room. The developers who laid out Southmoor in one sixteenth acre plots and houses of twelve-hundred, fifteen-hundred, and eighteen-hundred square foot floor plans had omitted the dining room from the smallest homes and substituted a family room. This was a "starter home" and Jack and Rae were a "starter family".

The guests, the dogs, the host and hostess milled helplessly around the kitchen, trying to assemble a dinner gathering from a melee. Simmy, Lee, and Dinah abandoned their isolated togetherness in company with the TV and stood at the entrance to the kitchen to watch the crowd groping for a plan of action.

Isaac further disrupted the search for order with, "Aha, and who are these people?"

Rae chimed immediately with, "Simon, Lee, and Dinah, say 'Hello" to Rabbi Abrams, Sage, and Lev."

The three smallest members of the mixture mumbled an obligatory, "Hi," and faded back into the family room where they were safe from strangers. The two dogs merged under the kitchen table and fell to the floor with deflating sighs, head to head in the spaces intended for human feet.

Jack ushered Lev and Sage toward the wall side of the kitchen table, placed Isaac at the head, near the door to the living room, and pulled out a chair for Rae near the sink with mock chivalry.

"Won't the children eat with us?" asked Isaac.

"It would be a little crowded, so we fed them first," replied Jack.

Looking under the table, Isaac commented, "And you didn't feed the dogs first, as well?"

Missing the comment, Jack simply observed, "Oh, they're always there when we eat. That way, when we drop a morsel of food, we never hear it hit the floor. All you hear is the snapping of jaws. Now," he went on, "Gefilte fish is on the table and you can . . . Oh, excuse me! Isaac, would you like to say a grace over the meal?"

Lev and Sage raised their eyes in mock horror.

"Did you invite me over here to work?"

"Well, no, I just thought that you probably say something at home and that you might like to say it here. That's all."

"Would you like me to say a blessing?"

"Only if you feel comfortable, of course."

Rae and the boys watched the negotiations with amusement. Finally, Rae pleaded, "Oh Rabbi Abrams, Rabbi Abrams, won't you please grace us with a blessing - or bless us with a gracing - or something that will magically permit us to eat dinner?"

Isaac laughed with his mouth and his eyes and rose from his chair.

"In that case, what we need here is not just a simple grace - the kind I would toss off at a Rotary lunch. No, no! What we need here is the ganze megillah, the works, the full priestly ministration."

"Dad," began Lev, "everybody's hungry and we have homework. How 'bout a simple blessing over the bread so we can eat before malnutrition sets in."

"Well, first we begin with the blessing over the washing of the hands. But in order to understand the fulfillment of the commandment to wash the hands, we need a story . . . "

"Malnutrition, Dad, malnutrition."

"O.K. I'll just do the blessing and the washing of the hands."

He sprung to the sink and filled a cup with water. Pouring it over his hands he said, "Blessed are You, Lord, our God, King of the Universe, who has commanded us to wash our hands before eating."

Rae leaned over to her husband and whispered, "Is this real?"

"I don't know."

Leaping back to the table, Isaac grabbed the wooden board on which the garlic bread sat and lifted it up. "Blessed are You, Lord, our God, Master of the Universe who brings forth bread from the earth." He tore a piece of bread from the loaf and stuffed it in his mouth. Passing the bread board, he said, "Boy, after a workout like that, I could use a piece gefilte fish. No?"

Jack sat dumb. Rae, Lev and Sage laughed. Isaac dived like a shark for the fish laying innocently on the plate, hiding under a slice of carrot and nestled against some purple horseradish. Emerging with a forkful of fish, he exclaimed, "I now find this dinner officially in session." All laughed.

Isaac ravished his fish. He turned to Rae and exclaimed, "My Dear, this is not a bad piece of fish! No doubt, you caught the pike and the whitefish yourself, filleted them, and chopped and boiled them according to an old family recipe."

"Jack smuggled it into town in his briefcase from Chicago. The state police are still looking for the guy who's the brains behind the illegal gefilte fish trade."

"Do you get to Chicago often, Jack? Oh! Before you answer that, you'd better know that if you do, I have a long shopping list."

"Well, yeah, I do. I have a research project at Jewish Hospital that's about to transmigrate to Cook County Hospital and I get up there every other week for a day."

"Really . . .!" the rabbi observed, "and exactly what do you do at Jewish and Cook County Hospitals?"

"I have a project on hypertension in the Black community. I'm trying to identify styles of personal coping with stress in families and their relation to the incidence of high blood pressure and then with peoples' compliance with the drug regimen."

"That's fascinating, Jack. Now could you tell us again - this time without the psychologese, what it is that takes you to Chicago every two weeks, so close to a supply of gefilte fish?"

"All right. Look, you have a large community of Black people in Chicago . . ."

"Half of whom would prefer to live in Bloomington," chimed Sage.

"Be quiet and listen," scolded his father.

"Well, the rate of high blood pressure is exceptionally high in the Black community . . ."

"And getting higher in the white community nearby," observed Lev.

"Lev, stop it!" The rabbi snapped.

Jack's eyes darted around the table. The agenda wasn't clear.

"Well, these are people under a great deal of social stress: Poverty, crime, violence, crowded living conditions, and people have different social psychological styles for dealing with stress. You know, some people internalize it, some act it out interpersonally, some accept it as God's will, and I hypothesize that some somaticize it - that is, they convert it into physical symptoms, like high blood pressure. You understand?

"And then," he went on, trying to avoid being professorial, "people vary a lot in their willingness or their ability to follow a treatment regimen like taking their pills and restricting their intake of salt. So, the next logical question is whether these coping styles not only predict who will get high blood pressure, but which ones will be compliant with the prescribed treatment regimen."

Sage rose to the discussion. "Why do you go all the way to Chicago when there are so many blacks here in Bloomington?"

"Well, that's a good question, Sage. The social stresses in Chicago are really intense and, of course, those hospitals have very large treatment facilities with all the programs that will support research like this."

"And in Bloomington, the Blacks have less stress so they import their problems from Chicago in a race to make life just as difficult here," Sage agitated.

"Sage! We'll discuss this later at home." Isaac glared at his son.

Sage stared down at his plate. "I'm sorry."

Jack lifted from his seat as Rae and Isaac squirmed. He moved to the top oven of the Kenmore stove, donned two oven mitts and announced, "Well, enough of this. Now for the main course." With a flourish he wrestled the Corning casserole dish from the oven and placed it next to the salad on a trivet on the table. The silence was evident, and Jack tried to fill it with food.

Isaac laughed at the kasha mit varnishkes. "This is some of the best kasha I've had since I came to Bloomington."

Rae smiled with, "And how many times have you had it in Bloomington?"

"Never!"

She turned to the boys, "Sage is such a lovely name . . ."

"If I had been a girl, he would have named me Marjoram, or something equally spicy."

Isaac mastered his pained look.

"Lev, you're a freshman?" she went on, struggling.

"Yeah, first year at the new high school. Fortunately, I have a big brother to look after me."

"Why do you need looking after?" Jack followed.

"It's a tough school. There's a lot of rough kids that they bus in from the north side."

"I don't understand. This is a sleepy little university town."

Sage took over authoritatively, "I wrote a paper about this last year for social studies, you know? I did interviews with whatever kids would talk to me. Some of the black kids that I knew from student government kind of told me. They said that they had moved down from Chicago and Gary when Beatrice moved the baking factory down here. They offered them jobs and a lot of them wanted to get out of Chicago 'cause it was so rough. I think they were probably nice people. But there's this family thing that if your nephew or your cousin gets into trouble or his black mama wants to keep him out of trouble in the projects, they send him to live with a relative somewhere else. Lots of them came here and the next thing you know, there's a gang, a black street gang operating in Veterans Memorial High School in Bloomington. You can't believe what it's like. Five years ago, nobody had locks on their lockers. Now kids carry knives to school, which is stupid because I've seen these black guys with their do-rags on their heads carrying guns. And the teachers and the principal are fools who have no idea how to handle these guys and we get all the heat. We get shaken down and pushed around and nobody, not our parents, not our teachers, nobody seems to understand that there's a problem here."

"Sage! Thank you that's enough. I think you're exaggerating a little," snarled the rabbi.

"Dad, you don't understand either. You've still got your old lefty ideas about oppressed Negroes and you need to think about oppressed white kids who are afraid to go to school!"

"That's enough!"

"Dad, he's right. If he wasn't at the school and everybody didn't know I was his brother, I'd never make it to lunch with money in my pocket. As it is, I can't leave anything in my locker. It just gets stolen. And it's not just white kids that get pushed around. The black kids who aren't in the gangs get pushed around even worse."

"Lev, please, that's enough. There are solutions to these problems."

"Dad, Sage is right. You don't understand. We need police in the schools or something."

This was their dining room and they were alone, each generation torturing the other with its history. Voices rang off the suspended Tiffany lamp and resonated through the kitchen. The dogs shifted uncomfortably under the table. There was only an uneasy resolution, a pregnant pause in the drama that permitted the audience an exit.

"Let me grab these plates . . ."

"Yes," Isaac sensed the cue. "I promised to get these guys back to their homework. I hate to leave."

"Dr. Israel," Lev chirped, "I'm sure your dogs would like to walk us home. I'd be glad to walk them for you as far as our house."

"Sure. Rae, do you mind if I leave you to start cleaning up without me while I walk these guys home with the dogs?"

"Somehow, this was foreordained," she groaned.

CHAPTER 8

Six souls exited the house. Sage walked silently ahead, chin down in the wind. Lev followed, stumbling over leashes, dragged left then right, pulling and being pulled, making irregular progress toward home. Dogs sense amateur dog walkers and torment them. There is a rhythm to the walk. The practiced human comes to sense the spots to stop -where some other canine has left a splash of pee as a signal for pause, where the wind picks up velocity and a canine muzzle requires a moment - two, perhaps - to sample the smells from miles distant, where a leg is to be lifted, a butt dropped to the grass to leave yet another message for dogs to come. The well-trained human walks on a loose leash, constantly attuned to the needs of his canine master. Lev was untrained. The dogs knew and showed frustration, pulling him by the leash, but to little effect. He was stubborn, slow to learn and had a bad attitude. He had no idea who was in control.

Sage patted the raised fender of the Chrysler Cordoba in the drive.

"Do you get to drive it?" Jack asked.

"Only when he's in the car," was the impatient reply.

Lev relinquished the reins to Jack, faced him and with a half-elegant semi-bow said, "Thank you for dinner and for the walk home. I'm sorry if we got excited in the conversation. We have a family disagreement."

"Not at all; it was an animated discussion."

The rabbi stopped and shooed the boys in. Turning to Jack he exclaimed, "So! Now for a nice little walk. What do you say? The evening has cleared up a little and I'd like to talk to you."

"Let's go."

It was like dancing now. Perhaps the March of the Tin Soldiers. They had rehearsed, learned one another's moves; tendered their complaints to one another, and created a cadence that was their own. It was a four-part dance, for even the dogs knew the steps and paced the rhythms. It seemed somehow genetic, some inherited remnant of Eastern Europe, some feature of physical dimensions: short legs, long bodies, rolling hips. From behind, one could even see their hands in sympathetic motion, choreographed by a power neither knew without the other.

"They're beautiful boys, Isaac. You have to be very proud of them."

"It's funny. As you can see, they're a pain in the neck sometimes. You know? But when they're gone, I really miss them. I really miss them."

"When are they gone?"

They were at the end of Crosscut now and had made what was becoming a habitual turn onto Pinecrest toward Bill Rothwell's house. Cady smartened her stride in anticipation of a rendezvous with Sandy.

"They go away for Christmas vacation and then for most of the summer. They go to visit their mother in Costa Rica."

"From the look of them, she's clearly a Central American."

"Yes, well" He breathed a deep sigh. "Maybe. I guess."

"Did you ever happen to look? I mean while you were married to her?"

"You have all the subtlety of an interrogator for the FBI. What kind of a psychologist are you? A confrontive shmeggegah?"

"What did you call me?"

"Oh. Never mind. Yes, she's a Central American, of course. But from a curious, curious people. Ach! It's complex. You see in 1492 the Spaniards expelled all the Jews from Spain. You've heard of the Inquisition? Under Torquemada, the Grand Inquisitor, the flower of Jewish civilization was given the choice of leaving Spain or converting to Christianity. Lots left and went this way and that. They became what we now call the Sephardic Jews - Jews with a Spanish heritage who speak a language called Ladino - it's a . . . a . . . a low form of Spanish. Well, lots of them converted to Christianity and stayed in Spain. And lots of the converts maintained their Judaism in secret. They met in secret, taught their children in secret, married in secret. You understand? These were called Marranos or Conversos. But even showing the outward uh . . . uh . . . manifestations of Christianity, the Spaniards suspected them and kept the heat on to find them out. When they found them out, they tried them for heresy and had an auto da fe - they burned them at the stake. At this time the New World was opening up and lots of Marranos went to the New World to escape the pressure. Like always, they were running from. Some of them wound up in Central America. Including the family of my former wife. And for four hundred or so years they practiced these little family customs. Every Friday night they would light a candle and drink some wine. On special days of the year they fasted, or they ate no bread. The old women arranged marriages for them - always with families who practiced these rituals. Mind you, most of them didn't even know why they did these things. They had really lost their Judaism as such. Only the old women knew the secrets."

"These people knew they were Jews? Or didn't they?"

"Well, I can't answer that exactly. But there are pockets of them all over the Western Hemisphere. There's even some in New Mexico. Then, a funny thing happened. Just when the Nazis were taking over in the thirties, a bunch of Jewish businessmen in Poland either saw what was coming or by accident invested some of their money in Costa Rica and opened up factories. In 1939 they were able to bribe their way out and they moved their families to San Jose where they already had businesses set up. The Costa Ricans never called them Judaeos, Jews; they called them Polackos, Poles. Now you had these two groups: This little group of secret antique

Jews and this community of Polish Jews. In some ways they had some things in common. They were both rich communities by San Jose standards and they began to do business together. And the old women in the Marranos made an amazing decision. They began identifying these newcomers as suitable marriage partners. The Jews, the Polackos, didn't. They wanted their children to marry Jews, and to them, these Marranos were gentiles, but of course the supply of eligible Jews was limited, so there was a lot of pressure to intermarry. Then, these Marrano families did something very brave for them. They broke the tradition of secrecy and invited Jewish families for dinner on Friday night and the Marranos - you know, nobody ever called them that but me - lit a candle and brought out a special cup of wine. The Jews thought they were being hospitable and quaint. But there was a curious kind of communication, you know? And a couple of marriages occurred and the Marranos moved unsteadily toward a kind of Judaism as the Polackos tried to preserve their own Judaism in Costa Rica - it was a very interesting phenomenon. You could write a book about it."

"Your ex-wife was one of these women."

"Yes. Nominally Catholic, descended from what was probably a Marrano family. Pressured by her family to marry into this community of wealthy Jews."

"But how did you get there? You were in the camps in the war. This was Costa Rica."

"I got there after the war".

"How?"

"I was living in Paris - if you can call what I was doing 'living'. I was one of lots of what were lovingly called DPs, displaced persons. I didn't have a passport and I was being fed in the soup kitchens and sleeping wherever I could find a short-term friend. I say short-term because I had no money; the French had no money. They were suffering the after-effects of the war like everybody. When I wore out my welcome, I moved on. Then HIAS - you know them?"

"No."

"The Hebrew Immigrant Aid Society, a blessing by Jews upon Jews. They do what they are called - they aid immigrants. They told me that there was a business opportunity in Costa Rica. Some manufacturers were looking for a young man to manage a factory. Someone who knew leather. They asked me if I knew leather. 'Leather!' I told them, 'Yes, I have an intimate acquaintance with leather, courtesy of the SS. What do they manufacture? Boots for colonels who like to ride horseback on their inspections? Gloves for feeding bodies into the ovens? Aprons for shoveling ashes out of the ovens? Leather! Ha! I have the equivalent of a doctorate from Auschwitz University. I am your man."

"They helped you get to Costa Rica?"

"They got me to Costa Rica; they helped me get Spanish lessons; they helped me find a place to live; they got me the job - they saved my life - a life, I might add, which seemed to need perpetual saving."

"And they got you a wife?"

Isaac stopped. Jack stopped in concert, a pause in the dance. The dogs, sensing an intermission, likewise stopped and sat obediently awaiting further direction from the choreographer.

"Better if they had. You know, whoever traded in the idea of arranged marriages for romantic marriages was a complete fool. In the Hasidic community, every marriage is arranged. Oh, the groom and the bride have a veto power, but generally speaking, they marry who their parents choose for them. You know what happens when you marry for love?"

"I have the feeling you're going to tell me something I never thought about."

"When you marry for love you think that it will make you happy and you expect everything from your wife. Everything that you don't get disappoints you and eventually you wind up unhappy and you blame your wife."

"And . . ."

"When you have an arranged marriage, you don't expect to be happy and you frankly don't expect very much from your wife. The result is that anything that you get from her is a true blessing, which makes you very happy and you also realize that your happiness is by and large your own to create."

"And what happens to love in all of this?"

"Love? Love is a curse. Love is having your heart pound, your face flush, and your armpits sweat. It's like having a heart attack only it lasts longer."

"Did you love this woman?"

"Yes, of course. My heart pounded and my face flushed, and my armpits - you know. I was young, I had lost years of my life, I wanted, uh . . .uh . . ."

"To get laid. It's OK, Isaac. You can tell me these things. After all, I am a psychologist."

"Are you making fun of me?"

"No, but your rendition of a horny adolescent is truly touching. Can we keep walking? The dogs are getting comfortable and may want to bed down for the night. You can keep talking; you married for love?"

"Well, I did. I had seen her in town, and she was quite beautiful, and I found myself very attracted to her."

"From looking at the boys, I would say that she must have been very beautiful."

"But you didn't just ask a girl out on a date. There were certain formalities you had to go through. Her family wanted to arrange a suitable marriage for her, but they didn't have a lot of money for a dowry. She was headstrong and hard for them to control. So, I asked the owner of the shoe factory that I worked for, and to whom I was like a son in many ways, to approach them for me and to ask if I was an acceptable suitor. They were looking not so much for me . . . they were looking to marry her into money. But she was interested in romance and so Fichter, my boss, served as my father-surrogate. I was the right age and he told her family that, that I had . . . you know . . . prospects and they were satisfied."

"And they believed this?"

"Well, I did."

"You told the family that you had been saving up for years and they thought you meant money."

"You are making fun of me!"

"No, I'm not. Go on. Go on."

"I courted her and her family encouraged her and we got married, had two boys. And . . ."

"It didn't work."

"Sometimes that's the problem when people get divorced." Isaac went on, "No, I mean, I was a European and she was Latin. I wasn't what she expected. She wasn't what I expected. I couldn't speak Yiddish to her and that was the language in which I . . . eh . . . eh, in which I expressed what was inside of me. You know? I could do business in German. I could run a factory with Spanish. But I couldn't conduct a marriage in Spanish. You understand?"

"Yeah, I really do. And her?"

"And she couldn't speak Yiddish and . . . and . . . she had expectations for a lifestyle that I . . . wasn't a part of. It just didn't work. And I did things that young men do that are acceptable in Latin society - and that I suppose she expected. But for me it wasn't right. I couldn't be married and carry on and I hated myself and I hated her and so it ended. She hated me and I hated her and it went exactly as a divorce should go."

"And her family disowned you?"

"No, they disowned her. She was supposed to stay married to me and be faithful. Before the divorce was final, which in Latin American takes forever, she had taken up with another man, a Catholic, and that was totally unacceptable to them. For them, to marry outside the tradition was unthinkable, despite the fact that they lived their daily lives as Catholics and practiced this ersatz, clandestine Judaism. She even married him - is still married to him - and her family has never forgiven her. When I went to Cincinnati . . ."

"Wait a minute! Wait a minute! How did we get from Costa Rica to Cincinnati?"

"There was a scholarship offered every year to the Hebrew Union College in Cincinnati for a Latin American to come and study for the rabbinate. Nobody ever applied for it. I heard about it, actually through HIAS, and I applied and got it. It was wonderful, Jack. I was going to America. Someone was paying me to come. Of course the assumption was that the recipient of the scholarship would go back to Latin America as a rabbi, but that was not what I had in mind."

"And the boys? How did you get them out?"

"Well, her family had no use for her, and they still liked me. And for them, this was an opportunity for their grandsons to come to America and to be Americans. It was a dream for them. They would be able to say, 'My grandsons in America.'"

"But I assume that that's the reform seminary. How could you go to a reform seminary?"

"I sort of didn't know from reform, if you know what I mean. What I mean is that where I came from, there was no such thing as Reform Judaism. You were a Hasid or Orthodox. There was nothing else. When they told me 'seminary', I thought, 'Oh, Orthodox, not Hasidic, but that will have to do. When I got to Cincinnati, I learned about Reform."

They were well along toward the Holston School by this time, nearly halfway around the circumference of Southmoor. The night was sharp and clear with little breeze to chill the metal fittings on leather jackets and parkas. They walked easily in habit now, so subtle had been this marriage of souls. The houses along the streets were pleasant irrelevances, inhabited by the anonymous engaged in inane conversations while these two explored the individual intricacies of life lived in history.

"Someday there'll be no Reform. There'll be no Conservative or Orthodox. We'll all be Jews again."

"That's hard to envision, Isaac."

"Don't be silly. Reform was an invention. It's maybe a hundred years old. Conservative was an invention. It's less than a hundred years old. In another hundred years, we'll un-invent them both because we won't need them. They were responses to the difficulties of being Jewish in a secular world. But we've learned how to do that now. Even the Orthodox can be Jews in a secular world. We don't need Reform or Conservative after another hundred years or so."

"This is wonderful prophecy. I don't see it myself. It seems to me that you, being mildly schizophrenic, I mean a Hasid who's a Reform rabbi running a schizophrenic temple, with Reform services on Friday night and Conservative services on Saturday morning. You're the perfect embodiment of the contradictions and incongruities of modern Judaism. In case it has escaped your attention, we Jews don't seem to like one another. You can't even get your crowd together in one service. You don't have a temple. You have two temples and for each one that you have, the congregants wouldn't be caught dead in the other."

"Then you don't understand the nature of a synagogue, shmeyer. A synagogue is like an umbrella: Different people can stand under it and keep from getting wet, but only if they're willing to be close to one another. There's no room for hatred. You have to have a tolerance for every single other member of the synagogue or it falls apart."

"What about your friend, Phil Dorfman, whom you sicced on me like a hunting hound. In your lexicon, he's the personification of evil. He would tear the place apart and you with it."

Isaac stopped. He positioned himself close to Jack. He put his palm flat on Jack's chest and began, "No, Jack, Phil has a kind of sadness, but he is not evil. Believe me, I know from evil and he is not evil. Do you understand? I have seen evil. Phil is . . . is . . . wrestling with the ghost of his dead father and he's angry at his father and he feels his father's anger at him, but he's not evil. He's running from. Only for Phil, he's running from himself - and that's the hardest person to escape from."

"Have you been talking to Myron Tabanov?"

"Myron Tabanov is no fool. He may be crazy, but he's not stupid. You'll find out. And Phil Dorfman is not evil. He may be tormented and he may act it out in funny ways, but he's sad, not evil."

Jack turned to resume the walk. "Watch out for the sad guys then, rabbi. He makes noises like he'd get rid of you in a flash if he could."

"He can't. People who come from big bureaucracies think that you can hire and fire rabbis at will. It's not so. This is, unfortunately, an American disease that comes from business success. A rabbi gives a congregation a personality, a character. Even bad rabbis can be good for congregations. You don't just hire and fire."

"Rabbi, unless I miss my guess, you work for a board of directors. Those guys vote and I assume that you work on a contract which they renew periodically. And if you don't get renewed, you walk. And if you get one or two committed agitators, you are history. Am I wrong on this?"

"You're right and you're wrong - on a lot of things. The board of directors is just another theater for individual ambition. People get to the top and they get bored with it. Presidents, boards, they come and they go. But what you have missed is the sense of synagogue or church for that matter or anything else as a community. And a community is a lot more than a board of directors. If you don't believe in the notion of a community, you can't succeed as rabbi."

"Isaac, great philosophy. I love it and I believe in it. But you get one powerful, committed and, dare I say, evil person talking about change and you will be faced with an insurrection in your community."

"Phil isn't evil, he's narcissistic - and perhaps that is the ultimate evil. What is it that you believe in your psychology? You think that everybody is basically good and that all you have to do is to understand their pathology and give them therapy. That's not true - I saw people who were guards in the camps. They had an evil in them that wasn't psychopathology, but it was evil. They loved their children, their dogs, and they murdered Jews and communists and homosexuals and intellectuals and Christian Fundamentalists and Gypsies without a care. There was an evil in them that wasn't a product of their pathology, it was just evil. There is evil in the world, Jack and it captures people. There is evil. But people are not evil and Phil is not evil. Do you understand what I'm saying?"

"Point conceded. Phil is not evil. Sick, maybe. In need of help, maybe. But not evil and still capable for reasons that are sick and not evil of making a lot of trouble which in its outcomes will be—watch out now, evil."

"Point conceded. Evil deeds, done for reasons that are not themselves evil, bring evil into the world. You know what I believe? I believe that there are good angels and there are evil angels and we make them ourselves."

"More please." They were most of the way home. The dogs tugged at the leash to complete the journey. But Jack held them back, slowed, patiently waited for what might come from his friend.

"Every good act that we do - every mitzvah - every unselfish act of devotion to something greater than ourselves creates a spiritual entity that is good, and you can call this an angel. And every good angel that we create, creates more good in the world. But every selfish act that we do - every time we ignore what is good and right to do that which is self-serving, mean spirited, uncaring or whatever- every such act creates an evil spiritual entity that you could call an angel of evil. And these angels of evil create more evil in the world. And the person who creates many such angels of evil is eventually consumed by them himself and suffers terribly, and the world suffers as well."

"Do people become captives of these evil angels?"

"Yes and no. Every person has the option at every moment to create good angels or evil angels. The more of one kind you create, the more you become like them. But you never lose your ability to change what you create."

"And your job as a rabbi?"

"Is to teach people how to create good angels."

"Isaac, I don't know whether you're naive and charmingly quaint or very insightful."

"When you figure that, you will have found wisdom of one kind - or of another kind. Good night."

CHAPTER 9

"You had a strange phone call," Ilene began, before even a 'good morning'. "Get this. This guy calls and says, 'Is Professor Israel there?' 'No,' I say, 'can I take a message?' 'Well, he goes on, 'have you looked for him under the desk? In the wastebasket? Is he crouched somewhere in fetal position, sucking his thumb?' Then he gives me this funny little laugh. Do you know this guy?" She handed him a pink message slip.

"Myron Tabanov. Who would have guessed? Is this his home number or his office?"

"I know how you can find out."

Jack hung his coat and dropped into the armchair. Several fourteen-inch piles on the desk wavered threateningly. He dutifully drew an item or two off the top of each, examined them and re-distributed them to other, more stable piles. He reached for the telephone and called the number on the slip. A female voice answered.

"Hellowwww."

"Hello, is Dr. Tabanov there, please?"

"Whooo is calling please?"

"Jack Israel. Is this his office or his home?"

"Ohhhhh. Jaaack. I've heard about you. This is Roseanne Tabanov. I've been looking forward to meeting you. You sound like such an interesting person."

"Well . . ., Thank you, uhhh. I'm returning a call to Myron. Is he there?"

"Oh, yes, just a minute."

"Hello?"

"Myron? Jack Isaacs returning your call. How are you doing?"

"Jack! Jack! How are you? I was wondering if you'd like to have lunch today?"

"Well, actually, I have a racquetball date with Pat Dunphy, my graduate student at noon."

"Wonderful! Perhaps you wouldn't mind if I joined you. I have a locker at the gym and a racquet tucked in it. Can I meet you there at noon?"

"If you don't mind playing a threesome."

"Fine. Fine. I'll see you there at noon."

Jack wondered what he meant by that.

The professor and the novitiate walked to the gym from McCormick Hall. The weather had chilled, the wind had risen and swept across the campus tucking its cold fingers in between buttons and under hats. They checked in, offering identification cards, collected fresh towels, nodded at naked men standing in front of lockers, and eventually made their way to adjacent metal closets, which were the symbols of their masculinity. Myron was already there, parading around with nothing on and prattling nonsense to anyone who would listen. He was being politely ignored when he noticed Jack and Dunphy.

"Oh good. I'm just about ready to play."

"What? No sneakers!" snorted Dunphy.

"Oh. Hi. I'm Myron Tabanov. You must be the Vice President for Academic Repairs."

"Pat Dunphy," he said, extending a roughened hand.

Jack and Dunphy opened their lockers and dressed in close-fitting nylon shorts and t-shirts with low cross-laced athletic shoes. Myron donned shorts that tied with a string and extended halfway down his thighs. His shirt had three-quarter length sleeves and three buttons at the neck. He tugged at his high-top Converse basketball sneakers and announced his readiness to take on all comers.

Once in the court, it was clear that this was to be a battle of tactical styles. Dunphy preferred to serve. He was built powerfully and low to the ground. He leaned over the ball as if keeping its whereabouts a secret from his adversaries, dropped it mere inches to the floor and whaled at it with vicious precision. Jack, standing to the rear and left, deferred to Myron as the ball ricocheted off the back wall with a sharp, "Thwack." Myron took an easy step away from the wall, reached low to the ball and lofted it up, up, up in an easy arc where it kissed the front wall, slid down its face, bounced high off the floor, and continued in a repetitive arc.

Dunphy charged to the side, leaped into the air and smashed the ball down and into a corner with force and conviction. The ball bit the wall, bounced the floor, and came back up in another high arc. Myron stood, simply watching it for a long moment, raised his head with the ball's arc, lowered it, moved his racquet to the side with agonizing deliberation and tapped the ball which dutifully went into a forward corner and dribbled out.

"Aw, Jeez. Another old man who's gonna play shitcan racquetball. I can't even work up a sweat if you're gonna play like this. Come on, willya? Just hit the goddam ball."

Myron now owned the serve. The pattern was set. He entered the service box, turned to smile at his opponents, gave the ball a long drop from his outstretched arm and hit it high onto the front wall. It came back in a looping curve directly to the right rear corner of the court where Dunphy stood developing purple hues. The ball rattled around in the corner and never really came out. Dunphy flailed at it, but the point was evident.

"You know, I got a stats class after this and maybe I'll just let you geezers pass gas at one another. There's no sense in my trying to get a workout when you two geriatric cases would rather play billiards with racquets. Boss, I'll catch you back at the office."

He grabbed at the small semi-circle that substituted for a handle and ducked though the miniature door into the hall.

"I'm sorry," began Myron, "do you think I should have gone easier on him?"

"No. That's just Dunphy," Jack laughed. "We can play by ourselves for a while."

Myron took the next serve. Jack was prepared for the high lob that would dribble out of the corner. He charged the ball before the bounce and got off a straight return to the front that skimmed along the left-hand wall. Dashing to the center of the court he stationed himself for Myron's return. Myron took one half step forward and to the left, twisted hard to hit the ball with a sweeping backhand and executed a graceful follow- through that connected his racquet squarely with the bridge of Jack's nose.

There was color and music everywhere. Jack lay on his back and saw flashes of light yellow, bright white, red; round, jagged like lightning. And he heard sounds: Bells, echoes. He cautiously opened his eyes and looked up to see Myron's bobbing head and pinpoint blue eyes looming overhead and heard him laugh.

"Are you all right? I hope I didn't hurt you. We can replay that volley if you like. Are you OK?"

"I . . . don't . . . want . . . to . . . play . . . anymore." He propped up on an elbow, rolled over on his hands and knees and pushed himself up from the floor. The room swayed slowly, but with well-placed steps he was able to find the door and exit. Myron pursued him.

"Well, I wasn't really up for a game anyway. Say, are you all right? I didn't hurt you, did I?"

Jack spun. He had a racquet in his hand, but it was a lousy weapon and he had already been bested in his first bout. He didn't dare strike out with it, but he thought about it for a sweet second. His nose throbbed with the piercing intensity of a smoke alarm. His ears rang and his eyeballs felt loose in his head.

"No, you didn't hurt me. If I were lying there on the floor dying, I would not give you the perverse satisfaction of telling you that you hurt me. I'm not hurt at all. I always feel this way. It's just that today is your day to make me feel this way. Do you understand?"

"Perhaps we should talk about this".

Myron graciously offered lunch and several more weak apologies along with advice about smash-proof glasses, nose guards and protective head gear. Jack had difficulty maintaining his show of anger in the face of diminishing pain. They showered, dressed and walked together in stiff conversation out to Myron's car.

In the parking lot sat a dark green Volvo sedan. It was the larger model. As they approached from the rear Jack noticed red line tires, dual exhausts, and a lowered look to the car.

"Myron, this car has dual exhausts. It comes with a straight six engine. Why does it have dual exhausts?"

"Oh, this is sort of a . . . new model."

"Myron. What is this?"

"Well, seeing as you asked, I'll show you." He opened the door, unlatched the hood's catch and walked to the front of the car, where, with great ceremony, he lifted the hood.

Jack looked, and laughed, "That's a 351 Ford Cleveland V8 if ever I saw one! Where did you get this?"

"I had it made. See it's a great chassis, but it lacked power, so I had this engine installed - it's been breathed on a little if you know what I mean - and then, if you look under the fenders, I mounted fat red-line radials on it but they're offset toward the inside, so you don't see them really, and I lowered the suspension about an inch and toughened up the shocks, but the only transmission that I could find to take the torque was a Jaguar and I have problems with the CenterForce clutch getting hung up
and . . ."

"I understand. I understand. I understand. If Dunphy ever talks to you again, you've got to show him this car. He'll appreciate it."

They drove downtown to a small Oriental restaurant, the only one in Bloomington. It was called the Peking and was an accident of American education. The son of a Chinese family from Boston that ran an outstanding restaurant in suburban Medford had come to study engineering in Bloomington. When the market for engineers looked bleak at graduation, he opened a branch of the family business in Bloomington. It was engineering's loss. The lemon chicken was known for counties around. With some notice Peking duck could be had. Pot stickers, pork-filled dumplings, were a regular item on the menu as well as Moo Shi Pork, hot and sour soup and other delicacies to delight an emperor. There was little on the menu Jack would eat.

He ordered the Chinese vegetable soup, the Buddha's delight, white rice, and water to drink. Myron seemed to know the small Asian woman who waited on them. He ordered the hot and sour soup, a plate of pot stickers, and the pork lo mein Szechuan style.

"Who's at home beside your charming nurse-wife, who will soon need a nurse midwife?"

"Three kids and two head of dog."

"Hmmm. What kinds of heads on dogs?"

"Newfoundlands."

Myron stopped in mid slurp. He laid down his lacquered soup spoon with clear deliberation. "Jack, I knew when I met you that you were a very sick man. I now believe that you are critically deranged and that even I cannot help you. You definitely need to see a specialist and, frankly, I don't think there's any hope at all."

It was suddenly clear. It was worse than clear. It was iridescent, translucent and, at the same time, mind-boggling. Jack understood. "What's your Newfie's name?"

Myron grinned the grin of recognition, "Schweniak."

"That means 'pig' in Polish."

"Yes, my mother-in-law's Polish."

"So's mine, but I didn't have the courage to name one of my dogs after her."

The two of them laughed the laugh of long-lost relatives reunited. They slumped back from their protected positions, giggled and told utterly stupid dog stories that would have bored or gagged other people at lunch. They told stories of dog spit and dog poop and dog hair in food and dogs that snored and dogs that twitched in the night and dogs and children and dogs and cats and dogs that died and made them cry. And then they talked about cars: Cars that ran fast and cars that ran bad and cars that were never allowed to run but were there to be polished and loved. And then they talked about wives.

"Do you know any Mafia hit-men?" Myron began brazenly.

"No, can't say that I do. You know there are less complicated ways to end a marriage, Myron."

"But you see, I can't divorce her. I would lose my children and I'd have to pay her alimony and she'd get the house and it would make her happy and then she'd be miserable, and I don't want her to be miserable."

"Wait a minute. Back up. I was with you 'til you got to the happy-miserable part."

"Well, you see, Roseanne is a person who's not happy unless she's miserable. Do you see? She hates herself - but she doesn't know that. And so, when she's miserable, she feels like she's getting what she deserves and she's happy - but she doesn't know that she's happy, of course; she thinks she's miserable. Now on the other hand, when she's happy, then she's tormented by guilt so she's really miserable and she feels the need to screw up her life hopelessly by doing all kinds of destructive things so she can be miserable again. Am I making sense to you?"

"I'm . . . not . . . sure."

"Well, Jack, there are a lot of people out there like that. I make my living on people like that. There are thousands of them and I must admit that I'm very good at treating them."

"Then why not treat Roseanne?"

"Because I'm her husband. And a key part of her life. And in order to make herself miserable, which is the only way that she can be happy, she has to screw up our marriage. Thus, I'm not at all in a position to be a therapeutic agent in this. She goes off and cheats on me and is mean to our children and throws my money away to make me angry so that our marriage can be miserable. And that's what makes her happy. You see divorce is out of the question. It would end in the most horrific, endless court battle imaginable which would make both of us miserable which would make her happy and me miserable. Jack, I fully expected that you would understand this if anyone would - being a psychologist with a Newfoundland and a Polish wife, I mean."

It was frightening, because Jack thought that indeed he might understand. Fortunately, his roster of Mafia hit-men friends was low at the time and so he begged off. Lunch came and went. Myron carefully halved the check and announced to Jack his fifty per cent including tax and tip despite the fact that Jack had eaten less than one-third the cost of the lunch for two. He accounted the loss as good-will and began to collect himself to leave.

"Hang on a minute, Jack."

"Yes?"

"How's Rae doing?"

"Average. She's tired and nauseous and has headaches - you know. You saw her."

"Who's her obstetrician?"

"Maria Acosta. Do you know her?"

"No. Has she seen Dr. Acosta lately?"

"Yes. Just the other day."

"Did she ask about the fatigue, nausea, and headaches?"

"Yes."

"What did Acosta say?"

"She apparently told her that she was an older pregnant woman who was under a lot of stress and to take some Darvon and don't worry about it."

"Jack. I don't know this Dr. Acosta at all and I'm sure she's a very good obstetrician. You know, I would never second-guess another physician - especially in something that's not my area. You understand?"

"Yes. I understand."

"Well, I'm not second-guessing Dr. Acosta. But a persistent headache and nausea and fatigue is a real set of symptoms, pregnant or not. And you might - you just might - want to talk to somebody else. Naturally I wouldn't say any more than that, but there's a good neurologist at the Creditor Clinic, a guy named Ian MacKenzie that you could talk to. He trained in Chicago and spent some time at the Diamond Headache Clinic. I have a lot of respect for him."

"Are you trying to tell me something specific?"

"No. No. But call his office. Tell his secretary that you're a friend of mine and that you'd like to be seen relatively soon. If there's any difficulty, tell them that you're on the faculty of the medical school and if that doesn't work have them call me."

"Why all this, Myron?"

"Nothing specific. I like Rae. She's one of the best nurses that I see on the floor and she appreciates fine dogs. Leave it at that. Just do it. Huh, Jack?"

CHAPTER 10

"Hey, Boss. You're a popular man today,"

Ilene looked up from her novel long enough to pass a pink slip to Jack as he came in the door. She made no pretense of working when there was no work to do. To feign business would have been dishonest and there was no room in her soul for dishonesty. She was at work on time every day. If she missed, she made it up. She took advantage of the liberal university policies on free tuition and released time for employees. But never more. Tasks were begun early and completed on time. Not only was there an orderliness to her life, she brought order to the lives of those around her.

Dunphy was different. His rhythms were not of the clock. He rose when the sun came up - early in summer, late in winter. He worked when there was work to be done; the closer the deadline the better. When his stomach gnawed, he ate; when he was bored and lethargic, he went to the gym. Life was an endless round of fixing machines and tending to the little problems of daily existence. A career was only an accident to be capitalized upon if profitable.

The other secretaries in the department were mostly farmers' wives. They worked to provide a steady income for families who lived in an endless cycle of boom and bust, feast and famine, bumper crop and drought or flood. They described their husbands as men who liked to work six or eight weeks a year - getting the crop planted in spring and getting it harvested in fall. The rest of the year was spent at the grain elevator checking on the momentary fluctuations in the prices of corn or beans or in the barn maintaining the tractor, the harvester, the baler, whatever. These women adored Dunphy. They would have liked to take him home for their daughters, perhaps for themselves. They disliked Ilene. She baffled them.

She was different where they were the same, urbane where they were rural, quiet when they cackled. It was a burden that she wore comfortably.

Jack snatched the message and read, "Rabbi Abrams, 659-8522, Eastern European accent, rather peremptory, no manners. Please call."

He dialed to get, "Temple Beth Jacob. Roseanne speaking."

"Hello, this is Jack Israel returning Rabbi Abrams call."

"Hello, Dr. Israel. I'll see if he's available."

"How did she know I was Dr. Israel?" he noted, silently.

"Jack, Jack. Thank you for calling. Look I have someone here right now and I can't talk, but it's important that we chat. You'll come for a walk with me tonight?"

"Sure, Isaac. What time?"

"Oh, the usual."

"I'm sorry if he was gruff on the phone," Jack called into Ilene. "He sort of has a right and he exercises it freely."

"Does it come with ordination?"

"No, if comes from having survived the concentration camps."

"I'm sorry that he went through that. But having been victimized doesn't confer a license to victimize other people, even in small ways."

"Ilene, you're a dear and I treasure you, but there are some things that go beyond your understanding and mine."

"Boss, you're a dear, but there are some things that go beyond your understanding too."

She stared at him directly, eyes locked. It was as silent and aggressive a gesture as she had ever shown.

"My father was in a concentration camp, Boss, only you didn't call it that because it was located in the Nevada desert and not in Europe and because America won the war. And he was not there because he was a Jew, but because he was a Japanese businessman living in California. And he lost his business and something of his psyche in the Nevada desert."

"I'm sorry, Ilene, I never knew that."

"I know."

"I've heard about the internment camps. What happened to him?"

"He survived, thank you. He got out, went back to Petaluma, my hometown, and tried to start again. His house was gone, his business was gone. But he met this nice farm girl from Iowa, my mother, and for reasons that I'll never figure out, he married her. Two kids later, he realized that as far as the rest of California was concerned he was still a nasty little Nip and it was going to be a long time before he'd be allowed to forget the atrocities that he personally committed at Pearl Harbor and Guam and Guadalcanal and in Malaysia and China and Korea. He left and went back to Japan. Divorced my mother and decided that it was easier to be Japanese in Japan than in California."

"I'm sorry. Do you still have contact with him?"

"No. He used to send birthday cards to me and my sister every year. Then we grew up and started to move around and we lost track of one another."

"Ilene, I'm sorry. I had no idea."

Jack knew when to back-pedal, but the actual skill of back-pedaling was another matter entirely. He wanted to leave, to be somewhere else, anywhere else; but there was business to be done here and only Ilene could complete the transaction.

"Hey. It's not a trauma. But history gives licenses to grieve only to the winning side. My father was a casualty too, you know?"

The driveway was crowded with vehicles of - two, three and four wheels - one bicycle that belonged to Simmy, one bicycle with training wheels that had once belonged to Simmy that now belonged to Lee, one Big Wheel trike that had once belonged to Lee that now belonged to Dinah and one Volkswagen bus that had belonged to a half dozen strangers, none of whom ever had it serviced. Jack parked the truck in the street, normally an infraction of neighborliness sure to irritate Jim Bascom, and charged through the door.

Each child got an appropriate kiss which they studiously ignored. The dogs cornered Jack until each had gotten major physical affection. Watching their obvious disappointment, he hung his coat in the closet and called into the kitchen, "Do these guys have to go out?"

"No. I just had them out and if they say they need to go, they're lying."

"Okay, how are you?" He needn't have asked. She was gray and thin everyplace but her belly and he knew.

"Fine, I guess. By the way - did you take the Darvon out of the bathroom cabinet?"

"No. Why would I do that?"

"It's gone. And I asked each of the kids - very, very carefully and not confrontively - if they had taken it and they say they didn't."

"That's crazy. What do you think happened to it?"

"I know damned well what happened to it. Our little friend, Merrill, the newsboy, asked if he could use the bathroom this afternoon. Came in as pleasant as you please. Brought the paper to the door with a smile and asked if he could use it. He took a long time in there and I never heard the toilet flush. That little bastard rifled our medicine cabinet and made off with the Darvon. That's what happened!!"

"Oh, Rae. Rae. Easy, there. He's a kid. His father's the principal of the school. He wouldn't do that. Are you sure?"

"Got a better explanation?"

"Oh, I don't think that's possible."

"I'll tell you what I think. I think we ought to call his parents and have a frank discussion with them. And if they don't like it, we call the cops."

"Rae, we have no evidence that he took it. Take it easy, here."

"Your home has been invaded, Professor. You need to think about this."

They cleared the table together and stacked dishes in the dishwasher. Rae moved slowly. The Midwest night sucked the light out of the kitchen into the back yard. They could see their heads in shadow outline, lying on the brown grass in the back. Southmoor lay far enough away from the center of Bloomington that the pollution of streetlights didn't rob it of the night. The streetlights in town gave a mobility to its residents at night. One was never locked in by the dark. Southmoor was different. The sentinel houselights were no match for the night. Families closed their doors and stayed in, sifting with one another the meanings of the day. Only those who were different left the nighttime protection of a Southmoor home.

"I had lunch with Myron Tabanov today. He took me to the Peking as an apology for beating me over the head with a racquetball racquet."

"He's a very strange man."

"How so?"

"He's the only board-certified psychiatrist at St. Mary's as far as I can tell. The rest are refugees from malpractice suits in anesthesiology, shot nerves in the ER, or whatever. And he prescribes meds about half as often as everyone else and then in half doses."

"How do his patients do?"

"They seem to like him. But they're crazy, so what do they know? Besides, do you know anything that does work for those folks?"

"He was asking about your headaches. He said there's a neurologist at Creditor Clinic that does a lot with headache and you might want to see him. Name's Ian MacKenzie. Myron pushed it real hard. What do you think?"

"I think I need to make an appointment. Jeez, I hate to do it this way. Maria Acosta is a dear and she should be making a referral if she thinks there's something wrong, but damn I hurt and it's not getting any better."

"Myron says to tell him that your husband is on the faculty of the medical school and that you're a friend of Myron's and to get an early appointment."

"I'll call tomorrow."

There was a banging on the front door. Rae smiled a tired smile, "It's either the Seventh Day Adventists or the Mormons, I'm sure."

Jack was ready. He grabbed a coat from the closet, the leashes from the hook, shackled the dogs and checked to be sure that there was an ample supply of plastic bags in his pockets. He did not so much open the door for his guest as blow through it, bowling Isaac over as he made his practiced exit.

"Hi, I was ready for you," he said, one quarter of the way down the drive.

"I see. What's your hurry? It's a nice night, no?"

The foursome collected in formation and began their practiced route.

"Isaac, do you get the Courier?"

"Yes, of course. I'm a rabbi. I have to know what's going on in town."

"Do you get it delivered?"

"Yes, like everybody."

"Who delivers it?"

"Merrill. He lives up on Hyacinth. I know his father. He's the principal at the junior high school. A nice man. What's this about?"

"Does Merrill ever ask to use your bathroom?"

"Yes, sometimes. Is this not allowed?"

"Well, he often asks to use ours and Rae noticed that there are drugs missing from our medicine cabinet and she suspects him."

"No. That's foolish. He's a kid, from a nice family. Tell me . . . you know, I mean no offense . . . I mean only to ask: Is Rae, uh . . .uh . . . uncomfortable around black people?"

"Isaac! Absolutely not. There's not a racist cell in her body."

"Well, you have to ask. You know there's this kid I wanted to talk to you about. He was in my office when you called, and I need to talk to you about him. He's kind of a strange kid and he has some definite, how do you say— attitudes toward black people and I don't know what to do with him."

"Are you doing race relations on the side?"

"No. No. It's a funny story."

"Before you start your funny story, do you know any more about Merrill?"

"No, but I have to talk to you about this kid. Maybe five months ago, the end of the summer, this kid shows up at Friday night services. That's a slow time of the year, so you notice who's new in the congregation. I would say, he's seventeen years old, a big kid, clearly not at ease in the shul and he comes up to me after services and introduces himself, he says, 'Rabbi, I'm Matt Cowan.' As though I'm supposed to recognize the name. I say hello and he goes on, 'I think my father used to come to this temple, Aaron Cowan?' I tell him as politely as I can that I don't remember Aaron Cowan, but then I've only been here a few years and it might have been before my time, but he doesn't stop there. 'He was a major in the Air Force. He was stationed at Cardiss Air Force Base in Montrose.' I explain that, indeed, I am a chaplain at the Air Force Base, but that I don't know his father. He asks if he can come and talk to me and, of course, I agree."

"Big kid? Seventeen or so? Was he at the service that I came to a couple of Saturdays ago?"

"Yes. That's him, he comes to see me in my office and launches into this story. He tells me that his father is Jewish, that he divorced his mother, who is not Jewish, when he was about six years old, that he has no contact with him now, but that after going to Sunday school at the Evangelicals for most of his life, he has decided that he really is Jewish and wants to—you have to listen to this. He says, 'I want to be a Jew.' Not, 'I want to be Jewish' or 'I want to convert to Judaism,' but, 'I want to be Jew.'"

"What do you figure that means?"

"That he doesn't know a Jew from a whistle, but that's not the point. If he asks, I have to respond."

"Doesn't he have to go through a formal conversion, I mean if his mother's not Jewish. My understanding is that this is passed down from your mother."

"Yes and no. In Orthodox and Conservative circles, it's assumed to be matrilineal. However, there's an active movement in Reform to accept patrilineal descent. That's not the issue. Conversion or not, this kid has no foundation in Judaism, but feels he has a membership ticket because his father, whom he hasn't seen since he was six, is Jewish."

"Why does he want to do this?"

"Well, frankly, being a psychologist, I was hoping you would tell me that."

"I get it. You need me to administer the Jack Israel Litmus Test for Sincerity in Judaism to this kid."

"No. No. I'd like you to meet with him. Talk to him. Tell me if he's crazy. My boys go to school with him. They say he's a loner and a little - you know what 'meshuggah' means? Crazy. Anyway, I told him to call you for an appointment. Is that all right?"

"Well, seeing as you cleared it with me beforehand, certainly. Look, Rabbi . . ."

"Don't call me Rabbi. Call me Isaac, seeing as you don't belong to my shul."

"Okay, Boss," Jack laughed to himself, "you have to understand that I'm not a clinical psychologist. I'm a social psychologist and I don't evaluate people for personality problems."

"Good. Then he won't feel like you're psychoanalyzing him."

"Why don't you send him to Myron Tabanov? He does belong to your temple. No doubt he pays dues. He surely addresses you as 'Rabbi' and is a bonafide psychiatrist."

"Because Myron, whom I do not have to call 'Doctor' because I am his Rabbi, which is a higher calling, is also a businessman. Every time I ask him to talk to someone, he asks me if they have insurance. I tell him it's a favor to me. He wants to know if I call Samuels and ask him for groceries for a favor or if I call Gartner and ask him for hardware for a favor. I tell him, I ask them for money, and he tells me he'll send me a check. You, I know, will do me a favor."

"If I'm not mistaken, you've already given Matt Cowan my phone number."

"I knew you would do it."

"Prophecy is not dead."

There was no longer a physical dimension to their walks. Every step was routine. Every house was familiar. Every pee stop and hydrant was known. Even when they varied their route, was not in the walk. It was in the space between them. It lived less in the words than in the silences, the cadences, the pulse. It happens best when people have languages that they share: Men who have grown up in the same village, married couples who no longer need to speak, friends who say nothing and are lonely when parted.

The shared path is a way of navigating the rocks and obstacles of a hard world. It is a way of owning and being owned by another, being property without contract. Its enforcement comes only in violation of the contract with the plaint, "How could you?" Such was the nature of these walks.

"What do you know about women?" It was an introduction, an entrée, not calculated for response, but to elicit invitation.

"Aha! I am a psychologist. How do I know this? Because I have an intuitive sense that you do not expect an answer to that question - at all! You, my dear Rabbi, friend, and freebie client, are about to ask me about a particular woman and, dare

I say, it is one for whom you have the hots. OK. You asked for it, but I will warn you for the last time: I am a social psychologist not a clinician. I will advise you for free - no cost, nada. And my advice will be worth exactly what you pay for it. Who's the lady?"

"Ahhh. She's a lovely young woman, a secretary in the English department at the university. Moved here a short while ago from Chicago." He lingered long over the last word cherishing every syllable, mulling her over in his own mind, tasting her identity in words, savoring her in senses that were not yet senescent, but most of all sharing with his friend his own joy in her.

"This is a long-standing relationship of mutual respect and admiration?"

"Well, let's just say I've known her for a while. We seem to like each other. She finds me, you know, a sympathetic listener."

The dogs had stopped at the edge of the cornfield. They had business of their own to complete. It had become so remarkably routine that Isaac didn't even notice anymore. If he harbored rank disgust, he kept it to himself.

"OK. Let's get the demographics down first. Age?"

"Late twenties."

"Jewish?"

"No."

"Diagnosed by a competent psychiatrist?"

"Well, there's some things I need to talk to you about."

"Oh, look, buddy. How old are you?"

"A young fortyish."

"You're pushing fifty if you're a day."

"I am not. I'm forty-five."

"And she's only twenty or so years younger than you and not Jewish - what your mother would have called a 'shiksah' - a non-Jew."

"Don't talk about my mother, Jack." The rabbi had snarled. Even the dogs took note. They discreetly lowered their flag-like tails, prepared for the next steps, the baring of teeth, the arching of backs and the inevitable thrust for the neck. Sasha moved into a defensive position between Jack and Isaac, prepared to shield her master from attack. Cady, ever loyal, positioned herself between Sasha and Isaac, prepared to defend her friend Sasha. It was a set of defensive maneuvers comparable to the Maginot Line and just as effective.

"I'm sorry, Isaac. That was insensitive of me on all counts. I really am sorry. Please go on."

It was too late for now. The flesh was rent. It had to heal. Perhaps only a chafe that needed a moment, perhaps a cut that would take time. Jack knew the signs. He had inflicted such wounds often enough to find familiarity with the dis-ease.

They walked in silence.

"You asked about the paper boy? My boys aren't close with him. They say he's scared of everything."

"What do I do? Rae wants me to call his parents. I don't think I've got any evidence."

"Talk to him. He's a decent kid. You can talk to him. Tell him that you suspect that he took something that he shouldn't have, and he should return it."

"That's law-suit material. I don't want to do it. I just don't think we should let him use the bathroom anymore."

"That's OK. They have a long history of separate bathrooms."

"So how did you meet her. Come on. I won't yell at you."

"I met her in a bookstore. Downtown. We struck up a conversation. We had a cup of coffee. We've been out to dinner a few times. Like that . . ."

"Is she your Chicago connection?"

"I drove her to Chicago for Thanksgiving. She needed a ride and so I took her, and I stayed with friends and then I drove her back."

"What's she like?"

"Well. That's what I wanted to talk to you about. She's a little young, you know? She's very attractive. She's small and she's shy. She comes from a place called Berwyn. Her family is a 'bissel tzerdrayt.' Do you know that that means?"

"No."

"A 'bissel gor meshuggah'. That, you understand?"

"Try Latin."

"They're a little crazy. Her father drinks a lot and pushes her mother around. Her mother sounds like she's depressed. She has a sister who ran away."

"How'd she wind up here?"

"She was working for a publisher in Chicago and was doing some liaison with the University Press here and heard about the job and applied for it. She wanted to get away from Chicago and her family. I think it was a healthy move, no?"

"But she goes back to Chicago to see her family - with you at the wheel. Did you perhaps meet mom and dad?"

"No. It's not at that stage. We're just very close friends right now. But I really like her, and I don't know quite where to take it from here. You know, Sage is almost seventeen. If he took her to the movies, they would look like a couple of college freshmen."

Jack took a long, long breath and blew it out ever so slowly through puffed cheeks. He created a small cloud of frosted breath before him, a defensive fog that would not hide him from counterattack.

"Isaac," he began with measured, deliberate syllables, "Isaac. It doesn't sound like she has a healthy family background. It sounds like she's left home but is on a long leash. It doesn't sound like she's about to bring you home to mom and pop as her knight in shining prayer shawl. And it doesn't sound like she's in a hurry to show them off to you either. She doesn't sound like she's fully functioning, and she may be quite vulnerable in a lot of ways. If you bring her home to your boys, they'll wonder about you. And if you bring her as a bride to your temple community, they'll roll you in breadcrumbs, fry your Jewish ass in Mazola, and sell you for Kentucky Fried Rabbi."

Isaac stopped dead in his tracks. He looked at Jack. His teeth shone as a smile of beauty crossed his countenance. He threw his face to the night sky and laughed. "Well, I hope you were being honest, Jack."

Jack laughed, raised his two plastic bags in an offering to the gods of darkness and the two men embraced, leaning precariously over the heaving bodies of Newfoundland dogs.

CHAPTER 11

"You miss all the action," Rae shook her head.

Her neck barely showed from the pink terry robe as she sat at the kitchen table. Jack realized that it was the robe that he had bought her when Dinah was born. It was time to buy her a new robe. That was forever ago - a different house, a different city, a different world.

Rae had never balked at leaving Milwaukee. It was an incredible turn of luck. Jack had spent six years in a joint appointment between the medical school and the department of psychology at the university. When it came time for a tenure decision, the rule was clear: "Up or out". Get promoted or you have one year to get a job. He found that he had friends in neither place. At the university he was that guy who wasn't a real psychologist. At the medical school, he was that Ph.D. who didn't see patients, who wasn't a real clinician.

There are people who live on the margins. They never belong. They like to watch, to learn the language, to savor the spices of life in groups, but never to commit. Living on the margins works in the years of plenty. In times of famine it's costly. It was a tenure decision that was guaranteed to go bad. There was no substitute for political alliances: Not funded research projects nor publications nor high student evaluations. He had not built the alliances. He believed the dean's words when he accepted the jerry-built job, "Just get your scholarly work done and you'll have no trouble getting promoted."

Jack had been caught in one of the lies that people repeat often and that the naive believe. Promotion was political, not scholarly. No, it really didn't matter what he had done. Yes, it really mattered who he was - and was not. The pain of rejection had been enormous. It was a year of banishment. Every person in each school with whom he had ever shared a kind word shuffled out of his way in embarrassment. People offered to write him letters of recommendation for new jobs and in their caring, concern, and kindness, helped the leprosy spread.

The job in Bloomington was a fluke. A late notice on the back pages of the American Psychologist, "Search re-opened . . ." In contrast to the pile of rejection letters from such notable institutions as St. Catherine's College and University of East Ottawa, he got a phone call from Bud Blumberg asking, "Can you be here day after tomorrow for an interview?"

It had been a non-interview. Bud made it all clear. "Look, psychology has sent four candidates over here and they may be fine psychologists, but they have no idea about medical education. You're the only person I've seen who can tell a mandible from a munchkin and I need to get this job filled. I'll call their chairman, Dick Kraus. If you're OK with him and you guys can work out the details, it's fine with me."

Kraus had negotiated a reasonable deal on the phone. The papers flowed. And Jack had never asked, "Rae, may I . . .?" She left her family and friends, the only city she had ever really known. She had no choice. Jack was sick in spirit and this was the cure. It was a step up to a major university from a dead end, the kind of move that happens only to the best - which he was not.

He said nothing to any of his colleagues. On the last possible Sunday afternoon, he packed both offices, loaded the boxes of books into the truck and posted his forwarding address on office doors at both the medical school and the department. He wanted so badly to see their expressions as they read the address. It never occurred to him that he had left an unworkable joint-appointment in a medical school and a psychology department to go to an unworkable joint-appointment in a medical school and a psychology department.

He began healing then. She, newly pregnant when they moved, caring for three children and two dogs, had kissed her mother and father and gone with her husband.

"What'd I miss this time?"

"Dorfmans again."

"Services on Saturday?"

"Better. Sabbath dinner on Friday night."

"You didn't accept, did you?"

"Wrong again, Professor. I told them that we couldn't possibly get a babysitter by that time and she told me that – get this - 'No, no, we want you and your children.' Dead in the water. Sorry."

"Oh, I can't do this, Rae. She's a really nice lady and he's a powerful player at the medical school and I simply can't inflict us on them. It's not a decent thing to do and besides, I just don't want to spend a Friday evening with them."

"You know what, Jack? I don't really know her, and she was really sweet on the phone. It was a very nice gesture and I think we should go and be just as gracious."

"Rae, you are a sick woman!"

"Jack, I need another human being to talk to in this town beside you and three children."

The Newman Center's basement cafeteria was known affectionately as "The Vatican". It was not frequented by undergraduates, who took what substituted for nourishment in their residential cafeterias. As a result, the clientele had a peculiarly catholic make-up with emphasis on the small "c": Faculty out for a cheap sandwich, graduate students looking for an escape from their privileged rabbit-warrens, secretaries, building superintendents, skilled workmen, and an occasional priest or nun. The set-up was primitive: A high sandwich bar at the front and long, narrow tables and wooden chairs in rows through the large, square room. Posters of Rome plastered the walls without adding beauty.

Jack and Dunphy arrived late enough in the lunch hour to avoid the rush. The dampness of the gym's shower had chilled on the skin and Jack needed warmth and nourishment before he could face the persistent breeze that crept through his office window. There was still plenty of vegetarian chili left in the pot - there was always plenty still left - and he ordered that and hot tea. Dunphy opted for the liverwurst.

"Did you have any luck with Imogene Ulrich at Bernie Frederick's shop?" Jack asked as he pulled a wooden chair in under his crotch and crouched over the chili.

"Yep! We're supposed to show up there a week from Wednesday. That's their clinic day. We get to grace the waiting room all day and ask people if they mind being interviewed while Fredericks keeps 'em hanging. I think we're the substitute for last month's Good Housekeeping."

"Have you got your troops lined up?"

"Everything's been set for three months. We've got questionnaires." He paused to assault the liverwurst and continued talking, smears of wurst swimming across his teeth, "permission sheets, directions on how to get there. Even got a state car reserved for transportation."

"Do you need me to come?"

"The research assistants always like it when you come. It makes them feel like they're being observed. Come next time."

"I'm not interested in observing them."

"What do you expect from people who had a choice between working for you or testing rats? These are college graduates who, of their own free will, chose to become psychologists. There's no such thing to them as an innocent motive. If there was, they would have become economists."

"Why are you here then?"

"Beat's workin', Boss."

They finished and headed for the corner of McCormick Hall that was now their estate. Ilene sat at her desk eating her usual lunch, a cup of plain yogurt, sliced vegetables, a pear, and tea. She looked up from Daniel DeFoe to greet her men.

"Hunters! Home with the kill. What have you brought your womenfolk for their nestlings?"

"Sorry, Snow White, I got the last of the liverwurst."

"Boss, popularity's growing!" and she handed him a telephone message. "This one's good. He was at a pay phone and couldn't figure out how much it would cost for another three minutes, but I think I got the essence of his desires. Can I leave when he shows up?"

The message read, "Matt Conlon (?) says the rabbi sent him. Coming this afternoon after school. Clearly a failed pugilist."

To see Matt Cowan enter was to watch the elephant dance. He was large in height and broad in bone. He was at the age when young men don't yet believe they have to shave every day, but, in fact, they do. In his behavior, he was small; Not frightened, but awed. He looked at the bare walls and examined the tiles on the floor. His steps were tentative as he entered, bent over Ilene's desk twelve inches too far, and whispered hoarsely, "Is this Dr. Israel's office?"

She leaped from her seat with, "Well, you have come to the right place! You must be Matt and old Doctor Israel has been waiting for you. Oh, Doctor Israel, your appointment is here, and I have to go off to do some photocopying or check the mail or something like that. See you tomorrow."

Matt entered the sacred cubicle tentatively. His bared head was crowned by brushed wire with matched stubble on his jaw. His face carried an assortment of moles, beauty marks, and adolescent pimples that marked him as no girl's mystery man. On his shoulder was the requisite backpack, army surplus, and he wore a khaki wool coat left over from some monstrous war in which fashion did not determine the victor. He extended a hand tentatively, not sure of the etiquette. Jack grasped it firmly and motioned him to the only available seat.

"I'm Matt. Rabbi said that I should come to see you." He called Isaac "Rabbi" in the same way that Roseanne, Isaac's secretary, did. "I'm not really sure what I'm supposed to tell you."

"Relax, Matt. I'm not really sure what I'm supposed to ask you, so we're even. Please call me 'Jack'. I think Isaac - Rabbi - just wants you to get a chance to meet some of his friends. I'm his neighbor and we walk together in the evenings."

"You're the guy who had the little girl at services."

"Yes, that's right. You have a good memory. What were you doing at services?"

"It's part of my training. I'm in training to become Jew. My father's Jew, you know?"

"Rabbi mentioned that. Have you talked to your father, or your mother, about . . . about becoming Jew-ish."

"Yeah. I talked to my ma some. I think it's OK with her. I don't talk to my dad much. He's in the Air Force and he's stationed somewhere in California. He's a colonel now. Big stuff, you know? Fought in 'Nam, two tours. Big time, you know?" He lolled back in the chair and raised his chin. He had a half-smile now.

"Do you think he'd want you to become Jewish?"

"I don't know. It's something I wanna do. I started hearin' about Jews in Sunday school at church and my ma told me that my dad was Jew. I got interested and I started lookin' around. There were some kids at school that were Jews so I asked them about it and they told me there was a temple on Diana Road. One day, I rode my bike out there and there was this nice secretary and she introduced me to Rabbi. He talked to me and told me I should start coming to services. So I did. And he gave me stuff to read and I been readin' it. I don't know what he told you, Doc, but I can tell you this, I'm gonna do this, I really am. This is hard, but I can do this, I really can."

"I'm convinced. Tell me what you like about it."

"Well, you know like he said that if I do this, I get to choose a Hebrew name, right? He gave me this book about Chan-noo-kuh". With this he pulled from his backpack an elementary introduction to the Jewish festivals, "and I been readin', like about Matt-tis-yoh-hoo? It's a really neat story, man. Like this guy had cojones, brother. You know what that means? Guts! He fought for freedom! For religious freedom! My father's a freedom fighter. He fought to keep freedom in this country and in Vietnam. You know what my name is, man? Matt! And that's gonna be my Hebrew name too! Short for Matt-tis-yoh-hoo".

"Impressive. Impressive. Tell me more about yourself. How does school go for you?"

"Okay. Lotta problems at school, man. Gotta watch yourself. Some bad dudes around there. Watch your back all the time, you know?"

"Where do you go to school, Matt?"

"Veterans Memorial."

"Tell me about the problems there. Do you have any problems?"

"Not me, man. I keep to myself, watch my back, and don't let anybody - not anybody - move on me. I got my secrets, man, and they know it".

"What secrets, Matt?"

"Kung-fu, man. I take lessons. I'm up to blue belt. Next is green, then brown, then watch out world, I'm a black belt. Hoo-eeee!" His face, at times leaden and serious was cracked by a smile that demonstrated his dentition. He squirmed with the glee of a small boy contemplating his fifth birthday party complete with pony rides.

"You say, 'they know it' – about your secrets. Who's 'they'?"

"Hey. You gotta spend some time there, man. Who's 'they'? They ain't even blacks, Doc, they're no foolin' around Gangbangers. Useless tough guys who know how to talk the talk when they got a gang with them, but, boy, you dare them to walk the walk when they're alone and they're just shit like the poor bastards they push around. You know?"

Jack couldn't help the recoil. It was just too tender. "Matt," he was a gentle as he could possibly be, "there have been lots of times when people have used harsh words for Jews. You know? Kike? Hebe? Hymie? You can't say words like that, Matt. You just can't."

"Hey, Doc, I didn't say 'Niggers', but that's what a lot of people would say, 'cuz they're black. But that ain't it at all. Look, I got lots of black friends. I ain't no racialist, Doc. But these guys are something else, and it ain't just black, and I don't have another word for it."

The most hopeless pain came from his sincerity. There was no way to disentangle the words from the facts, to disassemble old oppression from current, day-to-day hatred. It wasn't their skin that he hated, nor their differentness. Nor was it fear. In awful realization, it seemed that he had identified something that according to his decalogue, no matter how primitive, was unjust, and he hated them for it. To them, to it, he ascribed the only taxonomy that seemed appropriate.

"What do you think ought to be done, Matt?"

"Kick their black butts all the way back to Chicago and Gary, Doc. Every white kid - and every decent black kid - in that high school's gotta put their ass on the line. You know"?

"Yeah, I know, Matt."

"I said something bad, didn't I? I know, I'm sorry. It's just the way I feel".

"No apologies, Matt. I understand. I really do."

Jack had missed the racist rhetoric growing up. It was a failing in his education and it reoccurred routinely as an inability to condemn when condemnation was required. The fringes of the Jewish ghetto commingled with the fringes of the black ghetto. They lived together, went to school together, worked together. and learned from one another. It had been Barxtell Sidney, the long lean man behind the deli counter, who had taught Jack to listen to the soft-settling piano beat of Ahmad Jamal and how to play the daily number at the bookie's around the corner. Jack's father had brought black sailors home for dinner from the Navy Yard during the war. His mother had hired black help for the cleaning chores on Saturdays in their tenement apartment and worked alongside them. At the end of the day, she made sure, they had clean towels to bathe with and insisted, that, they stay to eat with the family. His father had paraded him before the Robert Gould Shaw memorial across from the state house, pointed out the black soldiers that had died in the Civil War and told him, "Don't forget." It wasn't that he was made of finer stuff, nor that he had made intellectual progress in a personal fight with himself against racism. He had simply failed to learn it correctly in the first place.

"Matt, what are you going to do with your life? What year in school are you?"

"Hey, I'm a senior, man. My grades are OK. C's and B's. You know. And the day I get out - it's the US Air Force for me! I got a family tradition and I believe in the need to defend my country."

"Tell me more about being Jewish."

"You know what I'm gonna do, Doc? You'll think I'm crazy, but I'm gonna do it, you watch. Before I leave this town, I'm gonna get me a bar mitzvah. I can do it. And I want you there to see it. What do you think of that?"

"Matt, I think that's not an impossible dream and you know what, man? If you do it, I'll be there to watch you!"

He edged the truck in next to the VW bus. The brown of the truck and the mustard yellow of the van stood out against the forest green of the house. It was a combination that reeked of human discharge. Muttering silent vows about building a concrete house with an underground car port and a revolving front door, Jack again braved the storm door, braced for the assault. There was a resistance from inside the wooden door. He pressed harder and made no progress. Now with shoulder, knee, and head to the task he threw one hundred and sixty pounds of social psychological force against the door and felt it slowly, slowly give way, just enough for him to peek around the edge. There were two large canine butts solidly against the door, immobile, their owners asleep. In between them, asleep herself, was Dinah a total perhaps of three hundred pounds of child and dog. He oomphed himself into the house and heard only one tail whack! whack! whack! against the floor. He loved making an entrance.

There was no other sound. The boys were nowhere to be seen. He hung his coat and crept into the bedroom where Rae lay on the bed. Softly, carefully, he slid open the closet and hung his jacket and tie. He stepped out of his shoes and was on his way out of the door when she spoke.

"The boys are at Bascom's, playing with Jimbo."

"You OK?"

"Same."

"Got any news?"

"Appointment with Mackenzie for Thursday."

"Can I come?"

"If you need to."

He dutifully cleared the dishes off the table, rinsed and stacked them in the dishwasher, swabbed the table with a sponge and breathed a final sigh. The rituals of evening were long but definable. This was the beginning of the end of the day. Bloomington was famous for its sunsets. The sun took its delicious time sliding into its prairie bed. These days, Jack could watch it happen as he drove home from work: It was a dramatic event that timed human biological cycles. In the summer, it happened so sweetly late. Dinners occurred after the lawn had been mowed and the boys had had a bike ride and he and Rae had walked the dogs together. They had had a few evenings like that before their first fall season in Bloomington had settled in. It had been a new beginning, a honeymoon. The anguish of Milwaukee was over, and this was to be a sweet new start. Dinners were earlier now as the winter solstice bore in at them. The sun closed early for the season and left humans huddled inside, waiting for the late dawn.

"I'm going to head out with my friends," he called to Rae, in the bathroom with Dinah. Three children made bath times an assembly line. Simmy could now be relied on, more or less, to keep himself clean. Lee was the transitional child, young enough still to need coaxing into the tub but too old to watch to be sure that he scrubbed. Dinah still relished her bath toys and her private time with Rae.

Jack picked up the phone and dialed. "Ready or not here we come. I'll meet you at the corner in two minutes".

He slipped into a hooded parka, checked for plastic bags, and grabbed the leashes off the hook. The trick was to click the metal segments of the leashes together. It took only this subtle clarion call to muster the troops. Out they went into the night.

Isaac waited at the corner of Tamarack and Crosscut.

"You're early tonight. I like to go later."

"Got stuff to discuss, monsignor. I met your boy today, Matt Cowan." They fell into step easily.

"What do you think?"

"I don't know! He certainly seems to want to 'become Jew'. I suppose that makes him certifiable right then and there. He could be crazy. He could be looking for a way to link himself to his father who he says is 'Jew' and Air Force - both of which he intends to become. On the other hand, why does any of us do anything that we do? I suspect he's no crazier than you or I and I'm not so sure about either of us. Does that make any sense?"

"It does and it doesn't. Which leaves me exactly where I was. You see, I have a very funny feeling about people who convert."

"You mean they're not real Jews."

"No! No! No! You don't understand at all. Let me explain. You see, we have an interesting cultural life, us Jews in America. There's a majority of us who've lost sight of what it means to be Jewish. All right, that I understand. The rest of us are Jews for different reasons. Some of us are Jews because our fathers and our grandfathers came from Eastern Europe and we remember the yiddishkeit. You know? You had a Bubbeh, you had a Zaydeh, you remember the songs, the smells in the kitchen, you know some yiddish swear words like schmuck and putz and that makes you Jewish."

"Then there's others of us," he went on, "who remember the Holocaust. Maybe I'm one, maybe I'm not. I don't know. But for some of us, that unspeakable nightmare means we have to be Jews. We can't ever forget. We can't ever, ever let the world forget what happened to us. The Sho'ah defines us in history. It means that we had our choice taken away whether or not we would be Jews. History made the choice for us, we're Jews."

"Then there's some of us that are Zionists. We believe passionately in a Jewish homeland; we believe that Jews will always face persecution and that we need a nation of our own. We're bound to our Judaism by the dream of Israel. Israel right or wrong. Israel forever. You know?"

"Yes, I see."

"All of this is very nice, and I think five, ten years ago, I would have stopped there. But I met a very interesting young woman in Minneapolis. Her name was Jennifer. She was a newlywed. She had married a man named Aaron Weissman. She had been Jennifer O'Toole, O'Malley, O'Keefe, I don't know, something like that. She had been raised as a Catholic and married this Aaron Weissman, a Unitarian. And he had explained to her that his parents were German, had left Germany during the thirties, had him late in their lives and he had grown up in New York where his parents had spoken German at home. Now, Jennifer wasn't an aggressive young woman. On the contrary, she was sweet and a little shy, but she was also curious. They left in the thirties. They spoke German at home. Why did they leave? She asked her groom and you know what? He couldn't tell her. He really didn't know. They went to visit in New York, and he asked his parents, in front of Jennifer. He didn't press them, but

Jennifer, who genuinely cared for them, did. And you know what? They told their son, Aaron and their daughter-in-law, that they had been Jews in Germany and had fled the Nazis."

"Wow! And he didn't know that?"

"No. They had never told him because they were afraid. They didn't want to be Jews anymore. They didn't want to run from. They joined the Unitarians and they never told him he had been born a Jew. He had no idea."

"That's amazing. What did he say?"

"He was angry. He yelled at them. He had a big confrontation with them. For a long time he couldn't talk to them. But then there was Jennifer. And Jennifer was an interesting woman. When they came back to Minneapolis, Jennifer came to see me. She told me the story and she said that she wanted to learn about Judaism. This poor, shy, Catholic girl who found herself married into a tormented family, decided that she had to find out about Judaism - about what this was that was so terrifying and so powerful. I enrolled her in my conversion class - not to convert her - that wasn't the object at all, but because it was the easiest way to teach her a lot in a short time. And she came faithfully and every once in a while her husband would come too. But for him it was difficult. He had no knowledge. He had very complex feelings and he just couldn't . . . couldn't . . . he just couldn't. You know what I mean?"

"Yes. Please go on. What happened?"

"At the end of the class she approached me and told me that she intended to convert. I asked her if Aaron intended to practice Judaism. She said no. And being the noodnik that I am, I asked, so why did she want to become Jewish? This young, shy, Catholic woman, who would have made a very good nun, educated me, Jack. She told me that in Judaism she had found a commitment to a God that she could relate to. That the God she had come to know in Judaism was a just and ethical God and that she had come to love the sheer spiritual beauty of the - get this - the relationship between God and the

Jewish people. And she wanted to share in that relationship. You know what happened to me, Jack? I cried. And you know why I cried? Because I had forgotten that. Or maybe I never knew it. Maybe we all forgot it. Maybe we forgot it a thousand years ago. Maybe in between the praying and persecutions we forgot about the relationship between the Jewish people and God. It doesn't matter. What matters is that she had to teach it to me."

"Wow."

"You know what Abraham Joshua Heschel says, Jack? He says that God tries in so many ways to reach out to man and that if one way doesn't work, He tries another and another and another. And in Jennifer Weissman, I think God found me. After all that I had seen and all that I had gone through, it took this shy young woman to teach me in one sentence what I hadn't learned in the seminary or in all my self-important studies."

"What happened to her?"

"Did you hear what I said?"

"Yes, but I want to know what happened to her."

"She converted. And she came to shul often. Sometimes Aaron came, but it was hard for him. His anger at his parents was more important for him to maintain than his Judaism. And it was hard for Jennifer to do this alone, but she did. I get a card from them once in a while. I think they had a child and they're raising it as a Jew. That's not what's important. What's important is that I realized that there's a whole new people that are coming to Judaism. Lots of them are coming because they've married Jews and that doesn't matter. What matters is that in the synagogues of America there's a whole movement of people who are Jewish not because their fathers and mothers are Jewish, not because of yiddishkeit, not because of the Holocaust, and not because of Israel. They're Jews because they have found a beautiful and just way to relate to God, and it's a way that the rest of us Jews have lost track of."

When Jack had been in the depths of despair, when he had been told he had to leave his job in Milwaukee, he had grown pathologically depressed. Rae had been to him what she could, but it was not enough. She had insisted that he seek help. This wasn't easy. He knew all the good therapists in town as colleagues and he would not, could not, go to a bad therapist. Finally, Rae had gotten a referral from one of the psychiatrists at Divine Mission Hospital, where she worked part time: A man in Chicago, an existential therapist, a kind man. Nathan Zadok. Jack had gone to see him for nearly a year, making the two-hour trek to Chicago by train. The issue had never been one of analyzing the situation and making sense of it. Jack had analyzed the situation and had made sense of it. Together he and Nathan Zadok had wrestled not with the situation, but with the meaning of it. Jack had asked at one point, "When will it all sink in? When will it all feel better? How long will it last?" Zadok had told him, "What you're seeking is not knowledge. You have knowledge. What you're seeking is wisdom. Wisdom takes time. Years maybe. But when it comes, it will all be better and it will never leave you and then you'll be able to share it with others." What Isaac had said was not knowledge. It was wisdom. Jack recognized it. He knew it when he heard it. He knew that it would be with him forever and that he would share it with others. But he simply could not respond to it. He was built of patterned responses as we all are. He interrogated because he was an interrogator. Had he been a disbeliever, he would have sought inconsistencies. Had he been an arguer, he would have taken issue. Had he been a jester, he would have made a foolish joke. People are captives of their patterns, even when they're faced with what they know is wisdom. Such is the burden upon the wise.

Jack interrogated, "So you think this is what has happened to Matt Cowan?"

"No, Jack," he evidenced exasperation, "Matt, I suspect hasn't yet found the abstract principles of Judaism that will bring clarity to his relationship with God. But Matt has come to Judaism and for him, at least for now, for whatever reason, it makes sense. And I am no man to question why any of us comes to Judaism. If he wants to be Jewish and if I'm the gatekeeper, my job is not to say 'No!' My job is to say, 'How can I help you to be the best Jew you can be?'"

"Do you think he's good material."

"Who is and who isn't? I don't know. He's no worse than a lot that I've seen except when he starts talking about the African Americans at school. Then I get scared. He says some of the same kinds of things that Sage and Lev say - but the phrasing is a little different, if you know what I mean."

"He says 'Nigger' straight out loud, doesn't he?"

"Yes, and it turns my stomach."

"It's okay. He doesn't mean it the way you think he does. He's an adolescent and he's saying something about what's right and what's wrong and he thinks there are some bad players at school and that they're doing something wrong. He is, after all, an adolescent. Better yet, he's a crazy adolescent."

"Do you think he could be dangerous?"

"Isaac, I think you might listen to him and listen to your boys as well. Apparently, there are some tough black kids at that school."

"There are tough kids there; there are tough kids anywhere. There were tough Polish kids and tough Costa Rican kids, so these are tough kids. Do you think all of a sudden this is a different order of toughness?"

"In a word, yes. Tough Polish kids were a majority pushing around a Jewish minority. Tough Costa Rican kids were probably a couple of bad hombres. These guys come from a permanently oppressed minority. There's no way up for them. They have nothing to gain from the white system. It offers them nothing and takes away everything. They believe that any white kid is an oppressor and that any black kid who accepts a white value system is a fool who'll eventually get reamed by the same white society that won't let them in. The street kids from Chicago are a very angry bunch and they have absolutely nothing to lose by being nasty."

"What shall I do with Matt Cowan."

"Looks like you're going to make him Jew."

CHAPTER 12

Rae was already in MacKenzie's waiting room at the Creditor Clinic. Every medical facility in the world smelled the same. It was the solvents, the alcohols that permeated the atmosphere and made even the blind and deaf acutely aware that they were in a treatment facility. She sat with her traditional air of calm, reading a magazine in her lap, legs crossed. The seat next to her was empty and Jack dropped into it, gently planting a kiss on her forehead as he did.

"Hey, babe, got a man at home or are you available?"

"That's two questions."

"Hey! It's one question or you're in trouble."

It was a half hour of silent magazines until the nurse came out and invited Rae in with a smiling, "Dr. MacKenzie will see you now."

"Shall I come with you?"

"No, if he attacks me, I'll see how good he is. If he's no good, I'll call for reinforcements."

The wait was interminable. MacKenzie and associates had sprinkled a variety of magazines through the rack. There was one called Wooden Boat and several old Sports Car Graphics along with the Mademoiselles and Good Housekeeping. Normally, Jack could be expected to lose himself in the car or boat magazines, but they didn't suffice. He disliked waiting rooms, disliked waiting, disliked Rae being in there without him.

The nurse came out. "Mr. Israel, would you like to come in?" Jack followed obediently.

Ian MacKenzie was large; not simply tall, but large. Though he could not have been more than forty, he carried a substantial paunch on his large frame. Sandy curls covered his head and a shy smile graced his round face. Jack had known lots of neurologists in Milwaukee and he liked them a great deal. They were a curious bunch. Invariably intellectual, they were the true detectives of clinical medicine. Neurology was, in many ways, an infant science. Our understanding of the nervous system was insubstantial compared to, for example, the cardiovascular system or the reproductive system. Neurology was struggling with diagnosis, nomenclature, observation, and classification. Treatment was incompletely understood for many neurological disorders. The standard joke was of the neurologist telling the patient with glee, "Eureka! I know what your disease is. Of course, we have no treatment for it." And yet, Jack's best students had chosen residencies in neurology. It was where the students who loved art or literature went or those who had some intellectual heritage far from medicine. These were as much philosophers as scientists and he liked them.

"Ahh, Dahktuhr Issrahale," he began in a Scottish brogue that warmed the heart like a single malt Scotch whiskey, "I'm glad tuh meet ya. I'm Ian MacKenzie and I been havin' a lovely chat with Rae, here."

Jack shook hands and dutifully sat down in the spare chair of MacKenzie's office. He had been prepared for the exchange of credentials. It was a ceremony that he loved. He would ask where some poor unknowing physician had trained and would follow with his teaching appointments at medical schools in Boston and Milwaukee, generously offering observations on the quality of their residency and fellowship programs. It was much like dogs sniffing at the rectums of other dogs before deciding if they would wag or lower their tails in friendship, warning, or deference. Jack was a master at it, occasionally to Rae's annoyance. Clinicians, even in academic settings often deferred to Jack's credentials in academic medicine. There was no need this time. MacKenzie's degree from St. Andrew's and his training in Edinburgh hung as documents on the wall. Jack had been disarmed both by his Highland charm and by his own real need to hear what the Scotsman had to say about Rae.

"Well, Rae's been complainin' of headaches, I hear-uh. An' a bit ah stoomach oopset an' some verrrtigo. Well, I looked her oop and doown, ya know, and she's a strong heifer," he laughed. "I've doon some preliminary obserrvayshons and some little tests, ya know. Now, I hear-uh as how yer a perfesser at the medical college - a psychologist as I hear-uh. So you'll know of what I'm speakin'."

"Yes, yes, please go ahead." Rae sat silently, virtually an observer in this process while her advocate, her champion, recently acquired, described her body to her husband. She had willingly offered her signet to this knight. The rose flush on her cheeks and Mona Lisa smile made clear that she was more than comfortable. She had one foot in the stirrup of MacKenzie's horse and was making up her mind whose saddle she belonged in.

"I don't know as I kin say with ashoorance what the problem is, orr even if tharr is a problem, ef ya know what I mean. What I'd like ta doo, ef ya doon't mind is to have a test orr two doone as soon as we ken. I'd like to see an EEG, ya know, an e-lec-tro-en-cephalo-graaam, joost be be sure, and soome radiographs - X-rays, ya know. Doo ya suppose thet we can git this yoong lass in here tomorrrow?"

Jack and Rae nodded in simultaneous agreement. They exchanged thanks and left little comforted for what they had learned.

"What do you make of it?" he asked.

"He's cute!"

"Thank you, I hadn't noticed. However, I did notice your little blue eyes light up. What did he do to you and what did he say?"

"He asked a lot of questions about the nature of the headache. It was a good interview on that. He looked at my eyes a lot - back and forth between them with the ophthalmoscope. Then he did a pretty standard neurological exam - you know: Stand on one foot, stand on the other foot, close your eyes, squeeze his hand with my left hand and with my right, press against his hand with my right leg and with my left. Standard stuff."

"What do you think he's looking for?"

"I don't really know. With neurologists so much of what they do is 'rule out'. Rule out multiple sclerosis, rule out stroke, rule out vasospasms, rule out this, rule out that. I think we're in rule out mode."

"Would you like me to come back with you tomorrow?"

"No, thanks, Jack. I think I'd like some time alone with Ian, Dr. MacKenzie."

Rhonda had been quite specific about arrival time. The sun went down very early. Shabbat candles had to be lit one-half hour before sundown; the latest she could possible justify for lighting them was 5:30 and they should not be late. Rae had gotten back from the Creditor Clinic at 3:30. It had taken forever to collect Simmy and Lee and scrub faces. Dinah was enjoying a late nap and was reluctant to awaken. She was in transition: Too old to nap every day and still go to bed early, too young to stay up with the boys and not crash into contagious petulance the next day. A nap was a mixed blessing today. She was foul to awaken, but once awake she would be charming.

Simmy and Lee no longer napped. They crashed emotionally each day promptly at four in the afternoon as their stores of sugar depleted from lunch. The time between four o'clock snack and the rise in blood sugar was the daily monsoon, complete with thunder and lightning. Anguished screams filled the house followed by blows, tears and unrepentant anger. By five it had ended between them, but the parental fall-out lingered with despair and recriminations. It was a typical American family.

It had been hard to establish the outlines of the day in the midst of this anarchy. "How'd things go at Lochinvar's Neurological Testing Center?"

"Fine."

"What'd he have them do to you?"

"EEG and standard head and neck X-rays."

"How'd they do the EEG?"

"Clipped a couple of hairs and pasted on electrodes. No big deal. I had them be real careful with lead shielding on the X-rays. Asked them to check for cavities in my teeth at the same time."

"Any idea when they'll have results?"

"His receptionist said they'd call."

"So, we'll wait . . ."

By five the crowd was assembled in the bus for the short trip to the other side of the river. Established faculty lived on the east side of town in the older homes adjoining the campus. The streets had mature trees and sidewalks that rose in respect to the roots of old oaks and maples. Homes were set close to the sidewalk with little or no lawn to mow. Nary a garage could be seen from the street. There were no single or even split-level homes here. These had been constructed by carpenters, not developers. They had genuine staircases and attics and cellars. The house on Tamarack Court that so stretched a new professor's salary was graced with none of these. Jack had been in the attic once. There was no room to stand. It was designed to be a dead air space and, indeed, it was. Likewise, he had once been in the crawl space under the house. It was a plastic-lined area of pipes and wires and the remains of a long-dead field mouse. The space itself was dead. The family lived as the filling in a sandwich between two dead places, maintaining life as they could.

The Dorfman's house was a soaring stucco that smacked of Prairie School architecture with cantilevered cornices and porches and stained-glass insets. It was vaguely oriental with a portico over the driveway and a grand side entrance. This was a badge which the Dorfman's wore. It was the house for a faculty family of long-standing at the university, a place where one could entertain with pride and at the same time demonstrate academic nobility.

Jack parked the bus under the portico and began off-loading progeny. Rae had brought a bouquet of assorted flowers and a bottle of decent California pinot noir. Rhonda was at the door with a young man by her side.

"Hi, everybody. Oh, flowers! For me? And wine? I'll put it right in the fridge."

Jack practically gasped. It was an all right pinot noir. A couple of hours in the cold refrigerator would ruin it. He swallowed his amateur wine-taster's nose and remained silent.

"This is Jared. He's our baby. David and Miriam are off at school and this one's got one foot out the door already." Jared shifted uncomfortably as his mother insisted on his title as baby of the family.

"Hi, Jared, I'm Jack Israel. Who are you really?"

"A vagrant that they picked up at the bus station. I did some odd jobs for them and they've kept me here in slavery. I'm being held as a captive against my will. Please inform the Turkish embassy."

"You're good. It's nice to know you."

"I'm a part time student at the university. I finished all my high school credits and now I'm taking some courses and waiting to ship out to the New England Conservatory."

"What will you study there?"

"I'm a French horn player."

"That's impressive. What high school did you go to?"

"Bloomington South."

"Okay, school?"

"Yeah, just fine."

"When you get to Boston, I have friends and family there. You might look them up."

"Can any of them get me a chair with the Boston Symphony?"

"Certainly, padded or unpadded? Folding or not folding?"

Phil breezed in the door and passed around greetings. He shook hands with Jack—firmly. He took Rae's hand gallantly and touched her shoulder as he did, following this by greeting each child with a pat on the head. Rhonda called for an assembly in the living room. There, before the large central fireplace was a small table on which stood two braided challahs, two candlesticks, a glass of wine and a calico cat.

"Phoebe, get away from the kiddush," Phil grabbed a newspaper and feigned a swing at the cat. In horrified offense, it recoiled, lifted itself to its feet, and with diffidence descended to the floor.

"There, having done the preliminaries, we can make kiddush."

He motioned everyone into a circle around the small table. Dinah clung ferociously to Rae. The boys sought the seclusion and safety of a neutral corner while Rhonda donned a kerchief. Jared passed out yarmulkes to Jack and the boys and took a position beside his father. Rhonda struck a match, lit the candles, closed her eyes and waving her hands beckoned the light into her life. She sang a short prayer in Hebrew and turned to repeat it in English to the uninitiated, "Blessed art Thou, Oh, Lord, our God, King of the Universe, Who has commanded us to light the Shabbat lights."

Phil raised his hands and held them over Jared reciting something in Hebrew. He too translated, "May the Lord make you like Ephraim and Mannaseh. May the Lord bless you and keep you and cause His countenance to shine upon you and grant you peace." Then he picked up the wine cup, held it aloft and began to sing a long chant in Hebrew. He rolled his head and sang out in sonorous tenor and as he really got going Jared and Rhonda chimed in and sang a rousing final verse. Phil took a sip of the wine, said a few words in Hebrew over the two breads and tore off a piece of one, ripping it further into smaller pieces which he handed out to all assembled.

"Shabbat Shalom, everybody," Rhonda said with kisses and hugs and handshakes and smiles. It was charming. "Well, time to eat!"

Phoebe graced the table. Phil took another swipe and she exited, again gracefully. The table was set with fine china, fine flatware, and a slightly chilled bottle of pinot noir. Rhonda and Jared commenced a steady procession from the kitchen carrying serving plate after serving plate of chicken soup with matzo balls, salad, baked chicken with stuffing, potato kugel, vegetables, and condiments. There was something definitely familiar in Rhonda's "Oh, please try some of the [blank]. Tell me if it's any good."

Phil sat at the head of the table with official smiles. The conversation was light, collegial, academic, unimportant but gracious. They covered the medical school and academics in general, research and even dallied over Rae's work at St. Mary's and her Milwaukee origins. Simmy, Lee, and Dinah squirmed the obligatory wiggles of children in boredom and picked at their dinners. Rhonda smiled at them and insisted on telling them what good children they were. She had no perception of reality.

"How's your neighbor, Isaac, holding up these days?" Phil asked.

"Oh wonderfully," Jack offered, "Occasionally we go for walks together in the evening."

"My friends in the English department tell me that he's becoming a nuisance."

Jack saw it coming and tried to head it off, "I'm looking forward to the next Saturday service . . ."

Rae screwed up her face in a frown of quizzical intensity. It was too late. Phil was on a roll. "He's been mooning over a secretary there. Some twenty-something shiksa that he's infatuated with."

He had said it. It was too late. Even he realized it and turned a presentable vermilion. Worse, he assumed that he was safe in his own home on a Friday night at his own dinner table.

Rae smiled. "A shiksa no less! Hear that, Dinah? One of us! Probably a bead-swinging, ash-headed, palm-carrying Catholic, I'll bet. Why she might be descended from some old pogrom-plotting Polack. Or some Jew-baiting Guinea, maybe. Or maybe she's a Ni-."

"Rae! We get the point," Jack laid a heavy hand on her arm. Phil sat stymied. It was Rhonda who broke up the impending fight.

"Isn't he a pig, Rae? My heavens. You can take the Jew out of the ghetto, but you can't take the ghetto out of the Jew. His own son is living with the loveliest Protestant and you'd think he was a refugee from the dark ages."

"I'm sorry," Phil began, "That just slipped out."

"Who slipped it in, Phil?" queried Rae.

"Rae, I am sorry. I meant nothing by it."

Rhonda laughed. Jared laughed. Jack worked up the best laugh he could. Phil smiled a little and Simmy, Lee, and Dinah just stared.

Rae smiled. "Tell me all about this lovely young woman that our rabbi likes so much."

"Oh. I don't know," Phil began. "I don't mean to speak out of turn. He kind of really likes younger women and every once in a while you stumble on him in a restaurant with someone half his age and it's just uncomfortable, that's all."

"He must be quite a man," Rae snickered.

Jack wondered where he had left the job listings. His career in Bloomington was nearing an end. Rae was the most loyal and sensitive of partners. She had never done this to him before. She was justified, of course. It was all right if his mother and aunts called her a shiksa, but never in her presence. That was forbidden and they understood the rules of modern Jewish intermarriage: Accept the heathen into your midst, be as charming as you can and pray that someday she'll convert and turn your grandchildren from mamzerim, bastards, into Jews. To repeat the errors of their own parents, to sit shivah, the seven-day period of mourning for the dead - over an intermarried child was no longer fashionable. This was the era of tolerance and superficial devotion.

"I think he's probably very lonely," Rhonda began. "He's alone and he's done a wonderful job of raising his boys. He's been through a lot and I, for one, think it's nice that he has an interest in women. He can be a very charming man you know. Don't you think so, Phil."

The poor man shrugged and nodded as best he could. "He's not exactly my kind of rabbi. That's all. And sometimes I speak out of turn."

The joy of bringing children to an uncomfortable dinner is that they can be counted on to plead to go home. Though Jared delighted them with trips to the cellar and playing with the cat, by eight o'clock, an agonizing two and a half hours after arriving, there was a five-year old curled up in her mother's lap and two pre-delinquents hanging on Jack. Jack begged off and managed to crawl out the door as Rae kissed Rhonda and gently, ever so gently, clasped Phil's hand.

The ride was twenty minutes long. The first ten were silent.

"He's an asshole, you know."

"I know, Rae, and I'm sorry. He's an asshole and there are an awful lot of assholes like him out there and I apologize personally for every one of them."

"Are you becoming an asshole too?"

"I already am one and you love me anyway. Did you have to hit him quite as hard as you did?"

"Fuck'em. It was fun. You should try it some time."

"Are you the woman that I married? I have to look at this guy at faculty meetings."   "Au contraire, mon petit chou. He has to look at you!"

Chapter 13

Sleeping late wasn't something that dogs understood, Sundays notwithstanding. By pulling the thick plastic shades down all over the house it was possible to convince the dogs that it was still dark. Even children spared their parents an extra half hour with competent shades in alliance. It was an easy trick. If you want everyone up early, just leave appropriate window space showing and the light will awaken all concerned. Adjust shades for time of arousal.

There was no morning arousal to be enjoyed in the master bedroom this Sunday. Any sign of movement was taken as evidence of impending waking by the beasts. Jack tried. He rolled over and caressed Rae gently, nuzzling her ear. Just as she sighed awareness, he saw the assault. Cady jumped onto the end of the bed and walked on him up the length of the bed. One hundred and sixty pounds divided by four paws meant a weight of forty pounds per walking paw on his rib cage - enough force to bruise and disfigure. Carefully gauging the crevice which lay between Jack and Rae, she unceremoniously dropped her entire weight in the inviting chasm and forced her head between theirs.

"Oh, Gack! She's slobbering on my pillow."

"She loves you. She wants you to take her for a walk."

"Somehow, I knew that."

He slipped out from under the warm blankets and found Sasha lying beside the bed, a loyal carpet for his chilled feet. Rather than dressing, he grabbed a pair of sweatpants and a sweatshirt and pulled them on along with sweat socks and running shoes.

"You stay in bed; I'll take care of these guys."

The children were not yet up, and Jack was able to walk the dogs in the bright Sunday sunlight. It was a particularly nice day for December. Not too cold, not too windy. A day to take a breath and find one's center. He skirted the edge of the frozen pond and felt the warmth of the sun and the bite of the breeze on his face at once. He stepped carefully, savoring the frozen crunch of grass underfoot and reformulated his day. Back in the house, the children were roused.

"Hey, you guys, what do you say, we let Mom sleep and we all go out for breakfast?"

"Where to?"

"Foxy's Peppermint Pancake House."

"All right! Let's go!"

Unanimity was rare. Foxy's was disgusting. It was a local attraction that bordered on the bizarre. It was painted in peppermint colors that had nothing to do with pancakes. Worse, it boasted an entire room of pinball machines that had even less to do with pancakes. The food was terrible, a mix of soggy flour and artificial syrup. Most concoctions were topped with whipped cream. The kids loved it. The hostess fawned over Dinah and gave her paper and crayons and the boys could always find leftover change for the pinball.

Occasionally, Jack felt the need to bond with his children and he gave Rae a couple of hours' peace on a Sunday morning. He slid the door of the bus open and Cady bounded past the kids into the back seat. Sasha waited hesitantly and made the leap into the middle seat. Each dog now occupied space equivalent to three normal sized humans. That left room for the driver and one passenger. Simmy claimed the front seat based on seniority. Lee muscled Sasha over in the middle seat and left Dinah to fend for herself with Cady. Dinah cried as she slid into the seat and Cady dropped her wet muzzle into her lap.

Jack backed the bus out of the drive and out onto Crosscut. As he took the left to head to the main road, he could see Merrill coming up the street pulling a wagon laden with Sunday papers. He hesitated as he passed the paper boy. No wave this Sunday. A nod, perhaps, but no wave.

He tried to time it for about an hour and a half. Foxy's tried to time it until they had pried every last dime out of Simmy and Lee's pockets and a few out of Jack's. They were successful. Dinah waved a sheaf of Christmas pictures colored in blue and green and yellow. Leftovers, of which there was a surfeit, were deposited on the floor of the bus, styrofoam covers opened for immediate consumption. Both were overturned. The advantage of the rubber mats in the bus was that in spring you could simply hose out the entire mess. While waiting for her pancakes, one of the dogs had eaten an armrest off the middle bench. Sasha denied any knowledge of the event.

Jack tried as best he could to parent well. He had had lengthy discussions with Norman Zadok arguing that parenting behavior was determined in large part by how one had been parented. Bad parents engender bad parenting, thus insuring the perpetuation of evil in the world. Jack reasoned that he had been badly parented by Joseph Israel especially and that, therefore, he was doomed to be a poor parent to his children. Moreover, Jack had a Ph.D. in social psychology and a poor relationship with his father, who had a poor relationship to his father, thus buttressing his expertise.

Dr. Zadok would have none of it. He argued that what makes people human was the growth of consciousness. We can observe our own behavior, critique it, analyze it, see patterns in it that provide enlightenment. And what makes us civil human beings is our ability and our willingness to change behavior on the basis of the analysis we have constructed. Jack had already done the analysis and critique. That was the hard part, to get people to step back from their everyday behavior and to look at themselves objectively. Jack had done this. Now all he had to do was to change the behavior.

"So how do you change your behavior?" he had asked.

"You get up one morning and you look in the mirror and you say, 'Today I will change my behavior.'"

He had practiced changing his behavior. It had been apparent from the start that Zadok was childless. One does not simply change one's behavior with one's children. A relationship with a child is not something that a parent controls. It is a negotiated arrangement that takes into account not only the parent intent on change, but the other parent who is ally and audience, other children who are adversaries and confederates, as well as the complex treaties, contracts, working assumptions, cease-fires, mutual cooperation agreements and temporary armistices which have preceded the day on which one looks in the mirror and says, "Today, I will be a better parent".

Jack congratulated himself. He was working at being a better parent. He also lost faith in his offsprings' ability to respond to this better parenting. No number of visits to Foxy's Peppermint Pancakes, nor pinball coins, nor family outings, nor televised basketball games altered the complexities of their relationships. They were not disappointed. Surprised, confused, faced with a parent who clearly no longer knew his role in the family, perhaps. But not disappointed.

He backed the bus into the driveway so that the sliding door faced toward the house and away from Bascom's. If the dogs exited on Bascom's side, they would dart for his lawn and pee there, carefully marking the corners of their range. Over a short time, Bascom's lawn had acquired a series of dead spots ringed with lush green grass. Jack called them "angel rings" where the nitrogen-rich urine had at once burned out the targeted area and amply fertilized the circle around it. Jim Bascom called it inconsiderate and aggressive and insisted that Jack fix the offending areas. He declined and Rae came out every now and again on hands and knees and worked lime into the soil and sprinkled new seed on the scars. The Bascoms tolerated her, tolerated the children, and despised Jack. It made things symmetrical.

The door slid open with the rasping sound of a large file on fieldstone and all shapes and sizes dashed for the front door. The boys hit the porch first, tore at the storm door and forced the wooden door with their shoulders. It stayed shut.

"It's locked!" called Simmy.

"Here. Gimme that". and Lee tried the inner door. It stayed shut.

"It's locked? That's odd. It's never locked."

Jack fished the key out of the collection on his key ring and turned it in the lock. The bolt released with a "Snap", the handle turned, and the door gave way. All entered to unaccustomed silence.

Jack went directly to the bedroom. Rae lay on the bed in her robe, her knees tucked up into her chest, facing the wall without moving. Jack swung around the bed. Her eyes were open and large tears ran over her nose onto an enlarging wet spot on the pillow. She was motionless. Not even her eyes moved.

"Rae. Rae. Are you all right?"

"No," she croaked. "He came in here."

"Who did? What happened?"

"The paper boy. I was in the bathtub - naked. He came in here and came into the bathroom. He just stood there, I screamed, and he wouldn't go away." Her chest heaved and she disgorged a sob that lay in her chest, choking the breath from her. She wept the tears of fear and shook without control.

Jack cradled her in his arms. He held her as close as he could without breaking her. He interrogated. "Can you tell me exactly what happened?" But she could not. The sobs had not emptied their toxins from her chest, and it heaved like a stomach gone bad. Her vocal cords were victim to the poison, and it infected her eyes and her face. The children stood in the door, their faces white, the dogs milled about Jack's back anxious to lick and soothe. All the love in the house was mustered around her and it did not cure the fear.

He ushered dogs and children into the other room and closed the bedroom door. With a glass of water, he re-entered and sat at the side of the bed while she expunged the last of the pain.

"I . . . I . . .was taking a bath and the door to the bathroom opened and he was there."

"Who was there?"

"Merrill, the paper boy! And he was just looking at me. And I was naked. And I screamed at him to get out and he wouldn't move, and I screamed again, and he still didn't move. Oh, Jack, I've never been so scared in my life."

"Then what happened?"

"I grabbed a towel off the rack and covered myself and got out of the tub — just screaming my head off all the time . . ."

"Did he attack you?"

"No, he ran out."

"Do you think it was just a mistake? Do you think he came in and just didn't know what to do when he saw you?"

"No! No! No! Jack, he came in here to steal drugs and when he saw me . . . I don't know what he was thinking. I ran into the bedroom and locked the door. I put clothes on and came out and he was gone. I locked the door and I haven't stopped shaking yet."

"Do you think we should call the police?"

"Damned straight we should call the police. He's a druggy and a pervert and something has to be done about him, Jack."

Jack left the bedroom, went to the telephone in the kitchen slowly, picked up the phone book, and looked up the number. There was a choice of numbers - the emergency number and the normal business number. He methodically dialed the latter. When he got a response, he reported calmly. "This is Jack Israel at 2105 Tamarack Court in Southmoor. We've had an intruder in the house. No, he's gone. No, nobody's hurt, but my wife's pretty upset. Yes, we know who it was. Thank you, we'll stay here."

He returned to the bedroom. "The police will be here in a little while." And he held her again as she cried softly.

They reported everything: the bathroom visits, the missing Darvon, the entry into the house. The police officer dutifully took notes and asked pertinent questions. "Had there ever been any other drugs missing? Had he ever made an inappropriate comment to Mrs. Israel? Had any of the neighbors ever reported a problem with him?" He was thorough and at the same time reassuring. He comforted them and sympathized in the way that only small-town officers can do. In closing, he suggested that they could file a formal criminal complaint at the station which would then involve the juvenile officer and probably a trip for Merrill and family to the police station or he could stop by the house and talk to Mr. and Mrs. Ramsey, Merrill's parents.

Jack had looked at Rae to make the choice. She shook her head and said, "I can see this one coming. OK, go talk to his parents and see what you can find out."

The police officer left with a promise to report back to them. Forty minutes later the squad rolled back into the driveway. The officer now accompanied by a female officer knocked on the door. Jack and the dogs and Rae invited them in and shooed the children away. All adults and canines sat in the living room, the least lived-in room of the house, to talk. They passed the obligatory comments about the dogs. Both officers knew the dogs, neither knew any of the Israels. It was a common phenomenon.

"Well, I spoke with Mr. Ramsey," the male officer began, "and he tells me that his son came home from his route and told him that there had been a problem. He told his father that he had seen you driving out on the street and that you had waved to him as if to tell him to bring the paper into the house. He thought that you wanted him to bring it in for your wife and he came in and says that she was standing in the hallway with nothing on and that he got scared and ran out."

"I wasn't in the hallway, I was in the bathroom and in the tub. And did you ask him about the drugs?" Rae pleaded.

"Yes, Ma'am, I did. I told him that his son had used the bathroom previously and that you had noticed some drugs missing."

"What did he say to that?"

"Well, Ma'am, the boy said that you did let him use the bathroom once when he had to go really bad but that he didn't know anything about any drugs."

"So that's it, huh?" said Rae with disgust dripping from her lips.

"Well, no, it's not, Ma'am. First of all, if you like, you can still file a formal complaint and we can conduct a more thorough investigation, though I don't know that we'll get any further than we have already. And of course, I'll note this morning's events on the police blotter and if anything like it happens again, well, we'll have an informal record of it."

The female officer joined in, "I know how you feel. These things are so upsetting. It's like being violated. But I was there, and I watched the kid's face and I think he was as scared as you were."

She meant to be supportive, but her role was clear - give the police force a feminine face, cool things down, make it go away. And it went away.

Rae paced for the rest of the day. Her eyes were red, but she didn't cry. The paper delivery was cancelled for all time. All doors were to be kept locked at all times. Neighbors were to be warned about Merrill. The children were to say nothing to anybody. Everyone was to remain alert to anything unusual around the house. There were measures to be taken, but the lesion was there and no measure taken after would heal the wound. It was like so many scars. It was an event that changed a person and the change was permanent. She would never take a bath alone in the house again. She would always lock the bathroom door. She would never leave the front door unlocked again. And she would always see that fourteen-year old face staring at her naked in the tub.

Jack picked up a Courier at the drug store on his way home on Monday night. He came through the door and parked his coat. Rae was in the kitchen, one hand on her head, the other on the kitchen counter, steadying herself.

"Hi. Headache again?"

"Yeah. Real bad."

"Any word from MacKenzie?"

"Yeah. His office called. They want us to come in very early on Friday morning about 7:30. Can you make it? We need to get someone to watch the kids."

"Sure, I'll be there. That's a real odd time for an appointment, don't you think?"

"Uh-huh. I asked her about it, and she said that she thought that he wanted Dr. Acosta there too, where she was my OB and all and that was the only time they could set up."

"OK. I'll ask Ilene and Pat if they can come over and have breakfast here while we do this."

Jack decided to take the elevator up to the third floor. It was an uncharacteristic behavior. Walking the stairs was a matter of pride. Going to the gym was a matter of pride. Being aware of his physical body was an anchor to reality and the stairs were a link in the anchor chain. The complexities of that chain had not prevented an inexorable weight gain. Nor the progressive development of male-pattern baldness. But today's electrical ascension to the third floor was not a matter of age. The fatigue had overcome. It was December. The semester was nearly over.

He had survived moving, the new job, the start-up of the research project. He had diminished his reserves. He had spent them in McCormick Hall and had nothing else to dispense, not even at home. Rae had exhausted her reserves. Merrill Ramsey, at age fourteen had sucked her dry of whatever had remained after packing her house and children born and unborn and following her husband to Bloomington. There was no elevator for Rae.

"Ilene, I need your help," he began before even taking off his parka.

"That's what you pay me for."

"Rae has a doctor's appointment on Friday at seven thirty in the morning and it's real important. Do you think that you and Dunphy could come over around seven and watch the kids for about an hour or so until we get home?"

"That's not what you pay me for. But we'll do it anyway."

"Thanks, you're a sweetheart."

"By the by. Christmas break starts in about ten days and the heat will be turned off in the building for three weeks. If you're not planning on being in here working in your long-johns and mittens, Pat and I would like to take some time off and go to Wisconsin. Will that be OK with you?"

"Sure, no problem. We'll be going to Milwaukee, I'm sure."

"Also, don't forget that you're off to Chicago tomorrow with my paramour."

"I am?"

"Check your calendar. By the way, there's a new calendar on your desk. You and Boy Wonder are supposed to drive the interviewing team to Dr. Frederick's clinic and be there by nine. You'll have to be on the road by six-thirty if you're going to make it in through Chicago traffic. I have a state car reserved and your personal chauffeur will pick it up tonight. All you have to do is be at your door at six-thirty in something more formal than your bathrobe."

"Oh, that hurts. Any idea what time we'll be home?"

"Well, if you leave there about four, which is when they schedule their last appointment, you can be back home by about . . . oh, maybe seven-ish. Don't pack a lunch. You're having pizza at Uno's with Fredericks and a Dr. Harry Lannon from Cook County. Imogene Ulrich set that up and said you would know what it was about."

"How do you know all this?"

"Pat set it up last week when they were in Chicago for their first trip."

"Oh".

Pat loved driving the state cars. They were all big Dodge sedans, identical in profile and in the same shade of beige as the cars that the state troopers drove. They carried the state seal on the side and in smaller letters beneath Bloomington State University. In the rear-view mirror, the cars were dead ringers for cops and the traffic melted out of the left lane in front of them to clear a path. Dunphy always drove and never cruised at less than eighty. He felt immune.

The ride home home from Chicago had been eventful and Dunphy was still entertaining himself as he pulled into the driveway.

"Did you see the look on his face? Jeez I was doin' about eighty-five when we passed him, just parked under the overpass waitin' for some unsuspecting clod to slither by at seventy. Gawd, he musta hadda hit a hundert and ten to catch us. Oh was he pissed. Did you wake up in time to hear him? 'Good Gawdamm we have enough trouble out here trying to keep the citizens from speeding without having to chase the state cars! Fer Chrissake will you please slow down?' Damn if there wasn't smoke coming out of the little holes on that silly hat."

"Dunphy, you set a fine example for your student colleagues in the back seat."

"Oh, Boss. I'se jest havin' some fun."

As they turned into Tamarack, the lights were on at the house and the front door was open. A small figure in a leather jacket and a Persian lamb hat stood in the door talking to Rae.

CHAPTER 14

Jack got out of the car without saying good-bye to Dunphy. Like a wife left at the train station without a kiss, Dunphy waited with the engine running and the window down, looking expectant. Jack walked up onto the porch, a quizzical look on his face.

"Hi. Isaac, you're about three hours early. Everything all right?"

"No, I came over to see if I could get a ride from you. My car won't start, and Matt Cowan is at the police station and needs some help."

Jack glanced at Rae who stood with blank expression at another demand on her partner.

"What's the problem?"

"A big fight at the high school. Matt was involved. Lev too. Some kids got hurt and they arrested Matt. He had no one else to call so he called me. I need to bail him out."

"Well, I'm just getting home, but I guess I can take you over."

A third voice chimed in. "Hey, Boss. Can I come too? It sounds like fun and I haven't seen a good bar room brawl since the last family wedding."

"Sure. Rabbi Abrams, my faithful driver, Cato, will take us there in my secret car. Hop in the back seat. No doubt he'll be able to procure a state police escort for us."

"Rae," he went on, "are you OK for a little while."

"I've been OK for the last twelve years. What's different about tonight?"

Dunphy gunned the engine and Jack made a feint at introductions, "Rabbi Abrams this is Pat Dunphy; Pat, Rabbi Abrams." The interrogator took over, "Can you tell me what happened?"

"Yes and no. I got it from Lev and he's a little excited if you can imagine. There's been some tension at school, you know—black kids, white kids. I guess there's been some pushing and some shoving. It's kid stuff, you know? But the kids leave school and it's over. So-o-o-o this afternoon there's a student council meeting after school and the student council stays late and they're debating if kids should be allowed to wear . . . to wear . . . shmahtahs . . . rags on their heads. Apparently, the gang members all wear the same shmahtahs on their heads. And the student council is all worked up - they're going to pass a rule that no one should wear a shmahtah. They get over with their debate and they're coming out of the building and a bunch of black kids, with, of course, shmahtahs on their heads are outside. They've been playing basketball - and the two groups, the student council and the black shmahtah-heads get into an argument. I don't know what happened. Lev says there was a lot of pushing and threats and they were scared and all of a sudden Matt Cowan comes out of the building and he looks at this and he starts shouting and screaming and coming over to this argument. And the black kids gang up on him and start to push him and he drops his knapsack and takes out some special sticks - I don't know what they are - Lev says they're kung-fu sticks, and he starts swinging them around and all the time he's shouting, 'I am Mattisyohu. These are my people. You're Greek pigs and I'll kill you.' And he bangs a couple of them on the head and apparently really hurt them. So some lady across the street saw this happen and called the police who showed up and found a couple of black kids on the ground bleeding from the head and Matt swinging these sticks and screaming that he was going to take back the temple and drive off these heathens."

"Isaac, that's the funniest story I've heard in years."

"Hey, Boss, do you think somebody caught it on film? Can we stage a re-enactment? It sounds like a hoot. I wish I had been there. I gotta meet this guy. Who is he?"

"Gentlemen, this is not a joke. This is a racial incident. People got hurt. My son and a . . . a potential convert in my congregation were involved. One of them is in jail. This is very serious."

"Rabbi, with all due respect, you have obviously never enjoyed a good gang fight. It is, after all, a rite of passage among American teen-age males. I would judge from your trace of an accent that you missed out on this formative experience."

"Jack, where did you get him, from a juvenile detention center?"

"Actually, Isaac, I found him wandering the streets of Milwaukee looking for a fight."

They pulled up to the police station. There was no parking on the street, so Dunphy pulled into a space marked Official Cars Only. They exited the car, which Dunphy left unlocked, and walked into Bloomington's police headquarters. The reception area was small and rather dark. Jack looked around and saw a pay telephone on the wall, a single bench, and dominating the room, a glass window with a metal-shielded porthole. The glass itself was green tinted and Jack could just make out the form of an officer behind it. Isaac retreated to the back of the trio, leaving Jack to navigate the system. He approached the glass-protected desk and informed the officer,   "Hello, we're here to claim Matt Cowan. I believe he's being held here."

"Are you family?"

"Uhhh . . . Well . . . I'm . . . uh, his psychologist; I'm Dr. Israel and this is his . . . uh . . . clergyman, Reverend Abrams, and this is . . . uh . . . my assistant, Mr. Dunphy."

"I don't know if you brought enough people with you to handle him, Doc. Wait here and I'll check". He left the desk and was gone for about ten minutes. He came back and leaned toward the port in the thick glass window, "He's in with the juvenile officer now. You can come in through that door. Wait for the buzzer." He nodded toward a door at the far left and motioned for them to approach. As they did, he buzzed the door and they entered.

Past the door was a different world. In contrast to the dim beige of the reception, the walls were white and brilliant fluorescents illumined a large area. There were desks arranged in orderly rows, an aluminum urn in a corner with a red light announced the availability of hot coffee. People flowed around the room, men and women, all uniformed and all wearing guns. The reception officer met them on the other side of the door and guided them toward a closed room at the back. He knocked politely on the door, cracked it open and stuck his head in announcing, "God-squad. Come to claim the avenging angel."

He swung wide the door and ushered in the Wednesday comedy club.

"Ah, yes," a youngish man said, rising with an extended hand. He said to Jack, "Are you Rabbi Abrams?"

"Thank God, no! I'm Dr. Israel. I'm a psychologist at the university and I know Matt. This is Rabbi Abrams". He turned to collect Isaac from the back of the pack and drag him forward into visibility.

"And this is?"

"Oh, yes, this is my assistant, Mr. Dunphy."

"Well, I guess then that there's enough of us here to deal with the . . . um . . . accused. I'm Officer Haddack, Eddie Haddack, and I'm the juvenile officer in charge."

In a corner, in a chair, tilted back against the wall, his feet gently rocking off the floor sat Matt Cowan. He was smiling.

"Hi, Rabbi. Hi, Doc. Glad you could come. If you guys want coffee, they'll get it for you. They're pretty nice."

The juvenile officer was in his late twenties. He was tall, broad shouldered, and had a casual shock of blond hair that fell over his face. He wore a uniform whose seriousness was undermined by twinkling blue eyes and a grin that escaped his face even when he attempted to appear stern. He dutifully shuffled chairs around so that everyone could sit.

"Let me explain my role," Officer Eddie Haddack began, "I take care of juvenile matters for the department. This young man, Matt Cowan, has been involved in what appears to be a gang fight at Veterans Memorial High School. There were some serious injuries and he may be charged with a felony - anything from simple assault to assault with a deadly weapon. Not only that, but there were three other young men injured, which means up to three felony counts. Because he's within six months of his eighteenth birthday, he will have to appear at a hearing before a magistrate to determine if he'll be charged and if charged, whether he'll be tried as an adult or a juvenile. Do you understand so far?"

"Yes," the choir chanted.

"I assume that you're here to bail him out. But I must advise you, that he has been read his Miranda rights, he has not waived them and therefore we do not have a statement from him. As you know, he's entitled to an attorney and if he can't afford one, the court will provide one. It's my obligation to inform you, as potential custody-agents for him, that should he be tried as a juvenile, he still has a right to an attorney and to a trial by jury. He may, however, if he's tried as a juvenile, waive his right to a jury trial and appear before a judge. Do you understand so far?"

"With all due respect, officer," Dunphy began, "I'm just the driver on this little picnic and I don't care to have anyone released in my custody, thank you."

"I see. Well, is one of you gentlemen here to act as a custodial agent for Matt?"

"I will," said Isaac. There was no smile on his face.

"Fine, Rabbi. I can release him to your custody. That's not a problem. There are several important matters, however. There will be a hearing within the next seven days at which he'll have to appear to determine the nature of the charges against him and, if there are charges, to assess whether he'll be tried in juvenile court or adult offenders court. It will be your responsibility to see that he appears. Do you understand?"

"Yes. Go on. I'd like to get out of here, please."

"Fine. Now, if I'm not mistaken, Rabbi, your son, uh . . ." he rifled through is notes, "Lev . . . was involved in the incident. Is that correct?"

"Yes, what about it? He didn't hit anybody. He was a victim. What do you want with him?"

"Well, I'll need to get a statement from him as to what happened."

"So? You'll get a statement. Can we go now?"

"There are just a few papers that I'll need to have you sign to indicate that you are accepting custody and then you can go. Matt, are you ready?"

"Hell, yes," he answered, dropping the chair's front legs to the floor with a resounding bang and leaping to his feet with the skill of a gymnast.

"OK. Rabbi, if you don't mind, I could stop at your home this evening to talk to your son."

"Yes."

The university car now contained four. "Where to, Green Hornet?" asked the driver.

"Well, let's see," Jack calculated, "We have to get Matt home, we have to get Isaac home, we have to get me home, and we have to get the car back to the university motor pool."

"I can't take Matt home," began the Rabbi, with disgust dripping from pressed lips, "my car isn't running."

"Whassa madda wit it?" the driver challenged.

"How do I know? It doesn't start."

"Does it crank? Does the starter turn it over?"

"I guess so."

"Does it catch? Does it sound like it's gonna start and then die?"

"No. It just . . . you know . . . it goes eehheehheehh and it doesn't go."

"Oh that! What kinda car ya got?"

"A Chrysler. A Cordoba. Black. Three years old."

"Oh, black. That explains it. You got a bad ballast resistor. It's classic. You want me to fix it? I can get it running for you in ten minutes."

Isaac turned to Jack. "Is this true? Can he do this?"

"If it's black, I would guess that the ballast resistor is the problem. You can trust him, he's from Wisconsin."

"Boss, there's an American Auto Discount at the mall on the way home. It's a standard part. We can stop for a minute and the masked avenger in the back seat and I can get the part and have it swapped in no time. Whadda ya say?"

"Sounds do-able to me. If that doesn't fix it, we can always rebuild the engine. Right, Isaac?"

"You people are meshuggah."

Dunphy and Matt were in the American Auto Discount for only ten minutes. They came out proudly waving a small red and white box and regrouped in the car.

"There it is. Always keep a spare in the glove compartment. Black Cordobas eat 'em like Fritos."

Isaac directed them to his house. Dunphy fairly leaped from the car with Matt in close pursuit and manually lifted the garage door. He opened the hood of the black Cordoba and rummaged around the garage until he found a screwdriver. In seconds all that could be seen of the two delinquents were rounded butts hanging off the fenders like a quartet of melons. Isaac and Jack went into the house where the Rabbi summoned his youngest son to present to the interrogator.

"Hi, Dr. Israel. No dogs tonight?"

"Different breed. I left them in the garage. Can you tell me what happened at school this afternoon?"

"Sure. It was just amazing, let me tell you. I was in a student council meeting. We have them every Wednesday afternoon. It was a hot meeting and the whole school knew what it was about. These black toughs come to school and they all wear red do-rags. Do you know what those are? Well, apparently, that's the badge for membership in this street gang.

And we debated a rule to keep kids from wearing any head coverings in school. See the idea was to do away with symbols of gang membership. We had a really good meeting and we passed the rule. By the time we got out all the school buses were gone so we had to take regular busses. But when we came out of the school there was this gang with their do-rags on and there must have been eight of them and they started pushing us around."

"Exactly how many of you were there."

"There were six of us. Two were girls and they left them alone. We were four guys. The funny thing is that we were two Jews and two blacks. And these guys started beatin' on us real hard."

"Were you scared?"

"Absolutely. I was terrified. We knew these guys and they beat on us on a daily basis. They take watches, they hold us up for money, they push us around. They're scum."

"Then what happened?"

"I didn't see it coming, but I heard it. Matt Cowan came out of the building; I think he has detention about four out of five days for coming late. He saw what was happening and he shouted, 'Let my people go!' Can you imagine that? It was Moses and Pharaoh. 'Let my people go!' And the black guys, I mean the gang members, looked at him like he was nuts."

"Did they attack him?"

"Not really. It was more like he attacked them - by himself. He grabbed a pair of these kung-fu sticks - the kind with two pieces of wood chained together and he started swinging them in these fancy moves and the next thing you know, he was busting heads all over the place. Two of the gang members hit the dirt right off. They were hurtin' real bad and the rest of them just kind of backed off and left just as the cops showed up."

"Did Matt say anything? While all this was going on?"

Lev laughed out loud. "Yes! That's the best part. He was shouting 'I am Mattisyohu. You're Greek pigs and I'll kill you.

I'll clean the temple with you.' Just goes to show what too much Jewish education will do to you."

The hood of the car in the garage slammed shut. Dunphy poked his head in the front door and asked for the keys to the car. Isaac procured them and left with them for the garage. Moments later the engine cranked, caught and roared with satisfaction.

"Lev, you'll be getting a visit from the juvenile officer tonight. His name is Officer Haddack. He'll want to hear this story from you. Do you know if any of the gang members were seriously hurt?"

"I've been on the phone all night. I heard that one has a concussion, one has a broken collar bone, and one had a huge cut on his head and had stitches. I'm really sorry they weren't hurt worse, let me tell you."

Dunphy took off with Matt. Both wore smiles of satisfaction as they spun the wheels of the university car in front of the Rabbi's residence. Jack walked around the corner. It was now getting late. He had been gone since six-thirty in the morning and had spent the day on edge. The reservoirs were empty. He had had no dinner and the dogs would want to be walked. He wondered how much complexity a person could tolerate in their lives. Did people vary in their capacity for complexity? Was it a personality variable or a neurological variable? Isaac had said that Jack had never run from, always to. But he had run from Boston. The pressure had been terrific. He had run from Milwaukee or been run out of Milwaukee. Now he systematically placed foot before foot on the way home and wondered if his life was more complex than he could manage. He had taken job after job looking for the one where he wouldn't feel pressured, overcommitted, threatened. He had gone from place to place, each time with the sure knowledge that here, here it would feel better. Now he felt no better. The thought crept into his mind for the first time — it wasn't the job, it was him. This was a disease that he carried inside.

He crept in the front door. Unnoticed entry was not a concept in the meager minds of Newfoundlands. He was mobbed. He hung his coat. At last he loosened his tie and went toward the bedrooms. All the children were asleep. Rae lay in bed, the light on the headboard illuminating a trash novel.

"I'm sorry. I didn't mean to be gone so long. I really didn't. Are you okay?"

"No. I'm not. I'm sick somehow and I don't know with what. I'm worn out. I'm lonely. I'm scared. And I don't know where you are half the time - even when you tell me that you're walking the dogs. I don't know where your body is. I don't know where your head is. And you know what, Jack? I'm not sure that I even know where your heart is anymore."

A tear left her eye for the slow, sideways journey down the bridge of her nose. It hung on the curve of her cheek for a long moment and found a home on the pillow slip, just in time to have its path retraced by another.

"Rae. I'm sorry. I'm really sorry. I'll do better."

She doused the light and turned over, dropping her book on the floor. Sasha barked a muffled note from the front door. They had not been walked.

Jack's head hurt. It was the hurt of muffled sobs. He was too old to cry, and he hurt too bad to ignore the pain. He stepped into the bathroom and opened the mirrored cabinet, rummaging about for the aspirin. Floss fell out, followed by old boxes of bandages, followed by aspirin. As he grabbed for the aspirin he noticed in the last recess of the cabinet a yellow plastic pill bottle marked "Darvon".

CHAPTER 15

"I need to talk to you."

"Just a second and I'll get my coat and saddle up the ponies."

"No dogs tonight. I need to talk to you, just you. No dogs." There was no pleasantry in his manner. He waited on the porch nervously pacing, head bent, agitated.

"Look, I really do have to walk the dogs. I promise they won't repeat a word . . ."

"NO DOGS! We need to talk. NOW!"

Jack came through the door, pushing dog faces back into the house behind him. He closed the wooden door and vainly tried to latch what was left of the storm door. Before he could zipper his jacket and put up his hood, Isaac was down the driveway. Isaac stopped at the end of the drive to wait without looking back to see if Jack was following. When he caught up, Isaac didn't settle into his walk. He turned as an accuser and faced Jack squarely, toe against toe, nose against nose.

Americans have standards for polite conversation. They stand eighteen inches apart if they are acquaintances doing business or passing the time. If they are close friends, they stand twelve inches apart. Latin Americans have a different standard. They stand six inches apart for all conversation. To Americans this speaks of aggression, an invasion of private space. It's common to see an American backing down the street as a Latin tries to have a civilized conversation with him. This situation was hard to assess. Did Isaac mean intimacy? Did he mean aggression?

Isaac withdrew a gnarled finger from his pocket. "I walk with you and talk with you because I trust you."

"Of course."

"You're not a member of my congregation. You don't play in congregational politics. You're a psychologist. I assume there's some confidentiality between us."

"Of course. What on earth are you talking about?"

"You know Marty Feldman?"

"Sure, I met him at services."

"He's the president of the congregation. He's a nice guy. He came into my office today - no appointment. He sits down and chats about nothing. Then he says to me that my personal life is, of course, my personal life. By which he means that I have no personal life, you understand? Only a public life. Then he says to me that it has come to his attention that I have been seeing a young - he says, very young - woman in town who is not Jewish and congregants are talking about it and I need to be quite certain that I know what I'm doing in this matter."

"Oh, no."

"Now look, Jack, the only person who knows about Edna is you. You're the only one I've talked to about her. It couldn't have come from anyone else and I'm enraged that my personal life has leaked into my rabbinic role. It's not fair, it's not decent, it's not . . ."

"It's not me."

"What do you mean, it's not you?"

"I never said a word to anybody."

"Then how come he knew?"

"Look, you're not exactly an anonymous face in the crowd. You want to keep secrets? I'll tell you about secrets. There are three kinds of information systems: Open, closed, and mixed. Here's the deal. If you live in an open system, you assume that everybody knows everything all the time and you live your life accordingly. If you live in a town of seventy people and there are no window shades, you don't walk around the house naked - not ever. Because the one time you do, everyone in town knows if your belly button turns in or out. If you live in a closed system, you assume that nobody knows anything about anything, and you can do what you want. You live in a city of a million; you work downtown; you keep a post office box and you keep your shades drawn. You live your life privately and everyone else does too - but you don't go looking for emotional support for your problems either. If you live in a mixed system, then you never know who knows what or when you're going to bump into someone who knows everything about you but who you don't know at all. You live in a city of maybe twenty-five thousand. You are the one rabbi in town and you may not know everybody, but an awful lot of people know you. You're not anonymous. You never can be; you never will be. You're carrying on with a woman in public places and then you're surprised that people know about it. I never had to tell anybody about it. People know!"

"Has somebody told you this?"

"Yes!"

"Who?"

"What the hell difference does it make? Marty Feldman gave you a friendly warning. What did you do, throw him out of your office?"

They had not walked a step. They stood in front of the house on Tamarack Court and shouted at one another. Jim Bascom flipped on his porch light to inform them that they were violating his rights. Isaac backed off six critical inches from Jack and lowered his voice.

"This is gossip. This is the worst sin. It's the murdering of someone's good name and that's unforgivable. I told him that it wasn't anybody's business at the temple what I did with my personal life."

"Nice try. You flunk. Try again."

"Why is it not my right to have a relationship that's none of their business?"

"Well, you are what might be called a moral entrepreneur in the community, my friend. Sad to say, but one of your jobs is to set the moral standard for behavior in the Jewish community and worse than that to represent the standards of the Jewish community to the non-Jewish community. Now as

I see it, you're only violating two inviolable rules in this situation: You're seeing a non-Jewish woman and she's about half your age. In a moral sense, I guess that puts you and Matt Cowan in similar straits, except that he gets a lawyer and you don't. If you don't cool it in public with Ms., was it Edna? - I suspect that you're not going to get a gold watch from the temple at retirement. Got it?"

"It's stupid. It's not just. And I don't have to stand for it. I have very powerful allies in the temple and Marty Feldman can't control me."

"It's not a matter of counting guns for the showdown at the OK Corral. You can't afford a fight like this in your temple. You've already told me that you have a split between reform and conservative partisans and people have quietly let me know that while you are loved by some, you are not loved by others. And you know what else? You're not a fuzzy, cuddly rabbi, Isaac. You're cranky and crotchety and you insist on telling people what you want them to hear instead of what they want to hear. You may win Mr. Forthright, but you'll never win Miss Congeniality."

"You're a shtoonk."

"And you need to learn to offend people in English so they can respond properly."

"I can't give her up. I won't give her up. Weekend after next the boys will be gone and I'm taking her to Chicago. The university will be closed and so I'll get to spend some time with her there."

"Did she invite you for Christmas dinner with the family? Put your presents under the tree?"

"You're being cruel."

"You accused me of blabbing your secret love life all over Bloomington."

"What do you think I should do?"

"We've had this conversation before. You know what I think."

"Have you ever been lonely?"

"Yeah. I'm lonely now. I'm lonely always and I don't know what to do about it."

"Why are you lonely? You have everything."

"Everything's in danger of being taken away all the time. This is a great life. I've never had so much. Good job, great wife, nice kids, good home. It smacks of happiness. Happiness is a curse. It makes you vulnerable. You have too much to lose. You start working your ass off to stay happy, so it won't go away and the harder you work at it the more you're in danger of losing your happiness. But you figure that if you stop working at it, you'll lose it. You're caught. It's insidious. You're better off not so happy so that you can be happier. This is crazy."

"No. No. Let me tell you a story: 'A wise rabbi once saw a man running through the marketplace. He called out to him, 'Why are you running?' The man answered, 'To make a living.' The rabbi called after him, 'Why don't you stop running to make a living so that you can have a life.' So, stop running and have a life."

"I'm not sure I know how to do that, Isaac."

"I can tell you how, Jack, but you can't laugh, and you have to listen carefully."

"I'll put my giggle-guard and my ears on."

"First, go get the dogs and we'll walk a little."

They walked slowly along their accustomed route. It was clear that Jack was not the only one with depleted reserves. Where they had spent each evening together covering distance in time and space rapidly, filling one another's minds with arguments and images, tonight they paced themselves with serious deliberation.

"I don't mean to preach at you," Isaac began, "That's not what I really intend. I don't preach well anyway. I tell stories. People can take their own lessons from what's in the stories. It's better that way. But you need someone to tell you something that you should already know. I'll tell you. If you let life set its own pace for you, it will continue to accelerate.

You'll find yourself with more and more to do and more and more to think about until at last, you can no longer think clearly and you'll begin to fail. Do you understand?"

"So far."

"What you need to do is to create a sanctuary where life can't control you; where events can't reach you. And if you can do this, you'll be able to go to this sanctuary and you'll regain control."

"I need a cottage in the woods?"

"That won't do at all. You're talking about creating a physical sanctuary, a place in space. Now that's a good start, but it won't work. It won't work because you'll get a phone in the cabin and a TV and you'll have work to do to keep up the cabin and you'll get active in the village and it won't be a sanctuary anymore. No. A sanctuary in space won't work. What you need is a sanctuary in time. What you need to do is to take a percent of your time - say fourteen percent - one day a week. For that day, tell the world that it doesn't own you. Don't let the world intrude on what's truly important to you - your wife, your family, your friends, even your dogs. On that one day, you won't open your bills, you won't do business at the office, you won't work around the house. On that day, you'll be only for yourself and those you love. You understand?"

"Yeah, I think I can see where you're heading."

"Jack, this is not my idea. This idea is four thousand years old. We just have to re-invent it for ourselves is all. Every Friday night, you light candles and have a nice meal with your family. No TV. No arguments. No bickering. You come together as a family. And you spend the evening telling your children stories. You can read to them. You can tell them about their ancestors - whatever. But you engage yourself with them. And you let them stay up a little late so that they can watch the candles flicker and smell the smoke when they go out. And the smoke from the candles fills the house like perfume and I'll tell you why it's a special perfume. Because, when they smell that, they know that it's time for them to go to bed and your wife - no, your bride, your Shabbat bride - knows that this is her time with you. And you know what you're required to do, my friend? You're required to delight your Shabbat bride; to love her and seduce her as though it was the first time. You need to romance her and charm her and make love to her with special sweetness. This is required! You must treat her as a new bride on Friday night. Do you hear?"

"I love it when you talk dirty."

"You're not understanding. A person by himself is not complete. The unity in Judaism is the married couple. It's only when a man and his wife come together in union that each of them becomes complete, becomes capable of the act of creation. This isn't dirty. This is what life is supposed to be and it's not sex, it's a sacred act."

"This is part of the religion?"

"Jack, you need to listen. You need to think about this. On Friday night you start your life over again. And on Saturday, you give thanks for all the blessings of the last week. Maybe that means going to Temple, maybe it doesn't. It's not a requirement. What's required is that you take time and savor your breakfast and you look lovingly at your wife and lovingly at your children and you be with them. Maybe even you should be with your dogs a little. And you take some time to read something that has spiritual value. Maybe you study a little Torah. Maybe you read a little Jewish philosophy. But you spend time in contemplation of who you are, and who you're supposed to be, and how do you get from here to there. And you go do something with your kids. You can stay at home and do a puzzle, or you can go to a museum. It doesn't matter. You give them some special time. And you take a nap. You hear? You lie down and you sleep because your body needs rest as well as your psyche and your spirit. And you stay out of the mailbox and only when the sun goes down, do you even think about anything other than the Shabbat. Do you think you can do this?"

"I'm not much of a Jew, Isaac."

"You're not much of a person, Jack. You're tired. You tell me that you're lonely. You seem to be scared, though I don't really know of what. And you tell me that you need a way out. So, I've given you a way out. If you have either the wisdom or the courage, you'll at least try it. And if you don't, so you'll go on being tired and lonely and scared. You choose."

"It's a lovely idea. It makes a great deal of sense. Maybe I'll try it. What are you going to do about Marty Feldman and the sensuous Ms. Edna?"

"I'm a foolish old man, you know?"

"I didn't want to be the one to tell you. And the word isn't foolish, it's dirty."

"She's a mixed-up young woman. She's very attractive to me and I don't find women my age as attractive."

"Isaac, in your heart, you're twenty-five years old, and I dare say in a few other places as well."

"I suppose I don't really expect that anything would ever come of this relationship. In some ways, I'm afraid of being left alone. Sage is going to graduate in June. He has his college applications out. Lev is too smart to stay here. When Sage is gone from the house, Lev should go to a private boarding school that will challenge him. You know what that will mean for me? One of my primary reasons for living will have ended. I will have finished my job to make men out of my boys and I'll be alone in the house - I don't think I can stand that. I want somebody to need me and you know what? I need somebody too. I don't want to grow old alone."

"Oh, I know. But, I don't think Ms. Edna's gonna do it for you, buddy. What you need is a lot deeper than a mud puddle. Worse than that, I don't know that you can ever find what you need in Bloomington. It's a pretty snotty little town-a mixed information system if you catch my drift."

"Yes, I've thought about that. It was a good place to bring my boys, you know? For me it was better than Minneapolis. I don't want to run from. I just don't".

"I don't either, Isaac".

CHAPTER 16

Rae was dressed and looking out the window at six-thirty. Jack turned in the drive with the dogs in a treacherous trot. His head was stuffed down into his good winter coat and his collar was up in an effort to keep the freezing rain off his flesh. The trees were beginning to grow a molten coat of ice on each branch. The drive was slippery and wet. He pushed the dogs through the door and went back to the truck. He started the engine to warm the cab and to melt the accumulation on the windshield. The van would not do today. The defroster wasn't capable of melting ice. It was a fair-weather fiend, the last revenge of the Third Reich. A Chevrolet truck was a forever thing.

The Camaro slithered into the drive, its fat tires failing to grip the pavement. Ilene and Dunphy ran for the front door. Rae delivered the lecture about clothes and breakfast and schoolbooks and lunches for Simmy and Lee and by the way, thank you, thank you, thank you.

Rae was now unable to button her winter coat over her expanding belly. She and Jack held one another's hands tentatively as they inched across the drive to the idling truck. He helped her around to the passenger side, boosted her in and crawled over to the driver's door.

"Have you there before they've even warmed up their stethoscopes," he offered. There was no answer.

The receptionist wasn't in the office. Nor a nurse. Jack peeked into the office and MacKenzie saw him and motioned them in.

"G'marnin' to ya. We'll be meetin' in heere. C'mahn in. Thar's soome cahffee heere fer ya ef ya like."

Jack and Rae left their coats on the rack and walked back into the Neurology Department's conference area. Maria

Acosta wasn't there yet. They made themselves as comfortable as they could. Rae's medical record, collated in a large manila envelope, complete with EKG strip and X-rays peeking out, lay on the table. They left it untouched. A few minutes later Maria Acosta came in wearing a soaked coat which she doffed and draped over a chair. She nodded with a half-smile and greeted Rae and smiled at Jack. This was not her turf. She was more of a stranger here than her patient and her patient's spouse. It occurred to Jack that she had never been here, and he had. Maria Acosta was an invited guest. "How odd," he thought. This is back-stage.

In a moment, Ian MacKenzie returned. He was not alone. With him was an older man wearing a full-length white coat with his name embroidered in flowing blue script above the pocket: Dr. Gerald Byer. He exchanged nods and shook hands around without much of an introduction. It was clear that the stage had been set and the cast collected, but the drama itself was murky and impenetrable.

As Rae exchanged pleasantries with Maria Acosta, Jack assumed a rectum-sniffing pose.

"Dr. Byer, are you a neurologist also?"

"Well, of a sort. I'm a neurosurgeon."

Byer had the markings. He was a large man, portly perhaps, with olive skin and tightly curled salt-and-pepper hair. He made no eye contact. In his body language he signaled that he was the senior person in the room with little time for anything other than the technical mastery of his trade.

"I'm a neurosurgeon," he had said. It was the key line in the play. The drama was predictable at this point. The events on which the action would turn were evident. Rae had not heard the exchange; nor had Dr. Acosta. It was medical communication at its best. Physicians speak in cryptic codes, euphemisms, semantic swatches of technobabble which impress and exclude. If you have not been initiated into the veil, if you have not learned the language, you can't understand the motives, the roles, the action, or the outcome. It appears as chance, as random acts of God, but it's not. It's prophesied in the intricacies of the code. Jack had now read the playbill. Though he didn't know yet the last line in the script, he knew that the audience would cry. He couldn't convey to Rae the immediate danger. He was the barber in the concentration camp, shearing heads in silence, even the familiar heads of acquaintances, knowing what was to come, unable to speak.

"Well now! It seemes thet we're-uh all heere. Dr. Acosta, Rae, she's yer primerry care-uh physician and she needs ta be heere and Dr. Byer, heere, he's my fine consultant, ya know. I asked him to be heere a'coz he's got a fine eye for a radiograph and he can help me explain a bit."

Byer didn't wait for the period to expire at the end of MacKenzie's sentence before he jumped in. "Mr. and Mrs. Israel, Dr. MacKenzie asked me to look at his clinical findings and your test results. Basically, they all come together to form a somewhat clear picture, though these things are never definite. Here, let me review them with you. First of all, he's noted an asymmetrical pupillary response in reaction to light. What that means is that your left pupil, Mrs. Israel, responds rather sluggishly to a light stimulus. And he finds that your left side is somewhat weaker than your right side and that you seem to have a slight imbalance when you're standing on your left leg. Now these are clues that there's something going on, most likely on the right side of your brain. Is this clear so far?"

Rae barely nodded. Jack nodded for her. Dr. Acosta kept her eyes firmly on the conference table and Ian MacKenzie smiled appreciatively at the excellence of the presentation.

"Well, Dr. MacKenzie ordered the EEG and a series of cerebral X-ray studies. We can take a look at those and I'll explain what they show. See here on the EEG tracings: This line is from the lead attached in the area of the right frontal lobe and this one is from the area over the right temporal lobe. Now if you compare the electrical activity on these tracings to the electrical activity on the opposite side, you can see that there's a rather atypical pattern on the right. Do you see that? Now, if we turn to the X-rays . . ."

He slipped the films out of their dark manila envelope and took them to the fluorescent display panels. He flipped the switches and tucked the edges of the pictures under the spring-loaded lip of the lights. They shone out like pirate flags, like warnings on insecticides, like mummies from museum cases. This could not be Rae, these figures in grey and black. This was not her blond head, her blue-green eyes, her soft face.

"Now note over here, on the right side, you see a shadow. We think this is a tumor of some kind. This is quite consistent with the symptoms of headache, nausea, and vertigo that you've been experiencing, Mrs. Israel, and with Dr. MacKenzie's clinical findings. Now what we think is going on is that this tumor is exerting some pressure on the brain itself and I think we need to do something about it rather quickly."

Rae didn't speak. Jack took over for her. "Can you be more specific. What exactly do we do in this situation?"

"Well, frankly, Mr. Israel, this is not your typical situation by a long shot. If Mrs. Israel weren't pregnant, why we'd go at this thing full court press, if you know what I mean. But with a pregnancy, we really don't know some of the variables at all. For the moment, all I can say is that I wish she weren't pregnant. That would free up our hands a great deal."

"I'm not sure I understand."

"Well, let's take it one step at a time. In the first place, we have something that we know and something that we don't know. What we know is that we've got some symptoms and what appears to be some compression from a growing mass. And we need to reduce that compression. What we don't know is what kind of tumor mass we have here. It could be something quite benign - perhaps, and most likely, a meningioma. Normally, what we would do is to try some radiation to shrink the tumor just as much as we could and then we'd go in surgically and clean it out. At that point, we'd get some biopsy information and we might, depending on the tumor, want to do some chemotherapy to mop things up. But we have this pregnancy to think about."

Maria Acosta turned to Rae, "Dr. Byer is a neurosurgeon, Rae. We've been talking by phone and I've made some calls to the Cleveland Clinic and talked to people there. We really don't have a positive fix on what the effects of radiation therapy might be on the baby. What's more, though we have a hazy idea of what the effects of chemotherapy are, there are no studies to determine which chemotherapy agents cross the placenta. We just don't know what the effect on your baby would be."

"Rae," she went on, "one option is to give up the pregnancy."

There was a long moment's delay as the actors waited for an audience response. Rae looked at Maria Acosta with disbelief. She turned to MacKenzie, but he refused to meet her gaze. Byer stared straight at her with no emotion on his face.

"Fuck you all! Did you hear me? I said, 'Fuck you all!' I lost a baby two years ago and I hated it. I want this baby. I've carried it for almost six months and I'm not going to lose it now. Do you understand? I'm not having any radiation therapy and I'm not having any chemotherapy or anything else. I'm having a baby - that's what I'm having. Do you understand?" The tears filled her lids and spilled in rivulets down her reddened cheeks. She looked at Jack and at Maria Acosta and Ian MacKenzie and Gerald Byer and no pair of eyes returned her gaze. Dr. Acosta took a tissue out of her pocket and handed it to Rae and then took another for herself.

Byer picked up the pieces, "We all understand, Mrs. Israel. We really do. We're going to do whatever you want us to do and all we want to do is to help. That's all."

"Where do we go from here?" asked Jack.

"We need to decompress that frontal-temporal region very soon. We can do that under a general anesthetic and provide some relief of symptoms right away. Of course, there will be some effects of the surgery. There'll be some edema -

some swelling, some incisional pain, but we can manage that pretty well. Although, I can see now that Mrs. Israel will have some definite ideas about what drugs we can use to manage the swelling and the pain. But that's OK. At the same time, of course, we'll get some biopsy results and we can go from there."

It was a dialogue. Jack and Byer were alone.

"When?"

"As soon as possible."

"Will you do the surgery?"

"If you'd like me to."

"Do you know what your surgery schedule is?"

"Yes, I'm open the end of next week.'

"That's the start of Christmas vacation. That's good. I can take care of things at home. How many days will she be in?"

"Well, if we can get her admitted early on Wednesday and do all our pre-op, we can do surgery on Thursday and I would say that she might be able to go home with a headache on . . . oh . . . maybe Monday or Tuesday."

"Rae, honey? Are you OK with this?"

"It's nice of you to ask." And the tears still spilled.

The rain came in a cold mist that froze on the ground. The truck had not fit into the parking garage at the Creditor Clinic, so they walked the long block to where they had parked. He held her under the arm and around the shoulder as he would a grandmother. Still she cried. She said little. They mounted their sheet metal steed and proceeded home.

"Hey," he began, "I'll take care of dinner tonight and we'll have a quiet week-end."

"I'm working tomorrow."

"Oh, Rae, you can't."

"I'm on the schedule, and if I don't, I'll be there anyway as a patient. They might as well pay me instead of me paying them."

"If that's what you really want. I think there's a service at temple tomorrow and as long as you're working, I guess I'll go for a while."

She turned and looked at him and her lower lip trembled. She deliberately and fitfully spit out the words, "Please . . .please . . . say something for me . . ."

Ilene and Dinah were washing breakfast dishes in the sink when they came in. Dinah stood on a kitchen chair handing dishes and silverware to Ilene one at a time. Dunphy was watching a talk show on TV. Rae hung her coat and went into the bathroom without comment.

"You don't have to do that; we have a dishwasher."

"Yes. I know. But as you can see, she's too short to do it without a chair to stand on."

Dinah beamed. "I'm helping. I helped to make breakfast too. And to clean up."

"Thanks, Ilene. You're a friend in need. Can you guys vacate now?"

She shut the water with deliberation and turned slowly. "Bad visit?"

"Too complex for here and now. Maybe later at the office - if I even come in."

"Got it."

She grabbed coats from the living room couch, kissed Dinah on the forehead

and threw Dunphy's parka over his head. With an appropriate curse on his lips, she dragged him from the house.

Jack dressed Dinah in her winter coat and ushered her out the door to the still-warm truck.

"C'mon, Beautiful, if you're such a good cook, you can help me shop for dinner."

It was cruel to take a child out on this day of freezing rain. It was crueler still to leave her at home with her mother. Dinah sat in the front, her mother's place, from which she could see nothing but the dashboard in front of her. She chattered to someone who could not, much as he might have liked, hear her. They drove to Samuel's and parked near the door. He commandeered a shopping cart outside the door. It was cold and wet and still he boosted Dinah into the fold-down child seat. She complained and he relented, abandoning the cart for one already in the store. As they walked down the first aisle, Jack could see nothing. He was interrupted by a small insistent voice.

"Is Mom sick? Daddy, is Mom sick?"

He had no answer. He stood and looked at this child and could not formulate a response. To deny would be to lie; to affirm would be to place a burden on one too young to bear it; to vacillate was not his way; and silence is not acceptable to five-year-old girls.

"Is she?"

He stopped the shopping cart and leaned over it, resting his arms on the bar. They were nose to nose. He lifted his face and kissed her forehead.

"You know, I love you," he began. "Mom's been having headaches and we went to the doctor to see if he could help."

"I thought Mom's doctor was a lady. She told me that. My doctor is a lady."

"Well, that's true. Mom's doctor is a lady and we went to see her and there were some other doctors there. And they were men doctors. And they're going to see if they can make these headaches go away. Now that may mean that Mom has to go into the hospital for a few days, but it will just be for a few days and then she'll come home good as new. OK?"

"OK. I don't want her to be sick. Ilene said that I should ask her if I can take ballet lessons. She says I would be a good ballerina."

"Oh, I think you would be a fine ballerina."

They began their stroll through the aisles. He picked out a package of orange roughy, frozen. Fresh fish didn't exist in the Midwest. This would have to do. Lettuce, carrots, tomatoes, purple cabbage, a sweet onion - he would make an elegant salad; from the bakery department, a fresh bread, uncut; from the liquor department a bottle of sickly-sweet kosher wine. He was making select choices when they arrived at the ethnic foods section. Rae loved Mexican food, but the pickings were slim in Bloomington and they had made do with packaged tacos and canned tamales. The Chinese foods were all canned. In one corner, a silent tribute to the ancestors of the Samuels family, was the Jewish foods section. Jack stopped. He stooped to the bottom and picked up a box of sabbath candles, twelve, imported from Israel, and a box of Channukah candles, forty-four, also imported from Israel. He dropped them in the cart and wondered if he could find a menorah for Channukah.

Rae slept all morning. As he made soup and a sandwich for Dinah, he poked his head in the bedroom to find her lying on her side, eyes open.

"Care for some lunch? Dinah needs to see you act as if you're still alive."

She came out, washed her face and took over the stirring of the soup and the spreading of the peanut butter. She kissed Dinah on the forehead, in the same spot that Jack had kissed. And the rain beat on the windows and froze to the panes and threatened more misery than they could bear.

He put Dinah in front of the TV and came back to the kitchen. Slowly, he turned Rae from the sink toward him, gently placing two firm hands on her arms and demanding her attention.

"It'll be OK. I can manage things here just fine. It'll be OK."

"I'm going to ask my sister Leyla to come down while I'm in the hospital. Someone will have to watch the kids. I don't know what to tell my mother. There's no way we're going to be there for Christmas and we haven't missed a Christmas in years. She's gonna know that something's up and she's gonna be mad that the kids won't be with her for Christmas eve. Oh, this is such shit. What am I going to tell her?"

"You'll tell her the truth - after it's over. And you'll tell her that there was never anything to worry about."

The orange roughy was baking bathed in lemon juice and paprika. Boiled potatoes garnished with parsley were covered in a casserole on the counter. A salad of color was on the table amidst the plates and silverware and off to the side were two short stoneware candlesticks with Shabbat candles in each, the loaf of uncut bread, and a stemware glass of ghastly wine.

Jack called the family together. All assembled: Rae, Simmy, Lee, Dinah, Sasha, and Cady. Jack had limited knowledge of the correct procedures. He held out a book of matches to Rae and said, "Here, I think this is your job."

Rae lit the candles in silence. Jack intoned, "Blessed art thou, Oh Lord, our God, who has told us to light candles on Shabbat." Next, he picked up the wine and said, "Blessed art thou, Oh Lord, Our God, who brings forth wine." He tasted the wine and passed it to Rae who turned it down with a look of disgust. And then he took the bread and said, "Blessed art thou, Oh Lord, Our God, who brings forth bread from the ground. And bless you all my children, and my dogs. Okay, team, dinner is served."

He escorted Rae to her chair and pulled it out from the table for her. She smiled appreciatively. From the oven he withdrew the fish and placed it on a trivet in the center of the table, followed by the potatoes, and a bowl of green beans. Dinner was slow and even a little elegant. He turned out the lights so that all could eat by the light of the candles.

"I hate fish. Do I have to eat it?"

"Why don't we have any good food tonight?"

"How may bites of this do I have to eat?"

"You know what, guys," the loving father began, "When I was a kid and Grandma was still my mother, we would have Uncle Max and Auntie Riva and their kids over for dinner on Sunday, and Grandma wouldn't have enough food for everyone. So, she would tell me to say that I didn't want any fish or any chicken or whatever she didn't have enough of.

Then when dinner was over and I hadn't eaten any of the fish, she would say, 'All right, whoever didn't eat their fish can't have any dessert!'"

"Is there dessert?"

"Eat your fish and find out."

As dinner was consumed, he motioned Rae to stay seated and cleared the dishes for ice- cream. All were sated. All squirmed.

"And now, my dear children, how would you like to hear about the day that Irving Black, the little creep that lived next door to me on Lawrence Avenue, broke my nose?"

There was a chorus of groans as he began laying out in laborious detail the insipid events of thirty some years ago in a place they never knew existed and its relevance for the peculiar bend in the organ which graced his face. Children demanded respite before the electronic goddess in the family room, but Jack would not let them go - not tonight. They talked for nearly an hour as the candles diminished and when at last they sputtered and snuffed, he said, "Well, it looks like bedtime to me."

Rae supervised bedding them down as Jack finished up the kitchen and walked the dogs. This was an undo-able errand. The ice on the drive made walking quite impossible. He steered them toward Jim Bascom's lawn to pee and out to Crosscut, toward the pond, to finish whatever else was on their mind and then returned.

In the house he doused lights, turned the thermostat up an extra notch, and headed for the bedroom. Rae was in bed, reading.

"That was really sweet. Thank you for making dinner. How come the candles and the wine and all?"

"Sorry. Haven't got a rational reason I can give you. If it makes any sense, I feel like I lost myself somewhere back there and I need to take some time to find where I left me. That's not a particularly cogent answer, but it's all I can muster right now."

He took his clothes off and put on his pajamas as the furnace kicked in and pumped warm air into the bedroom.

"How's your head?"

"It wouldn't be so bad if it were somebody else's. You know, I've had a shitty day."

"Here, let me see if I can help." He came over to her side of the bed and gently turned her onto her stomach. With slow, careful motions, he rubbed her neck, placing his thumbs along the line that ran down to her back. Deliberately he moved his hands over to her right shoulder, kneading it, digging his fingers into the soft spots in front while his palms lay heavily in the back. He placed his right knee on the bed and shifted his left knee between her legs to repeat the kneading on her left shoulder. She sighed deeply.

"Oh, you're so tight in these muscles. Here, let me get some of the tension out for you." He stretched her right arm out straight and rubbed just a little hard into the long muscles moving from shoulder to fingertips. To do the left arm, he moved over to the other side of the bed.

Then he pulled the covers halfway down and began systematically working down the left side of her back. The room was warm now and he leaned over and kissed her neck. "You know, I love you. Would you like to take this nightgown off, so I can do the rest of you?"

"I don't know if this is the night for romance, Jack."

"I love you and I just want to make you feel better."

He pushed the nightgown up toward her head. She lifted off the bed enough for him to slip it over her head and she lay back down. He closed the bedroom door, came back and shut the light on the nightstand. Now, he worked on the right side of her back, down across the fleshy parts of her bottom, first on the right, then on the left. He began to work the large muscles of her right thigh, pressing the center of the back of her leg with his thumbs while he deliberately let his fingers grasp the inside of her thigh. He moved slowly down her right leg, massaging the ankle and the bottom of her foot and then repeated the performance ever so slowly on her left leg. As he finished her left foot, he moved up and kissed the backs of both her knees. Roaming up slowly, he kissed her in the small place in the center of her back and her shoulder blades. As he reached her neck, he kissed lightly and deftly removed his pajama bottoms. He dragged himself and his own arousal over her back, making sure that she knew, and whispered in her ear, "Would you like to turn over and I'll finish the job?"

He lifted off of her to let her roll over. Her shape was swollen with child and her breasts gave ample evidence that she had nursed three babies and was close to a fourth. He kissed her neck, first on the right then on the left and moved his face down to her breasts. The rigidity of her muscles eased and he circled her breasts with kisses. She rose to meet him and she squirmed delicately under him. He moved further down the bed, sliding off his pajama tops and rested his head on her belly. He felt movement grazing his cheek and he kissed her there. Down further, he kissed the inside of her thighs and she hesitatingly drew up her legs. As he kissed her closer to her center, she was dry, but warm. He pressed his face against her and felt her dampen, become wet and open.

She moved now, gently rocking as he tasted at the cup of their conception. He kissed and licked as she began slowly to deepen her breathing, to move in rhythm and they danced in this way and he adored her. She left the day and went away somewhere where there were no headaches and no pain and no worry. Her muscles tensed in waves beneath his face and she was wet with sweat and with love. She arched and relaxed and then arched again and again and then once more with moans and his face was damp as she gently pushed him away. And then she cried.

He crawled from his nesting place up beside her and held her in his arms as she wept. "Are you okay?"

"I don't know."

"Can you tell me why you're crying?"

"Because."

"It's OK then. Just cry. I'm here."

"C'mon. I want you inside of me."

And he rolled as gently as he could onto her and lifted her legs to his sides and they danced once more. And when the music had reached its crescendo and was softly fading, he kissed her eyes and tasted the salt and the wetness of her face and did not know what to do.

CHAPTER 17

He realized as he listened simultaneously to the sound of the Volkswagen engine through the heating system and the timbrel of freezing rain on the windows that the van had been in the garage all night. That meant that it would be warm for Rae, the windshield clean and dry, and that she would have no trouble getting to work. Then he remembered that the truck had been out all night. It would be armored in ice.

As he lay in bed, he rethought Isaac's little philosophy. He did not walk on Friday night, he led services. On this Saturday, he would lead yet another service. Was this not work? And if Jack was bound to get up and go to temple for a service, was this not an imposition on his own day of rest? And how was he to spend the day with his family if he was needed in temple, perhaps to be the tenth man? Then again, he had slept a sound sleep, his arm around the waist of his Sabbath bride.

He sensed the immediate need to clothe himself as he searched under the covers for lost pajamas and realized the acute need for a shower. The dogs would know. They would probe with their cold noses and accuse or worse yet snicker in amusement. He found his pajamas on the floor and slipped into them, grabbed fresh underwear from his half of the large dresser and headed for the bathroom.

The dogs ambushed him in the hall. Their sheer volume blocked his way and they looked at him with odd and mixed expressions. It was fortunate that they did not possess words. Pets with memories and vocabularies could be a liability. He muscled past them and arrived, alone, in the bathroom. Only as he faced the mirror did he reconstruct Friday. There was not an emotional response, only an altered list. He realized that each of his days had a table of contents, based carefully on the preceding day's chapter. He leaned on the sink and now understood that Friday had wiped out his prior agendas. This day did not have a full agenda; the next week would have an agenda that he could not foresee; and the outcome of the next week would create agendas that were unknown to him.

He was an expert at agendas. He had come this far in an academic career because he could always see the next logical step. His thoughts were linear; they stretched out in rational sequence that enabled him to foresee problems, predict events, calculate responses to situations long in advance of their occurrence. He was a master wordsmith. Not only could he locate ideas on paper, but he could carve semantic nuances that delighted an entire class of people who were linear thinkers and semanticists. Since he was a boy, he thought in lists - logical, rational lists. It was a fortunate accident for him that the world of the university, the world of science, the world of industry was ruled by the linear thinkers, the list-makers. He would never write poetry, nor play a musical instrument with passion. He would never write a novel that spoke to the soul. But he could construct agendas.

Poetry and passion were for people with emotions. There was not room for emotions on the lists, except perhaps in parentheses. If there were emotions, they would have to be discovered and dealt with accordingly, but they could not be foreseen.

His days in Bloomington were ruled by his appointment book, class schedules, research tasks, recommended service intervals, quarterly reports, timetables, calendars, and lists. That all had to be put in obeisance now. For today, he would go to temple and do something non-logical, non-rational, and perhaps magical. He would recite incantations to the Invisible. It made no sense. But it was the only item on his agenda and so he must be about doing it.

It was barely quarter past seven. He had put on a dress shirt and wool slacks, and a sweater over the shirt. No tie. No jacket. If today was a day of rest, he would leave critical elements of his work uniform in the closet. Cracking open the door to the boys' room, he could see Simmy peeking back at him. He walked in so as to leave Lee undisturbed and whispered to Simmy in the upper bunk, "Got to take the dogs out. You take charge 'til I get back."

Simmy croaked back, "Is Mom sick? Dinah keeps talking about Mom being sick."

"Tough pregnancy. Bad headaches. Went to the doctor yesterday. She's got to go into the hospital next week and they're going to see if they can fix her up. It'll be all right. We'll do fine."

Simmy was a linear thinker. They did not have an emotional bond; they were bound by common methodologies. Simmy was a maker of lists. Lee was not. When challenged to produce a list, he did not. He could, but he did not. He preferred to keep his lists private. He and Jack did not have an emotional bond. Nor did they share a methodology.

He shackled the beasts, pulled on his parka, taking special care to put up the hood and tie it tightly around his neck. As he opened the door, a layer of ice had built up on the step and on the porch. All three crept out. In the drive the dogs lost their footing. Sasha's back legs fell to the ice and she struggled to regain her stance. They made it laboriously to the edge of the pond, the wind shooting icy rain at hands and face. Jack stood there by the dark gray water, cold and wet, his body shaking and realized that the moisture on his face was not all rain. He shook his head and tried to clear his eyes, but as he shook, they filled faster, and he felt his cheeks chap as he cried.

"I don't know what I'm gonna do. Please help me," he said aloud, and the dogs listened in fascination and pulled him home.

A quick check of the truck confirmed his worst fears. It carried several hundred pounds of ice evenly distributed over its mass. The doors were unlocked, but frozen, nonetheless. The windshield was caked in a quarter inch of solid ice which no amount of hacking with a scraper would dislodge. It was a nice winter day in the Midwest. He would feed the kids and get the truck warmed up enough to melt the ice. For the mere price of a gallon of gasoline, he would get the beast moving.

The team was assembled in the kitchen by the time he got back. "All right! Mom's at work and we have permission to make whatever we want for breakfast. We have here the world's finest kitchen aid, the delightful dancer, Miiiiissss Dinah! Your orders, please."

"Pancakes!"

"I want an omelet!"

"Cinnamon toast!"

"And I, dear children, want a bagel, with cream cheese, if you please."

He and Dinah prepared three plates, each of which contained one pancake, one single-egg omelet, and one half-piece of cinnamon toast. Simmy and Lee set the table, ran to the fridge for necessary supplies, protected the finished product from marauding wolf-packs, poured juices and milk and critiqued culinary methods. Dinah cracked eggs, ran the toaster, and mixed the pancake batter. Remarkably, no one had yet demanded access to cartoons. They sat at the table and Jack spread the real Philadelphia brand on his thawed bagel as he prepared to orate.

"You know, I never told you guys much about Channukah."

"We know about it," Simmy began, "we learned about it in school. We learned about the light that burned for eight days and the evil emperor and the temple with pigs in it and all that stuff."

"Aha! But did you get the real story? I mean about the armed elephants, and the guerilla war, and the brothers who fought that evil empire? And did you learn about the eight days and the presents every day?"

"Ahh. Some of that. Can you tell us about it?"

"Well. I'm real rusty, you know. It's been a long time since I . . . since I . . . did much with Channukah. But I have an idea.

There's a library at the temple and I know that they have books there on Channukah. What do you say, we just dash over there and hunt down some books on it and let's get the real story? And if it looks good to you, we might even . . . uh . . . go shopping for some toys for Channukah. What d'ya say?"

Simmy backed away from the table with utter distrust on his face. Lee put his head on his arms on the table without comment, Dinah moved up and down in her chair, clapping her hands silently, a grin of sheer delight on her tiny face.

"Are you trying to bribe us to go to temple?" the chairman accused.

"Absolutely! Trust me through temple and the next stop is Wee-Bee-Toys."

"How much can we spend?"

"Tell you what: You take however much of your allowance you want to spend, and I'll match you penny for penny. You want to spend two dollars? I'll give you two dollars more. You want to spend five dollars? I'll put up another five."

"OK. I'll go."

"I'll go," sighed Lee.

"I want to go too," shouted Dinah, "but I don't have any money."

As they inched out the door the truck was chugging noticeably and belching black smoke. Jack opened the driver's door and reached in to poke the gas pedal. The beast roared and settled into an unsteady idle. He shepherded the flock around to the other side and hoisted in all those who could not climb in themselves, being sure that all three were belted in place in some fashion. The windshield had cleared, but not the outside rear-view mirrors. He inched backwards down the drive, heaved a sigh when he was clear and headed out toward Diana Road.

Cars littered the ditches at the side of the road. It was late and he was driving at a speed that would have been all right on a dry, clear day. As he neared the junction of Diana Road and County Trunk K, he felt the rear start to slide left on a patch of ice. Deftly, he corrected the steering wheel - a touch too much. The rear end corrected and then swung right. "Steady on the gas," he thought, "No brakes, use the steering, stay cool, you can catch it . . . . oh, no!"

The front tires lost their grip and the whole truck was now sliding to the left, out of control. It crossed the other lane of traffic, moving far too fast. There was a low berm on the left edge of the road. The front end lifted, and the Chevy went airborne, flying, flying, flying over the ditch. Four bodies felt their breakfasts rise in their guts simultaneously. The truck landed - THUNK - squarely on all four wheels at once, still moving west. The frame jounced heavily against the bump stops, groaning, and still they kept moving. They hit the hard-packed gravel access road that paralleled the pavement, separating it from the corn field. The gravel held, the tires gripped and Jack motored, at a slightly slower pace, along the access road to its convenient merger with the pavement at the junction of Diana Road and County Trunk K. He swung easily onto Diana Road and whispered, "Thank you . . ."

"Wow! That was fantastic! Can we do it again?" Simmy had no judgement.

"That was scary," objected Dinah.

And Lee remained silent and wide-eyed as Jack regained the road and drove toward Temple Beth Jacob as though nothing out of the ordinary had occurred. Pulling into the lot, it was apparent that Jack would not be the tenth man for the minyan. There were about a dozen cars and one bicycle.

"Oh, dear,", he thought, "Matt came on his bike".

He marched his patrol into the temple with military precision. Dinah offered with pride to show her brothers where the library was. Jack looked at her and realized that not one strand of DNA in that petite, fledgling body, was derived from him. He gave specific directions, "Lady and gentlemen, your job is to find books about Channukah. I will be in there," he pointed, "behind this door. If you need me, just come in and get me. I'll be by to check on you periodically. OK?"

Finding no objections, he crept into the back of the sanctuary. The door closed with a dull thud and every eye turned to assess him, including those of Matt Cowan. Matt rose with a generous grin on his face and walked purposefully to meet him, picking up a prayer book and a bible as he came.

"Hi, Doc," he offered in a coarse whisper, "Don't forget your tallit and keee-pohh."

"Thanks, Matt. I'm just gonna sit in the back here."

"Hey. No problem. I'll keep you company."

After a moment, he added, "D'ja read about me in the paper?"

"No."

"Hey. Big spread. I'm famous." He smiled.

They sat together as Isaac, assisted by Phil Dorfman, directed the group to the appropriate page for the Silent Devotion. All stood, including Marty Feldman, Myron Tabanov, Bud Blumberg, and a clutch of others that Jack didn't recognize. People began to gyrate gently back and forth and mumble something to themselves that sounded like a mantra. Matt leaned over toward him.

"Hey, I like that guy you work for."

"What guy I work for?"

"That guy the other night. The one that fixed Rabbi's car. Pat Dunphy. He told me you work for him at the university."

"Oh, that guy that I work for."

"Yeah. Him. He was amazing under the hood of that Chrysler. He knew exactly what to do. Then he took me home and showed me some driving tricks in that state police car."

"Matt, I think we're supposed to be silent in this part of the service."

"Yeah."

Minutes later, Isaac announced the beginning of the service for taking out the Torah. He proclaimed with seriousness, "For the honor of opening the ark, Mr. Matt Cowan."

Matt, who wore a kippah, but no tallit, rose and crawled over Jack to the aisle. Turning he said, "Watch this!" He held himself erect and put his shoulders back in a deliberate, visible act. He strode to the bimah and stepped up, keeping himself square to the ark. As he reached the top step, he turned to Phil Dorfman and reached out a large hand in greeting, saying loud enough for all to hear, "Shabbat Shalom!" He repeated the greeting to Isaac and proceeded to the drawstring at the left edge of the curtain covering the ark. Isaac nodded, Matt drew the cord, and Phil, singing beautifully, walked to the ark, opened the door and removed the Torah. Matt closed the door, re-drew the curtain and stood obediently to the rear of Isaac and Phil. Phil chanted a couple of lines which were repeated by the congregants and walked down off the bimah and up the aisles. Each man took the fringes of his tallit, touched them to the Torah and kissed the fringes. Jack grabbed a tallit off the rail at the rear of the sanctuary and tossed it over his shoulders so that he could mimic the gesture. Phil smiled at him graciously without missing a beat in the song he was singing. But it was an odd smile. Jack smiled back.

Phil returned to the bimah, uncovered the Torah and laid it gently on the reading stand. Isaac waited for everyone to descend to their seats and he took up a position at the lectern, four feet above the congregation. He was sufficiently small that only his head showed above the lectern as he began his remarks.

"This Shabbat, we approach Channukah, which we will celebrate by lighting candles Tuesday night and for the eight nights to follow. We usually assume that Channukah celebrates the liberation of the the Great Temple of Jerusalem from the troops of Antiochus and the re-dedication of the Jewish people to the service of God. I'll talk about that next Friday evening at our annual Channukah service and I hope you'll all come. But today, I want to address an issue that sets the stage for our celebration of Channukah. That is: Why have the Jews lost their Temple not once, but twice and why have they not been able in almost two thousand years to rebuild it?"

"Now this is a very interesting issue. If we have a Covenant with God and if we pledge ourselves to do His service, why is it that the Temple, the place where we dedicate ourselves as a people to God, is taken away from us? Now the destruction of the First Temple by the Babylonians is probably easiest to understand. We had defiled it by blood and by war and by quarreling among ourselves. But why did we lose the Second Temple? Israel was strong militarily. The city and the Temple were well fortified. What could have destroyed the building blocks and ramparts and fortifications that protected that holy place? Only one thing is powerful enough to do that and that is - gossip!"

"You see, my dear friends, no building can stand, no fortress can hold out, no army can withstand the insidious, murderous sin of gossip. The leading families of Jerusalem during the period of the Second Temple competed with one another for displays of riches and power. Two families in particular were at odds and were irreconcilable. And the story is told of a great feast that was held by one and an invitation was delivered by mistake to the other. The invited guest, believing that this was a gracious gesture of reconciliation, came to the feast. When his host saw him there, he ridiculed him for being so foolish as to believe that he would be invited. The rejected guest went to the Roman governor and told him that his host was plotting rebellion. And the Romans acted and began the war that destroyed the Temple. Gossip killed an entire nation."

"Gossip is the equivalent of murder. It wipes out a good name with no hope of contradiction by the person being gossiped about. When people who know nothing make up stories about innocent parties to amuse others and gain status for themselves, they rob the innocent - both the person being gossiped about and the person who listens to gossip. Both are deprived of the truth. The one who gossips is an assassin. The one who listens and repeats is his accomplice."

"Once upon a time there was a great rabbi. And he was a widower. Every Friday, a young woman, who was herself a widow, came to his home. She entered the back door and came out a little while later, always smiling. A noodnik, a neighborhood shnook, saw this - a few times. And he decided that the rabbi, to comfort himself in his loneliness, had taken up with this young woman. And he told his wife and she told her friends and they told their friends and it was cause for great laughter in the town. The young woman was accosted in the market. Her children were made fun of in the streets. She had done nothing wrong, but she fled the town in shame."

"Soon it was Yom Kippur. On Yom Kippur, one is accountable not only to God, but to one's fellow man as well. And the noodnik, the shnook, as he prepared to do penance for his sins, realized that he was guilty of the sin of gossip. But this was not such a big problem. On Yom Kippur, one is obliged, and one has the right to go to the person whom one has wronged and to ask forgiveness and to ask to make restitution. He went to the great rabbi just before the sun had set on Kol Nidre, and he confessed that he had seen the woman go into the rabbi's door and he had gossiped about it."

"The rabbi said to him, 'My dear shnook. The woman about whom you told this story came to me on Friday because she was a poor widow and did not have enough money to buy a challah for Shabbat for her children. And every Friday, she ate her pride and came to me to beg for help and every Friday I gave her a few kopeks to buy a challah for Shabbat. Now she is gone, in flight from this evil gossip. As for me, I was tortured by her pain and amused that anyone would think that I, an old man, was even capable of an illicit relationship. The sin is yours.'"

"'So, rabbi,' the shnook began, 'soon the sun will set. It will be Kol Nidre. I have begged your forgiveness. What shall I do to make restitution?' And the rabbi took a pillow off the couch in his study and he tore it open and he took it to the window and opened the window. Then he took the pillow and shook all the feathers out the window and scattered them to the wind. And he closed the window and turned to the shnook and said, 'Such is gossip, that once it is spread, it flies to every corner of the world. For restitution, go and collect all of those feathers and when you have collected them all, even as you would collect all the gossip you have spread, and bring it back to me along with my good name, then you will be absolved.'"

He was expressionless as he turned his back and walked to the Torah, which he opened studiously and with reflection. Phil joined him on the bimah. Matt turned to Jack and said, "Cool, huh?"

"Yeah, cool."

They went through the Torah reading, calling up seven people. After each, Isaac said a blessing in Hebrew and English for the reader and his family. Then Isaac rolled the scrolls together and announced, "For the honor of lifting the Torah, Dr. Jack Israel. And for the honor of tying the Torah, Mrs. Sooky Samuels."

Jack was ready and he was grateful. He walked quickly up onto the bimah and around to where he could grasp the Torah handles. He was followed by a portly woman with gray hair and a beatific smile. She greeted the rabbi with a warm handshake. Isaac turned to Jack and nodded.

Jack began, "Isaac, I need help."

"Come on you can do this. I showed you last time," he whispered hoarsely. Phil rolled eyes up in his head.

"No that's not it. I need you to say a prayer for Rae."

"What's the matter. She's all right? Look, lift the Torah and then tell me."

Jack grasped the handles and bent at the knee. He cantilevered the scrolls off the edge of the table and got his hands under them. As he raised them, he could hear Isaac, "Now open your hands and let the text show." Gingerly, he parted his arms and looked up at the text. Phil grasped his shoulders and turned him so that the text could be seen by all.

The congregation sung and Phil guided toward a chair at the back of the bimah, turned him again, and pressed him gently to sit. Sooky Samuels approached with the sash in hand. "That was wonderful," she said, smiling and tying the sash around the scrolls. She had large teeth and coarse skin and puffed cheeks that went naturally with her shape and she never stopped smiling with affirmation.

They dressed the Torah in its cover and breastplate, decorated it with the silver pointer and the finials and took it from Jack to put on the stand at the side. Isaac waited until Jack was free of his burden. He approached and leaned to him, "What's wrong?"

"Rae's sick. Can you say a prayer for her?"

He hesitated only for a moment, returned to the lectern, and announced that it was time to say a prayer for the sick and to include a special prayer for Mrs. Rae Israel. As he began, Myron Tabanov looked up from his prayer book and stared at Jack.

Isaac broke his rhythm to turn first to the congregation, "Is there anyone for whom we should say a special prayer?" Several nods and several mentioned names followed from the seats. Isaac turned next to Jack, "Does Rae perhaps have a Hebrew name?"

"No. I don't think so. Why would she?"

Isaac spoke her name, "Rae Israel" out loud and finished the Hebrew prayer.

Jack came down off the bimah and walked directly out of the sanctuary. He smiled at Matt who shook his hand with sincerity, dropped the tallit on the rear row, and headed for the library. There he found his gaggle of geese, spread about the library. Dinah was on the floor, belly down with her dress hiked up over her waist. Her pink tights brightened the room. Simmy browsed the stacks and Lee sat at a table, idly thumbing through a book. Jack went to each of them in turn and kissed their heads.

"Can we go now? There's a bunch of books on Channukah. We can take some home," reasoned Simmy.

"Not a bad idea. If we wait a few more minutes, there's cake and cookies to be had."

"I'd like some cookies," chimed Dinah.

"Ahh, let's do the cookie bit, team, and then we can go to Wee-Bee-Toys. OK?"

He was walking around the room, picking off books about Jewish holidays and Channukah, when Matt Cowan walked in. He beamed.

"Hey, Doc. These your kids?"

"Yep. Simmy. Lee. Dinah. This is Matt Cowan, King of Kung-Fu. Hey, Matt. What can you tell these guys about Channukah."

"Hey! I got it all, Doc! You want me to tell these guys about Channukah? You have come to the right dude!" He sat down at the table and the children moved in his direction. Lee straightened up and took in this loud stranger as he began to pour out tales of evil kings and brave fighters and chariots and armies and elephants and hidden caves and magical lights. Jack slipped out of the library and back into the sanctuary as Isaac led the mourners in the Kaddish prayer. He sat in the back and his head swam.

As the service ended, Phil collected Marty Feldman and Bud Blumberg and swept them down the aisle, followed by Sooky Samuels and a young woman that Jack didn't know. All shook hands with Jack briefly. Phil made no eye contact. He was a moving quarterback with blockers about him. Isaac walked down the aisle alone with deliberation and stopped at the last row to face Jack.

"Can you tell me what's wrong?" He placed his hand on Jack's arm.

"I don't really know. She's got some kind of brain tumor and she's going into Creditor Clinic next week for surgery. That's really all I know at this point."

He shook his head. "We'll talk." And he exited, following Phil's retinue to the social hall. Before Jack could turn, Myron Tabanov stood before him. He fixed Jack firmly with his eyes.

"Ian MacKenzie?"

"Yes, and Gerald Byer."

"The best. Tumor?"

"Yes. How did you know?"

"Well, frankly, Ian was upset and he called. Rae had used my name when she made the appointment. He told me that Rae might need some support and asked if she was a patient of mine. Of course, I told him that she wasn't and that if she needed emotional support she had two Newfoundland dogs. But I suspected as much when I saw her at the hospital."

"How?"

"No PERL. Usually people's pupils are equal in reaction to light - PERL. When I looked her over the day she fainted, she wasn't PERL. It had to be a small stroke or a tumor. I took her blood pressure and though she had a little tachycardia - rapid heart rate - her blood pressure wasn't way out of whack and she didn't report any hypertension or unusual bleeding problems. It just looked like it might be, that's all. Anything I can do?"

"No, actually you've done a lot. I thank you for pushing me to call MacKenzie. We might never have caught it."

"You would have. If it's anything, you would have caught it fairly soon. She might have seized or she might have shown odd behavior changes."

"What kind of behavior changes?"

"Depends on the site of the pressure. Language problems on the left temporal lobe, loss of facial recognition on the right. Do you have any idea of the location?"

"Yeah. Appears to be right frontal lobe."

"Impulse control - the brain's editor. Any loss of emotional control?"

"As you talk about it, yeah - but I just thought it was the headaches and the stress of moving and being pregnant and having three kids and two dogs in a strange community. You know, all the normal stuff that women are supposed to handle easily."

"I'm sorry. But Gerry has really good hands. Hang in there. By the way, do you know any Italians?"

"Myron, we've been through this. No, I don't know any hit-men."

"I thought I had one this last week, but when I checked it out, he was already in jail for loan sharking. By the way, your fingernails are growing. It's time to bite them." He walked away.

Jack went back to the library to find it empty. He checked the classrooms, but they were empty too. Wandering into the social hall, he found three ragamuffins following Matt Cowan in a circuit of the kiddush table, picking out the cookies that had chocolate on them. Phil Dorfman was gone, and Isaac was edging his way out of the hall. Jack collared Matt.

"Did you ride your bike out here?"

"Yeah."

"Okay. We'll toss it in the back of my truck, and I'll drive your home."

'Hey thanks, Doc. I'll probably be a lot safer with you than dodgin' cars on the roads, huh?"

"No doubt, Matt. No doubt."

Matt enjoyed Wee-Bee-Toys as much as any of the kids. While Simmy fondled the Red Ryder Little Beaver pump action BB gun and Lee played the electronic question and answer toys and Dinah cuddled the baby dolls, Matt examined each bicycle with exquisite care. Jack found himself in the baby section thinking about dragging the old crib down from the attic and the car bed and the wind-up swing seat. Would this child make it to birth? Would it be normal? And if it survived gestation and birth, would it ever have anything new that was bought just for . . . just for . . . it? Lee had had almost nothing in his life that he did not inherit. Dinah had dresses and dolls, but even her jumpers and turtlenecks and socks had been worn by others before. Rae was wearing maternity clothes, some for the fourth time.

He called his three together in a clump. With them came Matt Cowan.

"All right, you guys. It's Channukah and we need to start celebrating. You each get five dollars to spend on a present." He was interrupted by screams of delight. "Not so fast. It isn't that easy. Lee, you use your money to buy a present for Dinah - you can help her pick it out. Dinah, you use your money to buy a present for Lee - he'll help you pick out something that he wants. Simmy, you pick out a present for Matt and Matt, please pick out a present for Simmy." He received in return quizzical stares. "And then, dear children, we all together pick out a present for Mom and a present for the new baby that's coming!"

Simmy understood the logic and immediately reviewed the list in his head. "And who picks out the present for you, Dad?" Jack got blindsided. He shoved them all off toward the aisles in two pairs and dug deep into his pocket for the handkerchief that lay waiting for the tears.

CHAPTER 18

The middle of December brought the night abruptly and Rae was not yet home. The rain warmed during the day had washed away the ice that gripped the town. Still it fell, threatening to re-draw the frozen veil which had made the last two days obscure. The dogs had walked more than they wanted. The children rested more than they needed. In boredom, they assaulted sleeping dogs. Newfoundlands didn't mind. They were bred for insensitivity to child-inflicted pain, for patience to the point of indolence, and toward a gross incapacity for aggression. Jack often amused himself with the notion that people owned the breed of dogs which reflected their own human characters. Nervous people chose small, active breeds who yapped continuously. Fashionable people chose long, languorous breeds which required elegant grooming. Aggressive people chose large, menacing breeds. But the analysis ceased when he came to himself. If these behemoths reflected him, in his diminutive size, how so? What was it in them that he found in himself? What he finally reasoned was that Newfoundlands were one of the few breeds which did not, which need not, which could not, take the world or themselves seriously.

The dogs protected him from his children. When they might have crawled on him looking for attention, they crawled on Sasha or Cady. When they needed warmth and loving, they hugged the dogs and let themselves be licked. When they wanted play, the dogs chased balls and pulled at knotted socks. When they fought with one another, the dogs came between them, separated them, barked at them, and they ceased. And when Jack needed conversation, they listened.

The lights in the drive heralded her homecoming. Six bodies pressed against the door in eager anticipation, making entry a trial. She slipped into the yellow light of the living room and even there appeared gray. Jack grabbed her coat as she attended each need. Yes, she would make dinner soon; no she did not know about Wee-Bee-Toys; indeed, this was a beautiful baby doll which could share the tub tonight. Hugs for the dogs. At last she entered the kitchen where the windows were covered with steam as the water boiled for spaghetti and the chef poured the canned sauce into a pot.

"How're you feeling?"

"Same. Sorry I'm late. New admission. Very difficult."

"Spaghetti okay? Why so difficult?"

"Spaghetti's fine. I'm not hungry. Rhonda Dorfman."

"What about Rhonda Dorfman?"

"New admission."

He stopped pouring and turned down the burner. There is news that elicits response as canned as tomato sauce. The Packers won. Gasoline is up two cents a gallon. The vote was defeated in Congress. There is news that elicits response beyond control. Someone is dead. The grant has been awarded. The war is over. And there is news that elicits confusion.

"I don't understand. To five-east? To the psych unit?"

"With full suicide precautions."

"What happened?"

"Long story."

"Umm. You need to explain this to me. Now. Can you tell me what happened?"

"Can I go to the bathroom first?"

"Yeah. Would you hurry. I want to hear this."

She came back to find him re-entered into his sauce. She sat clumsily in a chair and exhaled deeply.

"Lord, I never thought I'd get home. What a day!"

"OK. Start at the beginning and explain to me what happened to Rhonda, will you please?"

"She was admitted last night. Hey, look, I'm not supposed to talk about patients. OK? This is more than confidential."

"She came in on Friday night? Shabbat?"

"You got it. Look, you have to understand. When she saw me on the unit, she got very upset. She didn't expect to find anyone she knew there. She has orders for no visitors. I showed up and she ran for her room and wouldn't come out. For most of the day I was told to steer clear of her, which, of course, I did. At the end of the day, she came out, but she wouldn't talk to me and I didn't touch her medical record. This is a sensitive situation and I'm bound by confidentiality. But at change of shift, we give report. I had to be there, and Carol Martinez asked for a full report on her because she was a new admission on PM shift and they hadn't been briefed on her. After report Carol asked me to stay and tell her what I knew that might be useful in managing her. But I couldn't tell her a whole lot and she wound up telling me everything that I'm not supposed to know. But none of this - I mean none of this - can get out to the community. Not to Isaac, not to Phil, not to your buddies in the department or the medical school — nobody. Got that?"

"So far you haven't told me anything."

"I'll tell you, but it's confidential."

"You're never going to make it as a canary. Could you just tell me now?"

"Jared brought her in, and she admitted herself. Apparently, she popped into Phil's office in biology unexpectedly on Wednesday looking for a free lunch. The door was closed, and she just walked in. He was there with a graduate student in full embrace. There was lots of stammering and mumbling and she ran out. That night they had a . . . well, it must have been a discussion or something and she finally put together that he had been going to a lot of conferences lately, had bought all new underwear, had started working out and lost some weight. You get the idea?"

"I get the idea."

"Well, Rhonda got the idea too. She threw him out of the house, this was Wednesday. On Thursday she went back to biology, apparently a wreck and found him with the graduate student in his office. Graduate student left and Phil told her that he was moving out of the house, wanted a divorce and that he couldn't ever go back to a marriage that left him so unfulfilled. Rhonda held out until Friday night and then decided that she couldn't take it and was afraid that she would kill herself. Jared, bless him, said that if she thought she might kill herself; she belonged in the hospital and drove her over. Now you know the story."

"This you got from the report?

"This I got when I went into her room and hugged her."

"Who's her psychiatrist?"

"She got Irene Marklin. She's the only woman on the staff. She wasn't on call, but Carol thought she needed a female shrink. She's got her on Elevil for now."

"Rae, Phil was in temple this morning acting like there was nothing unusual in his life at all. I mean he was singing and praying and carrying the Torah around like it was business as usual."

"So?"

"So how do you go to temple and pray when you've just told your wife of umpteen years that you're dumping her for a graduate student?"

"I don't know. I'm not Jewish."

It was Saturday night. Isaac typically didn't walk on Saturday night. Jack overflowed. He made a list of the things that he needed to talk to Isaac about and the things that he couldn't talk to Isaac about. Most of them were the same. He waded through Saturday night and Sunday. Rae was spent. She didn't tolerate talk. She placed long calls to Leyla in Chicago. Yes, Leyla would come down, probably by Thursday. She called her mother in Milwaukee. Yes, everything is fine, just calling to say hello.

He walked the dogs in the rain. On Sunday morning he retrieved a paper from downtown, thumbed idly through it, endured his children and waited for the evening to come. His wife didn't speak. She did laundry. She vacuumed rugs. It was Einstein's relativity. Time telescoped away from him, refusing to pass, assaulting him with boredom and confusion. Shortly after eight, he heard the storm door rattle and the pounding on the wood. With a leap he ran to the door to find his Cossack smiling at him.

"I saw your light on as I drove by. Can I come in?"

"Well, yes. Do you want to go for a walk?"

"Maybe later. I've been driving a lot. I wouldn't mind sitting someplace for a minute that's not moving. I could use a cup of tea. Is Rae at home?"

"Right here." Jack turned to see her behind him buttoning a housecoat.

"How are you feeling?" Isaac attended to her directly. The dogs didn't stop him from entering and taking her hand. He was family.

"Average, thanks. I'll put up some tea."

They converged under the Tiffany lamp in the kitchen. Isaac moved slowly. He hung his leather jacket over the back of the chair, doffed his Persian lamb hat, saw Cady sniff at it and put it back on his head. Rae poured tea. Isaac sweetened his and left it to cool.

"Jack says you're going into the hospital?"

"Yes. I have some kind of mass in my head - in my brain - that's probably all that's in my head - and they're going to take it out."

"This sounds serious."

"Probably not. I was at work yesterday and did some reading. It's probably a benign tumor. They'll take it out. I'll be uncomfortable for a couple of days and that'll be the end of it."

"You're not worried about going into the hospital?"

"No. It's not a completely routine procedure, but the surgeon who's doing it seems to be well regarded in town from what I've been able to learn. I'll be fine in a few days."

"Is there anything you'd like me to do?"

"Could you go in instead of me?"

"They wouldn't find anything to operate on. What do you need me to do?"

"Well, you could look after Jack. I called my sister and asked her to come down to give Jack a lift over the weekend. You could come by and visit if you're over at Creditor Clinic for anything."

"I get there, though I don't like hospitals."

"Why not?"

"I spent too much time in hospitals. It's a long story. I won't bore you with it now.

Some other time. We said a special prayer for you yesterday in services."

"Thank you. That helps. Does it come with a guarantee?"

"Rae, you work at St. Mary's sometimes, no?"

"Yes."

"What do you do there?"

"I work on the psych unit."

"Did you work there this weekend?"

"Yes."

"Did you see Rhonda Dorfman there?"

"Yes".

"Did you talk to her?"

"Hmmmm. Not exactly. Maybe."

"Well. Let me tell you. I got a call from her son Jared and I went to see her late on Friday night. You know, no doubt, that she's a patient there".

"Yes".

"Then you know that Phil has asked her for a divorce and that she's quite upset - maybe suicidal."

"Yes".

"Do you know her doctor?"

"Yes".

"Is this a good psychiatrist?"

"Yes".

"Ahhh. Look. I don't know about these things and I don't particularly like hospitals or psychiatrists or whatever. But I have some things I have to deal with. Jared is at home and Phil is in and out of the house. Sometimes Jared is alone and sometimes he's with Phil. I don't know. I talked to Jared and on the one hand he's a mature kid who is handling this well and on the other hand he's pretty upset, and I need to keep an eye on him. At the same time, I like Rhonda a great deal and I'd like to help her, and I have a good working relationship with Phil and I need to see if he needs me as well. If there's anything that you see going on that I can help with, could you just tell me?"

"You need to keep an eye on Rhonda. And probably Jared. From what I understand, Phil's got some support and he'll be just fine."

"I thought that might be the case." He looked at the counter and the box of forty-four Channukah candles. "Oh, you're getting ready for Channukah. Do you have a menorah?"

"Actually not," offered Jack.

"So, you'll take your dogs. It stopped raining. We'll go for a walk and go by my house. I have an extra menorah you can borrow."

"I need to talk to you, Isaac," he began, almost out the door.

"We'll talk."

He put his head down and his arms in his pockets and rocked along the walk almost as if he were alone. "You know, I was in Chicago with Edna. Just for yesterday and today. We went to the Art Institute. They have some stained-glass windows by Chagall that are marvelous. It was very strange. She didn't know Chagall. Can you believe that a cultured person in this day wouldn't know Chagall! You know that Chagall is a Jew, of course. The name Chagall is a form of Segal and that it's an acronym that means Levite? Did you know that?"

"Isaac, I need to talk to you about some things."

"Of course. We'll take a slow walk. We'll talk. I was telling you, I was surprised that she didn't know him. And it was very nice there. It's a fine museum."

"Isaac, I'm really worried about Rae."

"Yes, I understand. So on the drive up to Chicago on Saturday afternoon, I asked her if she would like to take me in to meet her parents and she said that she didn't think that it was a good idea and it struck me that that was very strange. You know, she didn't say that it wasn't a good idea 'yet'. You understand? She didn't say 'not just now.' She just said that it wasn't a good idea. I wasn't suggesting that I should come in to ask her father for her hand in marriage. I just wanted to be introduced. Is that so much to ask? And then, she met me at the museum the next day and she didn't know about Chagall."

Jack stopped. Isaac walked ten feet further and then realized that he was alone. He turned quizzically to determine what had become of his audience. "Are you coming?"

"I don't think you're hearing me. You're so wrapped up in this . . . this young shiksa, that you haven't heard what I'm saying." His voice sang a blues of lament and anger at once. It was raised and it was plaintive. It had tears and invective. It asked, "Why have you gone and left me when I needed you so?" It lacked only harmony and melody.

"You talk to me about shiksahs, mister? Who the hell do you think you are?" The dogs moved in between the two as their voices rose together in counterpoints of pain.

"That's not the point. I'm trying to talk to you about my wife. Remember? You're supposed to be a rabbi. I need to talk to somebody. Where the hell are you?"

"I'm not your rabbi. I'm your neighbor. Maybe I'm your friend. But I'm not your rabbi." Sasha herded Jack backwards. Cady confronted Isaac, her eyes intent, waiting for him to move in her direction.

"Then maybe you'll act like my friend for a few minutes and just listen."

"OK, so I'll listen."

"You already know. Rae's going in for surgery. I don't know what to do."

"What do you think you should do?"

"I don't know. There's nothing I can do."

"What would you like me to do?"

"I don't know that either."

"Let me do what I think I should do, and you do what you think you should do."

They resumed the walk silently, each unto himself, together, alone. Every human being feels his own fear, moves to the rhythms of his own pain. Every culture plies the myth that being with people reduces pain; that love, and partnership and family and clan prevent the loneliness that comes with suffering. It is a lie. The basic unit of pain is the person. A person and his pain are wed, never to be rent asunder. Pain is a jealous lover. It lets no other relationship intervene. The collectivity doesn't feel it. No other person feels it. Words do it no justice. Bonds of love in defense of pain share only the tearing of relationship - a kind of pain in itself - but they don't ease the suffering. There is nothing to do but wait.

They struggled with silence, something they had not known together. Silence is the test of relationship. It is when two are comfortable with silence that they are friends. Not before. Isaac and Jack encountered their silence for the first time. Coming out of silent anger requires a courage that few have. It is the ultimate expression of reason. To remain in silence is to wound further both the other and one's self. To come out of silence is to admit that the relationship is more important than the anger. The silence of anger and the anger of silence are the true human dilemma. It is not something that human beings do well.

"What do you make of Phil and Rhonda Dorfman?"

"I can't talk about it a lot. I went to see Rhonda and what we talked about is, of course, confidential. What can you say? People get divorced. People get hurt. So?"

"Isaac, this guys got a honey on the side. He dumps his wife and family for a graduate student on Friday and comes to temple on Saturday to lead the congregation in prayer. This is a little sick, don't you think?"

"I don't think. First of all, he leads the service like a musical instrument. You listen to the organ. It adds to your enjoyment of the service. You don't ask what color underwear the organist has on. He sings. He does it well. That's all. As for the rest, maybe he davens and in his heart, he asks forgiveness; maybe he says a prayer of thanksgiving for being rescued from a bad marriage; maybe he says a 'hallelujah' because he isn't impotent anymore. Who's to say? He comes to temple. He has some kind of relationship to God. How should I know if it's right or if it's wrong? You confuse a person's relationship to God with religion. They're two different things. A person has a private, personal relationship with God. Maybe someone goes to temple. Maybe he doesn't. The relationship is his and he runs it his own way. Nobody can tell him how to do it. Religion is something else. It's temple politics. It's power and prestige and a lot of dramatic posturing. He came to temple. He led a service. He said his loud prayers that everyone hears, and he said his soft prayers that only he and God hear. On the loud ones I can argue. On the soft ones I can't."

"What about Rhonda?"

"Maybe he did Rhonda a favor that she couldn't do for herself. Again. How should I know? Maybe she's lived half a life because she's always been Phil Dorfman's wife. Maybe she needs to find out who Rhonda Dorfman is, and he's forced her to do it. You can't judge. You do what you can, and you wait. That's all."

"It was really decent of you to go to the hospital on Friday night."

"I had to. It's my job. I work on Friday nights anyway. But I don't like hospitals. I don't like doctors."

"Why not? I train doctors. They're human."

"They have a license to kill. They tell you they're killing you for your own good."

"What are you saying?"

"I've seen them make decisions about people's lives that kill them. And they tell their patients and the families with all piety and devotion that it's for the patient's own good. They're deceitful and self-serving."

"You're wrong. They protect themselves from death. They try to protect their patients from death. Lots of times you can't escape death. It comes into the room whether you invite it in or not. They get confronted with their own mortality every day and it drives them into a kind of shell where they deny it to themselves and so they deny it to others."

"Have you been there? Have you been close to death and had some doctor tell you that he was doing something for your own good while he was killing you?"

"No."

"I have. I know. It may be a kind of shell. They may not mean harm. But they kill nonetheless, and I've learned that they can't be trusted. Not ever."

"When did all this happen?"

"A long time ago."

"Were you close to death?"

"We lived together. We were lovers."

"What was wrong with you?"

"Tuberculosis."

"Can you tell me more?"

There was a silence. It was the long, easy rests in the blues lament, the break between the verses that gives you pause to feel the sadness, to let it overcome you, mellow you and make you look into your own soul, the long, empty beat that makes you want to hear the rest of the story. Jack waited the long, empty rest and walked in the silence of friends.

"When I got liberated, in '45, it was the Russians. They fed us. Army food. Whatever they ate, we ate. They gave us clothes. Whatever they had, they shared. They de-loused us.

And somewhere in there, they examined us for medical problems and treated us as best they could. The ones that were healthy went into one barracks. The rest of us they put in a sick bay. People who went into the sick bay either died and were buried or they got better and went over to the regular barracks. This went on for a long time. Sometimes they transferred people around. I never moved. Nobody told me why I was there. I just coughed and stayed skin and bones and never went anywhere. Then they moved me to a hospital in the American sector, a place called Wolfratshausen. It wasn't a hospital like you see today. It was more like a big house with big open rooms that everyone slept in. It was a sanitarium, I suppose, though I never understood that then. The sisters - nurses - took care of you and they stayed away from you as much as they could. Every few weeks, some Polish doctor came in and looked at us and went away. It was the same story. Some of us died. Some of us got better and were discharged. I just stayed. I didn't know why. I ate the food - it was one step better than in the camps - not much more, and nothing happened. I asked the doctor what was wrong, and he wouldn't tell me anything. I asked the nurses and they wouldn't tell me anything. All they ever said was, 'A little longer. A little longer. For your own good. For your own good.'"

"One night, the nurse wasn't around. I broke into the office and looked at my record. It said that I had tuberculosis. Too serious to discharge or to transfer to another hospital. Just wait. He'll die soon. You hear that? They expected me to die. Just wait. He'll die soon. They wouldn't tell me that. They just expected me to hang around and die. They made the decision for me, like they make for everybody. They hold your life in their hands and let you die for your own good."

Jack prompted, "That's not the end of the story. What happened?"

"What happened? I'll tell you what happened. I decided if I was going to die, I wasn't going to die lying there every night. So that night, I found a door I could get out of and I left the hospital. I walked to the town, it wasn't far and I walked around. And you know what I found?"

"No, what?"

"I found an angel. You know about angels?"

"Tell me about them."

The Cossack laughed out loud. "I'll tell you about angels and this angel in particular."

He laughed again. "God needs help to accomplish all His labors, so he has angels. Only you see, angels look just like people. Why do they look like people? Because they are people. Only they're people on divine missions. They're doing God's work, only most of the time they don't even know it themselves and if you told them they wouldn't believe you. What's angelic isn't them, it's the mission. And they may never understand what it is they're doing or why. You see?"

"If you say so."

"Let me give you an example. Once upon a time one of the great rabbis sinned a great sin. He disbelieved that God had made angels. For his punishment, God transported him in an instant to a huge desert far from his homeland. The poor man wandered about in the heat of the desert and he was about to die of thirst. He was sure that his time had come when he walked over the top of a sand dune and there was a man, a servant, walking in a circle with a water bottle on his shoulder. The rabbi begged a drink from him and satisfied his thirst. When he was done, he asked the servant what he was doing in the desert with a water bottle and the servant said, 'My master has gone mad and every day he sends me here to walk around with a water bottle waiting for someone who never comes.' So now you understand - and he understood - that God provides angels. He makes angels of us all at one time or another and most of us never know it."

"Who was your angel?"

"Oh, yes." He laughed again. "I was walking in the town. It was on the German border with Poland, maybe sixty kilometers from where I was born, and a man saw me and he looked at me and he looked and he looked again and he said, 'Isaac, is that you?' I looked back at him. He was fat and he was well dressed and somehow, he looked familiar. It was Petr Bremski, the Pentecostal kid that had run away with me and my friend Lev into the woods. We had been stopped by a German patrol, but he had been able to talk his way out of it. Now here he was in front of me, seven or eight years older and fat. I couldn't believe it."

"Where did he come from? What was he doing there?"

"He had escaped the Nazis. He went back to his family's dye factory in Vilna. His father was in jail, but he eventually got out. He was valuable to the Germans for what he could produce. They asked him to set up another factory in Poland where labor was cheap to make fabric for the war effort. He did. He moved his family to a small town and set up a new factory. Meanwhile, Petr met the daughter of a rich merchant and married her. He was making money from his father and he was working for his father-in-law too. He was rich in a time when no one had money and he was fat when everyone was starving. And he was so glad to see me alive. He took me home that night and fed me 'til I burst. We talked all night. When it got very late, I snuck back into the hospital, but not before Petr made me promise to come back every night. For six months I went back every night and he and his wife fed me. And then, one night, I felt strong. I felt good. I felt like I wasn't going to die. I didn't go back."

"What did you do?"

"I got into a DP camp and found my way to HIAS, the Hebrew Immigrant Aid Society. They helped me get to Paris. I went to start life all over again. The Nazis had failed to kill me. The doctors had failed to kill me. It was apparent that God had decided that I should live. He had something for me to do. I accepted His judgement and decided to live."

"Did you ever talk to Petr again?"

"No. Someday I will."

Their circuit was nearly complete. They approached Isaac's house where the Rabbi asked Jack to wait for a moment. He went in and came back with a small Channukah menorah.

"Here. Do you know how to use this?"

"You plug it in, and it curls your hair, right?"

"Don't be a shnook."

He ducked back into the house and came out with a black book.

"This is a prayer book. It's the one we use in temple on Saturday mornings. Thumb through it and find the blessings for Channukah. Light one candle for a shamash and use that one to light one candle the first night, two the second, and so on. You understand?"

"I understand."

"Fine. Also there is a prayer for the sick. You'll find it. Use it. One more thing. I need you to be in court for Matt Cowan a week from Thursday."

CHAPTER 19

The snow and rain mixed across the campus. He had a feeling for rain. The fall rain filled the earth with water before the frost and the spring rain beckoned vegetation; but this ill mix disciplined the world for its inadequacies. It chilled and sickened and lay in the low spots. Where it should have run into rivulets and into rivers and on toward the Mississippi, it did not. It haunted paved parking lots, lying in wait for errant feet to dampen, freezing in the dark before tripping the innocent. It was the price paid for civilization.

Jack descended further into his hooded parka for the trudge to McCormick Hall. The Newman Center was dark and uninhabited as he walked through. It was the annual winter migration of students back to comfortable suburban homes, to farmsteads, to warmer climates, to places where they were cherished. In a few days, with the end of exams, Bloomington would be depopulated, as would Ann Arbor, Madison, Ames, Urbana, Lexington, Lawrence, the land-grant colonies of the American expanse. These outposts of intellectualism would revert to non-places where nothing happened, and time was a burden.

The bulletin boards in the corridors of McCormick Hall had been stripped of the paper foliage that decorated them. Left were the scars of staples that had held unread notices by hundreds. Over time, each bulletin board was encased in the light armor of finely placed staples until it was not possible to tack another notice. This was the inexorable sign that the building was soon to be torn down and replaced by a new building with new bulletin boards.

He stood in the corner of the hall. The stairs were to his right, the elevator to the left. He took the elevator. It meant a long walk around the entire periphery of the building when he got off, but he couldn't manage the physical labor of the stairs. The cold weighed on him. His muscles didn't move, nor his spirit. The wrought iron cage closed around, lifted him thirty-six feet to the third floor and released him. Slowly, he made his way through deserted corridors to his offices and Ilene.

"Morning."

"Hey, Boss."

"Don't call me that."

"Anything you say, Fearless Leader. Sancho Panza's looking for you."

"I thought you were Sancho Panza in this operation."

"How insensitive. I am the lovely Roxanne. How're things with Mrs. Fearless Leader?"

"Not so hot. She's got some kind of mass in her brain. She's going into Creditor for surgery on Thursday. I've got my hands full."

"Ohhh. Ohhh. Jack!"

She never called him Jack. It was as close to a nurturing comment as she had ever made to him.

"Is there anything we can do?"

"Thanks. No. I need to talk to Dunphy, just to figure out where we are with the project. I'm going to have my hands full for a while and I need to put things to bed for the vacation just so I don't have that to think about."

"Do you know anything more about what's wrong with her?"

"Not really. She's been having headaches and nausea. The doc says she's got some other symptoms. They're gonna open her up and look around on Thursday and then we'll know more. Pregnancy's a real complication. Can't use much in the way of drugs, can't use much in the way of radiation. Surgery's the only option for the moment. We'll get a biopsy done and then we'll know."

"Pat and I were planning on leaving on Wednesday. Would you like us to wait until Friday or so? We can help watch the kids."

"Thanks, that's really sweet of you. No. Rae's sister is coming down from Chicago to keep an eye on things at home. I'll be at the hospital. When she comes home, I'm just going to keep her quiet. You guys go ahead."

Monday hung in the damp air like wash that wouldn't dry. Ilene Mariko-Dunphy and Sancho Panza had seen to the details of work for the next few weeks. It was the winter hibernation, the dormant season of the intellectual class, when no one expected ideas. There was nothing to do. Jack couldn't call home. He couldn't go home. There were no conversations to be had and he couldn't bear the silence. He sat in his lair and shifted papers from fourteen-inch pile to fourteen-inch pile without system. When he could stand no more, he picked up the telephone book and looked in the classifieds under Physicians-Psychiatrists.

"Hello. Is Dr. Tabanov available please? This is Dr. Israel calling."

"I'm sorry, Doctor, Dr. Tabanov is not available. This is his answering service. Do you care to leave a message?"

"Yes. Would you ask him to call me, please. Best bet is at home this evening - 356-3227."

There was little to say.

"Do you need me to do anything?"

"Don't forget that the boys will need lunches. Dinah will be in day-care Thursday and Friday. Monday and Tuesday if we need it. Leyla will arrive Thursday on the afternoon train. Please don't tell any of the relatives until after. There's soup in the freezer. Sasha needs a pill every morning."

He was grateful for the dogs and hateful of the weather. They were his escape, but the discomfort was unrelenting. He walked by Isaac's house on Crosscut but it was dim. He and Rae passed dinner in silence, with only the voices of children to distract them. After dinner, after dishes, after dog walking, after and after - at last the telephone rang.

"Hello."

"Hello. I'd like to speak to the paranoid schizophrenic, but I'm afraid to ask and so am I."

"Hi, Myron. How are you?"

"Well, actually, I've been gaining some weight. I don't eat barbecued food anymore and I've lost my grill-ish figure."

"Myron, if this is a recording, please tell me now."

"Ach! You've found me out. This is a recording. How are you doing, Jack?"

"Average. Look, the students are leaving town. Want to play some racquetball tomorrow and have lunch?"

"Sounds great. Meet you in the locker room at noon. If I'm naked, don't mistake me for some strange putz."

"Myron, you need a new writer."

"Jack, I need an Italian contractor to fix my house."

They played for forty minutes before the ball found them flat-footed, gasping and unable to master even simple shots. Sweat made wet spots on the floor and footing chancy. Jack surrendered.

"That's all for me. I've had it."

"I was just getting warmed up. Oh well, if you're pooped, I can finish my warm-up in the sauna."

The university's one gymnasium luxury was a genuine Finnish sauna. It was large by any standard. Some wondered aloud when the administration would see fit to convert it into two offices. It was wood lined and had three levels of benches, each hotter than the one beneath it. The nails had been deftly countersunk on each bench to save the inevitable burn when soft skin spread across wood. At lunch times, seating was hard to find. Often people stood and waited, towel in hand for some scarlet, sweating man to vacate a spot. Today, Jack and Myron entered to find it hot and empty. They assumed seats on the top bench and proceeded to perspire together.

"Thanks for the game," Jack began., "It didn't get my full concentration. I've got a lot on my mind right now."

"That only happens to me when I have a hat on," he chortled. "What's going on?"

"Well, Rae's going into Creditor for surgery on Thursday - with Gerald Byer. I'm really scared, Myron. I just don't know what to do. I can't talk to Rae. There just aren't any words. I've got to do something, and I really don't know what to do. Do you know what I mean?"

"Oh, yeah. That's really too bad. But she's getting good care. It'll be all right."

"Myron, I'm terrified. And I don't know what to do. I really need someone to talk to."

"Talk to the dogs, Jack. They'll listen. Where do you want to go for lunch?"

There was nothing to do in the office on Tuesday. Ilene read the last of Pride and Prejudice. Dunphy roamed in and out asking questions to which he knew the answers. They dragged Jack out to the only open eatery, Parella's Pizza, for lunch. Jack and Ilene shared a cheese and tomato on whole wheat crust while Dunphy had an entire sausage pizza washed down with a Miller beer. Conversation was light.

"You have Bernie's telephone number in Dodgeville on your Rolodex. If you need us, just call. We can be here in half a day. There's a small bag of goodies for the kids under my desk. Bring it home for the holidays. There's something in there for you too. The project is all tied up tight for now. We'll be going back to Chicago right after the tenth of January to finish up Bernie Fredericks' shop and to check out Cook County. You don't have to do anything. We've got it under control. Are you OK?"

"Oh yeah. I'm fine. I sort of don't know what to do with myself, but I guess we just have to wait this one through. Look, if there's nothing else to do, why don't you two get out of town now. The weather stinks and if you leave a day early, you can take your time getting there. You can bring me back a cow pie for a present."

Jack paid for lunch and hugged Ilene at the door of Parella's. As he turned to shake hands with Dunphy, Sancho Panza pushed his enlarged belly against Jack's and keeping his back rigid and tight, hugged him, breathing the smell of stale beer in his face. It wasn't an easy hug. Men don't know how to relax as they hold one another close. It was formal and stiff, at once cold and warm - a gesture that no one would have thought Dunphy capable of. With no other word he turned, clasped Ilene's hand and walked off in search of a canary yellow Camaro.

It was early when he got home. The office had a chill - because of the cold rain, because the heat was shutting down, because Ilene Mariko-Dunphy turned no pages at her desk. The winter solstice loomed with early darkness; the halls of McCormick rang with silent echoes; and it felt that home could be no more dismal than this. The truck had been cold, and he entered the house with a coldness that his body couldn't undo. The outside light was on. Living room lights shone onto the lawn. The dogs didn't greet. They lay in place, panting. The house was warm.

A voice called to him, "They've been walked. Don't let them lie to you."

"Hi. How are you doing?"

"I'm all right. Dinner's on the way. Special surprise."

He hung his wet parka, dripping, in the front closet and headed in the direction of the cheery voice. He looked into the kitchen to see Rae and Dinah scraping potatoes on a grater. The counters were a mess of bowls, potato peels, eggshells, onion peels, and a box of Dickie's Donuts.

"What are you ladies up to?"

"Tonight's the first night of Chanukah and we're having a party," piped Dinah. "Want to come? It's like a birthday party with candles and presents."

"Really? And what else is there?"

"Well, me and Mom are making potato larkies for dinner with apple sauce and we got some jelly donuts and she say's we get presents - even you!"

He looked questioningly at Rae. "You lost something you haven't told me about?"

"No. You brought home the candles and the candelabra and that prayer book and I thought you might want to do something with Channukah. I looked in the Sisterhood Cookbook that your mother gave me and it said that the required menu was potato latkes and apple sauce or sour cream and jelly donuts. And that's what's for dinner. The rest is up to you." She leaned over to him, cupped her hand to her mouth and whispered, "And there's a bag of presents in the bedroom."

Simmy sat in the family room, a book open on his lap, unread. He watched the activities in the kitchen with male disinterestedness and full curiosity. Lee was in the boys' bedroom, the door half-closed engaged in some private and mysterious contemplation. Jack waved to Simmy without waiting for response. He swept through the narrow passage to the bedroom, tapping lightly on the door to Lee's lair to signal a human presence.

"Go away!" informed him that his second son was in his normal humor. In the bedroom he shed the uniform of the professor: tie, two years out of fashion, tweedy jacket, and khakis, swapping them for a wool shirt over stained jeans and old athletic shoes. He was now home.

In the corner of the closet was an unfamiliar bag and inside that were five wrapped packages. At once he realized that there were presents, Channukah presents, for Simmy, Lee, and Dinah, for him and for the dogs, and there was no gift for Rae. He was at once ashamed and angry. He had no gift for his wife who was grating potatoes in celebration of Channukah. But this was not a celebration that was a continuous piece of their partnership. He'd been had. Caught by surprise and made to feel guilty for it. He could ignore the slight that he would attribute to himself or go back out into the rain to forage for some token of his own ignorance. Even at that, he would appear the insensitive fool.

It was easy to be angry at caring people. They gave unselfishly and made the recipients of their gifts feel guilt at the lack of reciprocity. They were an intrusion on the management of one's own daily life. It was one thing if they were paid for their troubles. It was all right if they did this as part of a job and they did the job exceedingly well. It was another thing if they had the audacity to give unselfishly and without expectation of return. Nice people, they were called. An annoyance.

He remembered Ilene's comment. There was a bag under the desk. Back into the living room, he extricated his parka from the closet and slipped out into the dampness. Without a word, he ran from the house and mounted his waiting Chevrolet for the drive back to McCormick Hall.

CHAPTER 20

Time is the enemy to those who wait. He had left her at the Creditor Clinic on Wednesday evening and had kissed her goodbye. The ride home - twenty minutes perhaps, had been endless. Lev and Sage were watching the children and Jack knew that he had to be home promptly but dreaded his own arrival. How to walk in the door to children who had no understanding of where their mother had gone or why; dogs to walk; kids to tuck in; and no one to attend his own fears.

Leyla arrived early on Thursday. Jack had delivered the boys to school and Dinah to temporary day care. With Leyla to cover the home front, he could be at the hospital while surgery was in progress, if only to wait.

There are places where one is a stranger in one's own land, when knowing the language and the customs doesn't protect you from being a foreigner. The family waiting room in the surgery wing of the medical center is just such a place. There's no comfort; there's only waiting. There is no time; only waiting. There is no respite until the kind clerk says, "Mr. Israel, Dr. Byer will be coming down in just a few minutes to talk with you." It was after noon. If Byer had begun early, it had been a long procedure.

A half hour later, Gerald Byer walked into the family waiting room. He graciously invited Jack into a smaller conference room to talk. He was still dressed in his blue scrubs and wore a blue scrub hat. A face mask hung around his neck. Salt and pepper curls snuck out from under the hat and his arms were bare, dark, covered with hair. Black shadows nestled under his eyes.

"Well, we're done, for now. And she looks pretty good after surgery."

"How did it go?"

"Well, it was pretty complicated - more than I expected. Our Chief of Anesthesia sat in just to monitor because of the pregnancy issue. So, we made a triangular skin incision over the tumor area and peeled back a portion of the scalp. Then we drilled three holes in a triangle and made cuts between each of the holes. That gave us a triangular window through the skull and then . . ."

"What did you find? Were you able to get it all?"

"Well, I had hoped to find something nice and contained - perhaps a meningioma - tight margins, encapsulated, easy to dissect out . . ."

"And? Is that what you found?"

"Well, no, it was clearly not a meningioma. So, we went in deeper to access the tumor and it was a little more widespread than we had originally thought."

"What are you saying?"

"Well, it was clearly visible over the right frontal lobe, but there were . . . extensions of the tumor into the temporal lobe. In fact, we actually had to extend our window through the skull to reach those areas."

"Dr. Byer, can you give me a sense of what the tumor is? Is it malignant? Were you able to get it all out? What's happening here?"

"Now, give me a minute. We sent some tissue down to our own pathology lab immediately, of course. But we want to be absolutely sure of the diagnosis, so I'm going to send some samples up to Chicago to have them read there as well - just to be safe. That will take a few days and then we'll have a better idea of where we stand."

Waiting. There would be more waiting. There was no answer - not yet.

"Were you able to take the pressure off her brain?"

"Yes, I think we did a really good job of that. Now we have to manage the swelling and we'll be aggressive in doing that. Look, Mr. Israel, she's in Recovery now and if you ask the clerk, she'll tell you when you can go in and see her. I'll be in regularly to check on her and, if all goes well, we'll have her out of here in a few days to rest at home. Then when we get the findings from Chicago, we'll match them against our own and we'll know where to go from here. OK?"

"Do I get a choice?"

"I'm sorry, Mr. Israel. I know this is hard. Just know that Mrs. Israel is going to get the very best care we can give her."

Time doesn't exist in Recovery. No windows to see sun rises or sets. Clocks that tell meaningless hours. Lights that stay on at all times. Nurses present and busy at all times. Patients arriving and departing unscheduled. There is no rhythm; there are no days and no nights. There's not a time to sleep; not a time to be awake. It is a separation from the world more complete than prison. To be a patient in Recovery is to lose one's body; to hand it over to others to puncture and probe, to add or diminish fluids, to take blood, to give blood, to close old wounds and open new ones, to end mobility and truncate conversation. It is an end to existence until permitted otherwise.

Rae was difficult to find. Rae was not there. In her stead was a gauze turban with a clear plastic drain taped to the side of her face. Her skin was a desiccated gray. Her breath came slowly, seemingly with difficulty. Her blue eyes and blond hair were absent as though her soul had been sent to pathology for dissection, to be returned only if the microscope found it without blemish.

Jack reached out tentatively and held her hand. It was stiff, dry, hard. He squeezed gently, desperately hoping for response. Nothing.

"Rae, it's me, Jack. Oh, I love you honey." And the last word choked his throat as his vision disappeared in tears.

"It's the anesthesia and the diuretics. She'll be out of it in a day. She'll be groggy but she'll be good as new." It was Carol Martinez and behind her, Myron Tabanov.

"Oh, I am so glad to see you two. Thank you for coming."

Myron smirked, "I was actually looking for a men's room and took a wrong turn in here. What's Byer have to say?"

"Actually, not much. He found more tumor that he expected and he's sending samples to Chicago to identify the type."

Neither Carol nor Myron responded. "Look, Jack, Carol and I ought not to stay very long and frankly neither should you. The nurses need a clear field to monitor her and do whatever it is that nurses do. She's not going to wake up until tomorrow and she might be pretty cranky even then. Why don't you go home and persecute your children?"

"I'll go in a few minutes. And thanks."

It was dark when he exited the hospital and crossed the street to the truck. He glanced at his watch to find that it was 4:20 and the sun was down. It occurred to him only then that this was December 21st, less light than at any other day of the year. The boys would be in full melt down. The dogs would need to be walked. There had to be dinner. There was no time to cry, to feel sorry for himself, to find solace somewhere, anywhere. A light rain fell, and he didn't care. It was a day when cold rain didn't matter; it couldn't make things much worse.

Lights were on all over the house. Jack went through the door to unaccustomed quiet. No immediate kids. No immediate dogs. Murmurs crept in from the family room. He peeked around the corner of the kitchen into the family room and the voices of children burst upon him: "Look what we got! Look! Look!"

There, in a renovated corner of the family room stood a diminutive, innocent blue spruce, a Christmas tree. It was hung with streamers and cut outs of stars of David and Channukah menorahs. In the cacophony of shouts, he was able to make out, "We wanted to surprise you! We're decorating it for when Mommy comes home! Do you like it?" A sheepish Leyla hid in the opposite corner.

"They needed it, Jack."

The late evening knock at the door was all too familiar. Jack slept on the family room couch, fully clothed. Leyla wrestled past the dogs to find a small man in a Persian lamb hat standing, unsure of who had answered.

"Hello, I'm . . . Rabbi Abrams. Is Jack around? I thought he might need a walk."

"Oh, Rabbi, I've heard so much about you. I'm Rae's sister, Leyla," and realizing the presence of a non-kosher tree in the family room, she deftly blocked the entrance.

"Jack is passed out on the couch, Rabbi. Rae had surgery today and he was at the hospital all day."

"Do you know how she's doing?"

"Not really. Why don't I have Jack call you in the morning?"

With a casual "good night", she closed and latched the door and retreated toward the family room.

"Thanks, Leyla, I just couldn't talk to anyone tonight," Jack mumbled.

"I thought. You might like to go to bed, Jack."

"Bed's empty, Leyla. Rae's not there. My life's not there."

"We'll go tomorrow. She'll be better."

They distributed the children the next morning, Friday the twenty second. School vacation began on Friday. They had made feeble excuses as to why they couldn't be in Milwaukee for Christmas. Somehow, Rae would have to call them on Monday.

Leyla followed dutifully as Jack burst through the doors of the Creditor Clinic. He stopped at the information desk to locate Rae and was told that she was in the Intensive Care Unit. This was not what he expected. He rushed to the elevator and pressed the button. Had the elevator come immediately, he would have left Leyla behind. Instead he waited. Leyla caught up and they entered the elevator each occupying a back corner.

Where Rae was blond and blue eyed and pink, Leyla was auburn with dark eyes. They barely looked like sisters. Rae filled the shape of a woman who had borne and nursed three children and was now carrying another. Leyla was one half head taller, still slender and fashionable. She was well made up and wore a noticeable hint of cologne.

The elevator doors opened, and they followed the signs toward the ICU in quick step. The doors were locked, and Jack pressed the intercom. It rang and again he waited and waited for a response.

"We'd like to see Rae Israel. This is her husband and her sister . . ."

"Just one moment please while I check."

More waiting.

"Mr. Israel? Mrs. Israel is with the medical team right now. She'll be ready for you in about fifteen minutes. There's a family waiting room across the hall. We'll call."

Time. Time. Time is not a friend in the family waiting room. Fifteen minutes. Twenty minutes. The phone in the family waiting room rang.

"Mr. Israel? You can come in now."

Jack leapt from the chair. Leyla followed a step and a half behind. The ICU was partitioned by curtains. Privacy didn't exist. Rae was surrounded by Byer, the head nurse and a primary care nurse. Jack skidded to a stop, his rubber soles squeaking on the tile floor. Byer looked up.

"Oh, hi, Mr. Israel. How are you doing?"

"Fine. How's Rae?"

Rae opened her right eye and looked at Jack. Her left eyelid drooped and the eye itself seemed lethargic, clouded, unresponsive. She turned toward Leyla and managed a half-smile.

"Oh, this is my sister-in-law, Leyla Rosenbaum - Rae's sister."

"Nice to meet you, Leyla. You may know Rita and Irene. They're in charge of Rae's nursing care."

Jack pressed. "So how is she doing? Do we have any results from Chicago - from anywhere?"

"Well, things are a little slow. It's Christmas, you know. But I'm confident that we'll have some things to talk about on Tuesday. Rae's going to be with us until then while we manage the swelling and make sure that she's draining well and that the bone graft is healing over the incision. If you can be available Tuesday morning, I'm confident that Rae will be off ICU and we can have a team conference."

"Fine. I'll look forward to seeing you then."

"Oh, I've arranged the conference, but I probably won't be there. I've done my work and you don't need me much anymore. But I've asked Dr. Acosta to be there and another physician, Helaine Crane. You'll really like her."

"Who is she?"

"Well, I think she's the proper person to manage Rae from this point on."

"What is she? What does she do?

"She's an oncologist, Jack."

Rae offered Jack and Leyla one small laugh. Leyla asked, "Rae, do you want a visit from the chaplain - maybe a priest?"

Rae had laughed a weak half choke. "No, get me a rabbi, if he's not being held by the police."

Jack drove home and Leyla was silent for a while. "How long can you stay, Leyla?"

"I'll stay until Wednesday. I want to be at the conference if that's OK with you. I can go home on Wednesday afternoon."

"Can Mike get on okay without you."

"That's a definite yes, Jack. Mike is on his own path these days and I'm on mine."

The late afternoon traffic on Georgia Boulevard slowed their progress home and gave them time for the kind of car conversation that prevents eye-contact. Driver and passenger stay riveted on the road and can say what they can't speak face to face.

"Are you two . . . doing all right . . . together?"

"That's very polite, Jack. Thank you. Each of us fine but separate. We're not together in the sense that a married couple ought to be together and we haven't been for a long time. Mike had a very rough time with his cancer, Jack. It nearly killed him and frankly, it nearly killed me. And for sure, it killed a part of our marriage. I would never have left him when he needed me - never. But he's in remission. It's been three years. He's back up to his ass in his damned chemicals because that's the only thing that he really knows how to sell. And I don't want to wait around for the next bout of cancer and I don't want to live with a garage full of chemicals and I don't want to live with the fear and the anxiety and just not being able to talk about it." She rummaged in her purse for a tissue and blew her nose.

"Well, at least your marriage is sound."

She laughed a weak choke of a laugh. "You heard what the doctor said about Tuesday - about having an oncologist there. I've been in a conference like that, Jack. I went through all that with Mike. I just hope to God that you don't have to go through what I went through. And I just can't imagine going through that with my only sister."

Jack made a sudden turn into the parking lot of Gartner's Supermarket. The truck lolled around the corner and he heaved it into a parking space.

"What's wrong, Jack?"

"It's Friday. Dammit, Leyla, it's Friday and I need some candles and some bread and some wine."

"Since when do you light candles on Friday night?"

"Since I learned that my life isn't in my control and since I need all the help that I can get."

Friday night was the fifth candle of Channukah. It was Shabbat. Jack and Leyla did the best that they could do with Simmy, Lee and Dinah. Saturday and Sunday passed, and Jack ran off for a while to buy last minute presents to grace the humble blue spruce. The world had disappeared: Dunphy, Ilene, Isaac. All were gone. Rae was gone. Jack dashed back and forth to the hospital to see what remained of her. She emerged from the ICU to a patient room. She emerged from her turban of bandages. She shed her drainage tube and it became more white than gray. But whether it was Rae or someone else in the bed, Jack couldn't be sure.

Monday was Christmas. Presents were opened - all but the ones marked, "To Mommy from Santa." That would wait. Jack could stand the sadness of his children no longer. He called the Creditor Clinic and got the head nurse on Rae's floor, a veteran who was willing to give up Christmas to bring joy to a young mother who had been scheduled to work.

"This is Jack Israel, Dr. Israel, Rae Israel is my wife. Look, I know hospital policy about kids and all, but it's Christmas and I have three kids who don't know if their mother is ever going to come home. Please, oh please, can I sneak them in to see their mother for just a minute?"

"Well, Dr. Israel. You know our policy and of course I could not possibly permit children on my unit, now could I? However, we had Mrs. Israel up in a chair for a while today and I just bet that she would love to be in a wheelchair say in one hour . . . and we could wheel her into the family waiting room just down the hall and she could stay there for . . . let's say fifteen minutes. Do you understand, Dr. Israel."

"Nurse, you are a saint."

Only the adults cried. The children carried presents "To Mommy from Santa" and Jack and Leyla cried for the full fifteen minutes. Rae was there and she was not. Her left eye was unresponsive. Her mouth drooped slightly on the left side. Her speech halted as she grasped at the names of each of her children as though she struggled with the memory of them.

Jack and Leyla waited patiently in the family conference room on Tuesday. The conference had been scheduled for nine. The transport worker wheeled Rae in in her chair. She looked fresher, more awake, more in touch. Jack leaped to her side, but the transporter held him gently off. "Watch out for the head, please. This lady's been playing tackle for the Chicago Bears and she's showin' the wear and tear."

Jack leaned over and kissed her tenderly on her left cheek. The flesh was cool, flaccid, and yielding. Leyla came to her side and kissed her as well. She smiled a weak smile. Her voice was hoarse, but she said, "I suppose you wondered why I asked you all to be here today? Well, I have plans to turn this place into a full-scale looney bin and I'm going to be in charge."

Maria Acosta came in followed by another woman. Had she not worn a long white coat with her name, Helaine Crane, MD, embroidered over the pocket, she might have been a candy striper, a high school volunteer delivering flowers to patients. She was slender enough to be a candidate for either a swimsuit competition or an eating disorders clinic. She had huge brown eyes graced with long dark lashes and a smile that became her entire face.

"Hi, I'm Dr. Crane. I already know Rae and you must be Dr. Israel and you are . . ?"

"Leyla Rosenbaum, Rae's sister."

"Well, thank you all for coming. Dr. MacKenzie and Dr. Byer asked me to come aboard the treatment team. At this point the issues that we're looking at need Dr. Acosta and me to help guide some decision making. We have the pathology report back from our own Pathology Department and from Chicago and we have a pretty good idea of the biopsy results."

Maria Acosta didn't make eye contact with anyone. She sat silent as Helaine Crane took over the conversation and waited patiently for her cue.

"And?" Jack asked impatiently.

"Well the pathologists agree that the tumor is what we call a glioblastoma. This is an unusual type of brain tumor and we really don't know the epidemiology - what causes them to appear."

"How . . . I mean . . . are they . . . malignant? Did Dr. Byer get it all? What's the prognosis?"

"These are difficult tumors to treat. They grow tentacles that invade the brain tissue - like long skinny fingers. And that makes it impossible to treat just with surgery. You can get most of it, and that's what Dr. Byer did, but you can't get it all."

"Chemotherapy? Radiation? What do we do next?" Jack insisted.

Maria Acosta took her cue. Jack had pressed her start button. "This is an unusual case. Rae is nearly six months pregnant. Dr. Crane and I have gone through all the journals looking to see what the effects might be of chemotherapy on the baby and there's just no research, no case reports, nothing. Rae needs to be treated immediately and the pregnancy complicates things on both ends. We don't know the effects on the baby, and we don't know how her being pregnant will affect her response to chemotherapy. One of the options that we simply must consider is terminating the pregnancy."

"The fuck you will!"

It was Rae. Her voice was husky, raw and her attitude was more so. "This is my baby and you aren't going to take it away. Do you get me, Maria?"

"Rae! Easy. Easy," Jack reached a hand across to her, but she pushed it away.

"I told you before. I'm going to deliver this baby."

"Rae," the calmness of Helaine Crane began, "we need to begin treatment as soon as possible. This is very, very important. Dr. Acosta is very troubled in all of this. This would be a late term abortion, and frankly, we don't even know what effect that procedure might have on the tumor."

"Rae," Acosta chimed in, "if you won't permit us to terminate, we need to wait on chemotherapy. Waiting is dangerous, Rae. Do you understand?"

"I'll make my own decisions, Maria. Get it?"

"OK. If you insist on having this baby - let's see. You're twenty-four weeks now. We need at least another eight weeks, Rae. Maybe nine. March first if development is normal. That's about as early as we can take the baby and hope that it's not too early. That gets us to thirty-three weeks - six weeks early."

"March tenth and not a day before. I want this baby!"

Dr. Acosta released a long, audible, frustrated sigh. Jack and Leyla watched the agenda unfold without comment. It was two skilled boxers, each determined to make points, neither willing to concede.

Helaine Crane touched Rae on her right arm. She looked directly into her eyes and it was clear that she wasn't speaking as a physician. "Rae, I've been where you're sitting. I'm a cancer survivor, Rae. I know. I've also had to give up a baby, Rae. I didn't know what the medications were doing to my baby and I made a very hard choice and it hurt - probably as bad as you hurt right now. But I had two little kids at home that needed me, and I did what I felt was best not for that baby but for my family. Please, Rae, we don't have a lot of time and we need to begin treatment."

"I'm having my baby. That's it. Now get me out of here so I can be with my children."

"Rae," she ended with, "Maria and I are your physicians and we're women and we understand what you want. But Rae, there'll be no guarantees on this one. Do you understand? We'll do whatever we can for you - but no guarantees."

On Wednesday Jack brought her home. She was weak, but she walked up the drive and into the house. Leyla was there to get her past the dogs and into the bedroom. They closed the bedroom door and spoke as sisters, together and alone.

Leyla left in the late afternoon. It was the end of December. Bloomington was devoid of people. No students, no faculty. An apprehensive calm hung in the streets waiting for the return of faculty the first week of January and students the week after. Jack had time with Rae, time to be with the kids, time to walk the dogs. A visiting nurse came twice a week to re-bandage Rae and to be certain that she was being mobile.

Jack lied. He told the kids that Wednesday evening was the last night of Channukah. It was a day late. He set out the last of the small gifts and arranged eight candles and the shamash, the one that lit all the others, in the borrowed menorah. Rae made her way into the kitchen and sat down heavily. As Jack began to strike the match, Simmy said, matter-of-factly, "It says in the book that we read at the temple library that if all the candles go out at exactly the same time we get to make a wish and it'll come true. We gotta make a wish."

Jack choked. Rae choked. They looked at one another and couldn't speak. Dinah fairly shouted, "I wish I could be a dancer!"

Her mother looked at her and said, "You already are, and you always will be."

Jack did his research on glioblastomas. He went to the medical school library and Irene Turner, the librarian, worked her magic for him. His intensity was a giveaway. Irene was an older woman with gray hair and wire rimmed bifocals.

"Not your area of research, Jack. What are you looking for?"

"I just need information, Irene."

"Family?"

"My wife, Irene."

"I'm so sorry, Jack. I'm so sorry. Anything I can do?"

"No, Irene. I have the information and . . . and . . . Oh, I don't know, Irene."

She put a hand on his shoulder and held it there for a long moment. "Whatever you do, Jack, don't go through this alone. Don't be a typical man and think that you can't talk about this with your friends. You're new here, but you have friends already. Use them."

"Thanks, Irene. For the moment let's keep this between you and me. Okay?"

Each time he drove in or out of Southmoor, he took the long route and went by the house on Crosscut. He knew that Lev and Sage would be back in school the first week in January and that Isaac would have to be back. On Tuesday afternoon he saw the black Chrysler in the drive and lights on in the house. He drove home, set up dinner, spent time with Rae and the kids and watched the clock intently. He and Rae tucked the kids in together. Though it was still early, the fatigue diminished Rae and she retreated to the bedroom. Jack tucked her in with all the love that he tucked in the children.

"You've been checking out my diagnosis, haven't you?"

"Yeah."

"What do you know?'

"There's always hope."

"Fuck you. That means there's no hope."

"Oh, Rae . . ."

"Don't think I don't know. Doctors speak in codes and I know the codes. Helaine Crane is desperate because the chances are slim to none. This is a done deal, Jack, and I know it."

There was nothing more to be said. Each retreated toward sleepless exhaustion, the fatigue that steals the spirit. Jack gently disentangled himself from from his wounded mate, kissed her on her aching forehead and said, "I've got to take the dogs out. I'll be back in a few minutes. Just remember that I love you while I'm gone. O.K.?"

"Sure. When you come back, remember to wash your hands before you get romantic, O.K.?"

He rose and slipped out of the bedroom. Grabbing a coat from the closet, he leaped for the door. On the porch, the storm door still rattling in his ear, he leaned against the support pole, the coat in his hand. His arm was up, a cushion to his head, his chest heaved and he moaned. The bitter bite of the January night reminded him that he had not yet put on the coat. It numbed and at the same time it refreshed and cleansed. The night was quiet and clear. It provided a respite from the day's battle.

Jack rubbed his eyes. His chest still heaved. It hurt from the crying that was inside and wouldn't come out. He slipped into his jacket and headed down the street and around the corner at a pace that was neither run nor walk. In moments he was at the single door that he felt he could enter to find rest. He struggled past the black Chrysler that crowded the drive and up the stairs. The outside light was on; the inside lights were on. He pressed the bell. And again. The small Cossack peeked through the side window and opened the door.

"Jack! You need a walk?"

Jack burst through the door. "Oh, Isaac, oh, Isaac. I gotta talk to you!" He grabbed the rabbi by the arm. Isaac retreated slightly. He laid a hand on the hand with which Jack was gripping his arm.

"Sure, sure, sure, what's wrong, Jack?"

"Isaac, we went to the doctor - the . . . the . . . oncologist. Jesus, Isaac, Rae's tumor is malignant and she's gonnah die. Oh, my god, I can't believe it. Rae's got a cancer that's gonnah kill her and I don't know what I'm gonna do. I can't believe it. Jesus Christ, what am I gonna do?"

"Jack. Take off your coat. Come into the kitchen. Sit down. I'll make some tea."

"I don't want tea for Chrissake. My god,igawd I gotta do something. Do you understand? My wife's got a terminal diagnosis." He circled the living room - once, twice. He ran his fingers through his hair. He circled again. He repeated: "She's gonna die. I don't know what I'm gonna do. For Chrissake, Isaac."

Then he stopped and turned toward the rabbi. "Where the Hell is your damned God in all of this? Why the Hell does Rae have to have cancer for Chrissake? What kind of sense does that make? Where's your fine God of justice now? Huh? HUH?"

Isaac gently placed hands on his shoulders and said, "Jack, let me tell you a story."

Jack erupted. He threw Isaac's arms from off of him. "What the fuck good are you and your Goddam stories? You and your stories. All you do is tell stories. What the Hell good are you and your stories? My wife is dying of cancer and all you've got is stories! My children are going to lose their mother and you tell stories. That's all you're good for is stories! That's all you ever give anyone is stories!"

Isaac swung from the hip. His flat hand arced ballet-like across the stage and caught Jack squarely on the hard spot between ear and cheek. The slap of palm on flesh filled the room for a frozen moment. Jack moved in perfect partnership. His face swung right, his shoulder dipped, his left foot eased up from the floor and he balanced on his right for the long pause. Then he stumbled back onto the couch behind.

"Shut up, Jack!".

"Why did you hit me?" Jack's eyes filled with old tears. "Why do you always hit me? You always hit me. You don't have to hit me. I'm too old for you to hit me. I hate when you hit me." And he cried, his head in his hands, his arms on his knees, and he cried.

Isaac sat down on the couch beside the child. He grasped Jack's head and pulled him from his fetal pain and cradled his reddened cheek to his chest.

"It's okay, it will be all right. You'll see. You'll see. I'll tell you a story."

Jack sobbed softly as Isaac spoke.

"Once upon a time there was a wise and wonderful king who ruled over a poor country with justice and compassion. In order to do this, he had to understand the lives of his people. And they loved him, though they really didn't understand what made them rich or poor or happy or sad".

"The king had a daughter, a lovely princess. And when she was old enough, he sent her to live among the common people. She lived in the small villages and everyone knew that she was the princess and came to love her. And in her life in the village, she came to know each of the people. And she loved them for their strengths in the face of adversity and for their foibles. Every day she learned more about them and grew wiser and wiser. She came to understand when they hurt and when they were angry. Though she was never one of them, she knew them all so well".

"One day the great king summoned her back to the castle. She was sad to leave her people in the village - so sad, because she truly loved them. But her father, in his wisdom, explained to her that now she must learn the principles by which the kingdom was ruled and then with her knowledge of the people of the village and her love for them, she would be able to assist him in ruling the kingdom wisely and she would be a guardian for her people."

"The folk in the village felt lost without their beloved princess. She had brought them so much beauty and joy and they could only experience the sense of loss. They cried for her and never understood that she served them still and loved them still and was always with them. And their lives were richer for her being among them than they would ever be had she not come and lived with them and finally left. But she was with them always."

He trailed off.

Jack lifted his head from off of Isaac's chest and gently took his hands off. His eyes matched the red mark of the hand on his cheek as he turned to the small Cossack and said, "You know, you old goat, sometimes your stories just don't work." And he smiled a wry smile.

Isaac shrugged sheepishly. "Sometimes that's all I have, you know."

"I know. I know." And Jack cried again.

After a few minutes Jack blew his nose and said, "I've got to get back. Rae will wonder what happened to me."

"Wait just a second and I'll come with you," said the small man who also wore red eyes. "Perhaps you'd like me to come in with you to talk to Rae?"

"No, thanks."

The two donned coats and walked out the door and down the street.

"Jack," Isaac began, his words arriving at half-cadence with their hurried steps. "Jack, there's a prayer for the sick. It's usually said in temple over the Torah. I think it would be all right for me to say it myself for Rae. I can teach it to you in a few minutes' time if you want to say it."

"Thanks, Isaac. That'll help. I haven't got much else right now."

"Jack, the one thing that Rae doesn't need is to think that you're going to come apart and not be able to take care of the kids and yourself. You know?"

"Yeah, you're right. Can't let her think that, can we?"

"Jack! You can pray, Jack. Lots of times that's all we have."

"Yeah."

They were at the door of the small green house. Nothing more was said. Isaac gently put his arms around Jack and held him for a moment. It was not an easy, relaxed hug. It was stiff and formal. Everything was now said.

Jack went in by himself and snapped off the porch light as he entered. He dropped his coat unceremoniously on the couch and went directly to the bedroom where he had left Rae. She hadn't moved since he had left.

"Jack, you schmuck," she began, "You forgot the dogs."

CHAPTER 21

A very pregnant woman with a bare patch over her right temple walked into the family room. "Do you worry that I'm dead?"

"No, of course not."

"Why not?"

"Because you interrupted me to ask. That's a sure sign that you're not dead."

"I want a motorcycle."

"Of course, Rae. Every pregnant woman wants a motorcycle. What took you so long to ask?"

"I want it for this spring. I gotta learn to ride."

"Is there a particular reason for this immediate need for a motorcycle?"

"Yeah. I want a big black motorcycle and a black leather jacket and on the back of the jacket I want 'Born to Fuck'."

"Well that's a perfectly normal request. I'll watch our children while you ride around on your big black motorcycle with that feminine jacket and that's because . . . ?"

"Because I want to see the look on some trucker's face when he pulls up behind me on that bike with that jacket and realizes that it's somebody's mother."

"Most amusing. I'll put a big black motorcycle on your birthday gift list along with the leather jacket. You can have the lettering put on yourself." She waddled back to the kitchen.

Night came and Jack never knew quite what it would bring. Rae was healing from the surgery and the headaches seemed to have diminished. As January wore on, they reassembled their lives, he about his work and her about house and children. She no longer worked on the psychiatric unit; he spent more time at home. Approaches to her had to be cautious. At times she was more the loving mother that she had always been - gentle, soft, strong. At times her responses became unpredictable. A request from one of the kids might bring her to fulsome tears. A tired whine might produce unrestrained rage. The children became wary. They came more often to Jack.

Lee confronted, "What's wrong with Mom? She yells at us and she cries a lot even when we didn't do anything."

"Mom's pregnant, Lee. And sometimes that makes her feel a little sick - not real sick, mind you. Just a little."

"I don't like it. I want her to get better."

"Oh, she will. I promise. She'll have this baby and we'll all be happy again." He couldn't stomach his own distress. His breath was heavy in his chest, he had piercing headaches, he didn't sleep and he, himself, was irritable. But he would not permit his children to lose two parents.

The hordes migrated back to Bloomington. At the end of the first week, Jack went into the office to find a smiling Ilene Mariko-Dunphy waiting for him.

"Hey, Boss. You look awful."

"Don't call me that. I am awful."

"Want to talk?"

"No, I don't want to talk. I hate to talk and besides no one, that's no one, no one ever, ever, ever listens."

"Good attitude. Do you want me to go away, sit here silently while you suffer in the next room or do you want to talk?"

"Rae's got a malignant brain tumor. She won't let them treat it until she's delivered the baby. It's touch and go. We're losing critical treatment time, but she won't budge. I just don't know what to do."

"Oh, Doc. I am sorry." And Ilene Mariko-Dunphy, controlled, acerbic, unemotional, wiped her eyes, blew her nose, and came out from behind her desk and put her hand on Jack's shoulder.

Jack wiped his own eyes and turned to find Rhonda Dorfman in the doorway.

"May I come in?"

"Rhonda, of course. Good to see you."

Rhonda Dorfman was the color of her gray dress and the gray walls which surrounded her. The only color to her was the black under her eyes. She carried a small cup of water and looked as though she had ceased eating weeks past.

"Can we talk in your office?"

"Why yes, how're you doing?"

"Oh, I'm sure you know. Absolutely everybody at this university, everybody in this town knows that Phil left me. Not only that, but it seems that everybody in this town knew that he was involved with one of his graduate students except me - and that he'd done this before. Makes me look pretty foolish, doesn't it?"

"Oh, Rhonda, I'm so very sorry. Rhonda, you don't deserve this."

"That's not what Phil says, Jack. He says that our marriage was dead for years and that I was simply not interesting and exciting to be with anymore, that I had forgotten what marriage was all about." She began to cry. Jack reached for the box of tissues which he kept in his desk drawer. It was called the F-box, handed to students who had failed his course and came to shed tears for extra credit.

"I'm sorry. I'm actually doing well. I'm on Elevil for depression. It makes me thirsty all the time but at least I can function. Look, this isn't what I came to talk to you about. When I went into the hospital - I assume you know that I was in the hospital - Rae was there. She wasn't my nurse, but she was there for me. She was the one that I didn't have to talk to but who made me feel that I had a friend there and not just a team of nurses and doctors."

"Rae never said anything," he lied.

"The irony is that she knew what kind of person Phil was from the first moment and I, who'd been married to him for twenty-seven years, really didn't catch on. He made me a laughingstock, Jack. For all the anger inside of me, that's the part that hurts worst, knowing that all those other people knew, and I didn't"

Jack had very little to say but needed to do nothing but nod sympathetically.

"The Rabbi said a prayer at services for Rae. I asked him about it, and he said that she'd had surgery and was recuperating. Jack, she's pregnant. Is everything all right?"

How do the terminally ill ask help of the mortally wounded? Where is it written that no matter how great your suffering, you have the right to demand sympathy from those who suffer also? Those that are well, are too busy to listen, the ill, too weak to attend. To whom can one turn in acute pain if not those who are also in pain and those who are not in pain? One turns to those paid to listen to pain: psychiatrists, social workers, counselors, and, of course, rabbis.

"It'll be fine Rhonda. It'll just take some time. We're going to have a fine baby, and everything will be all right. And Rhonda, I know how much you hurt right now, but my dear, this pain will go away and you will have a new life and it will be a good life."

She rose with a weak smile and hugged Jack a genuine hug before she walked out the door, just a little straighter than she had come in.

"Liar!" Ilene muttered.

"Ilene's taking a couple of days off to go to a conference in Chicago. And Dunphy's running the data from our clinic interviews. I need to get in a little early tomorrow to cover the bases. I can drop the kids off on my way in. Will you be all right?"

"How could I be better?" Rae replied.

"I'll probably work with Dunphy over the noon hour. If you need me, I can dash home."

"I'll be fine. I have two canine companions and a kicking fetus. With all the conversation, I'll be busy all day."

Dunphy loomed in the door, reams of computer print-out in his arms. Unceremoniously he occupied Ilene's desk, which was the only clear surface in the office. He wore a wool plaid jacket and a leather cowboy hat, jeans and a turtleneck shirt. His boots had clearly seen duty in a cow pasture over the weeks of vacation.

"Well, the little woman's gone, so I guess I might as well work for you instead of her for a couple days. Got the first runs off the data and it looks pretty good. Wanna look?"

"After spending eighty thousand dollars to get this data, I'd have to say 'yes'."

"Well, take a look here. We have interviews with over three hundred patients. Got Israel Social Networks Inventories on almost all of them. Scanned their medical records and have a bunch of social psychological scales on them. Your graduate student elves did a fine job, Santa Claus."

"What did we find?"

"First of all, we have no differences in the data between Cook County and Chicago Jewish. The populations are similar for age, gender, reimbursement - everything is close enough that we can combine the samples and treat them as one."

"Great, get to the good stuff."

"We get a nice normal distribution on the size of their social networks and the amount of support they get from these networks. So far, so good. But when we look for an association between the size of networks and amount of support and the intensity of their high blood pressure, it's not there. Looking at these data, we cannot prove that the more support they have, the lower their blood pressure. Doesn't work."

"So far, we've wasted eighty thousand dollars of grant money - most of it on you and Ilene. What else?"

"Here's where it gets good. There's a lot of variation in their compliance with their treatment plan. The best indicator is whether they make their appointments or not. And there we find that people who have larger social networks and more support are good about making it to their appointments. But the smaller their networks, the less likely they are to get to their appointments, the more likely that they'll be no-shows."

"What do you make of it?"

"Well, could be a couple of things, Boss. For one, it may just mean that people with bigger networks and more support have an easier time getting rides, getting someone to watch the kids, or just getting someone to come with them. Could be that simple. But it could mean something else. Could mean that people who aren't connected to other people, just don't . . . well, they just don't function as well. They can't move; they can't behave; they're isolated and alone and they can't deal with the pressures, you know?"

"Can we test that out?"

"Sure, Boss, with another grant we can design a study and find that out for you. I'm gonna need support myself, you know."

It was the end of January. Rae must have been sleeping in the day because her nighttime sleep was sporadic. Jack would wake in the night to find her side of the bed empty, cold. He would find her wandering the house aimlessly. At bedtime she was often awake and alert.

The weather had warmed uncharacteristically. It was near fifty degrees. Just before ten in the evening, there was a familiar rap at the door. The dogs, now so accustomed to their neighborly companion walked toward the door. But tonight, they had competition to get there. Rae raced to the door. Jack and dogs followed. She turned to him and said plainly, "Beat it. I'll walk the dogs."

"What if I want to?"

"Beat it!" and she slipped into the parka which he held in his hand, shackled the dogs and went out to meet Isaac.

They were gone. It was a long walk. The air was fresh, humid, and warm. It made no sense for Rae to be out. Though this was not her way, he no longer recognized what was her way and what was not. He didn't know any more what was Rae and what was symptoms. What was her? What was disease? What was her response to disease? Dunphy said that people without social networks and support didn't function, didn't behave. Had Jack brought Rae to a place where she had no friends, no support, and where she had become someone that he didn't know? He had all the education in such things that a man could get, a Ph.D., a post-doctoral fellowship, his own research. But like so many well-educated people, he had no answers.

He had Dunphy and Ilene in his life, and Myron Tabanov, and, of course, Isaac. Not a large coterie, but he had always been an isolated person. Rae had been his soulmate and he tested his realities at home with her. He could survive. But she had only him and her family hours away. She had Leyla. But Leyla herself was losing her most vital connection.

How many people does it take to help one person survive? When life is easy, perhaps none at all. For some even when life is easy, the prospect of loneliness is itself too great a burden to bear. When life is hard and one is alone, the loneliness overwhelms. It exacerbates; it compounds, convolutes and leaves one helpless. Dunphy had numbers to prove it. People couldn't manage their illnesses. They lost the will to come get care. They waited. And Jack now understood. Waiting is dying. And Rae was waiting. And he was waiting. And they could not wait.

Jack stood out on the concrete slab that substituted for a porch. He searched the darkness for four familiar forms. In the dim, he made them out, walking so very slowly, the Cossack holding two leashes, Rae leaning on his arm.

"Jack, can we talk for a few minutes?"

"Of course, come on in. Thank you for walking the dogs. This is a real breakthrough for you."

"No, for them. They finally learned to accept me for what I am."

Rae handed Jack his coat and saying nothing retreated to the bedroom. She gave Isaac no particular "good night," not even a pat to the dogs. She just left. Isaac chuffed and dropped into a chair in the living room. Both dogs fell at his feet. He looked down at them and laughed.

"So, I have a favor to ask you."

Jack expected a review of Isaac's conversation with Rae. But that wasn't on the Rabbi's agenda.

"Sure, what do you need?"

"You remember that incident at the school with Matt Cowan?"

"Yes, sure."

"Well you know he was charged with a whole bunch of felonies: assault, assault and battery, assault with a deadly weapon, mayhem, God knows what. The district attorney has a bunch of charges and there's a hearing this week, Friday. Nine o'clock. At the courthouse. Judge McInerny. You know her?"

"I think I used to date her sister. Go on. I think this isn't going to be pretty. In fact, I bet Judge McInerny isn't very pretty either."

"Well, here it is. There's a hearing. As I understand it, the judge will determine if Matt is to be tried as a juvenile or an adult. If she decides that he's a juvenile, she can ask him for a plea and perhaps dispose of it right then. If she says he has to be tried as an adult, then he can either plead and if he pleads not guilty, she has to order a jury trial."

"From me you want what?"

"Well, his mother has too much money for a court-appointed attorney and not enough for a real attorney, so he has no attorney. I was hoping that if you and I came along as, kind of character witnesses, that we could get the judge to try him as a juvenile and give him a suspended sentence or something like that."

"My friend, a person who goes before the judge without a lawyer has a fool for an advocate. This is not a good idea."

"I agree. It's not a good idea. But what else can we do? Will you come and speak for him?"

"Did I mention that I don't have enough troubles of my own these days?"

"So, you'll come."

Jack had every intention of sharing Friday's courtroom festivities with Dunphy. He seemed to have bonded with Matt and would be good company. On Tuesday, Dunphy didn't appear. Jack assumed more data runs. On Wednesday at mid-morning the cowherd appeared, obviously in distress. He hadn't shaved and even at this hour he breathed a fog of stale beer. His clothes had been slept in.

"Hey! Are you OK? You look terrible. Something wrong?"

"Oh, no. The usual. Ilene called Monday night. Said she'd been in a hotel room all weekend with some guy she found at this meeting in Chicago. Said she wasn't comin' home. Told me to be away from the house today so she could come get her things and leave her key behind."

"Oh, Dunphy. I can't believe that! Did she say why? Did she give you any reason?"

"Well, Boss, it wasn't a long conversation. But she said I was a great guy and she'd always love me, but that she wasn't havin' much of a life with me and didn't think she ever would. And she just had to get out, that's all."

"Dunphy, I am so sorry. Is there anything I can do?"

Dunphy wasn't drunk. Neither was he sober. He was in that place where one has enough alcohol to loosen the strictures of communication and goes on to say what one otherwise one cannot say. It helps a great deal if the partner to the conversation has also had something to drink. Drink sharpens the tongue and dulls the memory. People can say what is otherwise beyond them to say and no one then remembers. Jack had not been drinking.

"Hey, Boss. I know about Rae, ya know? I know about the brain tumor and all. Ya know? And here you are thinkin' what a shit I am cuz I never said anything to you about it. Well, Boss, ya gotta know why. See, you been like a father to me. And in a way, Rae's kinda been like a mother. And I tol' you, my Ma died of cancer. She died of a brain tumor, Boss. And Bernie and me, we just hung on to each other so tight 'cuz if we didn't, we woulda died ourselves. I'm sorry, Boss, I just can't go through all this again, ya know? I just couldn't say anything."

Jack hurt deep inside. He was struggling desperately to contain his own pain and it took all his strength. He was devoted to Dunphy, but it was like talking with Rhonda. How do the terminally ill ask help of the mortally wounded? How many times could he spend his own spare reserves and still survive?

"What are you going to do, Pat?"

"Well, I tried begging and that didn't work. I'm gonna find a friendly tavern and spend the rest of the day there among the kindly customers keepin' the bartender busy while she skips town. Ya understan'? Then I'm gonna go home and sleep for a couple days. Then I'm gonna come in here and finish a final report for Morton. You with me? And then, my brilliant friend and mentor, I'm gonna pack up the Camaro and go back to Bernie and the cows in Dodgeville. I'm done, Boss."

"Okay, Pat. You get today to drink. You get tomorrow to sober up. Friday, I need you in court at nine o'clock sharp."

"What are you talkin' about?"

"Your little friend Matt Cowan is in front of the judge and you are to be there for support. Got it?"

"What does this have to do with me?"

"I have only a few days left to teach you, my friend. And one of the things that I have to teach you is that when you hurt so bad that you just want to die, that's the time that you have to give whatever you have to someone else that needs you.

That's the cure, Patrick, and you will be there if I have to drag you out of the drunk tank."

CHAPTER 22

Bailiffs come in two flavors - only two: Barrel chested, and portly. You don't get to choose. This one was barrel chested. Bailiffs are most often political appointees. They are the Highland Guards of every court in the country, there to offer an illusion of military authority when, in fact, all they do well is stand and demand that others stand.

"All rise for the Honorable Judge McInerney."

All stood: Matt, his mother, Kate Cowan, Isaac, Jack, Dunphy, Officer Haddack, and a similar array of families, attorneys, defendants, girlfriends, and, to Isaac's pleasure, two other clergy from around town. Far in the rear were three observers. Lev, Sage, and Merrill occupied the final row of the courtroom. Kate Cowan wore the facial lines of a woman who had tanned too often and smoked too much. She wore her hair tied back with a banana clip to hold it in place. Her blouse was bleached to snowy whiteness and her collar was frayed. Her skirt was two inches too high for her age and the occasion and she wore calf-length boots. Once upon a time she had been very pretty, and she wanted to be pretty again. But the old ways of being pretty didn't work for her now and she became odd instead.

Matt wore an indelible grin. After a lifetime of sitting in the back of the room, his was the main event. He was dressed in a white shirt and slender blue tie which he had not tied himself. Under his pressed khakis was a pair of worn army boots. He wore no suit jacket and moved visibly in his seat as if to music that only he heard.

In the row behind sat Isaac, Jack, and Dunphy. Isaac was busy acknowledging his clerical colleagues in the rows immediately behind. Each accompanied a family member more than a defendant. Isaac was clerical — dark suit, white shirt, modest tie, black shoes. Jack was academic - wool sweater over a long-sleeved shirt and Weejuns. Dunphy wore a headache and a heart full of sorrow. These showed far more visibly than his jeans and cowboy boots.

Judge McInerny had perfected solemnity. She smiled at no one. There was no evidence of any color other than black about her. She nodded to the bailiff as she took her seat on the bench and her loyal grenadier intoned, "You may be seated."

Matt was the first case called by the bailiff. "Matthew Cowan, please come forward."

Matt rose with a stupid grin on his face and, as directed by the bailiff, entered the inner sanctum of the court before the judge. His team of expert legal defenders, one rabbi, one professor, a worried mother, and a cowherd, attempted to follow but were restrained by the bailiff. Jack signaled that he needed to be beside Matt and the bailiff acquiesced.

"Are you Matthew Cowan?" asked the judge.

"Yes, Ma'am," he grinned through exposed teeth.

Jack whispered, "I think you're supposed to call her 'Your Honor.'"

"Oh," he whispered back, "That's me, Your Honor, Ma'am. And I got a Hebrew name too -"

Jack grabbed his arm, "Not now. You can tell her some other time."

"Bailiff, will you read the charges please?"

"Yes, Your Honor. Defendant is accused of assault, assault and battery, assault with a deadly weapon and mayhem, your honor."

"Mr. Cowan - Matthew, do you understand these charges?"

"Yes Ma'am, Your Honor."

"How old were you when the events which led to these charges took place."

"Uh, I guess I was seventeen, Your Honor, Ma'am."

"Cut the Ma'am, Matt," Jack implored.

"And how old are you now?"

"Just turned eighteen, Ma' - Your Honor."

"The court must decide, Matthew, if you are to be tried as a juvenile or an adult. Do you understand that?"

"Yes, Ma' - Your Honor."

"I have read the juvenile officer's report on this incident and on you, Matthew, and Officer Haddack has recommended that the court deal with this as a juvenile matter. However, if you prefer, you may ask to be tried as an adult. The difference, Matthew, is that if you are tried as a juvenile, you will appear before me in an informal hearing. In fact, given the thorough nature of the juvenile officer's report, we can dispose of this matter this morning. Should you wish to be tried as an adult, you may choose to be heard before a judge, or, should you plead 'not guilty' before a jury. Do you understand what I am saying?"

"I, uh, think so . . . Your Honor."

"Do you have counsel, Matthew?"

"What's that?"

"An attorney, Matthew."

"No Ma'am, I don't need an attorney - I mean, Your Honor. I'm cool about all this."

"Do you have a decision as to whether you wish to appear as a juvenile or an adult?"

"Oh, yeah. I'm a . . . juvenile, your honor."

"Who are these people with you, Matthew?"

"Hey, that's my Ma back there. And this is my Rabbi. And this is, uh, a friend, Doc Israel, and his boss, Dunphy. And I got some friends in the back."

Jack cast the kind of look at Dunphy that raises welts. Dunphy, for the first time in days, relinquished his agony and laughed. Isaac looked quizzically at both as the judge intoned, "We'll take a short recess while we move this case to chambers for consideration."

"All rise," croaked the bailiff and the case was removed to chambers.

Chambers is not an amphitheater; it is an office. It is a secure sanctuary where a judge, a public servant constantly subject to public scrutiny, can be private. There she can exercise all the emotions which are not permissible on the bench. It is a place to be angry, to be petulant, to laugh, perhaps even to cry, to be human within the limits of the law.

Matt's entire entourage clambered for space in chambers - Isaac, Jack, Kate Cowan, Dunphy, Lev, Sage, and Merrill. The bailiff in a rare moment of usefulness stopped the platoon in mid-charge and admonished, "Now who really needs to be in there with the judge?" Isaac, Jack, and Kate indicated their precedence over the ragtag assemblage and Dunphy retreated with a troop of disappointed cub scouts behind him to wait in the courtroom.

Judge McInerny seated herself behind a mahogany desk in a reclining leather chair. Office Haddack was already in the room, standing to her side. There were three leather armchairs in front of the desk and the bailiff carried in a fourth chair to accommodate.

"All right, Matt, can you tell me what this is all about?"

"Yes, your honor. See there's a lot of trouble at school. You know there are a lot of African American kids that are new to the high school. Like, they moved here from Chicago and Gary and places like that. And they're real tough kids, you know? And they got a gang and all. You know, they wear gang colors and they hang together and they're like real tough, except when you face 'em down mano a mano, you know? And they push the little guys around, Your Honor. You see those kids in the back of the courtroom, your honor? Well those two Jew boys and that . . . African American kid, they got pushed plenty hard by those gangbangers. Well I can't stand around and let people get pushed around by bullies, Your Honor. My father is in the US Air Force and I know what it means to defend freedom. And I'm gonna become Jew myself and I'm learnin' about freedom from slavery and fightin' against bein' oppressed. I came out of school and saw a bunch of these gang bangers beating on some really good kids and it wasn't a fair fight. Now, I got training in martial arts, and I was on my way to karate class, so I had my kung fu sticks with me and it was time to teach those guys a lesson. And I didn't mean to hurt no one. I really didn't. But I did what was right and I'll stand by it. I'm sorry if people got hurt. I really am. But I don't regret what I did."

Judge McInerny had spent years listening to the Matt Cowans of the world. She had heard stories of getting drunk and disorderly, of beatings and speeding and petty theft and grand larceny. She looked into the eyes in her chambers, Officer Haddack, Kate Cowan, Isaac, Jack - there was not a simple emotion to be seen. It was layers and layers of feelings. How could he be so naive? How could he be so brave? How dare he be so honest? How dare he be so dumb?

"Matthew, these are serious charges against you. You must enter a plea with regard to these charges. You may plead 'not guilty'; you may plead 'guilty'; or you may enter a plea which says that you do not wish to contest the charges but to enter your story before the court. Do you understand, and if so, what plea should the clerk enter for you?"

Jack nudged Matt hard and whispered loud enough for all to hear, "I don't wish to contest the charges."

Matt responded with, "Yeah, that's what I want."

"Officer Haddack's report indicates that you plan to enlist in the Air Force upon graduation from high school. Is that correct?"

"Yes, Your Honor."

"If you are found guilty as charged in this matter, you know that you will not be eligible for enlistment?"

"No. I didn't know that. Oh, please, don't do that. I want to go into the Air Force."

Matt shook his head in fear and disbelief.

"Can this court be assured that an episode like this will never happen again, Matt?"

"Oh, yeah, Your Honor."

"Matt, this court finds you guilty as charged in this case but will reserve judgement on this case until three months after your high school graduation. Should you graduate successfully and with no further problems in your behavior - no arrests - and should you enlist in the Air Force, I will vacate these findings and your record will be clean. Do you understand what I am saying?"

"Yes, Ma'am - Your Honor."

"Matt, you have broken the law and I cannot condone that. But I am sure that you have learned something important and that you will make a fine member of the Air Force. You may go now."

"OK, Boss. It's Friday and I done my duty to your boy. I'm gonna finish up the data for the research today and tomorrow and pack on Sunday. After that, I'm gone. Gonna find a new life."

"Any word from Ilene?"

"Word? Naw! But I woke up under my car on Thursday morning - remember Thursday morning? It was damned cold there on the ground. But I guess I had enough anti-freeze in me to keep me alive. Had a hell of a time finding my glasses. And I went home to clean up, and the door was unlocked. So, I go in and the place was neat as a pin and on the kitchen table was a red rose in a vase. That's all, Boss: One single red rose."

"Patrick, my lad, there's a message there. She does love you, Pat. Really she does. But she has her own . . . her own . . . well, I guess you could call them demons. She has her own problems that have nothing to do with you. They existed in her life long before she found you at the Humane Society. It's not you, little brother; it's all inside of her. And the hardest part to understand is that in a lot of ways she left in order to protect you from her demons."

"I could have helped, Boss."

"No, you couldn't. This is something that she has to work out for herself and this is the only way that she can do it. And all you can do is let go and take some time to heal. Life is losses. Without losses we're empty. With losses we reflect, and we grow and become more than who we were. Take the pain, stay away from the bottle, go breathe some fresh air, talk to the cows and let time heal. You have no other choice, Pat."

Dunphy's eyes watered noticeably. He took a red bandana from his pocket, one that needed an appointment with a washing machine, and blew his nose. He reddened, took off his glasses and threw himself around Jack.

"Oh, for God's sake stop it! Don't you dare get sentimental on me after all the crap you've handed me."

"Thanks for everything, Boss. If you need me, I'll be at Bernie's."

Small town newspapers create chaos. While big city rags bury the news of your neighbors where you can't find it and can't act on it, small town papers build circulation on police reports, divorces, and petty thefts. Matthew Cowan had been in the papers at the time of his arrest. His high school picture had appeared along with the minor headline: High School Senior Arrested in Wild Melee. Worse, when the local reporter had seen his own name as a by-line under such a story, he followed a blood trail that he couldn't abandon. Thus, it was that the Saturday Courier carried a second page item that was headlined: Cowan Guilty on All Charges. The accuracy of the headline was subverted by the article: "In a hearing in her chambers, Judge Sheila McInerny found Matthew Cowan guilty of charges of assault, assault with a deadly weapon, and mayhem. She has postponed sentencing until after the defendant graduates high school. McInerny proposed that her judgement would be vacated if Cowan, who is no longer a juvenile, successfully enlists in the US Air Force. School authorities refused to comment."

Without Ilene to protect him Jack was forced to answer his own phone. This gave him no boundary within which to hide. It is the bad dream of every academic - to have no protection from intruders: Students, graduate assistants, and worst of all, fellow faculty. These latter underemployed individuals have an endless capacity for intrigue which absorbs only perhaps fifty percent of the academic day. The topics for conversation are without limit and, in fact, are irrelevant. This is what is valued in the academy as "the free exchange of ideas".

The phone rang and Jack foolishly answered.

"Jack, this is Phil Dorfman. I need to talk to you. May I come over?"

"Uh . . . Phil. Well . . . yes, of course." It was not in his interests to deny permission. His personal feelings were irrelevant to the demand of a senior colleague for face time.

Phil strode purposefully down the hall. He was average in height and had earned the slender, athletic build of a man who has discovered his body later in life. The price that these late-blooming athletes pay is the sagging skin on face and neck that are the old evidence of a fleshier time. Phil's smile spread across his face in a way that only showed the wrinkles all the more. He thrust a boney hand at Jack for a hearty handshake that Jack couldn't avoid, but which made him feel guilty. Days before, Rhonda had stood in the office washing down Elevil with tepid water.

"Jack, I need to talk to you."

"About?"

"Well, it's about your friend, Isaac, the Rabbi." Spoken as if there were a surfeit of Isaacs in Jack's life.

"What about him?"

"It's obvious that he's a good friend of yours. And that's great. He needs all the friends he can get. I don't mean that as criticism. You know, when you're the only Rabbi in town, you just don't have a lot people to talk to. And you're Jewish, so you understand one another, but you don't officially belong to the congregation, so you're not involved in any way in decision making. That makes you very valuable to him. And that also means that you're in a position to do him a big favor."

"Oh?"

"Oh! Look Jack, he's announced to the congregation that there'll be a bar mitzvah coming up in a few weeks. Now get this. He announced that we were all invited to celebrate the bar mitzvah of Matt Cowan! Jack, this kid is as Jewish as Mahatma Ghandi and is a convicted felon! He has no Hebrew school training and he is an ignoramus. Isaac has truly overreached his authority on this one and the congregation is very upset."

"Matt Cowan considers himself a Jew. His father is a Jew. He's been studying with Isaac. I'm no authority, but I don't see what the problem is."

"The problem is that Isaac is not the best rabbi for this congregation. He's a storyteller and not a rabbi. His head is lost somewhere back in the old country. And he insists on acting like he's in charge of things at the synagogue which he is not in charge of - like determining whether this kid is eligible for a bar mitzvah, which he is not!"

"What do you want me to do about this, Phil."

"You can do Isaac a big favor, and yourself at the same time. Bud Blumberg is online with this and a few other very important people. Just take Isaac aside and explain to him diplomatically that if this bar mitzvah occurs, it will make it much less likely that his contract will be renewed for next year. This has to stop."

"Phil, you said, if I heard right, that it will be much less likely that his contract will be renewed. Does that mean that if he cancels the bar mitzvah that his contract will definitely be renewed or that it may still not be renewed?"

"I'm just one member of the board, Jack, and that's not my decision alone. I can't say anything other than that this bar mitzvah would hurt his chances. Now, can I rely on you to do Isaac and the synagogue a favor and deliver a subtle message?"

"Subtlety has no place here, Phil. It's a threat, pure and simple. You're just asking me to deliver the kiss on both cheeks that you're not willing to deliver. I'm supposed to warn Vito that the Godfather is pouring cement slippers for him."

"That's a little crude, Jack."

"Crude? Crude? You have the gall to use the term shiksah in front of my wife, to trash Rhonda in full view of the campus community, to assassinate the rabbi, to hijack a joyous event for a young man who wants only to become Jewish and then to tell me that I'm a little crude? Phil, were you ever a decent human being? For all your pose of piety and all your self-importance around the university I happen to think that you're not a very nice man. Will I speak to my dear friend and warn him about the Brutus in the Senate? About the stab that's imminent? You bet I will. Would I do the same for you? No way. Out of my office, please."

Jack stopped by the university library on his way home to look through the employment pages of the Chronicle of Higher Education.

Just after dinner Jack picked up the phone to dial Isaac's phone. After one quarter ring a youthful voice picked up. "Hello Lev or Sage, this is Jack Israel around the corner calling."

"Hey, Professor. That was great on Friday. It got passed around school instantly. The gang bangers were pissed. They were sure that Matt was off to jail. Oh, and this is Lev."

"Hi Lev. I refer to the two of you in one word, Levsage. Is the good Rabbi in?"

"Just got here. I'll get him."

"Jack, you just caught me. I had a meeting tonight."

"Let's go for a walk -- now."

"Jack, I just got in and I need a while to collect myself."

"We need to go for a walk. Now!"

"Okay, okay. Give me a few minutes and I'll come over."

Jack called to Rae in the family room, "Hey Love, I'm going out with my three walking companions a little early. Can you manage the chaos for a while without me?"

"Jack, I manage this chaos without you all the time. Sometimes you are the chaos. Take your dogs and leave us in peace." There was no lightness in the words, no hint of humor, no tones of love layered with laughter. It was like being cut while shaving, first the small bite and then the trickle of blood, all unintended, all sure to heal, but an abrupt indication of vulnerability, nonetheless.

He shackled the dogs and headed for the corner to wait for his friend. The earth was just beginning to warm during the days. The snow had melted leaving farmers' fields of stubble anxious to collect and store the spring rains. This was good earth. Jack would put in a garden in the spring, perhaps a pear tree in the back yard. The great migration from Milwaukee was done. He was in his new surroundings. His life with Rae was suddenly tortured. Now he stood on a dark street corner in a place no longer strange and didn't dare to predict what the months ahead might bring.

He had run from Milwaukee and to Bloomington. He had run for career, for job, for the salvation of his own self-respect and he had found it. Now it was time to calculate the cost. He could stay for five years in hopes that the Phil Dorfmans of Bloomington would leave him be. Or he could run. From? To? He no longer knew. Rae could no longer run with him. This he understood. She understood as well. Now they waited. Now he stood on the corner and waited.

Isaac ambled down the street, slower than usual but still with his rocking gait. The dogs rose at his approach in tail-wagging greeting. If he had won no other female hearts in Bloomington, these were his.

"Is everything all right?" he inquired.

"No. In fact, my dear Rabbi. Nothing is all right. I had a surprise visit from your dear friend Phil Dorfman, whom you allege is not evil. And he asked me to deliver a very direct message to you. It was something to the effect that if you bar mitzvah that convicted felon and would-be Jew-boy, Matt Cowan, he will agitate against the renewal of your contract.

And what's more, even if you cave in and cancel said bar mitzvah, that's no guarantee that your contract will be renewed. Not only that, but he has a fair amount of power to see to it that I never make it past third year review at Bloomington State and get handed my walking papers. Sorry, Kimosabe, but we are surrounded."

"Is that a Japanese word? Kimosabe?"

"No, it is not a Japanese word! Have you no memory of the Lone Ranger and his faithful Native American, formerly Indian, companion, Tonto?"

"Did he write a tractate in the Talmud?"

"Have you heard anything I've said?"

"Sam Gartner came to see me today and told me all of this. I have some friends in the congregation. If I choose to fight, I can probably beat them. In fact, I don't think I even have to fight, I just have to stare them down."

"The fact is that you're calling for a face off over a kid who, I hate to say this, is never going to be a great credit to the Jewish people."

"Jack, Jack. Let me tell you a story."

"Isaac!"

"No, Jack. Listen. One upon a time there was a shepherd and he found a protected little place to graze his sheep. But there was a problem. A huge deer came down to the pasture and grazed among the sheep. Now this was a big animal and the shepherd was . . . uncomfortable with this strange beast among his sheep. And he wanted to get rid of him. He went to the great sage and told him the problem and the great sage said, 'Welcome the deer among the sheep because he has chosen to be among the flock, the sheep have not.' You understand, Jack?"

"I get the idea, Isaac. I'm not supposed worry about your livelihood. Now, I just have to worry about mine."

"Jack, let's walk a little - but slow tonight." And they began the walk of two men who are ready to welcome spring into their lives, who need spring in their lives, who have endured a long, hard winter and are ready for renewal, even when renewal is slow to come.

"I'm tired, Jack. I thought this was the place that I would retire from. The boys will be gone very soon, and I'll be alone. Much as I like looking at the co-eds on campus, for whatever reason they aren't interested in a fifty-year-old refugee. I don't know why. I'm handsome, charming, intelligent. What more could a twenty-something year old beauty queen want? I'm lonely now and when the boys leave, I'll be lonelier. I can't be Isaac in this town because to every Jew for fifty miles, I'm the Rabbi. This doesn't work. And if they want to force me out, maybe it's for the best. Do you know that everything happens as it's supposed to?"

"Bullshit!"

"No, Jack, there's a plan and we may not see it but it's there. One of the rabbis used to say 'zeh gam tov.' Do you know what that means?"

"Isaac, to whom do you think you're speaking? Phil Dorfman? No. I don't know what it means and even after you tell me, I have no faith that I'm going to agree. Phil's right about something, Isaac. All you have are your quaint stories. There's not a rational discourse behind them."

"Seeing as you have just demonstrated your profound ignorance, I'll translate and offer you a commentary. The phrase 'zeh gam tov' means 'this also is for the good' and it implies that God's plan is perfect, at least for God's purposes. Even though we can't know those purposes, we must believe that this is so if only so that we can survive and go on."

"Look, my esteemed friend, you are about to be run out of town on the Atcheson, the Topeka and the Santa Fe. I'm in danger of losing my job. My wife is terminally ill, and I don't know what I'm going to do about any of this. And you're telling me that this is all for the good?"

"Someday it may seem that way."

"Oy! And I can translate that Oy! for you if you like, but not in polite company."

It was not a long walk. Emotion became fatigue. Jack headed up Tamarack toward the house where all the lights were on. Through the door he heard crying coming from the boys' bedroom. Simmy rushed out at him. "Dad, come quick. Something's wrong. Dinah's on the floor all rolled up in ball and Mom won't talk to me."

Jack dashed past the boys' door. From within he could hear Lee sobbing. He went into the bedroom to find Rae on the bed, eyes rolled up in her head, thrashing. Dinah lay on the floor in fetal position, too frightened even to cry. "Simmy, I need you to help me and you need to follow my instructions carefully. Run as fast as you can to your school kit and get me your wooden ruler. Hurry."

He knelt over Rae and brushed the left side of her face. The flesh was flaccid, but he could feel her jaw tensed beneath his hand. "Rae, Honey, it's Jack. I'm here, Baby. Come back, Rae. Please come back. I can't live without you Rae."

Simmy came back with the ruler and Jack gently forced Rae's jaws apart to put the ruler between her teeth. He rolled the blanket over her and dashed to the phone where he dialed for the operator. "This is Jack Israel, 2105 Tamarack Court. My wife is having a seizure and I need an ambulance immediately. Please help."

The operator repeated the information and forwarded the call to the Bloomington Fire Department.

"Simmy, you did great. Now call this number - it's Rabbi Isaacs. Tell him we need someone to watch you guys pronto. OK?" Simmy dashed for the phone as Jack knelt down beside Dinah. "I'm here, Honey. Mom's going to be all right. It's all going to be OK." Dinah looked up at him in terror. Next, he dashed into the boy's room where Lee was under his covers weeping out of control.

"Lee, it's Dad. Mom's not feeling well but she's going to be fine. I have to take her to the hospital for a bit, but she'll be fine. I promise. Lev or Sage will come and watch you while I'm gone but I promise I won't be long. I need you and Simmy to take care of things here. OK?" Lee nodded through his tears as there was a banging on the door.

CHAPTER 23

"Best thing you can do is go home. We've got her sedated, the seizure is over. We'll admit her and keep her overnight. We've got a neuro consult on the way and you can come back and see her tomorrow morning. Nothing more to do here."

He was a resident in the emergency room. These are masters of the critical moment, experts in sustaining life when nothing else matters. They spend much of their time telling patients on Sunday night that they are ill-trained to manage a tooth ache that began on Friday and they should have seen a dentist. They see people in crisis whether that crisis is acute pain or the lack of any other practitioner who will see them. They work through the night without sleep and without complaint. They ask little. This young man was simply asking Jack to go home and let him tend to his patients.

Jack now knew all the best routes between the Creditor Clinic and home. It was three in the morning. He had left his children in the care of a neighbor and faced once again an empty bed. The last words from Rae still cut deep, "Sometimes you are the chaos. Take your dogs and leave us in peace." Was this the woman he loved speaking? Was it some woman who had had a piece of her brain dissected, the piece where words of love used to live? Was this a patient about to have a seizure spewing brain static beyond her control? Was this a terminally ill woman grieving for her own death, a mother beside herself with worry for her children?

Jack was cold in the cab of the truck. The heater didn't help. The cold came from within and the only force that could warm him was lying, sedated in a hospital bed. Lev was asleep on the couch. Dogs barely stirred at his entry. It was the frontier of night when being awake stirs fear. No one else exists and the blunt reality of the loneliness of being human strikes hard at the heart. Isaac was right. Dunphy was right. Loneliness is a kind of death.

Jack managed to shed the fatigue, feed breakfast, walk the dogs, and drop the kids. What he failed at was answering the questions. "Where's Mom? Is she all right? Is she coming home today?" He had no answers. Neither had he the stomach for lying to children.

"She's at the hospital. She'll be all right. I'm not sure, but I hope she'll be home tonight."

He didn't know what to believe. They didn't know what to believe. Children don't do well with doubt. They have little sense of subtlety. They rely on adults for certainty. Sometimes that certainty is itself a doubtful gift to give a child. There is an ultimate recrimination that lurks in the future: "You lied to us."

He found a florist just opening and managed a small bouquet. It was a delaying tactic. He didn't want to enter the Clinic. He had been there too often and for too long. He had familiar places where he felt safe - home, office, the streets of Southmoor. Now even these carried a vague sense of unease. Certainly, the Clinic was the house of dread.

Rae was holding court in her room. Around her stood Maria Acosta, Ian MacKenzie, and Gerald Byer. She was again gray, groggy, struggling to be in conversation.

"Well, Mister Issssrael! Gud marnin' to yuh. Looks like you and Rae here had a little advenshoor last night, eh?"

"You could call it that. Can you tell me what's happening?"

"We waar joost talkin' 'bout thet. Had the EEG techs here furst thing this marnin', we did. And we looked ovah the tracin's, we did. Looks to us like this lassie's got a sorta different kindah brain wave ovah her right froont lobe and ovah her tempooral lobe. Not a surprise, yah know. Dr. Byer here, he says as how that's the area he was workin'. What we got is a little distoorbence in the electrical activity of the brain and it soomtimes can set off a seizure or two."

"Or two? Did she have two? Or are you telling me that this is going to happen again."

Byer was no lover of understatement. "Mr. Israel, Rae now has a disrupted electrical field showing in her EEG. That indicates a likelihood of possible seizures in the future. We can medicate her to prevent those seizures, but frankly we've got a very complex case on our hands. We have the pregnancy to think about and the tumor activity. I've talked with Dr. Crane and we've lost some precious time in treating this aggressively."

"Jack," Maria Acosta pleaded, "we've all been very attentive to what Rae wants. And we're in no position to make decisions for Rae, but I think we have to at least schedule a delivery as soon as is possible - I mean, as soon as possible. We can manage a pre-term birth but we're taking some terrible risks with Rae if we put off cancer treatment any longer."

"Thank you everyone. Rae and I'll talk."

The array of expertise left to care for less complex lives than Rae Israel and her unborn child. Jack handed Rae the flowers. They looked at one another in silence for a moment. Simultaneously each began to cry. Tears can be criminal mischief. Just when you want to show calm control, they overwhelm. They come in quantifiable characteristics for size and shape and rate of flow. They redden the eyes, curl the curve of the mouth, cascade the face and sign to all that life is no longer understandable. Jack and Rae cried with one another and a kindly nurse swept shut the door.

"I want to see Isaac, Jack. Get him for me now."

"What for?"

"I've got business I have to take care of."

When someone asks for clergy, you need not ask why. It is the pastor who carries the balm of the soul and not the doctor. The doctor may treat the body, but he doesn't treat the soul. The body may heal. But if the soul isn't healed, the life that has been saved isn't worth living. Sometimes, just sometimes, healing the soul is enough to heal the body. Jack dialed Isaac's house and got no answer. He called the synagogue, got past the secretary and through to Isaac.

"Isaac, this is Jack Israel. Thank you for sending Lev last night. Rae's here at the Clinic and she needs to see you. Please."

Rae breathed a sigh of relief and turned back to Jack. "When he gets here, I need to be alone with him."

It took Isaac only half an hour to get to the Clinic. Jack sat by Rae's side. She was clearly exhausted physically and groggy from anti-seizure medications. Still, she talked in a somewhat slurred delivery. They spoke of nothing. It was the conversation of those who know inevitabilities but refuse to divulge them to one another. One is left wondering if they divulge them to themselves. She broke out of small talk.

"The medical team knows I'm dying. The nurses all know I'm dying. You know I'm dying. I know I'm dying. Why the fuck won't anyone talk to me about dying? Fer chrissake, Helaine Crane is my friggin' oncologist and she has patients dying on her every day. What is this, some kinda state secret? Why the hell can't we get real here?"

Jack, voluble, witty, intelligent Jack, who always had a fast reply, sat silent. What does one say to an unpleasant truth that carries future agony? The nostrums fill volumes: There's always hope; perhaps a new treatment; sometimes people survive; we can pray for a miracle. Sometimes it happens that way. When it does, it diminishes the lies that we tell one another.

Physicians and nurses work behind a veil. In front of patients and families they are positive, optimistic, hopeful. Behind the veil, amongst themselves, they are cold realists who entertain themselves with crude images and cutting humor: Mr. So-and-So is circling the drain. Someone needs to tell Mrs. Nobody not to buy any green bananas.

One professional lives on both sides of the veil at the same time: The clergy. They know and they accept the reality and pray with the plagued for an unreality.

He came off the elevator in a determined stride. Isaac knew the corridors of the Creditor Clinic. He had been on this errand many times before and he was a practiced professional about it. He nodded to nurses, especially the younger ones, left a deft knock on the door and came into Rae.

"Get out, Jack. I wanna talk to my main man here."

Jack retreated to the family waiting room. He hated it there. How long would this take? He was supposed to be worried about Rae. There was nothing more to worry about. He worried about Simmy. Simmy was smart, he was strong. He would survive. He worried about Lee. Lee was a middle child. He was introverted, sensitive, vulnerable. He had never built the bond with Jack that was born into Simmy. He was Rae's boy even as Dinah was her girl. How would Dinah survive? She had no understanding of this episode in her life. And in this mix, there would be another life to protect and Jack couldn't even imagine who that baby could become.

He waited an hour. An hour and a half. Isaac came out of Rae's room and into the waiting room.

"She needs to talk to you. It's important. I'll check on you tonight."

Rae sat up in bed. Somehow she looked better. The braced muscles of her shoulders had relaxed. Her face was calmer. But the clear tracks of tears showed on her face through a curious smile.

"Well at least somebody is willing to admit that I'm gonna die! Look, my hero, I got some things I gotta get done and I gotta get 'em done right now. Maria Acosta's gonna bust in here any minute with Helaine Crane and they're gonna have loaded guns. Maria's gonna want this baby outta me and Helaine's gonna want quarts of chemo into me. I gotta act fast."

"What do you need, Rae?"

"First of all, I gotta convert, pronto! I want a Jewish baby and Isaac says that the only way I can have a legit Jewish baby is to convert before it's born. I want this kid to grow up in one faith with nothing confusing it. Isaac's gonna do the honors. Got it?"

"If you're sure this is what you want to do."

"Yeah, I'm sure. Something else. Will you marry me, Jack? Will you be my husband? Cuz if this is gonna be a Jewish baby, we need to be married by a rabbi. After all these years, I'm asking you if you love me enough to marry me."

Jack thought of himself as a strong man. Not today. He erupted in sobs and found himself buried in his dying wife's arms desperate for comfort.

"Okay, I'll marry you, but you have to know it's just because I knocked you up." And they laughed and they wept together.

They were summoned to a medical team conference late the next afternoon. Rae had slept at home, the sleep of the sedated. She was slow but she functioned. They waited in Maria Acosta's waiting room for three quarters of an hour until Dr. Acosta's secretary indicated that Helaine Crane had arrived and they were waiting in the OB-GYN conference room.

"They couldn't be here, but I've spoken with Ian MacKenzie and Gerry Byer. We're out of time, Rae. Dr. Byer and Dr. MacKenzie agree that this is probably the first of a series of seizures and that they're likely to get harder to manage. This isn't doing you any good and it's not doing your baby any good. We need to get that baby out and get you into treatment. Do you understand?"

"I have a couple of things I have to get done first. How much time can I have?"

"I can schedule you for a C-section end of next week. February 24th. That's as long as we're willing to wait. Can you get everything done that you need to get done by then?"

"I'll take it up with the God squad."

"Rae, this is nuts. It's February 17th for God's sake. It's cold out there. The ground's frozen and there's still ice on the pond."

"Shut up and follow me. Isaac said he'd meet us out there in ten minutes and he'd bring Lev and Sage as witnesses."

"You're not going in the pond, are you? We'll never get you out."

"I said shut up, wear a hat so God'll think you're a Jew and not some impostor."

Isaac and his boys were already waiting at the edge of the pond. It was sunny and warm for late winter. They stood by the pond dressed for the weather but still clearly cold. Lev carried a small plastic bucket. Jack and Rae joined them. Isaac assumed a rabbinical air.

"We have three mitzvot - one blessing we will do today. We're going to welcome Rae into Judaism as a full and complete member of the Children of Israel. And then, later we're going to change her name for reasons that I will explain. And then also later, I'm going to perform a Jewish wedding ceremony for Jack and Rae. All of this I'll explain. And I assure you that God won't let us freeze to death out here before we're done."

"So," he began in a sing-song voice, "we have here the convert and three male witnesses. And Rae Israel has asked to become Jewish. And three times in my conversations with her she has asked and three times I have tried to turn her away and she has repeated her request. And I know from her that she has studied Judaism and has a good knowledge of it. So now I am going to ask her, 'Rae Israel, do you leave and renounce your previous faith, and do you accept the One God and agree to live your life according to the law of Moses and Israel?'"

Rae nodded.

"Now, Lev, get some water from the pond." Lev leaned as far over the water as he could without going in and managed to scoop two cups of well chilled mix of silt and water to bring back to his father. Isaac took Rae's hands and dipping his own hands into the chilly mix, he washed her hands and asked her to repeat a Hebrew prayer with him.

"Now, we will assume that your Hebrew name is Rachel," which he pronounced "Rah-chayl." "But let me explain something important. This name is the name you were given by your parents and it is the name attached to your soul. But we will give you another name, a traditional name for someone who has chosen her Judaism and that name will protect you from any force which comes to take your soul. We will do this a little later. You understand?"

"I understand."

Lev and Sage turned for home. Rae, put her cold, wet hand in Jack's and the three walked away from the pond.

"Isaac, why not do the rest of this right now?"

"I want a minyan, a quorum of ten Jewish souls for the rest."

"Will that make it all kosher?"

"It'll be close enough for our purposes for now. Have a healthy child and bring it up as a Jew and that will make it all kosher. We'll finish this later."

Leyla came back. She arrived on Thursday by train and took over the household before the sun came up on Friday. Jack and Rae dressed, Rae for the last time in her maternity clothes. This would be a birthday. They drove to the Clinic in silence. Jack reached across to hold her hand. It was cool to the touch.

Their instructions were to go directly to the surgical suite and to be there by six. When they arrived, a large group was assembled in the family waiting room. Bustling about was Isaac singing an unfamiliar song, "Not one, not two, not three, not four, not five, not six, not seven, not eight - we need two more! Find me two more! I need them now!"

Arrayed in the room were Myron Tabanov, Bud Blumberg, Marty Feldman, Gerry Byer, Phil Dorfman, and in the opposite corner Rhonda Dorfman. The receptionist was on the phone to the ER,

"Are there any staff there that are Jewish? Can you find me two and get them up to the family waiting room in surgery? It's important."

It took ten minutes for two ER residents to straggle into the room. They wore the green scrubs and the gray faces of their profession. An ER doc is known by his ability to appear awake when he is not. Isaac resumed his negative count, "Not one, not two - are you two Jewish?" The strangers nodded.

"OK," Isaac began. "Thank you all for coming. One of the great mitzvot that one can do in one's life is to be present to support the bride and groom. For doing this, you all receive credit for a mitzvah. That it's six o'clock in the morning only adds to the mitzvah. We need you here to be a minyan to witness a kosher Jewish wedding. By being here, you not only participate in helping to make Rae and Jack's marriage Jewish, but you also help to make their child Jewish. This is a double mitzvah and with the extra points for being here at this hour, we're all grateful. Nu? Let's begin."

He began to chant in Hebrew. Jack recognized only a bit of what he was doing here and there - the blessing over the wine, the name of Jerusalem. Isaac went on for perhaps four or five minutes. He stopped and looked at everyone assembled, "We don't have a lot of time, so . . ." He now turned to Jack and motioned for him to stand next to his wife. He said simply, "Jack do you take this woman Rachel bat Shimon to be your wife according to the law of Moses and Israel?"

"Yes, I do."

"Rachel bat Shimon, do you take this man, who I assume is Jacob, to be your husband according to the law of Moses and Israel?"

"I do."

"Then I declare you married among the people Israel according to the law of Moses and Israel and now go have a Jewish baby."

There was nervous laughter in the room. Rhonda lurked in the corner. Her Elevil couldn't block the tears that washed her face. Phil, still her husband, ignored her and shook hands with Jack who was trying to follow Rae as the receptionist ushered her toward surgery and Maria Acosta. Rae was a Jew. Her baby would be a Jew. That was what mattered.

Maria Acosta came into the waiting room. It was nearly eleven in the morning.

"Congratulations, Jack, you have a somewhat small and slightly pre-term baby boy. He's in an incubator in the nursery. I asked Hank Vanzander, one of our pediatricians, to take a look at him. His Apgar's a little low - the viability score for newborns, but that's to be expected."

"How's Rae?"

"She's in recovery. Still sedated. She handled everything well - anesthesia, surgery - all routine. No more bikinis for her. Give her a couple of hours to wake up and you can go in."

"Baby?"

"He's small, of course, but for a pre-term he'll do fine, I think. He looks to be about two thousand grams, maybe four and a half pounds. Definitely early arrival, but I think he's big enough to do fine. You look like you need some sleep. Why don't you go home and rest before Rae wakes up?"

It was all too much. Jewish wedding. His colleagues showing up at six in the morning. A new son. Just too much. He started for the elevator and then stopped. He asked the receptionist to direct him to the nursery and took the elevator up the two floors to OB. The clerk at the OB desk pointed out the nursery. A large plate glass window permitted new parents to peek in at their newborns in bassinets. Jack stood next to a beaming couple, her in a bathrobe and him in overalls as they gloated over a pink girl. There was no incubator. He returned to the desk and the clerk, still patient, looked in her lists and found the name "Baby, Male, Israel, Pre-term." She sent him a little further down the hall toward the Pre-Term Nursery.

There was only one incubator and it was all enclosed plastic. There were connections all about: Thermometer, heat unit, humidity, filtered air. Within was a small package neatly wrapped in a blue blanket. He wore a yellow stretch cap which made him look ridiculous. His face was shut tight and was gray with a coating like cream cheese. Even within the swaddling blanket, he struggled for freedom.

"Oh, you poor, beautiful baby boy," Jack thought, "What will you do for a mother?"

Jack came back in the early afternoon. Rae was out of recovery and on the OB floor. Plastered on the medical chart at her door were red, orange and yellow stick-ons with special instructions. One red one cautioned "seizure watch". A yellow shouted "sterile precautions". Jack found her lying flat on her back with an intravenous line into her arm. She didn't appear to be a joyful mother.

"Hey, it's the Jewish bride. How're you doing?"

"How do you think I'm doing? I hurt like hell. I feel like a steam roller flattened me to the pavement and nobody's willing to let me get up. You wanna change places?"

"We have a beautiful baby boy," he lied.

"I wanna see him. Now!"

"They're holding off on that. He really needs a haircut and they want him looking his best for you."

"Don't give me a lot of your smart mouth. I want my baby and I want him NOW!" Her voice was raised enough that the nurse came quickly through the door.

"How're you doin', Rae, Honey," she began. "We're a little short-staffed on the floor, Baby; you ready to put on a uniform and come help us out, heah?"

"I want to see my baby. Please, please let me see my baby," and she began to sob. Huge tears fled her eyes as she struggled to raise herself.

"You know, Honey, we're gonna find you a way to see that baby of yours. You relax for jes' a minute and your hubby and me, we're gonna go out and see what we can do. You all right with that?"

Rae nodded as the nurse ushered Jack into the corridor. Jack glanced at the board with patient assignments posted and found that he was in the hands of Jennifer.

"Mr. Israel - got that right? - you know she's still comin' outah the anesthesia, you know? Don't you fret about her bein' upset and wantin' to see your baby. We'll git her up in a bit and git things all straight. You okay?"

"Oh, yeah. I'm fine. I do this all the time."

"We're gonna check her dressin' on her incision and get her cleaned up. Whyn'chou go on home for a little bit an' come on back in a couplah hours. She'll be a bunch bettah by then."

Once more Jack headed home. Fatigue weighed on him. He walked slowly to the truck, drove slowly home, and stumbled from drive to house. Two large dogs and one sister-in-law shook their hind quarters at him.

"Hey! C'mon, Dad. What's happening? Tell me," Leyla insisted.

"Well, let's see. I got married today - to a Jewish woman from Milwaukee as I recall, but it's pretty hazy. I mean it was early and I might have been hung over. And then, oh yeah, we had a baby just after the wedding. It was a short pregnancy so the baby's kinda pre-term and, uh, oh, yeah, it's a boy and he's real ugly; kind of looks like your side of the family. Sorry about that."

"How's my sister?"

"The Jewish mother? Mean. Damned mean. Also like your side of the family."

"Get straight, will you?"

"Leyla, I just don't know and I'm too tired to even think about it. She's under the effects of the anesthesia. I'm sure she's in pain. She just had major surgery. Her hormones are raging. And, oh, by the way, she's missing part of her brain. Other than that, she's just fine."

"When you go back, I'm coming with you."

"Gimme an hour to shower and nap. We'll go."

This time Jack walked into the Clinic in tandem with Leyla. There was not much conversation on the ride. Jack had napped, walked the dogs, picked up a babysitter to watch the kids and they drove slowly in the late afternoon traffic. As they stood at the elevator Leyla turned to him, "No flowers for the new Mom?"

"You're right. I'm a jerk. You go up. I'll be back in a while."

He now knew the whereabouts of the florist and dashed for some roses. The shop was still open, and he waited patiently for another customer to clear the way. It gave him time to wipe the fog from his mind. Too much. Too fast. No time to adjust.

"A dozen red roses, please."

"I got 'em but the reds aren't so great. It's Friday and they're pretty picked over."

"I'll take yellow."

"Careful, yellow's jealousy."

"Huh."

"Well, you know, red's for love, pink's for friendship, purple - hey that's hot, and

yellow's for jealousy."

"Yellow. A dozen. Please."

The door was closed when he got to the room. It made sense to knock. Rae lay on the bed half-raised to sitting. Her face was inches from her sister, and they turned in surprise at the stranger with the yellow roses who entered. There was no smile from them to the suitor.

"Hey, Mom. The flowers aren't as beautiful as you are, but they'll have to do."

"Oh, hi. I want to see my baby. They haven't brought me my baby."

"I went to see him, Jack. He's quite a boy. Did you get the yellow roses to match his dashing cap?" Leyla laughed.

"I'll talk to the nurse." Jack exited and deftly closed the door behind him. At the nurse's station, he found Rae's primary care nurse. "Can we get the baby in to be with Rae even for a few minutes? She's getting upset."

"Well, Honey, I don't blame her. These mean ol' doctors just give their orders and don't have a lick of sense 'bout what a Momma needs. That ol' Doc Vanzander, well you know he's the meanest one. Now he says he wants that little guy in an isolette for a couple days. But here's what we're gonna do. Let's get us a wheelchair and see if we can't get Momma sittin' up in it. Then we'll jes' wheel her down to the nursery and give her a peek at her little guy. Whatcha gonna call that little tyke?"

"Jennifer, that's a great question. I was thinking about Earl E. Byrd, myself."

Jennifer brought a wheelchair to bedside. She and Jack and Leyla gently raised Rae to a sitting position and swung her so that her legs hung over the side of the bed. She was dizzy at the change. Jennifer raised the leg supports out of the way and instructed Rae: "Now, Darlin', we're jus' gonna give you a lil' boost off this here bed and help you stand. Then we gonna help you turn and plop your butt right down in this here chair. Now, Poppa, you hold this chair good and steady and me and Sis, here, gonna work with Momma. You all ready?" In a smooth move they shifted Rae to the chair.

"Am I gonna hold my baby?"

"Not jes' now, Honey. That mean ol' Doc Vanzander got your boy on restrictions. But we gonna git you a good look on him, you hear?"

Jack wheeled Rae to the window of the nursery. The lower edge was just above her eyes. Her three caregivers lifted her to her feet and she stared at the diminutive bundle in the isolette, his blue blanket and yellow hat so hopelessly mismatched. His eyes were scrunched and he struggled in his casement.

Rae smiled, "Ohhh, it's my baby. I need to hold him."

"Not jes' now, Honey. You need some rest fer now and we'll see about tomorrow."

Rae turned to look at her. Her eyes grew large in their sockets and without warning her head snapped back, her body convulsed and she collapsed to the floor thrashing. Jack wasn't fast enough to hold her up but cushioned her fall. Jennifer got down on her knees, carefully laid Rae's head down and ran for the nurse's station yelling orders, "Charlotte, I need a tongue depressor, STAT. Call Dr. Acosta, please, we got a seizure on her patient. I think MacKenzie's her neurologist. Git 'im on the phone. I'll git a blanket and let's put in the tongue depressor afore she bites her tongue. Call for a float nurse. We're gonna need some extra hands up here."

In minutes both the OB/GYN resident and the neurology resident were on the floor next to Rae. There were no anti-seizure medications in the medication cabinet on the floor. The resident called down to Pharmacy for injectable anti-seizure meds. The OB/GYN resident stood by helplessly.

"Sorry, Buddy, out of my department. Tell me if you want me to do something."

The neurology resident turned to Jennifer, "She a C-section?"

"Oh, yeah."

"Better get a check from surgery just to be sure the sutures aren't compromised. Let's get her sedated and we'll get some help from Transport to get her back into bed." He turned to Jack, "You her husband?"

"Yes. She gonna be all right?"

"Any previous history of seizures?"

"Yeah, that, and neurosurgery for a brain tumor. Other than that, she's fine."

"Got your hands full, huh?"

"You can't imagine."

The resident, perhaps a decade younger than Jack, put his hand on Jack's shoulder and said, "Well, let's get her past this and take things one at a time. She'll be OK for the time."

"Yeah. But I won't."

Leyla wept all the way home. Jack was silent. There was nothing to be said nor was he able to speak. There's a time when fatigue and sorrow combine so that existence becomes elemental and words can't reach the reality of feelings. There is just nothing to say.

Red eyed and weary they put the children to sleep. Jack shackled the dogs, needy beasts who were now one more burden on him. He donned his coat and set out the door. Halfway down the block he spied a familiar figure rocking along toward him.

"Jack! I was just coming to check on you."

"Isaac. What day is today? Is it Friday?"

"No, you shnook, it's Saturday. Today was Shabbos and we missed you. What happened with Rae? Do you have a baby?"

"Oh, Isaac. Oh, it's been a hard, hard day."

The tale of the day was told. "Is there anything I can do to help? I can come see Rae tomorrow if you think that'll be all right."

"She'll be glad to see you. I'm sure she'll be awake. Probably groggy, though."

"I'll come. We need to talk about a brit milah."

"A what?"

"He's a Jewish boy. He needs to be circumcised. It's usually done at eight days, but we can wait until he's strong enough. What will you name him?"

"Haven't got it all figured out yet. We talked about some names, but no closure yet."

"Your father . . . He's deceased? Yes?"

"Yeah."

"Has there been a child named for him?"

"No."

"Well, you could name this child after him. What was his name?"

"Joe. Joseph."

"Not a bad name for a son of Rachel."

"I'll talk to Rae tomorrow - if she's up to it. But I'm getting scared. Real scared. Look, Isaac. I know in my head what I'm facing. I haven't got answers to what I'm gonna do, but I can figure out what the problems are gonna be. I just don't think I can go through all of this and survive."

Isaac laughed a sardonic laugh. "You don't know what you can survive until after you've survived it. Ask me. I'll tell you. God spares you from knowing what's in the future. You can only look at the past and be astonished at what you were able to endure and how much strength you found to make it through. If we could see the future, we'd all commit suicide."

"Now there's a positive suggestion! If I didn't have three, no make that four kids that are gonna need me, I just wouldn't want to be here. I just . . . I just couldn't keep on going just for myself. It just hurts too much, Isaac."

They assumed their customary pace, their normal path. It was an unhurried pace. As tired as Jack was, as deep the pain in his heart, walking with Isaac was healing. The dogs now trod easily next to Isaac, Cady brushing her flanks against his leg. He hardly noticed.

"Someday, Jack, a long time from now maybe, but someday, you'll look back and you'll see that this too was what it was supposed to be."

Jack stopped in his tracks so abruptly that he choked both dogs. He turned to Isaac with tired fury, "How can you even say something that . . . that . . . stupid? Is that supposed to be comforting? You can't possibly believe that!"

"Jack, I've had long conversations with the Angel of Death. He's come for me more times than he comes for most people. I've been where you are - maybe even in worse places than you are now. I know what I'm talking about. There are things you can't see - that you'll see only much later in life. Let me tell you a story."

"Oh, I don't know that I can take a story from you tonight, Isaac."

"Not only can you take one, my friend, but you need one badly. Here is your story: Once upon a time there was a young man who was very wise in all the ways that the rabbis teach. He knew Torah, he knew Talmud, he was a wonderful scholar. But he wanted to know so much more. He prayed and prayed and prayed and one night at the stroke of midnight, a figure stood before him in his room. He was astonished and asked, 'Who are you and why are you here?' And the figure said, 'I'm the Prophet Elijah. You prayed for wisdom and I'm here to answer your prayer.' The young man said, 'Will you give me wisdom?' and Elijah answered, 'This I will give you: You may accompany me on my journeys from now until Shabbat. The only condition is that you must not question me about anything that you see on these journeys. You may watch and you may learn, but you may not question.' Well, our young friend was beside himself with joy. Shabbos was three days away. He had three days and two nights to watch and wonder at the works of the Prophet Elijah. His prayers were answered. So, they set out together and walked a very long journey. At the end of the first day they were very tired, and they were lost in a forest. But they came to a small cottage and in the cottage lived an old man and an old woman. They were very poor, but they survived with one cow who gave milk. They sold the milk in the village and had barely enough to eat. The two travelers came to their door and asked if they could stay the night and the old man and old woman welcomed them. They set out their best dishes and as much food as they had. And the old man and the old woman told the Prophet and his companion that they weren't all that hungry and made sure that the travelers ate most of the meal. At night the old couple insisted that the travelers have their bed to sleep in and they slept on the floor. When the sun came up, the young man woke up and found the old couple sobbing. He woke Elijah to tell him and the Prophet said, 'I know, I know. The cow died.' The young man was perplexed. How could the Prophet have permitted this to happen? But he had sworn not to ask. So, the next day the travelers went on. They walked and walked along the road and came to a fine inn which was filled with singing and laughter and they went to find if there was a room for them. The innkeeper greeted them at the door and took one look and said, 'See here, more trash from the road!' The Prophet asked for a room and something to eat and the innkeeper said, 'Room for the likes of you? Never! You can sleep in the back with the cows and the goats, for that's what you deserve. And as for food, you can chase the dogs away from the swill and eat from that. And for the privilege you can pay double!' The Prophet led his pupil to the back of the inn and they bedded down in the straw. They fell asleep but the young man awoke late in the night to find the Prophet up and busy. He was working furiously at the back walls of the inn where the bricks had come loose and were in danger of collapsing. He was huffing and puffing and sweating and working as hard as he could. And after a few hours, he had repaired the decrepit walls so that they were in no danger of falling down. In the morning they left toward home and the young man was furious. He was consumed by anger at the Prophet. Finally, just before they arrived at home and just before the coming of Shabbos, his anger exploded. 'How dare you? How could you? You're the Prophet Elijah. You have the ear of God on High Himself. You permitted the old couple's cow to die and then . . . and then . . . you had the . . . the . . . the foolish audacity to keep the wicked innkeeper's wall from falling. Has the compassion and judgement granted you by God escaped you?' The Prophet listened in silence. And he spoke slowly, 'You're a fine scholar, my son. But the wisdom of the Lord is beyond even the finest scholars. You see, on our first night, I awoke to find in our midst the Angel of Death. He had come for the woman, to collect her soul. And I engaged him in argument that the compassion of the Lord wouldn't tolerate the suffering that would befall her husband. And the Angel of Death was so moved by my words that he, himself wept. But, he said, he couldn't return without collecting a soul and so we looked about the cottage at the old man, at you, and at the cow. And we agreed that he would take the cow. As for the innkeeper: I awoke from a dream and saw in my dream that beneath the crumbling wall lay a great treasure stored there by an evil landlord. When the wall collapsed the innkeeper would find the treasure and use it for wicked purposes. I arose and repaired the wall to hide the treasure from him. So now my scholarly friend, you have a bit of wisdom. A guten Shabbos.'"

Jack turned toward Isaac who was clearly pleased with himself.

"Do I fall on the ground overcome by the wisdom of this or do I just throw quarters into your hat? With everything I just told you, what you have to give me is another story?"

"You're the young scholar, Jack. Some things you just can't change. You struggle to find the meaning in what you can't change. I can't cure Rae's cancer. I can't make her seizures go away. I can be here next to you and do one of two mitzvot. I can either be silent and just be present or I can give you whatever small bits of wisdom I've collected in my own sufferings. Which would you prefer?"

"Let's just walk . . ."

Close to home Isaac slowed noticeably. They had been silent. Sasha observed the close discomfort and nudged Jack. Isaac turned to speak,

"We have some things to do. We have to get this child strong enough to have a brit milah and then we have another circumcision to do."

"Someone else have a baby?"

"No. I need you to help me with Matt Cowan. We need to do a conversion for him and then he needs a ritual circumcision."

"You're gonna do a circumcision on Matt? On an eighteen-year-old? That's a kind of animal sacrifice. That's ritual murder. I won't have any part of it - and you know which part I mean in particular."

"You don't learn so fast. Or you're over your limit and aren't thinking rationally. Maybe I prefer the last explanation. Let's start with the easy stuff. You need to have a name for this baby. That has to be done. When he's let's say six, seven pounds, if he looks strong, we need to bring him to the brit milah. We'll do that. Yes?"

"Yes. Then what?"

"As soon as Rae is home, we need you and her to come back to the pond. She'll be a witness, it's a mitzvah, and we'll do for Matt what we did for her. Yes?"

"So far, easy. Now let's get to the good part. You then take out a rusty razor, I hold Matt down on the ground, you yell something in Hebrew that nobody can understand, and you attack his penis with the blade. Right?"

"Remember, I'm forgiving you because I know you're over your limit. No. Fortunately, his mother or his father who is in the Air Force - had the sense to have him circumcised when he was born. We don't have to take any more flesh from him. All we have to do is a symbolic circumcision . . ."

"Wait. I got it. We tattoo a star of David on the tip of his penis!"

"Way, way over your limit. No, schmeckel, we have my friend Dr. Vanzander take a sterile needle and draw a single drop of blood while I recite the brochah. Do you want to be a witness?"

"No. No, Isaac. I can be there for the conversion at the pond, but the less time I have to spend in a hospital for the rest of my life the better. Got it?"

"I understand and you are over your limit. Good night, my friend."

CHAPTER 24

It was Sunday morning. Jack crept out of the door over the Sunday Courier that Merrill had dropped on the doorstep. Paper delivery had resumed. He no longer asked to use the bathroom. The dogs were out early; Leyla would watch the kids. He needed to see Rae.

The hospital was quiet. He headed for the OB/GYN floor and found Jennifer on duty.

"Hi, Jennifer, how's Rae looking?"

"Well, hi Poppa. Rae's not here, Honey. They transferred her up to a medical floor, six as I recall."

"And the baby?"

"That lil' guy's still here. You gonna go take a peek at 'im?"

Jack walked to the pre-term nursery. No form filled an isolette, but in the corner he could see a nurse in a rocking chair holding a bottle to a small bundle in blue blanket and yellow knit cap. From the isolette next to them he could see a bright fluorescent light. He walked back to Jennifer.

"Has Rae held the baby at all? And what's with the bright lights in his bassinet?"

"No, Poppa. She ain't been back since they transferred her to medical. But she'll be down here. You jes' wait. You'll see. And Doc Vanzander, he ordered the light. It's called a bilirubin light. It's like sometimes, these lil' guys get lots a' bilirubin jes' after they's born - you know? - and that there light shinin' on 'em makes it all go way. But we're real careful, we put eyeshades on 'im. You come on back later and you'll see."

Jack took the elevator to six. Where OB/GYN had a joyful air to it, the medical floor was far more serious. There were more people and fewer smiles. He asked at the desk for Rae and was directed to room 619. Rae was there. She sat up seeming somewhat dazed. Next to her was a solicitous Ian MacKenzie. He was the first to greet.

"Ahh, Mr. Israel, Jack. Good to see yah. We had a toof evenin' didn' we?"

"We did. Can you tell me what happened?"

"Sure. When we took Rae, here, in for the delivery, ya know, we backed off ah her anti- seizoore medications. Can't be doin' full anesthesia and anti-seizooore meds in a procedoor like that, ya know. Bad fer the mom, bad fer the baby. We backed her down a wee bit. And then we wanted tuh be sure that she had cleared all the anesthetic afore we got her back on the anti-seizoor meds. It was jest a bit o' time, ya know, jest a bit to get her back aboard. But sometimes somethin' sets off a seizoor, you never really know what it is. It kin be somethin' as simple as a flashin' light or an emotional upset o' some kind. Hard to say. We got her back on meds here and she's seemin' OK fer now."

Jack looked closely at Rae. She was there. She was present. But she also wasn't there. He looked at her left eye. The pupil was large, blown out. Her right eye was fine. He looked in her face and grasped both her hands in his and squeezed. Her right hand squeezed back. Her left did not. He leaned over and kissed her and turned to MacKenzie, "Can we talk outside?"

"Sure."

They walked out to the conference room behind the nurse's station. They collected at the corner of the table, less a confrontation than a collaboration.

"How long do you figure she was out?"

"Well, I spoke with the resident about that fer a bit. He's a good man, ya know. In a situation like this, if a patient's ooot fer let's say more than maybe five minutes, it's a problem. Ya start to get some neuron damage."

"You haven't answered my question. How long was she out and what does it all mean?"

"The resident says she was oot for a good five minutes. He got some diazepam in 'er and that was a good call. It was the right drug fer 'er, ya know. But five minutes is a loong time with somethin' like this."

"Her left eye?"

"Ahhh. Ya saw that, did ya. Yaaa. She's had a bit o' damage there, I'd say."

"Can you just tell me what this all means?"

"It's Sunday, lad. It's a church goin' day. There's stuff in this business that's not in my control, ya know. I talked to Helaine Crane - another good one. Rae's got some tumor activity. We dinna have much of a chance from the beginnin'. And Rae chose to wait until she could deliver. That gave the tumor a bloody good head start, ya know. I looked over her EEG tracin's. We called in the EEG tech last night to get 'em. Her right frontal and temporal lobes are all static ef ya know what I mean. We haven't had a radiologist look at any new films, but I can tell you now, it's late in the game and we're way behind on the score. We'll get her oop and 'round for a bit more. We'll keep her medicated and she'll have a bit o' time with that new baby. But it's not a lot o' time, lad. We'll give you what we can."

"Well, thanks for the honesty. Thanks for coming in on a Sunday."

"Rae's my patient. I jus' wish I had more to give ya."

Jack knew nothing more than he had known before. Only now he had to admit it all to himself and deal with it. He left the conference room and went into room 619. Rae was sitting up looking dazed. She was in slow contact, medicated, aware, but slow.

"OK, My Lovely. You look like crap to anyone else, but to me you're still beautiful. We got some things to talk about. There's this kid downstairs who's calling for his Mom and you and I are gonna get a chair and go down to see him. OK?"

She nodded and laboriously smiled.

"However, my sweet, the ladies in the nursery are calling him John Doe. Now I don't particularly dislike his being a John, but I hate being Father Doe. What are we gonna call this child of my declining years?"

"I talked to the Rabbi about it." She struggled to get the words together.

"The Rabbi? I think you mean that strange man from around the corner."

"That one. My Hebrew name is Rachel. Rachel had two sons, Joseph and Benjamin. She died giving birth to Benjamin. I can't name this kid Benjamin. If I do, he'll grow up thinking he killed me. Your father's name was Joseph. How about Joseph Isaac Israel?"

"Joseph Isaac? Oh, no. Who's the Isaac for or dare I even ask?"

"He's my friend, Jack. And I'm gonna die. And I need some honesty. He's the only one that doesn't lie to me."

"You're not gonna die."

"Jack, I'm gonna die."

"Oh, Honey, don't say that."

"Fer Chrissake, you ass. I haven't got much time and I need to get things settled. Don't lie to me and keep me from doing what I've gotta do. Jack, I want my kids raised as Jews. I want this one to be a Jew. Do you understand? My father was a Jew, Jack. He could have given me some of that, but he didn't. It was my gift and he never gave it to me and he never even told me that it was mine. This little one's a real Jew. And I want the others to be Jews too. And you know what, Jack, I want you to be a Jew too. 'Cuz if you're not a Jew, they won't be either. Promise me, Jack. Promise me that you'll be a Jew so that my children can be Jews. Promise me."

"I promise."

"When I'm gone . . ." as she said this Jack winced. It was involuntary.

"When I'm gone . . . you wait a while, a nice sensitive, diplomatic time and . . . you marry my sister, Leyla. You hear?"

"I'd sooner rot in Hell for eternity."

"Don't you smart mouth me! When I'm gone you're gonna go out with some cute gentile graduate student who's gonna think you got some beautiful kids who need a mother and all her hormones are gonna flush and the next you know she'll be pregnant and you'll be married to some non-Jew who's not gonna care a snot for my babies. And you're not man enough to stand up to that. I wanna know that my children'll be raised by a Jewish woman who'll tell them good things about their mother. You have to marry Leyla!"

"You haven't by any chance mentioned this to Leyla, have you?"

"I made her promise to look after my babies. For God's sake, Jack, you can take care of yourself. You always do. But I'm not gonna be here to take care of my babies. I can't die in peace if I don't know that they'll be taken care of. You have to promise me."

Dams burst. Thunderstorms hit. Volcanoes erupt. Hurricanes and tornadoes hit. The world changes cataclysmically in an instant and there's nothing that you can do, nothing to stop it. You're left powerless before a force beyond comprehension. You find whatever shelter you can and know that your life is going to change forever. You just can't foresee the changes. A mother's dying wish for her children is a force equal and equivalent to any other force in nature. Jack promised. He might marry Leyla, some day.

He left the room for the nurse's station.

"Excuse me. I'm Rae Israel's husband. We have a baby downstairs in the nursery and my wife hasn't even held him yet. She's upset. Can we get a wheelchair and take her down there just for a little while?"

Medical floors are not OB/GYN floors. OB/GYN nurses love bringing life into the world. They teach new mothers how to hold their newborns, how to nurse them. They josh with new fathers. They check sutures with a smile and a light pat. They make compromises with policy because policy gets in the way of the joy of new life.

Medical floors are different. Medical nurses are alert to the threats to life. They monitor, they watch, they dispense. They share information guardedly. Above all, they are the seraphim to the physicians. To them policy is important and there are few compromises. If things go bad, the nurses are the first suspects. They know this.

"Just a minute. Let me check the record and see if we have any orders."

She thumbed through the record. "We do have some orders to try to get her mobile, up out of bed and in a chair. We've got a serious seizure watch on her. We got orders from the neuro resident, Dr. MacKenzie, and Dr. Crane. She's got a lot of doctors watchin' her."

"Can we please get her down to the nursery?"

"Wow, I don't know, Mr. . . . Israel. If we send her off the floor and something happens, it could be a real problem."

"Can we get our baby up here?"

"I'll call down to the nursery." She checked the number, dialed the phone and found someone to talk to.

"Mr. Israel, your baby is a pre-term. It's in an isolette. There's no way they're gonna let an isolette off the floor. They're not even gonna let that baby out of the pre- term nursery."

"OK. If I go back into my wife's room and tell her that you're not going to let her see her newborn son - our newborn son - Joseph . . ."

Suddenly Jack's emotions had found the cliff and without being pushed, they jumped. His eyes filled and his throat choked. He had a son and this minute person had a name and it was his father's name. Jack felt the simultaneous presence of his father, his son, and his dying wife, and could not hold it all back. He was smart enough not to speak, but he didn't have to. Nurses are also able to see the descent off the cliff even before the jump.

"Mr. Israel, I'll call the shift supervisor and see if she can spare someone off a floor that's light right now. Maybe we can get a nurse to take your wife down to the nursery. I'm really sorry. It's policy. But I know how you feel and we'll find a way."

It took a platoon. A transport worker came with a chair and a float nurse came with the transport worker. The head nurse came into the room with the transport worker and the float nurse and the nursing shift supervisor trotted in behind. The shift supervisor wore invisible sergeant stripes and barked orders, "Don't you leave her for an instant. Transport, you stay with them and supervise all the transfers. Rochelle, you keep track of pagers and be sure that the nursery has all the pager numbers if we need them in a hurry. You know, I'm not sure we should be doing this. We've got a half dozen violations of policy and procedure here."

Rochelle, the head nurse, nodded and kept the platoon marching to bedside. Rae was there but she was not. Part of her was missing. The right side of her mouth lifted in a smile and the left did not. She was soon into the chair, down the hall, visibly dancing as they waited for the elevator. Rochelle went with them to the elevator, as far as her leash would permit. She understood.

They wheeled Rae to the pre-term nursery and the nursery team was there waiting. Joseph Isaac Israel was waiting as well, lying under a fluorescent light with his eyes covered, wrapped in blue with a silly yellow stocking cap still on his head. The nurses lifted him from his isolette, took off his eye shades, and handed him to Rae, still in the wheel-chair.

For the first time in months Jack watched Rae smile. It was the smile that began on the right side of her face and stretched so wide that it drew the damaged left side into a smile as well. Her right eye filled with tears and then her left as she looked down at her son for the first time. She cradled him in her left arm and with her right hand gently pulled his silly yellow stocking cap from his head. He was dark haired, and his face was red and blotched. He yawned and she loosened his bindings as the nurses hovered in concern.

"Isn't he beautiful?" she asked no one in particular.

At the sound of her voice his tiny eyes opened, and it was as if he saw for the first time the source of the voice that he had heard the long months before his birth. His eyes drifted up to Rae's and he squirmed. The pre-term nurse spoke,

"It's 'bout time fer him to eat. You wanna feed 'im?"

"Oh, yeah. He wants his Mamma to feed him. Oh, I just wish I could nurse him. Just for a little while."

"Well, Hon, he's on a pretty strict diet of supplements right 'bout now, so's ahh don't think thet's gonna work. But here, let me gitcha his bottle an' you kin feed 'im and make my job a lil' easier."

She prepared a small bottle and helped Rae position her baby. He sucked eagerly at the bottle as Rae wore a smile seen only on the Madonna.

"We need to go home," she began. "My baby and I need to go home. When can we go home? We need to go home soon. When? When can we go home?"

The pre-term nurse spoke deliberately, "Ahh dunno, Hon. You got that Doc Vanzander and he's watchin' this lil' guy like a cat contemplatin' a fat sparrow. Now don'chou git me wrong. This lil' guy's puttin' on the pounds real good and I don' figger that ahm gonna git to play with him a whole lot longer. But you give us a leetle bit more time with him and we'll jes' ship him to you special delivery. Fer now, far as I heerd, you jes' gotta git yourself home and let us take care o' him for a bit."

The float nurse and transport looked at one another and signaled that this visit had to be over. Jack asked the pre-term nurse,

"When you see Dr. Vanzander, can you ask him to stop up on the medical floor to talk with us?"

"Sure kin. You positive you got enough time to talk with him? He's a long winded one, he is."

Back up on the medical floor, Jack returned to Rochelle at the desk.

"Can you ask Dr. MacKenzie and Dr. Crane to see if they can spare me some time during the day? I need to talk with them, if I can."

Dr. Henry Vanzander was not a young man. His hair had gone AWOL some time back and his shoulders bent as though he had been carrying concrete. But his eyes lit with mischievous laughter and he had a permanent wry smile on his lips. He was a typical pediatrician. He loved children and he was patient with parents, and he avoided the hardest cases.

"Hi. I'm Hank Vanzander. I'm sorry we haven't met. I've been spending a lot of time with your son. He's a cutie. Got a name for him?"

"Joseph Isaac Israel," Rae spoke up.

"Wow. That's a strong name!"

"Dr. Vanzander, I'm Jack Israel and . . ."

"Oh, I know who you are. You wouldn't remember me, but I saw you at Bud Blumberg's new faculty reception."

"Oh . . . Well, Rae and I were wondering what we could expect about bringing . . . Little Joe home. And there are some other things too. We need to get him circumcised and . . . I don't know if you're aware of Rae's medical history . . ."

"I think everyone in this hospital knows her history by now. She's our poster gal for the intrepid mother, you know. Joe's lookin' pretty good, I'd say. He's gained a pound already. He's up to about five and a half pounds. If we're gonna do a circ on him, I'd like to see him closer to seven pounds anyway - maybe seven and a half to be sure. They usually lose a little weight after the circ - not from the tissue loss, you understand."

He chortled to himself, thinking he had made a joke. It went flat. Jack had little left of a sense of humor. Vanzander went on,

"I'd like to hang on to him here for another week if we can. Any idea when Mom here is going to be going home?"

"Hope to have an answer by later today."

"It'd be nice to have him home, but given the circumstances, if you want me to do the circ, I'd like to do it here and that means we need to keep him at least another week. Have you thought about the circ at all?"

"No."

"Well, here's your choices. I can do this as a simple surgical procedure here in the hospital. It takes a minute and I can do all the follow up. Or, if you prefer, we can have a religious ceremony where Rabbi Abrams officiates, but I do the procedure. He does the prayers and drinks the wine; I do the cutting, and I get a beer afterwards. Or, he can call in a team of religious professionals from Chicago and they do the prayers, the cutting, drink the wine, and I just stand around and make sure they don't mess up."

Jack turned to Rae, "Have you ever discussed this with Isaac?"

"I did. It's hard for me. I don't want anybody to hurt my baby. But he says it has to be done and that it doesn't hurt. Does it?"

Vanzander spoke confidently and convincingly with no assurance that he wasn't lying, "Oh no, there's no pain. Their nerve tracks are immature at this age and they don't really feel it. They cry, but that's because we unwrap 'em and they're cold. And we anesthetize the tissue and it feels cold to them. But it's not really pain."

He turned to Jack, "You got any recollection of pain from yours?"

"No, but it hurt like hell when I got the damned thing caught in my zipper at about age seven."

"See. There you go. So how do you want to do this, Mom?"

He handed the decision to Rae. It was a gentlemanly act. He could afford to be gallant knowing that the procedure would be his to supervise in any event.

Rae hesitated for just a moment, "I . . . want the religious ceremony with the guys from Chicago and I want Isaac there and I want you there."

Vanzander passed pleasantries and asked if Jack wanted to walk him back to the elevator.

"You OK? Everyone here understands your situation and if you need anything, you just need to let people know. Bud Blumberg's been a prince about making sure people here are watching out for you."

"I had no idea."

"That's the way things work in this town. We don't talk much, but we take good care of one another. Hey, you aren't a biker are you?"

"Beg your pardon?"

"You look like you might ride a motorcycle."

"No. . ."

"I ride with a bunch of guys and we're always looking for new riders."

"Well, if Rae makes it through all this, maybe she'll join you."

MacKenzie and Crane came into the room shortly after noon. It was apparent that they had little time. Jack lay in wait.

"Can Rae go home?"

MacKenzie smiled at Rae and began, "Ahh yoop. I think wee're joost about ready to talk that oop. Rae, Loov, would yah be wantin' to git yoourself hoome, now?"

"Only cuz the food sucks. I wanna go home and I need to take my baby home."

Helaine Crane shot a piercing look at Jack and suggested, "Jack, perhaps you and I and Ian can chat in the conference room about what arrangements we can make."

She threw her head toward the door and Jack understood the need to move the conversation. The three of them went to the conference room. This time Helaine Crane and Ian MacKenzie took seats next to one another across from Jack. Jack sensed the difference in tone but was unsure what it meant.

"Jack, lad. We goot the seizoores oonder control, hear? Rae's on a lottah anti-seizoore medication and it'll make 'er a wee bit groggy. But that don't mean as how the basic problem is gone, ya know."

"Jack, managing the seizures means controlling a symptom of a basic underlying pathology," Helaine Crane began. "There's active tumor growth and it's disrupting normal brain function. Ian's seeing quite atypical electrical activity. She's got a blown pupil, which you know. With tumor growth we're likely to see - anything."

"What's anything?"

"For one thing, we could see some very drastic seizure activity - maybe even leading to what we call status epilepticus. Ian knows much more about this than I do, but basically the brain's electrical activity gets short circuited and the patient goes into a sort of permanent state of seizure and . . ."

"And the patient dies, lad. Pure and simple."

"Or?"

Helaine resumed, "Or we get advancing tumor activity and we see what's called 'coning' where the tumor displaces the brain itself and the physical pressure causes changes in function that we can't even anticipate. But it's also an end-stage situation."

Jack breathed deep. He felt no emotion whatever. He was on automatic intellectual control, that place where the emotions are relegated to someplace remote and inaccessible while the logical mind searches for information that will change the situation that the emotions cannot bear.

"Treatment options?"

"None really."

"OK then. I need you to help me save my family and I need that help now. My kids have seen their mother in full seizure. They've seen her carted off to the hospital three times and they can't endure the back and forth. I can't let them see her seize again. I can't permit their last image of their mother to be one of her lying on the floor thrashing and foaming at the mouth. I can't have them waving goodby to her as the ambulance pulls away. I can't have them come to the hospital to kiss their mother one last time while she lays in a bed with a dozen IV lines going into her. Do you get my picture?"

"We do, Jack. We do. Look, Jack, I have two kids. I'm a cancer survivor. I understand."

"Then if you can't save my wife, for God's sake, help me save my kids from the agony will you please?"

"And we got to help you as best we can too, Jack." And with that Ian MacKenzie ended the conversation.

"Am I going home?"

"You sure are. And we're gonna get that cute little guy downstairs home as well, but it'll take us a week to do it. You're going home cuz I can't stand our children for another day without you and frankly, they can't stand me either. And the yard's full of dog poop and cleaning it up is partly your job. You tell me what outfit to bring you for your grand re-entrance and I'll go get it."

Jack smiled the smile of an accomplished liar. He drove home, packed a fairly loose pre-maternity dress, some combs and brushes, a lip stick off the dresser, comfy shoes and a light jacket. Instead of his trusty truck, he decided on the VW Minivan. It was more nearly Rae's and she would be glad to see it. It hadn't been run in weeks. When he opened the garage and started it, it groaned and spit in defiance. On the fourth try it caught and cast a pall of oil smoke into the neighborhood. Every neighbor knew when the van left the cul-de-sac.

At the hospital he dessed her lovingly and helped her to straighten. The nurses insisted that she be wheeled to the front door in a chair by a transport worker. On the way she insisted on a stop at the nursery. Little Joe was asleep, but she pushed her hands hard against the tires of the chair and entered the nursery where the nurse, knowing oh so well, took him from his isolette and placed him in his mother's arms.

"Hi, Joey. I'm going home to get a room ready for you. And I'm gonna be back every day to see you 'til you come home. Don't you worry, Honey, Mama's here." And she went home.

Jack failed post-natal preparation. There was no crib waiting for Joe. There were no new-born disposable diapers, and only the neonate clothes left over from three older siblings. Simmy, Lee, and Dinah had received little attention in the past week and less explanation. The dogs were restless from lack of exercise and the house had acquired a musty wet-dog smell that was a slap in the face to all who entered. When the children asked why the house smelled funny, Jack explained that is was like the smell of fresh-baked cookies at their friends' houses, only different.

He helped her through the door and past the dogs. The children were at school or day-care. Rae simply dropped her coat on the couch and headed to the bedroom where she collapsed, exhausted by the trip from bed to bed. Only then did Jack realize that he was a captive. Rae was in danger of seizure at any time. She had to have someone with her always. She couldn't be left alone with the children. They had been traumatized once and couldn't tolerate such an assault again. She needed to be driven to the hospital once a day to see her son. There was shopping to be done and kids to ferry about and baby preparations to do, but Jack dared not move away from Rae and Rae herself was barely movable. He couldn't manage by himself. He tucked Rae in to nap and went to the kitchen to make calls.

"Rhonda? Jack Israel. Rhonda, I need a big favor. Can you please come over this evening and watch Rae and my kids for about an hour so that I can do some shopping?"

"Leyla? Jack. Rae's home. The baby, Joseph Isaac to those of us who know him, has to stay in the hospital for about a week. If he gains enough weight, we're gonna have a circumcision ceremony. Look, Leyla, I can't manage Rae on my own. If she tosses a seizure and I'm out shopping it could get bad. Can you take some time and come down, at least until after the circumcision?"

"Bloomington Visiting Nurses? My name is Jack Israel and I'm in need of some serious help here."

Leyla arrived the next day at the train station. Jack bundled Rae and took her to meet the train. From the station they went directly to the hospital. Rae sat in the rocking chair in the pre-term nursery and fed Little Joe. Halfway through, she looked at her sister and asked if she might like to hold him and feed him. Leyla took the chair and the baby and the bottle and smiled in a way that Jack had never seen her smile.

With Leyla there, Jack was able to haul out the portable crib stored in the attic space over the garage. He found the box of old baby clothes and washed them all, rinsed out the big plastic waste basket and scrubbed the baby tub. This child was entering a second-hand world - someone else's crib and clothes, tubs and baskets. There was a serious question if even his mother would be his own.

That night, just after the kids and Rae were tucked in, there was a familiar knock. Jack was the first of three to the door. "Oh, I am so glad to see you! Wait while I get a coat and a couple of spare dogs and we can walk."

"I thought you might like some fresh air. Is Rae OK?"

"Well, yes and no but her sister is here so we can go."

Leyla appeared in the background and Isaac muscled his way through the door.

"You're Rae's sister? I'm Rabbi Abrams, Isaac Abrams. We met briefly and I've heard so much about you."

He grasped her hand between his two hands and smiled generously at Leyla. Jack had seen this ritual before.

"Isaac, walk. Remember? Walk?"

The four of them tumbled down the street in a jumble of leashes. Sasha and Cady were out for their first long walk in several weeks. The first bouquet of spring was in the air, the smell of vegetation struggling to emerge from earth; grasses greening and daffodils poking noses, joyful at the world warming and still frightened of the frost. The two friends walked a fast trot released from the bonds of winter.

"Nu, Rae is okay? Your son is okay?"

"Rae is what Rae is, Isaac. And Little Joe . . . You do know his name, right?"

"You could tell me."

"Joseph Isaac Israel. How many kids are there who have your name sandwiched in between their mother's fantasies and their father's genealogy?"

"Must be thousands. It's a good name. When can we do a brit milah? How much does he weigh?"

"He's lookin' pretty good. They're moving him into the regular nursery. Must be over six pounds by now. Could be ready in a week. Rae wants the full shebang, the luxury version, the Cadillac of cuts. How do we do this?"

"OK. I have to call the mohel in Chicago and ask him to come here. He does this, but we'll have to set a date. Then we'll have to organize a minyan. And I need to get Matt set up."

"Not so fast, please. Who do you have to call?"

"The mohel. That's the Hebrew for the ritual circumciser. It's a very honored role in the community. Nowadays it's most often a specially trained rabbi or cantor or sometimes just someone who understands the importance of the ceremony and has dedicated his life to it. It's a great mitzvah."

"OK, you have Dr. Vanzander there?"

"Always."

"And what's this about Matt?"

"If we're going to have the mohel here, it would be a great mitzvah for us to do Matt's conversion and then do a brit milah for him at the same time. That way the mohel can do the blessings for Matt with no trouble and he'll have a kosher conversion."

"But he just loses a drop of blood?"

"Just a symbolic drop of blood."

"Do these guys give group rates?"

"Don't be disrespectful. It's an honorable profession."

"I don't trust them."

"Why not?"

"I think that when I was getting done, my father must have gotten into an argument with this guy over price and he cut too much. I've felt shortchanged ever since."

"Was that a joke?"

"Was that a joke? Was that a joke? Why yes, my dear rabbinic friend, that was what we in the Western Hemisphere call a joke. Did they take out your sense of humor in rabbi school?"

"You're making fun of me."

"Good. Good. You're catching on. I am making fun of you. You're about to supervise the shortening of my newborn son's winky-tink and you think this makes perfectly good sense in the modern world. What sense does that make?"

"I'll explain. Let me tell you a story."

Jack stopped and bent over at the waist. "Oh, no. He has a story. He has a story. He's got another story!" He stooped over further and finally fell on the ground and rolled around to the total confusion of the dogs. "Lord save us from another story." he yelled.

A door opened and a male voice yelled. "What's goin' on out there? You drunk?"

Jack got up off the ground and said, "How come, just tell me how come you always tell stories? C'mon, you can tell me. Why do you always, always, always tell stories?"

"To answer that question, you shmuck, I'll tell you a story."

"There! See? I knew it. There is not a person in that head. All that's in there is the Children's Golden Book of Stories. Nothing else."

"So many years ago, there was a peddler. And he went from door to door with a big suitcase yelling out, 'Shoelaces, combs, matches; shoelaces, combs, matches; shoelaces, combs, matches.' And nobody ever bought. One day someone says to him, 'Okay. I want to buy a comb.' And the peddler opens the suitcase and there's nothing in it. The guy says to him, 'All these years you lug around an empty suitcase and you have nothing to sell. Why?' and the peddler says, 'Look, I'm a peddler. I'm marketing.' So, shmuck, I'm marketing."

The two of them stood in the emerging evening of spring and laughed out loud. Jack put his hand on Isaac's shoulder and said, "Isaac, that is either a feeble joke or one of the most profound pieces of religious philosophy I've ever heard. And I have no idea which it is! Let's go cut some poor kid's winky-tink and tell him it's for his own good."

Isaac called the next day. "We've got a date for the brit milah. The mohel can come early on Friday the tenth of March. But it has to be early because he needs to be home for Shabbos. He wants to know if he can bring two people with him. He's training two new mohelim and they need to observe. This is Okay?"

"Yeah sure. What else?"

"We have a lot to do. We have to set up a room at the Clinic that we can use. We have to be sure we'll have a minyan. We need to get Matt converted the day before and have another room set up for him next door to where we'll be. And we need a sandek."

"What's that?"

"This is a very important role. This is the person who holds the baby as the procedure is done. It should be a righteous Jew, a pious person because it's believed that he has an important effect on who the child will grow up to be. You need to pick someone."

"No contest, Don Quixote. Will you be the - what it is again?"

"Sandek. It will be an honor. There's some other things we're going to do while we have a minyan there but you'll see when the time comes. Now go find me, let's see, we need at least five more Jews. Can you find them?"

"In Bloomington? Wait, I'll check the Yellow Pages under 'J.'"

Thursday, March 9th was blustery, but it was clear that the winter had passed. The afternoon sun had warmed the earth by the pond enough to make the mud magnetic to shoes. It was an odd assemblage: Matt Cowan, Lev, Sage, Isaac, Merrill, Jack, Rae, Leyla, Simmy, Lee, Dinah and two Newfoundland dogs. Counting the dogs there were thirteen souls.

Isaac had an audience. Matt stood like a boxer now in the ring. He wore a long khaki coat that the army surplus store had sold at a fire sale. On his feet were rubber sandals. That should have been the tip-off. Merrill stood at the back with Matt's army surplus backpack bulging at the clasp. Lev and Sage looked nervously at one another, the dogs looked longingly at the pond, and Isaac looked long and hard at Leyla.

Isaac began the now-familiar service in his best rabbinic tones:

"So, we have here the convert and our witnesses. Matt Cowan has asked to become Jewish. Three times in my conversations with him he has asked and three times I have tried to turn him away and he has repeated his request. I've given him books to study, and I know that he has studied Judaism and has a good knowledge of it. So now I'm going to ask him, 'Matt Cowan, do you leave and renounce your previous faith, and do you accept the One God and agree to live your life according to the law of Moses and Israel?'"

Matt crowed, "Yeah!" At which point Jack realized that there was no bucket to retrieve water from the pond. Isaac nodded at Matt; Matt nodded to Merrill, Lev and Sage. Suddenly, he unbuttoned his coat to show that he had on only a bathing suit underneath. He dropped the coat off his shoulders and ran headlong for the pond taking a full-length dive into cold water four feet deep.

Jack was caught off guard, but not the two rescue bred Newfoundlands at his side. They responded instantly and raced for the water without giving Jack the option of untangling the two leashes from his wrists. Like practiced canine lifeguards they hit the water paws pounding furiously followed by an ungainly professor whose shouts of "No! No! NOOOOOOO!" went unheard. In the pond was a convert headed for shore as fast as possible, two dogs wholly committed to rescuing a young man who needed no rescue and one professor soaked to the waist and caught between hilarity and rage. The rest of the assemblage was paralyzed with laughter, especially Rae.

As Matt emerged, Merrill drew a large towel from the backpack and ran to him like a trainer to his champion pugilist. There were no towels for Jack or the dogs.

Isaac intoned, "Your Hebrew name is Mattisyahu. May you be protected by the God of Abraham, Isaac, and Jacob!"

Lev, Sage, Merrill, and Matt dashed for the warmth of the rabbi's home. Rae reached out for Jack and said, "Let's get you dry, dog-master." Cady and Sasha looked longingly at the pond hoping for another swim and Isaac accompanied Leyla toward the house on Tamarack.

CHAPTER 25

Rae navigated in a medicated fog. She was slow but not paralyzed, capable of short periods of clarity with effort, but not long periods. The entire household labored through the days as Jack and Leyla struggled to maintain some kind of normalcy for the children. Dinah was too young to reason, but she felt the tidal change. Lee retreated to his room as his safe harbor. He came out seldom and spoke little.

Simmy stopped his father at the door late in the afternoon. "Can I walk Sasha while you walk Cady?" It was an astute request. Cady had twice the tonnage of Simmy and never really got her steady bearings. Sasha was older, wiser, gentler, and forty pounds lighter. Simmy could manage her.

"Sure. You're old enough to help walk these guys."

They each took a leash and an attached dog and went out into the lowering sun. A light breeze freshened Southmoor and carried on it the aroma of plowed earth. The farmers were disking the fields preparing for the early planting. Dog noses fetched the scents of spring and quickened their steps. Cady looked longingly at the pond as Jack tightened the tether.

"Dad, what's goin' on with Mom?"

"Whaddaya mean?"

"She sleeps all the time. When I try to talk to her, it's like she's halfway there. One of her eyes looks really funny. I know she's been sick and all, but I wanna know when she's gonna get better."

Jack looked at this man-child in confusion. When do you stop talking to your child as child? When do you put aside your own childhood hurts, bury them forever and shepherd your own child into manhood? When is the time when you're not a pillar to be leaned on, but a partner who can be leaned on and who can lean in return? Was Joseph Israel, his own father, ever

Jack's friend? He couldn't remember the sound of his father's voice. They never spoke. His only recollection was of Joe Israel yelling out his name in anger or disappointment, "Jack!" He never told him he loved him; or was proud of him; or missed him; or was happy for him; or was worried about him. Never.

Jack recalled Morton Zadok in Milwaukee. Mort was his psychiatrist and debate partner. When he ended therapy, they lunched together occasionally and they debated. Jack argued still that if one was poorly parented, one would become a disabled parent.   "Look," he said, "as a social psychologist I believe that we learn our most powerful lessons about how to behave from role modeling. If we have flawed parents, we never learn the lessons about how to parent well." Jack was lecturing to himself; displaying his own fears.

The psychiatrist punched back. "You're wrong. I told you. As soon as a person can say 'I was poorly parented' he's begun the process of healing. He can get up and look in the mirror every morning and say 'Today, I'm going to be a good parent. It'll take effort but I can do it.' The whole premise of psychotherapy is that people are capable of change."

The walk with Simmy was a time of test. Could Jack Israel overcome the sadness that his own father had bequeathed to him?

"Simmy," he sang, "I'm so sorry. This has gotta be so hard for you. I wanna make it better. I want it to go away and all be O.K. - but I just can't. And I can't because it's out of my control and because it's so hard for me too. Can you understand that?"

Simmy wore his mother's face and her luminous eyes and he began to contort that beautiful face in the same way that Rae did when she cried. He was nearly twelve, that terrible age when a boy is too old to cry without shame and too young to stifle his anguish.

"I . . . want my . . . Mom back." And he wept the tears of a lost little boy.

Jack leaned into him and put his arms around him and held him so very tight.

"You know I really love you. And you're a great help to me in a tough time. Simmy, this is hard, but we're gonna make it through this, you know? Somehow, we're gonna make it through this."

He then knew that Morton Zadok was right. He also knew that he was now about to rob his eldest son of his youth, but it was something he had to do.

"I need you right now, Simmy. We have to take care of Lee and Dinah and we're gonna have Little Joe to take care of. And I need all the help I can get and you're part of that."

Through the tears, as his childhood was ending, Simmy was able to ask, "Mom's gonna die isn't she?"

"Yes. Mom's gonna die. I can't lie to you."

Each of them took a dog to his side, took the other's hand, and each of them cried as they walked.

The anti-seizure medications were a poisoned apple in Sleeping Beauty's mouth. As Rae slept her narcotic sleep Jack made the necessary calls for what should have been a joyous event. But Friday's brit milah, the ritual circumcision, was one more burden that Jack had to bear. He made the critical calls.

"Rhonda? Jack Israel. I need some help - please. We're going to have a bris for our new son at the Clinic early on Friday. The Rabbi is setting up the rooms and all the medical stuff, but I need to round up about half a dozen Jews. Can you help? And would you feel comfortable calling over to St. Mary's and asking Carol Martinez to come over? Rae likes her and she's probably gonna need some support. And can you bring some - I don't know - bagels and stuff for people?" Rhonda was saintly, probably the reason that a flawed husband left. She agreed without a breath in between and it was done.

Jack woke on Friday before the alarm. This had to be Rae's day. It just had to be. She slept next to him, on her back. Never, before being sick, had she slept on her back. Now she lay, flat, breathing deeply, unmoving. There was a great deal to do. In his dash for the bathroom he collided with Leyla in the narrow hall as she emerged from her shared bedroom with Dinah. They stopped in the morning isolation that envelopes people with the smells of sleep and stale breath and the ravages of unkempt hair. They looked at one another for just a moment.

Jack said, "Good morning. Hey. Thanks for being here. I couldn't do this by myself. Just . . . thanks."

Leyla nodded. "She's my sister. You know?" And she put her arms around Jack and hugged him. Hugs are odd things. They say a great deal that can't be said, perhaps ought not be said, in words. Jack smelled her smells of sleep, breathed them in deep and in a fleeting moment remembered how long it had been since he had held a woman in embrace. And then it was over.

A small conference room was reserved on the OB/GYN floor at the Clinic next to a second, smaller conference room. By the time Jack shepherded his three children, Rae, and Leyla into the room, a small but significant crowd had gathered. Rhonda was scurrying about, setting a distant table with coffee, bagels, and spreads. She greeted Rae warmly and introduced herself to Leyla. Hank Vanzander wandered about the room. Myron Tabanov occupied a corner and watched as if taking notes. Gerald Byer was officiously present. Carol Martinez came in accompanied by an elderly woman in a modest blue dress. With them was a dark-skinned man with a narrow face and a thin trimmed mustache. Carol approached Rae and offered a genuine hug. Rae returned a slow, deliberate smile. Carol brought her entourage to Jack.

"Dr. Israel, I'd like you to meet Sister Mary Roman. She's the Vice President for Nursing at St. Mary's. Oh, and this is Dr. Muhammad Attah, who's new on our pediatric service."

"Dr. Israel," Sister Mary Roman began, "I hope it's all right for us to be here. Neither Dr. Attah nor I have ever been to one of these ceremonies and we both wanted to watch and learn. I know Rae and I'm fascinated by what this all means and Dr. Attah wanted to watch the procedure. Is this OK with you?"

"Oh, uhh . . . Rae and I are just glad to have you here. Sure, by all means."

They shook hands all around and it slowly began to sink into Jack's head amidst all the confusion. Here at his youngest son's circumcision would be, at the least, one rabbi, three mohels, one nun and a Muslim physician. Only the Dalai Lama could have made it more religious.

The door opened and Isaac led in a cast of many. Lev and Sage were with him as were three men, one rather old and two young. The three were slightly bedraggled. It was evident that they had been traveling. The older man carried a small instrument bag with him. Just behind them were Bud Blumberg and Irene Turner. There was one key person missing.

Isaac took immediate command. "Could someone bring the baby in please?"

A nurse who had been standing sentinel by the door turned to locate a bassinet which most recently had been moved out of the pre-term nursery and into the main nursery. In the bassinet was a bundle, slightly larger than it had been the week previous, with a small sign which read, Baby Boy, Israel. The nurse took the bundle and, instead of handing it to Rae, handed it to Jack who stood next to Isaac. Rae half turned, buried her head on Leyla's shoulder and began to cry. In a moment, she and Leyla left the room. Rhonda followed.

Isaac began, "Hello, everybody. I think I know all of you. So today we have a great mitzvah to perform. I'm so pleased to tell you that we are honored by the presence of Rabbi Mordechai Tillman from Chicago and these two gentlemen whom he is training to follow in his footsteps in this honored profession. I'm going to let him do his job and then we have some other things to do."

Rabbi Tillman took his lead. "Nu, Jack. You know that the Torah teaches that it's the father's obligation to bring his son into the covenant between God and the Jewish people through the ritual of brit milah. This is for you to do yourself. But, if you appoint me to do this ritual circumcision for you, if you ask me to do it in your place, I can do it. So, do you want me to do that?"

Jack nodded while Rabbi Tillman went on, "And to do this, you must also choose a sandek, someone to hold the baby who will be his sponsor. And this should be a righteous man in Israel. Do you have someone?" Jack nodded again. "If you will pass this baby who does not yet have a name in Israel to your chosen sandek, we can begin."

Jack handed the baby to Isaac, who appeared very serious. The mohel conferred with his two trainees. He extracted from the instrument bag a bottle of Magen David grape wine and soaked a gauze pad. He put the soaked pad in the baby's mouth and the child sucked eagerly at the sweetness. He then stood erect and turned with a serious face to Isaac and spoke in Yiddish - directly, almost aggressively. Isaac responded in Yiddish, also directly, almost aggressively. Jack wondered at the exchange in an ununderstood tongue.

The mohel opened the blanket and the baby immediately began to squirm and to cry. Hank Vanzander produced a plastic board with straps attached and he and Isaac worked to strap the child onto the board so that his legs parted, and he couldn't move. It was clear that they had done this as a team before. The mohel applied an anesthetic cream to the end of the penis and five heads leaned over the site of the impending trauma - Rabbi Tillman, Isaac, two trainees, and one supervising pediatrician. In moments the cutting was done, the penis was bandaged, and the child continued to cry but now with added reason.

Isaac resumed his command. "Usually, Rabbi Tillman does the honors at this point, but I have asked him if I might officiate for personal reasons." He sang some in Hebrew and then said, "We now confer a name on this baby who, according to Jewish law has not had a name until this moment. Let him be known in Israel as Yoseph Yitzchak ben Yaacov v' Rachel, Joseph Isaac Israel. Now please understand that this is a very meaningful, a powerful name. He is named for Joseph, the son of the patriarch, Jacob, and his wife, Rachel. He is also named for our forefather, Yitzchak, or Isaac, who was the father of Jacob. Joseph was the dreamer. He could see what God's plan was for the world about him. Isaac was a mystic, a meditator, a man of prayer who was in communion with God. So, in giving this boychik the name Joseph Isaac, we confer on him great powers of insight and wisdom."

Isaac was not done. "It's customary for the sandek to give a short drash, a sermon, and I would like to do that now. And what I would like to tell you all is that this is a very emotional ceremony because the father, Jack here, is required by Jewish law to cut flesh from his baby son. He is required to draw his blood and to at least some degree to cause him pain. Every Jewish man has experienced this loss and this pain and has a right to ask his father, 'Nu? Why did you do this to me? Why did you hurt me?' And every Jewish man, no matter how much he loves his father, has a right to this question, why did you hurt me?"

He was on a theme that spoke to every Jewish man there and he was gathering mystical velocity. "It's only when a man brings his own son to the brit milah - it's only when he sees the need - when he knows the importance of bringing his own son into the Covenant of Abraham - it's only then that a man can forgive his father for the pain that he caused him. And not just the pain of the brit milah, but the pain that every parent puts on their child for the child's own good. So, this is a wonderful ceremony for the community and for the baby and for the family. But more than that, it is a mitzvah for the father of the child and for the grandfather because at this moment, the father forgives his own father. Most often the sandek is the grandfather, but Joseph Isaac's grandfather is now of blessed memory. I have substituted for that grandfather and in this room, there is joy, celebration, and forgiveness."

He still wasn't done. "Could someone bring in the mother?" The nurse went into the corridor and brought back a tearful Rae, a tearful Leyla, and a tearful Rhonda Dorfman. Isaac intoned, "Now we have a minyan and we need to do a couple more very short ceremonies."

The circumcision team and Hank Vanzander snuck off through the door. They had business in the next room. Isaac was now fully in charge.

"As long as we have a minyan here today, we can do a couple more things that are important but that will only take a minute. Jack, go stand next to Rae." Jack moved toward the corner by the door and stood next to Rae. "Now," Isaac continued, "I hope you all know that Jack and Rae are legally married, and that Joseph Isaac is not a mamzer, an illegitimate child. And Rae has gone through a conversion and Jack and Rae had a private Jewish wedding with me. As long as we have a minyan here, I'm going to conduct a very quick renewal of their Jewish marriage. Jack, do you take Rae to be your wife according to the Law of Moses and Israel?"

"I do."

"Rae, do you take Jack to be your husband according to the Law of Moses and Israel?"

"I do."

"So now I pronounce before this minyan that you are husband and wife according to the Law of Moses and Israel." He was not done. "Two more things we have to do. We're going to confer a different name on Rae to protect her from anything adverse in her life. I will now recite a brachah, a prayer, and we will change Rae's name to Sarah bat Avraham, Sarah daughter of Abraham, because Sarah is the first woman to choose Judaism and Abraham is the father of all Jews." He recited a Hebrew blessing and instructed, "Please all say Omayn!"

All replied with a resounding, "Omayn!"

"Now, someone go next door and bring me Matt."

Sage slipped out and came back with Rabbi Tillman, his students, Vanzander and a sheepish Matt Cowan.

Isaac questioned Tilllman, "Nu?" Tillman nodded somberly.

Isaac turned toward Matt, "So, we have in front of us Matt Cowan who has gone through a ritual immersion and who chose to become a Jew. And just now, he has gone through a symbolic brit milah to complete his conversion. All that's left is for us to give him his rightful Hebrew name. Let Matthew be known among the people Israel as Mattisyahu ben Avraham. All say 'Omayn!"

All responded with "Omayn!"" And Mattisyahu ben Avraham Cowan grinned and kept his hands in the pockets of his baggy trousers.

Most left. Some stayed for bagels and coffee. Myron Tabanov remained in the corner smiling softly to himself. Jack approached to thank him for coming. Myron spoke before Jack could speak. "Lost a lot of business here today."

"Beg your pardon?"

"Lost a lot of business. Isaac absolved all these guys of their problematic relationships with their fathers. Some of my best customers."

"Myron, you're much crazier than any of your patients, but I think you're harmless. Thanks so much for coming."

"I looked at Rae. I'm here when you need me. You understand?"

"Yeah. I understand. Thanks, Myron."

Rhonda was next on his list. She was supervising bagels while Rae was sitting in a corner holding her wounded baby.

"Rhonda, thank you so much - so very much. How're you doing?"

"You know, Jack, this was good for me to do. I'm really fine. It took me a while, but I realize that I gave up a lot of myself in my marriage. I never got to be anything. So now I'm starting a new life. It's not easy, but it's good for me. Look, when you need help, let me know. It's good for me to be able to do things."

The room cleared. Vanzander was in a corner with Rae and Leyla discussing care of a clipped penis. Rae was clearly fatigued and in need of relief. Jack realized that in the back corner of the room were Simmy, Lee, and Dinah, huddled together. Simmy was reading to them. Jack approached slowly and Simmy looked up.

"I brought some books for us to read and some crayons and coloring for Dinah," he offered. Of all the moving moments Jack had known in these months this might have been the most poignant. His oldest son, to whom he had spoken as a confidant for the first time only yesterday, had assumed the role that Jack had begged of him. He knew at once, gratitude, pride, and guilt. Truly he had robbed his son of his childhood.

They all went home. All of them. For the first time Cady and Sasha sniffed at Little Joe and were disgusted. Their comments were all but audible, "He smells bad. He's noisy. Why did you get him? We don't need any more litter mates!"

Rae went to bed. Leyla remained isolated in meaningless housekeeping, avoiding conversation. An odd silence quieted the house broken only when Joseph Isaac Israel slept off his wine-induced trance and woke to find himself in unaccustomed discomfort.

Jack ran for the portable crib in the bedroom next to Rae. Even the frantic cries of her son didn't wake her. Leyla was on Jack's trail, the second hound in the pack. As Jack lifted Joe from the crib, she elbowed her way in and said, "I can do this" and made it clear that Jack was to leave the room. Twenty minutes later Leyla and Joe rocked in the rocker in the living room as she held a bottle awkwardly to his mouth.

"Jack, can you move the rocker into Dinah's room? That way I can feed him quietly and not disturb Rae."

As afternoon wandered toward four o'clock the boys began to enjoy their hypoglycemic whining. Leyla, who showed signs of fatigue, made brownies and fed them to children for whom a serious life-long risk was diabetes. Jack ricocheted off the walls of the house, bouncing from Rae's bedside to Joe's crib-side to the truck's curbside. He knew no place of comfort.

As dinner approached, he announced, "Hey, whaddayasay Simmy and me go and get some Chinese takeout?" To roars of approval father and son gathered themselves for a hunting expedition in the forest of fast foods.

It was after nine on Saturday night and Jack had put off walking the dogs deliberately. At last the expected knock came at the door. It was so routine that no one noticed. Dogs and master assembled to greet their guide and the foursome wandered off once again.

"Thanks for yesterday. It was really, really good. When Simmy and Lee were born we just had them done at the hospital. No religious ceremony."

"Will you have them convert? And Dinah too?" Isaac asked.

"Oh, oh. I don't like the nature of the question. Exactly what do you mean?"

"They were born to a non-Jewish mother. The boys didn't have a brit milah. Dinah didn't get named in a synagogue. In some circles there would be questions about whether they're Jewish. If they go through bar mitzvah, they're automatically accepted in Reform Judaism. Conservative and Orthodox Judaism won't accept them without a formal conversion and for the boys the kind of ceremony that Matt had today."

"That sucks. They'll be Reform Jews."

"If they're Jews at all. That part's up to you. If you're a Jew, they'll be Reform Jews with ease. If you're not much of a Jew, they won't be Jews at all. And if you make them Reform Jews and they don't convert, that'll work unless, of course, they fall in love with a Conservative or Orthodox Jew."

"Then what?"

"Then, they're not Jewish and they have to convert, or the families will reject them. And even if the families don't reject them, your grandchildren will be mamzerim - bastards in your language - to Conservative and Orthodox families and therefore not suitable as marriage partners. You have a choice. You can live as a Jew, get them converted and if they fall away from Judaism, that's their choice. If you don't get them converted, you've pretty much made the choice for them."

"They can make that choice when they get older."

"It's possible but by that time it's very difficult. If they get to be young adults and they aren't comfortable in a synagogue and they don't know any Hebrew and they haven't grown up in a Jewish culture, it's very hard to become a practicing Jew. It takes a lot of determination and frankly, they'd face a lot of opposition."

"So, I could end up with just one Jewish child."

"You almost missed on that one."

"What do you mean?"

"Do you remember yesterday Rabbi Tillman spoke to me in Yiddish?"

"Yeah. What was that all about?"

"He asked me if this was a kosher penis, I had asked him to come and cut."

"That's hilarious. Kind of like a kosher salami only smaller."

"You can joke if you like, but he's committed to a difficult mission and he adheres to Torah law. He wasn't about to do a brit milah on a non-kosher petzel."

"What'd you tell him?"

"I got angry at him. I told him I was a rabbi and that I knew the Law and I wouldn't drag him here from Chicago only to have the child rejected by the mohel as unsuitable. Then he asked about Matt and I told him the same thing."

"Hey, Isaac. You swore to a colleague that these were two kosher penises. Are you sure? Or is this the Reform standard for kosher?"

"I'm fully sure in my heart that I did exactly the right thing. Now go back to your other three children. Go back to yourself. The Jews in this town came out for you today. The rabbi came out for you today - by the way, you owe Tillman four hundred dollars plus travel. You don't belong to the synagogue and you barely count yourself a Jew. What are you telling your children when you do this?"

"You've been talking to Rae."

"Rae's been talking to me, Jack. She's forgiven her father. She's making her peace with God while she still has a little time. And you?"

Jack slowed the walk and shook his head from side to side with sad resolve. "What you said today was very . . . very . . .," he waved a hand through the air, "Very insightful. At some point we have to forgive our parents and accept that they did the best that they could for us. None of our parents are ever ideal. If they do the best they can, that's all we can ever ask, and we have to forgive them for not giving us more."

"Jack, you ever read the Ten Commandments?"

"Oh, Isaac, c'mon. No sermons tonight."

"No sermon. A moment of Torah study, OK? The fifth commandment starts out, 'You shall honor your father and your mother.' Remember?"

"OK. I remember."

"You notice it doesn't say 'You shall love your father and your mother.' It doesn't say that you have to love them or that you have to stay in their lives or anything of the sort. It says that you have to honor that they brought you into the world and that they did the best they could. Your parents did the best they could. Now, my apostate friend, are you doing the best you can for your children?"

"I . . . am . . . doing . . . what . . . I . . . can at this moment. I know what I have to do but I have to take this one step at a time. Just give me some time. I have more than I can handle right now. Just give me time. OK?"

"I'm not the one handing out time, Jack. God hands out time. How much time have you got? If you're not a member of the synagogue, you owe the shul a donation and if you're thinking of joining, you owe the synagogue four hundred dollars in dues and your kids get Hebrew school for free for one year. "

"That's extortion. Isn't that a felony?"

"If you belong to the synagogue you get the rabbi for life cycle events for free. If you don't belong, you pay. This isn't about synagogue membership. It's about how much time you have left before your kids grow past you and what do you need to give them to survive in the world. The Talmud teaches that you have to teach your kids two things: How to swim and how to make a living. That's so they can survive in a hostile environment. The rabbi says you have to also teach your kids how to find meaning in their lives. Without a way of understanding the world, life is meaningless. You once asked me how people survived the camps. I told you the Orthodox and the communists survived. They had a way of finding meaning. So, give your children a way of surviving. Teach them to swim in a life that has no meaning if they don't have any faith."

"Is that what you're doing for Matt? Teaching him to swim in a meaningless world?"

"Matt's going to live in the Air Force, probably for the rest of his life. He's going to be part of a military machine that kills people for meaningless reasons. Not only does he need a way to survive, but he has to show other people around him how to survive."

"What's next for him?"

"One more step. I need to bring him to bar mitzvah. He's been converted. He's had a brit milah. He's got a Hebrew name. Now he needs a bar mitzvah and then I've done what I have to do."

"Tell me I have no role in this. Please."

"Sorry. You're already implicated in the crime. You'll show up and he'll probably want you to have an Aliyah, to come up and read from the Torah."

"I don't know how."

"You have barely enough time to learn. I can teach you - but only of course if you're a member of the synagogue. Otherwise I have to charge you for lessons." Isaac laughed at his own little joke.

Jack and his friends came back through the door. Leyla was in the corner of the family room with a contented Joe in her arms, bottle in mouth. She wore a beatific smile as he looked at her. The dogs headed her way and she exclaimed, "No dogs. Get the dogs away, please. He doesn't need dogs."

Jack was prepared to argue. Of course, Joe needed dogs. All his children needed dogs. Jack needed dogs. Rae needed dogs. Even Isaac had come to accept dogs. And then he remembered that without Leyla, he was paralyzed, unable to cope. Silence was a wiser course.

"Any sign of Rae?"

"Out cold."

"She's not awake much. Doesn't eat much. Doesn't drink much. We can barely get the meds into her. Don't like it. Not much to do, I suppose. Just wait. Just wait."

Monday morning Rae roused for a short time. She was able to kiss her children as they left for school. She held Joe in the rocker. She had little conversation with Jack and only a few words with Leyla. Together they got her into a tub to clean her up. She took her meds and went back to bed in the same way, on her back, breathing slowly, deeply.

Toward afternoon, Joe awoke to be fed. Jack went back into the bedroom to rouse Rae, sure that being with Joe was the best therapy for her. Rae was breathing very slowly, too slowly for Jack's comfort. He sat next to her and stroked her brow. There was no response. He leaned over and whispered in her ear. Again, there was no response. Now he patted her cheeks. No response. Time. Barely enough time.

He went to the phone on the wall. On a scrap of paper by the phone was a series of number - Dr. Vanzander, Dr. Crane, Dr. Acosta, and Dr. MacKenzie. Who to call? He opted for MacKenzie and dialed.

"Creditor Clinic Neurology Associates. How may I direct your call?"

"This is Dr. Israel. My wife, Rae Israel, is Dr. MacKenzie's patient. I think we have a problem and I think it's urgent. Can you get him for me?"

"He's with a patient, Doctor. May I have your number and have him call you back?"

MacKenzie called back within ten minutes. "Ahh, Jack. Is there a problem, lad?"

"Rae's not responsive. She's breathing slowly, very slowly and I can't wake her up. What do I do now?"

"Ahhh. I seeee. OK. You need to get her in here. It's not like you need tah come in through the emeergency room, ya know. I'll call doonstairs and we'll just admit 'er to ahhh . . . I doon't even know that we need an ICU bed, if ya foller. We can joost put her in a neurology bed fer now. You jest bring her here an' we'll see what we kin do."

Jack called the Bloomington Fire Department to ask for an ambulance.

"Sir, can you tell us the nature of the situation?"

"It's my wife. She's . . . she's not waking, and her doctor wants her in to the Creditor Clinic and I need an ambulance to get her there."

"If this isn't an emergency, sir, you can call MacDowell Ambulance Service. They can take her in, sir."

MacDowell Ambulance arrived in about twenty minutes. There was no reason for haste. That time was past. They put Rae on a stretcher and moved her out to the waiting ambulance. Leyla cried. The dogs milled in their perplexity. Leyla stayed at home to receive the kids as they made their way home from school, left to explain to them why their mother was gone again.

Jack drove behind the ambulance so that he could manage the paperwork and see to the details. Time was getting late. MacKenzie showed up with Helaine Crane in tow at the end of the day. This time she was in charge. "We'll get an EEG and do a head X-ray series. It may just be the meds, or it may be more. We'll have some answers tomorrow."

"I have to go home and tell my kids something. Is she going to be coming home?"

"Realistically?" she intoned, "Unlikely. We'll have a better idea in the morning. Go home. Reassure them as best you can for now. Prepare them for something worse if you can do that. We'll have more information tomorrow. Don't stray too far from the phone in case we need you."

Jack stopped at bedside. Helaine Crane followed him into the room. She added, "Hearing is still operative, even at this point. Don't hesitate to talk to her." And she left.

Jack sat on the side of the bed. There was no response from Rae. He began slowly, choking on each word, "Rae. It's me, Jack. Rae, I love you. Thank you for all the years of love and all the support. I don't know what I'm gonna do without you. But I remember everything you asked me to do and I'm gonna take care of things. Every thing's gonna be OK." He got up and hurried home.

Leyla was waiting by the door. The three older children stood around her, haunted looks in their eyes. There are times when men bottle up what is inside and cork it firmly. They go into their command mode and take charge, issuing directives and advice, seemingly oblivious to their own emotions. Those emotions seep out of a tight bottle into the sinuses and the chest and the stomach and the back as pain. Jack hurt everywhere, but he was in control.

"Leyla, why don't you go to the Clinic and sit with Rae for a little while? I can cover things here. Take the truck and go. Now."

Leyla understood what he said and searched for her coat. In minutes the taillights of the Chevy were gone, and Jack had his time with his children.

"Kids, we need a family conference." There are manuals written by such well-meaning people as social workers, child psychologists, clergy and the like for helping children cope with death. They are written for people who are rational, composed and capable of assessing the child's needs, fielding their questions, and providing the stable adult supervision that they need at a critical juncture. None of this described Jack Israel.

"Mom's back at the hospital. She's pretty sick. You saw that she's been sleeping a lot - a whole lot. And now she's gone into a deep sleep and I don't know for sure that she's gonna be able to wake up."

"What Dad's trying to tell us is that Mom's dying, and we need to be really brave and really good right now." Simmy did what Jack could not do. "This is really a tough one. I know a kid at school whose dad died, and he was out of school a lot and he was really sad. But our teacher, Miss Lenehan, explained it to us and told us that we had to be really understanding to Benjy cuz of what happened. And we gotta be really good and do what Dad tells us we have to do. Got it?"

Jack was so grateful, and so ashamed. Simmy was Rae's son. He could survive under pressure. He could do what had to be done and he could be the rock for those who needed one. Lee sat mute. He turned to Jack, who was no longer leading the conversation, and asked, "Are you gonna die too?"

"No! Absolutely not! I'm your Dad and I'm gonna be here forever for you. You need to know that you're safe with me."

Lee would not be put off. "You are too gonna die. Everyone does."

"Well, let's say I have no immediate plans and I expect to be here to see you grown up and adults all on your own."

"Dad's not gonna die, Lee. He's fine. It's Mom that's sick."

Dinah didn't comprehend. "I wanna go see Mom."

"Can we see her, Dad?" Simmy asked.

"Ohhhh. Maybe tomorrow. Maybe tomorrow. For tonight, Aunt Leyla's gone to see her, and I'll go over first thing in the morning to see if she's any better and can see you all. For now, let's have dinner and wait for Aunt Leyla."

Jack was beginning to function as he would have to: Feed and change Joe, make sure the kids get to school, get the dogs out, make meals, shop and call for help often. His mainstays were Leyla, Simmy, and Rhonda. This was to be a night like others. He fed dogs, children, and baby, left food out for himself and Leyla and watched for lights in the drive.

At mid-evening the truck lumbered into the drive. He was at the door to greet her.

"Hi. What's happening there"

"Nothing with Rae. She's not just sleeping, Jack. That doctor, MacKenzie? Well, he came in and looked at her and just shook his head. I asked him what was going on and he used the word 'coma' a couple of times."

"Did you talk to her? Dr. Crane was there and said that she might still be able to hear."

"Yeah. I talked to her and I made her some promises, Jack. Oh, Jack!" And she broke into sobbing tears and leaned heavily onto his chest. He held her as she cried and wondered whose chest he was to cry on.

The call came at about two in the morning.

"Mr. Israel? This is the charge nurse on the neurology floor at the Creditor Clinic. Our neurology resident has been looking after Mrs. Israel and he suggests that you might want to come in right away."

"Yeah. Yeah. I know. I'm coming. I'm coming." He sat for just a moment on the edge of the bed. This was what it felt like at the bottom of your stomach at two in the morning. Joseph Israel had the kindness to die at home. Just as Jack was making his way into a relationship with him, the old man had a heart attack in the middle of the night and died in Jack's arms. It was the final insult, "Don't think you can have a relationship with me. I'd sooner die."

And he did. Just as Jack was overcoming the trauma of death visiting in the night, it had returned. He dressed as quickly as he could and knocked softly on the door to Dinah's room.

"Leyla," he whispered, "Hospital called. Gotta go. Right now. Watch everything here." He left once more for the clinic.

There was no one at the information desk but he knew where to go. When he arrived on the floor, the head nurse followed him into the room. Rae was flat on the bed, her breathing alternately rapid and very slow. The nurse observed, "This is a particular breathing pattern. I'll call the resident. He'll explain."

Dr. Block was young but wise past expectation. He ran for the room but when he was there, he immediately slowed his pace. He spoke with deliberation. "This is what we call Cheyne Stokes breathing. It's an abnormal pattern of breathing with a gradual increase in depth and sometimes in rate and then you get a decrease in breathing almost to apnea. We see it in comatose patients, especially if they have tumor activity that hits the nerve centers that control respiration."

"How much longer?"

"I've looked over her medical record and she has a lot going on, Mr. Israel. Her EEGs have been all over the place for a while now. We're not talking about a long time. Maybe as little as hours. At most a day or two."

"She in pain?"

"I would say not."

"She gonna seize again?"

"Probably not. She's on a ton of anti-seizure meds."

"I have kids. They want to see their Mom. Have I got time?"

"Can't say for sure. Can you bring them in first thing in the morning? She might still be here by then."

Jack kissed Rae on the cheek. It was cold. Clammy. "I'll be back in just a bit with your children, Mrs. Israel. Just know that I love you, OK?"

It was six in the morning when he got home. Leyla was up with Joe. Jack roused the rest and got them dressed in haste. He instructed Leyla to bundle up Joe for the run to the hospital. He gathered everyone at the front door.

"Now listen all of you very carefully. We are going to the hospital to see Mom. They don't let kids in, but we're going anyway. Got it?" Heads nodded. "When we get there, we're going into her room for just a minute. Understand this - just a minute. No more. She's gonna be sleeping. She's not awake at all, but she can still hear you. You get to go up to her and tell her that you love her and then we're out of there like a shot. Okay?"

Dinah asked, "Are Sasha and Cady coming with us?"

"No, Honey, but I'll lick Mom's face and she'll think they're there."

He backed the microbus out of the garage, and they all piled in, with Leyla and Joe in the front seat. It was a fast trip as morning traffic had not yet built. It was the seven am change of shift at the clinic and no one was at the front desk. They hit the lobby on a dead run and crowded into the elevator. The nurse's station was empty as the staff were in report. They all made it into Rae's room un-intercepted. The head nurse on the day shift peeked out of the conference room and saw what was going on. She retreated into the conference room to explain that report would require a few extra minutes this morning.

Leyla positioned herself on one side of the bed holding Joe. "Rae. Rae. It's Leyla. I got Little Joe here, Honey. I'm gonna put him down next to you." She placed the wrapped baby on the bed. Simmy, Lee, and Dinah waited hesitantly near the door. Jack moved to the other side of the bed and nodded obviously to Simmy. Simmy approached and placed a tentative hand on Rae's left arm.

"Hi, Mom. It's me. Simmy. I love you." He looked up at his father to ask, "Can I go now?"

Jack motioned to Lee. He shuffled forward uneasily, hesitantly. Taking up his older brother's place he mumbled over a downcast chin. "Hi, Mom. It's me, Lee. I love you too." and he shrunk back.

Dinah stayed back, fearful of approach. This was not her mother. This was something else. It wasn't shyness. It was fear. It was the unknown and though she couldn't understand it she knew it was dreadful. This was not being done to her for her own good, it was for someone else's good; to relieve someone else's fear and horror.

"Dinah," Leyla whispered, "just come say hi to Mom and tell her you love her."

"Why can't she say she loves me? She always used to."

"She can't right now, Honey. But you can tell her."

Dinah took a small step forward and said from a distance, "Mommy! I love you." and retreated to the company of her brothers.

"Okay, guys. That's all for now. Let's go home." Leyla picked up Joe and all left for home with a renewed sense of emptiness, loss, and foreboding.

Jack returned late in the morning. Ian MacKenzie came by. Rae was still in Cheyne Stokes breathing, but slower now.

"So, Doc. How much longer now?"

"Hours. Might last the day. Somehow, they always wait 'til night, ya know. It's good you brought in yoor kiddoes. They'll need to know they did that one day. You might want to stay a good bit, ya hear? When you have tah, take a little break fer sum coffee an' such. But stick aroun', eh."

"I understand."

The nurses brought in a tray.

"She's entitled to meals and we thought you might like something to eat. We've got coffee in the nurse's station. Just help yourself. Can we call anyone for you? Minister? Priest? Family?"

"Oh, no. Thank you. I just need to be here by myself with her."

He shook his head to cast off the sorrow, but it didn't work. In the small hours of Wednesday, Rae's breathing changed noticeably. He heard liquid noises from the back of her throat and went to sit by her. He held her hand and rubbed it gently.

"I'm here, Rae. If you need to go, Honey, it's OK. I understand. You can go if you have to."

After a few moments he realized that he could no longer hear her breathe.

He rose slowly off the bed and walked to the nurse's station.

"Thank you for everything. It's time for me to go home now."

CHAPTER 26

He went through the door as quietly as he could. Even the canine security system didn't go off. The streets were empty; the skies were black; it was a time for rest and not for sorrow. He chose not to wake Leyla. There was no need. He would have felt unfaithful to Rae to enter into her sister's sleep. The bed was not a place he could be. He grabbed a blanket and headed for the couch in the family room. The sun would be up all too soon.

Dinah was the first. She crawled next to him on the couch. Exhaustion was no protection from this day. She was followed by hot dog breath and soon after two more warm bodies and the murmuring of children who know not to wake but who do so anyway. This was always their pattern on Christmas morning. This morning would be different.

There were five bodies next to him; five souls emerging from sleep waiting for his soul to rise as well. He lay, eyes tight shut, at first dreading the day. In his own head, he began to realize that these souls were not his burden. They were his strength and his solace. He would be denied self-pity because these children needed more from him than self-pity. He would immerse himself in the details of ending one part of his life and beginning another because these children would demand that he be responsible to them and so to mend himself. He had promised their mother no less.

Jack cracked one eye open to find Dinah staring at him. As his vision cleared and he opened another eye, he could see Simmy and Lee. He sat up in his rumpled clothes and rubbed his eyes.

"Good morning, my beloved children," the red-faced man began, "Everything will be all right. I promised it would be all right and it will be."

Simmy stared him straight in the face. "Is Mom . . . okay?"

"Mom and I talked last night," he fabricated, "and she told me how great it was to see you all and that she heard everything you said to her. And she told me how much she loved you all. And she went to sleep, to sweet dreams, and she didn't wake up."

Dinah crawled in closer. "Is she gonna wake up?"

"No, Sweetheart, she's not. She's gone."

"Where did she go?"

"She's in Heaven, Dinah."

Simmy wouldn't quit. He wouldn't let his father down easily. "Did she die? Is she dead?"

"Yes, she died last night."

Lee opened his eyes wide. "You lied. YOU LIED! You said everything would be all right. You know what? You're . . . you're full of SHIT! You always lie!"

Jack grabbed for Lee and tried to hold him close, to hug him, to reassure him but he mustered all the strength of which a nine-year-old is capable and wrenched free. He ran to his room and Jack could hear him moving his bed and bureau against the door to keep the awful reality out.

"I'm sorry," Simmy began, "I shouldn't have asked. It's my fault."

"No. Not anyone's fault. He's got a right to be angry. We all do. But not at one another."

"Who do we get to be angry at?"

"Nobody. Just nobody."

"What on earth is going on out here?" Leyla held a squawking Joe in her arms, and she wore a look of unhappiness.

"Mom died last night, Aunt Leyla," said Simmy. "Dad just told us, and Lee got really upset."

"Jack! Jack! What happened? Tell me."

"Not much to tell. Got a call in the middle of the night. Went to the hospital. It was all very quiet and peaceful. Not much to say. Got to pick up the pieces and start to heal. That's what she would have wanted."

"Why didn't you call me?"

"What would you have done? Left the kids and come to sit next to Rae to wait for her last breath? There was no point."

"The point is that she's . . . was my sister. And I would have wanted to be there!"   "Is there anyone here who's not mad at me?" Two dogs looked lovingly at him.

He began making phone calls at nine. Even an anticipated death permits no preparation. Even the most prepared is not prepared for what needs to be done. Funeral directors and clergy earn their fees at times of death. No one ever anticipates the small details and carries it off by himself with grace and dignity. He called his neighbor, his friend, and, by now, his rabbi.

"Isaac? Jack. Rae died last night."

"Are you home? I'll be right there."

He was moments in coming. In those moments Simmy crashed through the door of his bedroom to be with his sulking sibling; Dinah sat with Leyla as she fed Joe and Jack just sat. Isaac didn't knock. He walked in unannounced and found Jack. He said nothing.

Jack opened, "So what do I do now?"

"Now we take a deep breath and then we see about a funeral."

"How do I do that?"

"There are some little problems. You're not a member of the synagogue so I can't offer you the use of the synagogue. I'm sorry but that's the case. You can hire a funeral home and they'll do what they do. I can guide you through it - there's a lot to know. But if you want a chapel service, it will have to be at the funeral home."

"Have I got an option?"

"Graveside service. We can do a tasteful graveside service that won't be too hard on your children and will give you a sense of closure."

"Can you run it - even though I'm not a member of the synagogue?"

"Yes. Of course. You'll have to arrange for a burial site - a grave. There's a corner of the Bloomington Cemetery that's reserved for the synagogue. You can buy a plot there. If you were a member it would be free. Best thing for you to do is to. . . never mind, I'll call the funeral home; we use Coutts. They'll arrange everything."

"What's everything?"

"Well. They'll pick up the body and prepare it for burial. They'll arrange to have a grave opened. They'll arrange a hearse and a limousine. They'll want you to come over to enjoy their counsel, to sign a contract, and to pick out a casket. Don't worry about the casket. I'll tell them what you want."

"How do you know what I want? What if you pick a color for the lining that she didn't like?"

"Among Jews a casket has to be special. It's supposed to be a plain pine box - no nails, no metal. Wood, yes. Rope handles, OK. Wood handles are OK. But no metal."

"How come?"

"Everything's supposed to decompose. Everything's supposed to return to dust, to the earth from which we came."

"I don't want a pine box with rope handles."

"Nobody does. We have an arrangement for special caskets—very nice, tasteful, good looking - but all wood. We need to pick a day. Ordinarily we need to have the funeral as soon as is possible, but not on Shabbat or an important holiday. How long do you need to get people here?"

"Probably two days at least."

"Today's Wednesday. I don't like to do Friday. We can if necessary. Better would be Sunday. It's too far away, but it's the best we can do. Can you call people and get everyone here for a service on Sunday morning?"

"Yeah, yeah."

"OK. Now, I'll call Coutts and get this started. Be sure to get there today."

The next call was to Rhonda.

"Rhonda? Jack Israel. Rhonda, Rae passed away last night. Isaac, the Rabbi's been here and we're setting up a funeral for Sunday morning. I need some help at the office that's really important. Can you have the secretary let you into my office. On my desk, under the rubble is my rolodex. Just go through it and see who needs to be called, who needs to know. You can ignore the photocopy center and my plumber but use your own judgement and call as many as you think need to be called. And could you ask the secretaries if they can have someone cover my office phone for me. I'm out of commission for a while. Oh, and be sure to call Dunphy in Wisconsin."

"Sure, Jack. I'm so sorry. I'll make the calls and I can cover your phones for a few days. My schedule is real light right now and people can search me out in your office. I'll take messages in case anything comes up. Will you be sitting shivah at your house?"

Shivah. Jack remembered. When Joseph Israel had died, they had sat shivah. It was part of the Jewish ritual of mourning. Mourners were at home for up to a week and people came to pay their respects. Old friends of Joe's, family on both sides, friends of Jack's, neighbors all came in hordes to pay their last respects. The funeral was over.

Shivah was not for the dead. It was for the living. If the mourners were too overcome with grief to go back out into the community the community would come to them. It was a joy; it was a prison. The family had to be at home. He remembered covering the mirrors in the house, at once dreading the entry of the first visitor and being so grateful for people coming; being exhausted as the last person left and lifted up by their kindnesses. The last day of shivah had been a catapult. He was so glad to be freed from it that he ran back into the world.

After shivah, then what? He would go to the synagogue to say kaddish for Rae. He would stand and recite again the words spoken by mourners. He would make a public affirmation of his grief and every year on the anniversary of her death he would repeat the act of affirmation - I have lost, I have lost.

Over five thousand years the Jews had perfected grieving. Get the burial done as immediately as possible. Strip the mourners of their daily tasks and permit them only to mourn. Deny them their private agony. Make it the responsibility of the community to tend to their needs. And then force the mourners back into the community. Force them back to the synagogue, back to the prayer service, and keep them from their self-pity. And then, year after year, remind them of their loss so that they never forget. He would sit shivah for Rae and he would remember her year after year.

Coutts Brothers Funeral Home was professional. Kevin Coutts was a portly man in a white shirt, understated tie, and nearly black suit. He had worked closely with Isaac and knew what had to be done, quickly, quietly, diplomatically. Rae was already in his care. The limousine would pick up the family on Sunday morning. They would drive past the funeral home where the funeral cortège would be waiting. Isaac would lead to the cemetery in his car and the hearse and limo would follow. Private cars would line up behind the limo. The grave would be open, the service brief, and the grave diggers would wait out of sight for everyone to leave to cover the casket.

Isaac had a casket waiting. Coutts always kept a few Jewish caskets available for such needs. Members of the Jewish community unknown to Jack would stand watch over Rae until the funeral. This was a secret society of men and women who prepared the body for burial and stayed with it for as long as necessary, reading psalms in shifts. They were known only to one another. No one else knew the membership in the group. They might have been local to Bloomington; they might be drawn from outside towns. No one knew. It was their gift to the deceased.

A few family members came from Milwaukee. No one came from Boston. Jack anticipated only perhaps a dozen or so at the cemetery. The limo arrived at Tamarack Court at ten on Sunday morning. The death notice in the Courier called for an eleven o'clock service. Jack, Leyla, and the kids were dressed and ready. All were clean and neat and gray in color. Leyla carried Joe in her arms. Jack wanted him there. He wanted to be able to tell him someday that he was present for his mother. The boys were fascinated by the limo. The gravity of their own loss escaped them. Dinah clung to Leyla as they climbed in the back. The boys occupied fold out seats.

The ride to the funeral home was brief but they were required to wait while the staff lined up the cars behind them. Through the limo windows Jack could see Bud Blumberg, Myron Tabanov, Marty Wolf, Lev and Sage, and Matt Cowan who unceremoniously waved to him. Carol Martinez was there with several nurses from the psychiatric unit at St. Mary's. Leyla knew no one, not even Rhonda Dorfman who waited with Jared for the funeral procession. Isaac pulled to the front in the black Chrysler, the hearse was just behind him. Next came the limo followed by a dark green Volvo sedan that burbled with a hot rod V-8. It carried Myron and Matt. Perhaps a half dozen cars followed. The parade headed east toward the big Bloomington cemetery.

Along Maplewood Boulevard the street was parallel to the interstate highway. An exit ramp intersected at Market Street. Jack looked out at the highway and saw a canary yellow Camaro wearing Wisconsin plates hurrying down the highway. It grabbed the exit and ran the red light at the intersection to assume the last place in the funeral line. Two forms could be seen in the seats hunkered down, hidden in the gun turrets of the car, an old Wisconsin dairy farmer and a young cowherd.

It was eleven o'clock. Isaac had practiced this enough to know the time from Coutts to graveside. The hearse and limo entered the cemetery. The rest of the cars parked on the road and somber faced congregants filed in, eyes cast carefully to ground. Waiting for the assembly was a freshly dug grave, a mound of earth beside it, six folding chairs, and a chrome plated device for lowering the casket oh so gently into the earth.

Isaac motioned for Jack, Leyla, and the children to assume the seats and he himself took position at the head of the grave. There is a crude ecology at graveside. The officiant is at the head and the family is close and then relatives and friends find their own distance from the gaping emptiness of the grave, from the gaping emptiness in the lives of the family. They array by closeness, by emotional proximity, by the magnitude of their love and their pain and their intimacy - and by their own sense of loss.

Rhonda stood close. Near her were Jared and Lev and Sage and Matt. Behind them stood Bud and Myron and with them members of the synagogue. Bernie and Dunphy stood at the back away from the crowd. They wore wool jackets and broad brimmed hats and boots. Isaac looked to Jack and asked, "Do you have specific people you want to be pall bearers?"

Jack had no time to answer. Matt Cowan took a bold step toward the rear of the hearse. Dunphy and Bernie circled around the crowd to join Matt. Lev and Sage on a nod from their father followed. Rhonda Dorfman took a count of them and joined them. She would be the sixth. Together they lifted the casket from the car and carried it to the chromed square over the grave and set it gently in place.

Isaac began slowly. Fold-over papers were handed out. He offered no prelude.

"The dust returns to the earth as it was, but the spirit returns to God who gave it. Please join me in responsive prayer . . ."

They read together: "There is a time to be born and a time to die, a time to laugh and a time to cry. A time to forget and a time to remember. We remember one who enriched our lives with love and beauty, kindness and comfort. As we reflect on her whose memory moves us this day, we seek consolation, and the comfort of our tears.

God knows how we are fashioned, remembers that we are dust.

The wind passes over it and it is gone, and no one can recognize where it grew.

Three score and ten our years may number, four score years if granted the vigor.

What are mortals, eternal God that you should be mindful of them?

The sounds of infants attest to your power, the magnificence of life reflects your glory.

Teach us to use all of our days Oh, Lord, that we may attain a heart of wisdom."

He stopped for a moment and looked around. He looked at Jack and Rhonda. He looked at Leyla and the children. His eyes stopped for a moment as though he were looking at himself. He counted losses.

"Together" he asked.

"At the blowing of the wind and in the chill of winter, we remember her.

At the opening of the buds and in the rebirth of spring, we remember her.

At the shining of the sun and in the warmth of summer, we remember her.

At the rustling of the leaves and in the beauty of autumn, we remember her.

At the beginning of the year and at its end, we remember her.

As long as we live, she too will live; for she is now a part of us, as we remember her. When we are weary and in need of strength, we remember her.

When we are lost and sick at heart, we remember her.

When we have joy, we crave to share, we remember her.

When we have decisions, which are difficult to make, we remember her.

When we have achievements, which are based on hers, we remember her.

As long as we live, she too will live; for she is now a part of us, as we remember her. We are grateful for the gift of her life. And we are grateful for her life in us."

"Would anyone like to share here their remembrances of Rae?"

The small crowd avoided eye contact. For a long moment no one spoke. Then Myron Tabanov's voice opened, "Rae was a fine, compassionate nurse. She was a professional in every sense."

Carol Martinez picked up the beat, "Rae was one of the best listeners who ever worked on the unit. If I had a problem patient, I sent in Rae."

Rhonda lifted her gaze and looked at Carol and the psych nurses,

"I was one of those patients. And Rae was there for me - just there and I'll always be grateful for knowing that she was there. I'm better now in part because of her."

Isaac was a pro. He knew when to cut in and move to closure,

"Let the memory of Rae Israel be a blessing for each of us. And let us say Amen. I have a few words."

"Let me tell you a story. When Sarah, the wife of Abraham passed away, our forefather needed a place to bury her. He negotiated with a chief among the Hittites, Machpelah, for a choice burial cave. The cave is in the city of Hebron in Israel. And when Abraham died, his sons Isaac and Ishmael buried him in the Cave of Machpelah. But when Jacob's favorite wife, Rachel, died he buried her along the road that leads from Bethlehem to Jerusalem. Later, he buried his wife Leah in the Cave of Machpelah. When he went down into

Egypt, he met with his long lost son, Joseph. And the rabbis tell us that Joseph was upset with his father, Jacob, because he had failed to bury his mother, Rachel, in Hebron in the Cave of Machpelah, with the rest of the family. And Jacob, who was old and wise, told his favorite son, Joseph, that he buried Rachel in a strategic spot so that when the Children of Israel went into exile from the Holy Land, Rachel would watch over them and shed her tears for them. So here we are, my friends, in a kind of exile in a little town in the Midwest. And we're here to bury Rae Israel in a grave by the road. And someday, when we have left this place once and for all, these children might turn to their father and ask him why he buried their mother here. Children, she's here so that she can watch over you and shed her tears for you when you need her."

"We close with the twenty third psalm after which we will recite the kaddish."

"The Lord is my shepherd; I shall not want.

He gives me repose in green meadows.

He leads me beside the still waters to revive my spirit.

He guides me on the right path, for that is His nature.

Though I walk in the valley of the shadow of death, I fear no harm, for You are with me. Your staff and your rod comfort me.

You prepare a banquet for me in the presence of my foes.

You anoint my head with oil; my cup overflows.

Surely goodness and kindness shall be my portion all the days of my life.

And I shall dwell in the House of the Lord forever."

He motioned for Jack, Leyla, and the children to rise. "Now we say kaddish. Tonight, there is a shivah at the Israel household and please, all of you come so that we can have a minyan and say kaddish. The kaddish isn't a prayer of mourning, it's an affirmation of our faith in God. Even though we are in grief, we still praise God."

He intoned, "Yiskadal, v'yiskadash, sh'mei rabah . . ."

Jack followed as best he could. He was the only one muttering syllables. He had only the vaguest recollection of the words, but somehow the rhythms took over and he seemed in some small way credible.

Dunphy and Bernie stood close, perhaps at this moment closer than they had ever stood as men together and together they wept. At moments like these it becomes difficult to identify the source of the tears. Dunphy and Bernie wept for Rae. They wept for Jack and for Simmy and Lee and Dinah. They wept for Ilene Mariko-Dunphy and they wept for the loss of a wife and mother so long ago. They wept for the pain of loss that was old but never went away and they wept for the pain of loss that was new and would not abate. They wept for a life that always includes losses. They wept for the loss that is the cost of love. For loving is a dangerous enterprise that promises pain always.

"So now we lower the casket into the ground."

Two large men appeared as if on cue and ratcheted the casket into the grave. Leyla wept as it went down. Isaac was nearly done.

"The last thing we do at this time is to shovel a spade of earth into the grave. It's our responsibility to bury our dead. For those of you who wish, you can take one of the two shovels that are here and put a little earth into the grave. It's a mitzvah, a blessing, to do this. And when we're done, please form into two rows and let the mourners walk through to go home to the house of shiva."

Isaac stepped forward, took a shovel and dug in, using the back of the shovel to put a cup of dirt into the grave. He motioned Jack to do the same and then Leyla. Without being asked Simmy and Lee followed but Dinah stayed clear of the gaping grave.

One by one the rest of the crowd came forward and put in a little dirt. Isaac motioned that all should form two lines for the mourners to exit. Jack, Leyla and the children walked this gauntlet of grief and Jack opened the car door for his family. After they were in, he stuck his head in, said something, and closed the door. He ducked around those leaving and went back to the grave. Isaac looked questioningly at him, but he motioned that everyone was to leave him there. He stood for a long moment by himself staring into the grave as the two workmen approached.

He turned to them and said, "Hey guys, grab a cigarette and give me a minute here, huh."

And then he took a shovel and began furiously shoveling dirt into the grave. He was stopped for a moment by a tap in his shoulder.

"Hey, Boss. Lemme have that for a couplah minutes."

"Don't call me Boss!"

"Who cares what you want. Me'n Bernie are better at this than you are." And with that, the Dunphys, senior and junior, began, with Jack, to bury Rae. After a while they had done enough. The workmen came back to find a pile of wool jackets and cowboy hats and one dark suit jacket on the ground. Three sweating men leaned on shovels and it was clear that they had done all that they needed to do. There was plenty left for the workmen.

"C'mon, Boss. Let's throw Bernie, here, in the back seat and get you home. Sorry we were late in gettin' here, but the Camaro was startin' to overheat up aroun' a hunnert and I had to slow down."

"You'll be late for your own funeral too, I imagine."

The three crammed tired, smelly bodies into the Camaro and took the slow ride back to Tamarack Court. Bernie and Dunphy were not exactly dressed for shivah and Jack had no change of clothes to offer. Nor did he have a cold beer or even a cheerful word.

These three suffered the disease of men. They were set adrift without the women they loved. Their compasses, their clocks, and their calendars were broken. They would wander from bad meal to dusty corner to empty closet without complaint until some hapless woman took pity on them and set to reorganize their lives. They would know the loud laughter that lives among men but not the soft smiles that spice the lives of men with women.

Dunphy pulled into the drive and they went in the door. Jack introduced Dunphy and Bernie to Leyla. Bernie barely nodded in recognition. It had been a long time since he had been in a house with a woman in it. The boys ringed Dunphy demanding that he find them a race to watch on television. Dinah clung to him and asked, "Did you bring Ilene? She was supposed to teach me to be a ballerina!"

Dunphy looked at Dinah and swept her up in his arms to the level of his face.

"Ya know what, Princess? Ilene decided to go back to dancing school to become a ballerina herself."

"What about you?" she asked.

"I got the best part of the deal. I get to play with the cows all day. You ever milked a cow? I get to do it twice a day. Now that's fun! Wanna come home with me and help?"

"No. I'm gonna be a ballerina, not a cowgirl."

They stayed as long as necessary. As the afternoon wore on, Dunphy said, "Sorry, Boss. Gotta go. Can't leave the cows for too long. Gotta take it slow on the way home and it's a long ride to Dodgeville. Whyn't you bring these guys up for a weekend? Sure, could use the help." And they were gone.

Shiva is an odd assemblage of law, custom, and superstition. The lines between are indistinct, the separations unclear. No one knocks or rings a bell. They just come in. There's little conversation directed to the mourners. More so people just listen. There's no need to provide guests food. They bring it. There's no need to serve nor to clean up; guests are expected to do that. The mourners sit, preferably on low seats, and mourn. This would sound like a dismal scene. But it's not. Amongst themselves the guests are animated, alive, engaged. It's as if not only the mourners must heal, but that organism called the community must heal as well. And the treatment for pain is laughter. People tell stories.

"She was a great nurse. Had terrific instincts. Did you ever hear about the light of the world? Well, it seems there was this patient on the psych unit who kept telling Rae she had the light of the world in her womb. And we just thought this lady was having religious hallucinations. But Rae kept insisting that we call a gynecology consult and so after about a week, when we could sniff something bad happening, we called in Dr. Wildebrand who did a pelvic on her - and he took a Bic lighter out of her!"

"Oh, and do you remember the time that we had that patient who kept dancing around the unit flipping her fingers and singing "Cigaretteh, bitte, cigaretteh, bitte?' Rae came out of the nurse's station and she was standing there, and Rae starts dancing around singing, 'Cigaretteh, bitte, cigaretteh, bitte' and the patient just fell in a heap she was laughing so hard and she never did it again."

"Remember the towel thief? We had this guy who was stealing towels wherever he could and hiding them in his room. Under the bed, in the closet. He just kept copping towels. Rae got us all together and we called laundry and got a stash of towels and every time we saw this guy out of his room one of us handed him a towel and told him to put it in his room. In two days, there was no place for him to sit or sleep in his room and the next thing you know, he brings Rae out a towel. And then another and another and another. Got himself down to two towels in his room in two days time and he never copped another towel."

"Oh, do you remember the college girl who was hearing voices? Oh, that was something. See this girl, like maybe a freshman, came in and told us that she heard voices and they were telling her to do bad things. So, the docs wanted to medicate her. But Rae sat down with her and asked what the voices were saying, and she told her. Rae asked her if she ever talked back to the voices and she said, 'No.' Rae goes, 'Why don't you explain to the voices that they're upsetting you and ask them to stop?' She did and a couple days later when we're in group she says that the voices stopped bothering her. No drugs, no therapy. They just stopped."

There's no place to hide in a house of shivah. Jack rattled between living room, family room and bedroom. There were knots of people everywhere. The bathroom was the only real escape and that wasn't totally foolproof. At times he joined the dogs in exile in the garage. They were miserable. But then people began wandering into the garage.

Sunday evening the house overflowed. Isaac came with Lev and Sage and there were enough Jews for a minyan. On Monday fewer came and there were barely ten to pray the evening service so that Jack and Leyla could say kaddish. Tuesday there were not enough. At the end of the evening Jack asked Isaac, "How many nights do we have to do this?"

"Which answer do you want? The law or the custom?"

"The one that's shortest and doesn't involve a story."

"The law says up to seven days or the beginning of Shabbat. The custom in Reform Judaism is until you don't have a minyan and you're tired of it."

"That means we're done!'

"Hang around tomorrow night for a while and if no one comes consider it done."

"Then what?"

"You're obligated to say kaddish three times a day with a minyan for eleven months and one day. But seeing as there isn't a daily minyan, let alone a three-times-a-day minyan for three hundred miles from here, and seeing as you wouldn't do it anyway, it's all irrelevant. Come to shul when you can, when you know there'll be a minyan and say kaddish as often as possible."

"When's the next time?"

"You're coming to services this Saturday. It's a special Shabbos for a lot of reasons and you have to be there."

"So why is this special and I have to be there?"

"Because I said so! Look, it's Shabbat HaGodol, a very important service. It's the Shabbat just before Pesach, and traditionally the rabbi gives one of his most important sermons of the year. And you have to come to say kaddish. And it'll be Matt Cowan's bar mitzvah. Given that he was there for you, the least you can do is be there for him. And there'll be some other things of great importance that day. No excuses."

"I'm not sure how long Leyla can stay and that's gonna leave me pretty stressed. I gotta find someone to take care of Little Joe."

"You'll bring all your children to shul on Saturday. It's important."

"Can I go back to work tomorrow?"

"Do you need me to decide that for you?"

"I'm going to work tomorrow."

"And you owe the shul four hundred dollars."

"You're charging me?"

"It doesn't go to me. The arrangement is that you make a donation to the synagogue."

"And they pocket it?"

"It goes in the rabbi's discretionary fund. Your check will cover a nice after-service
    kiddush to celebrate Matt's bar mitzvah."

Wednesday morning Jack stumbled into the office. Children were apportioned to appropriate elementary schools. Leyla was relieved to be at home with Joe. The dogs had a pleasant morning walk and there was an illusion of normalcy to life. He took the stairs to the third floor and felt the burn in his thighs as he crested the climb. Barging into the office he found Rhonda sitting at the desk formerly occupied by Ilene. Without missing a step or taking a breath he rounded the desk, threw his arms around Rhonda and kissed her on the cheek.

"Thank you. Thank you. Thank you. You're my guardian angel. You're the most wonderful person. I'll be grateful to you for the rest of my life. I'd ask you to marry me, but you deserve better."

"Well that's certainly true. Look at this office. It's a fright. What can you possibly accomplish in a mess like this? Do you ever throw anything away?"

"Rhonda, I'd like to withdraw my proposal of marriage. It was a wonderful romance, but you could never tolerate me."

She laughed and hugged him, and they sat for a half hour and just talked. Finally, she said, "I think you have some important messages. They're on your desk."

Jack went to the pile of pink message slips that were on his desk. Much was expected: Dunphy - "Will be there"; Bud Blumberg - "Full sympathy, will come with colleagues." And then there were two tacked together. Bernie Fredericks - "So very sorry. How can I help?" Randall P. Morton — "So sorry. Please call immediately."

"Rhonda. Did you take these messages from Bernie Fredericks and Dr. Morton?"

"Yes. Is something wrong?"

"How did they know?"

"You told me to call everyone on the rolodex that looked like they needed to know except the plumber and the copy center. By the way, your Volkswagen mechanic wasn't very nice."

"Did you call Bernie Fredericks?"

"I think so."

"And did you call Dr. Randall P. Morton of the Regional Medical Program?"

"Yes. Shouldn't I have called them?"

"I suppose it's fine that you called. I just never . . . anticipated that."

He sat down at the desk. Morton asked him to call immediately. He had done no work since submitting his report. He had been out of touch with work for weeks. Calling Morton took all the courage he could summon. He lifted the number off the pink slip and dialed.

"Good morning. Regional Medical Program."

"Hello, this is Jack Israel calling. Dr. Morton asked me to call."

"Oh, Dr. Israel! We're all so sorry to hear about your loss. This is Cindy. How are you doing?"

"Well, uhhh, it's OK, Cindy. You know, it's . . . it's very hard but I have help and we're going to make it. Thank you so much - but how did you know?"

"Oh, we got a call from your office and Bernie Fredericks called us and he was very upset. I know Dr. Morton wants to speak with you. He's in a staff meeting right now, but I can slip him a note that you're on the phone. Hold on."

A few minutes later a gravelly voice came on the other end of the phone. "Jack, Jack, I'm so sorry to hear about your wife. Can you talk for a few minutes?"

"Of course, Dr. Morton."

"Cut the Dr. Morton, crap, Jack. My office got a call from your office and then Bernie Fredericks from Jewish called. You know, he thinks the world of you. And I read your report and - well, I don't know exactly how to say this, but it's not just a good research report, Jack. It says something pretty profound about people, about loneliness and social isolation. I really liked it, and Bernie and I agree, that it needs a lot more exploration. You with me so far?"

"Oh, yes."

"Jack, I don't talk about my personal life, but there's something I need to tell you. Many years ago, probably when I was about your age, I lost my first wife to breast cancer."

"I had no idea."

"I don't talk about it much. But it was a long, hard battle and I got left with two teenagers and we had a very hard time of it. A couple of years later, I met Uma, my current wife, and she put us all back together. But Jack, I know what you've been through and I know how dark life must look to you now."

"You're right. It's been hard and I frankly don't know what I'm looking at in the future."

"Well, Jack, this is where Bernie and I come in. You did this project on a young investigator award and we invested a lot in you and your career. The project turned out really well and we don't want to risk losing you. You've become valuable to us and valuable to the field. But if you stay put, you're not going to make it long term. You're in a very small community far from your data sources in Chicago and far from the kinds of help with things like childcare that you're gonna need to get back on your feet."

"That's probably true."

"So, here's what I'd like to propose. Why don't you and Bernie put together an expanded grant application for your project. More data, more time, more staff, more resources and we'll see if we can fund it. But instead of putting it in through Bloomington State and Bud Blumberg's shop, let me talk to the folks at Morton-Methodist-St. Mark's here in Chicago and see if they're willing to take you on board."

"Oh, I don't know if they'd really want me."

"Let me make some calls. You may know that before the merger of Methodist and St. Mark's I was Chief of Neurology at Methodist. When Charlie Radison put together the merger of Methodist and St. Mark's I was central to the process. Then when Charlie decided he just had to have a medical school in the mix, he came to my family's foundation for help with the initial funding. And that, my friend, is why it became Morton Medical School of Morton-Methodist-St. Mark's Medical Center."

"I had no idea."

"Not only that, I trained Frank Wachtel, the current Chief of Neurology. Let me call over there and see if Frank's interested in you. If I explain to him that you'd come in with a link to Bernie and with funding in hand, he'll be glad to talk to you. Here's my question: Are you movable to Chicago?"

"Dr. Morton - Rand - that's a big question. I need some time to think this through."

"Fine, Jack. Take whatever time you need. Here's my agenda: I don't want to lose a talented young investigator that I've put a lot of money into. I have your report and it's promising. Bernie's willing to support additional research. We think you ought to be in Chicago. While you're thinking, send me a fresh curriculum vitae that I can show Frank Wachtel. If I have to go to Radison, I'm glad to do that too."

"Wow."

CHAPTER 27

"I need to go home. How will you manage with Joe and the kids?"

"I'm not totally sure. I put an ad in with student employment looking for help. If I can hire two students who're comfortable with babies and they can swap off shifts, I think I can manage it."

"What do you think about the offer to move to Chicago?"

"It's the only intelligent thing for me to do in the long run. I sent off my papers and now it's just a matter of waiting to see if it all works out. If they want me and if Morton will continue to fund me, it's good for my work. It's good for the kids."

"And for you?"

"You know, Leyla, in all of this, I stopped worrying about what's good for me. What's good for you?"

"I made promises to my sister. If you're in Chicago it makes it much easier for me to live up to those promises. I hope you come, Jack. I really do."

He drove her to the train with Joe in her arms. At the station, he put Joe on the seat of the car to give her a hug and to say, "Thank you, Leyla. But for you" She stayed in the hug longer than courtesy demanded.

Most people live in a bubble of egoism. They calculate what's good for them. Everything else is weighed in balance with the egoistic bubble. Sometimes life unbalances the scale and bursts the bubble. What's good for one's self ceases to be what has to be done for others. There are two possible responses. The first is the feeling of being cheated. The child inside screams, "But what about me? Where's mine?" The second response is a kind of enlightenment. A person realizes just how small and how insignificant they really are. Others become so much more important in the balance. The bubble re-inflates. Only now, ego is outside, looking on in wonderment and gratitude for just being there to watch others. Women understand this better than men. Jack now understood how truly small he was. He loved Rae and missed her. The pain was excruciating. He would love her always. Now he had four children to watch. They were bigger to him than he was to himself and he was happy to be able to see that.

Life took planning. He laid out everyone's clothes on Friday night. Everyone got baths. Joe's bath required four humans and two dogs and took place in the kitchen sink to the accompaniment of laughter and stories about each child's babyhood. The events of Saturday were foretold and rehearsed. This was a team. Everyone had to know not only his position and play but everyone else's as well. Simmy was team captain to Jack's coach and Dinah was the cheerleader. Only Lee, dark, brooding Lee, who was always being cheated out of stardom, was slow to assume his position.

Lee was Mom's baby for the first three years of his life. When Dinah was born, he was no longer the cherished baby. He couldn't be Dad's boy, Simmy was that. The older brother was always better at everything. He could talk to Dad better, play ball better, help with chores better. There was no place for Lee to go. He could never please Dad the way that Simmy did. Mom, his true love, had left him for his baby sister. Some hurts are not healed with words. There were no words to help Lee.

"Simmy, I'm out to walk the dogs. While we're gone you are the chief guard dog. Please stay out of the kibble while I'm gone. When I come back, we go off to services."

A few minutes later all were assembled, including Little Joe, for loading into the microbus. Simmy now occupied Rae's spot in the front passenger seat. Dinah and Little Joe in his car seat occupied the middle row and Lee sat by himself in the third row which was redolent with the smell of dogs. The trip to synagogue was minutes long. Dinah recognized it immediately,

"I've been here before. They have books! Remember?" She turned to her two older brothers, "C'mon guys. I'll show you!"

Jack packed Little Joe into his baby carrier and shouldered the plastic diaper bag. He had fed Joe before leaving and he was napping peacefully, hopefully for the duration. Jack shepherded his flock into the synagogue where Dinah raced for the library with Lee in tow. Jack opened the door to the sanctuary to find Simmy at his back. As Jack grabbed a kippah from the box by the door, Simmy did the same. Jack snatched a tallit from the rack and placed it over his shoulders and again Simmy followed suit. This time Jack motioned that Simmy did not require a tallit. "You're not old enough," he whispered. It was only then that he considered whether Simmy might ever qualify as a Jew.

The minyan was there. Jack, Simmy, and the baby carrier took seats at the very back. All turned to see who had entered and a choir of smiles opened before them. Katie Cowan sat at the front with Matt. Matt wore a tie, a sport jacket one size too small, and a self-satisfied grin. Isaac looked up and nodded and the regulars, Bud, Phil, Myron, Marty looked back and nodded as well. In the opposite rear corner were Lev, Sage, Merrill and three girls. Rhonda sat by herself.

Jack picked up the Hebrew prayer book as did Simmy. Simmy fumbled with it in confusion, taking a long few minutes to comprehend that it was bound right to left and not left to right. He managed to open it but was confounded by the pages numbered backwards. Jack watched him and laughed and Simmy laughed back. The service was just beginning. After a few minutes of Hebrew prayers, Phil ascended the bimah and took over the lead.

He was in full voice. It was a sequence of "Please turn to page _____." "We now rise for _____." "You may be seated. We read responsively on page _____." As it went on Joe wriggled in his carrier and Simmy idly turned pages. The sound of the door behind his head alerted Jack to the two small forms that joined him. Isaac caught the entrants and, in a moment, stood and announced, "For the honor of opening the ark I would like to call upon Simon, Lee, and Dinah Israel."

There was panic in the pew. Simmy looked at Jack with terror; Lee shook his head. Dinah smiled broadly as Isaac beckoned her forward. Jack pushed them out into the aisle and toward the bimah. Lee balked and bolted for the library. Simmy and Dinah walked up the aisle and followed Isaac's smiling directives to open the ark and then please return to their seats. Phil Dorfman watched expressionless. The Torah was taken out and Phil rendered the appropriate prayers. He carried the Torah around the sanctuary and placed it on the reading table on the bimah. As Jack had watched before, Isaac and Phil called a series of men and a few women to come up to recite the blessings over the Torah. Among them were Lev and Sage. Isaac read from the scrolled parchment and shook hearty hands with all.

After a while, Isaac took a long moment, retreated from the reading table and called out in a loud voice, "Calling the Bar Mitzvah, Mattisyahu Cowan!" Matt rose from his place next to his mother, stood to his full height, and bounded up the three steps. He wore a tallit that had clearly been borrowed from the rack at the back of the sanctuary. The fringes flew with his steps. Under Isaac's direction, he took a corner of the tallit, touched it to the Torah and kissed the fringes. Phil retreated a full stride from Isaac and Matt and looked sour. Isaac directed Matt to the large print transliteration of the Hebrew prayers on the reading table and Matt began to sound out the syllables like a first-grade child laboring through a reading primer. Phil looked down at his feet and moved his head critically from side to side in disapprobation. It was agony to watch.

At the end of Matt's blessing, Isaac read from the Torah after which Matt repeated his strained reading of a Hebrew blessing. The agony continued. The Torah was closed, lifted, and covered. It was now time for Matt to recite a blessing and to read a segment from the prophets, the Haftorah. Once more he stumbled and mumbled through the blessing and then began a halting recitation of the reading in Hebrew. After a single sentence, he looked up, appraised his situation and began to read the segment, only now in English. There was simultaneous relief and dismay. It was supposed to be read in Hebrew. That would have imposed a penalty on the ears of the assembly that was unbearable. But the shame of it! It was a ghastly performance, only slightly less so in English than in Hebrew.

When the trial was over, Isaac shook Matt's hand eagerly and invited him to say a few words to the congregation. He made no excuses.

"Hi. And Shabbat Shalom to you all and thanks for coming - especially my Ma and my friends in the back. Thanks, guys. You know, I'm not good at this, and this is hard for me. And it's not just this, that's real hard for me. Anything at school's always been hard for me. I'm pretty used to not doin' this stuff so well. But I gotta tell yah, this was important to me. I got Jewish friends who did this cuz their parents made 'em do it and they didn't care about it at all. But I did it cuz I learned what it meant to be a Jew and I wanted this more than anything I ever wanted in my life. I did it. An' I'm really glad that all of you came to share this with me. Thanks."

Isaac shook Matt's hand and ushered him off the bimah. He returned to the lectern from which he cast an obvious scowl at Phil Dorfman. And he began.

"I'd like to tell you a little story. Once upon a time there was a little village in Lithuania called Kupiskas. And there were a few Jews who lived in this little village. Not a lot, but a few. And there was one shul and one rabbi and maybe a few dozen Jewish families and everyone knew everyone else. But there was always a threat to this little village and that was the Tsar. The Tsar always needed soldiers for his army, so every once in a while, the army came around and they searched the village for any young man from say fourteen on up who hadn't been drafted and they took him away to become a soldier. And the families were left in horror, because the length of time that such a young man was required to serve was twenty years. If they came home at all, they came home broken. They were broken physically, and they were broken spiritually for what the Tsar's army had made them eat forbidden foods, kill, persecute, you understand. For some of you, your own grandfathers came to this country to escape the Tsar's draft. Over the years, lots and lots of young men disappeared and most were never heard from again. One day the army came to Kupiskas and they took away a young man. We'll call him Iddle. And he was just . . . gone . . . and no one ever heard from him and they forgot all about him. So, one year it came time for Yom Kippur, the day to repent for our sins, and the remnants of the Jewish community gathered at the only synagogue in Kupiskas and did what Jews do on Yom Kippur. They fasted, they prayed, they afflicted themselves, they promised repentance. But the rabbi watched, and he knew his people and he knew their false pride and their self-importance and the little ways that they cheated and how hard their hearts were when the beggar was in front of them. He knew. Into the back of the shul came a stranger. He was decrepit. He was in rags. He was dirty. He wasn't shaved. His hair wasn't cut. And everyone stood as far from him as they could. And the people in the congregation were praying so hard in their Hebrew and the stranger was struggling. He didn't know the Hebrew prayers. He didn't know how to daven. Somewhere in his past he might have known, but that was long ago. But what he remembered was the aleph-bet, the letters of the Hebrew alphabet that we teach our five-year olds. And while the congregation davened their complex prayers for forgiveness, the stranger began to sing out in a child's song 'Aleph, bet, gimel, daled, hey, . . . ey, . . . ey, vov' and everyone looked at him and laughed. But he kept on and through it, and he wept.

So came the end of the day, the Neilah service, the last minutes of Yom Kippur when the Gates of Heaven are closing, and the final judgement is being written in the Book of Life. And the rabbi, at the front of the synagogue stood up on the bimah and he shouted, 'Stop! Can you hear? Can you hear? All of your prayers, all of your pleas for mercy, all of your promises for repentance for your sins have fallen short of the Gates of Heaven. They didn't make it into the heavenly realm. The Gates are closing. But one voice, one voice here today was so filled with devotion and repentance that it moved God on High. And as God Himself heard the aleph bet, those simple letters carried all your hypocritical prayers for forgiveness through the Gates of Heaven. And because of that simple song, your prayers were heard. Welcome home, Iddle, and he sat down."

And Isaac sat down as Phil Dorfman glared at him.

The rest of the davening was routine. Phil carried the Torah around once more. It was returned to the ark. Jack wasn't invited to participate. Little Joe remained silent and Dinah fled in search of Lee. It was only Jack and Simmy who remained in the back when Isaac said, "At this time we turn to the Mourner's Kaddish. We recall with sadness the loss of Rae Israel and extend our heartfelt condolences to the Israel family. Let those who mourn now rise as we recite the Mourner's Kaddish."

Jack stood uneasily and for the first time since the funeral, still able to feel the fit of the spade at the grave in his hands, his eyes moistened to overflowing, began slowly to read the transliteration of the prayer from the book in front of him. Ten words into the prayer, he realized that Simmy stood beside him, stumbling along the tongue-twisting transliteration. He was a boy stung with loss, dragged into manhood, desperately trying to find meaning in all of this strangeness.

Jack and Simmy sat down. Father looked at son and at baby stirring in the carrier. Simmy's lip shook as tears ran rivers down his round face. His mother's eyes sat in slits on his face as he looked to his father for an answer to a question that neither needed to ask.

Isaac once more took the lectern. "It's time for the announcements. Announcements are . . . announcements. Nu? But this week I have more than just announcements and I apologize for taking a few minutes of your time, but I have several stories to tell . . ."

Phil still sat on the bimah, prayer book in hand. At the mention of stories, he not so much slammed his book as detonated it. It felt like he fired a shot in the sanctuary. He sighed, loud, openly, with obvious disapproval. He tossed his head back as if to ask, "How much longer do I have to endure this?"

Isaac was not to be put off. "First, you need to know that in the old country, the rabbi didn't give a weekly sermon. The rabbi spoke twice a year from the bimah and only twice a year. Once was on Yom Kippur and the other time was on Shabbat HaGodol, the Great Sabbath, which is today. And on that day, on this day, the rabbi would speak to his congregation about how to prepare themselves for Pesach, for Passover. In that tradition, I would like to speak to you, even though this is supposed to be about announcements, about Pesach. Are you ready?

"You all know the story of Pesach, of the Exodus from Egypt. The text is specific, and it tells a story and it's a story you all know because you've heard it at every seder you've ever been to. But the Torah is full of secrets. If you're going to understand the secrets that the Torah has to tell, you have to read it closely and with a different kind of mind than just looking for the facts. Let me show you what I mean. You see, the story is about leaving Egypt. In Hebrew, the word for Egypt is Mitzrayim. Now, you can see easily that Mitzrayim doesn't just transliterate to Egypt. Mitzrayim is a Hebrew word and it has a literal meaning. It means, the Narrow Place or the Narrows. Now this makes sense on an obvious level and on a not-so-obvious level. On the obvious level, Egypt was, in fact, a narrow place. The only areas that could be cultivated for crops and the only areas that had reliable water were along the Nile River. Egypt, other than the desert, was a long, narrow place. Makes sense, no? But the text plays an interesting game with the meaning of the word Narrow Place. It says that God brought the Children of Israel out of the Narrow Place and in that meaning you can see that God brought them out of a place where their vision was narrow, where they were boxed in, closed in and no longer able to see outside of their daily slavery. They were so deep into their oppression that they had lost the vision of their forefathers of what life was really about. They served their taskmasters and not God. God brought them out of the Narrow Place and into the desert. At the Red Sea, the Sea of Reeds, they were caught in between the sea and Pharaoh's army that was chasing them to bring them back to

Egypt. It looked to them as though there was no escape. They had a narrow outlook and they couldn't see that there might be something more than slavery in front of them. Now the text says that the Red Sea parted, but the rabbis say that it didn't part until one man had the vision to walk into the water up to his lower lip - and then the sea parted. One man had to be able to escape the mentality of slavery in order to show the entire nation a path back to God. For Pesach, we have to escape our own narrow mentality in order to find our own path back to God. You understand?

"Now, more stories. Up until the Holocaust, with which I am all too familiar, there was in Lithuania a city called Vilna. On your map today, it's called Vilnius. Vilnius was the intellectual center of Eastern European Judaism. It was called the Jerusalem of Europe. There were about a hundred thousand Jews and hundreds of synagogues and dozens of yeshivot, academies of Jewish learning. It was every peasant boy's dream to go to study in Vilna. And the head of the community was the Vilna Gaon, the great rabbi of Vilna who was a world authority on Judaism. In the Holocaust, this flower of Jewish life was exterminated, but not completely.

Most of the synagogues were destroyed, the academies wiped out, the people killed in the camps. What remains today is a remnant of maybe six thousand Jews and the Great Synagogue in Vilna.

"So, my friends, you ask why I'm troubling you with all of this during the announcements. I have an announcement. The government of Lithuania has a position which is supported by the state. It is the Chief Rabbi of Lithuania. It has been open for a long time. A few months ago, I applied for the position and was offered it. I was offered it because I speak the languages of the community - German, Polish, and Yiddish and because no one else would possibly want the job. I conferred with the president of this synagogue and explained that I was not running from Bloomington but that I was running to a community where I have a deep history, and which needs me badly. So, I am here to announce that I am leaving Bloomington to become the Chief Rabbi of Lithuania in Vilnius."

Every mouth fell agape. Jack listened and laughed - out loud. Myron Tabanov plastered a gigantic grin across his face. Bud Blumberg smiled. And Phil Dorfman sat expressionless. Isaac stood on the bimah and a glow surrounded him. He was inches taller and years younger. The etched lines on his face disappeared as he found the lost years, as he shed the pain and suffering and walked with confidence into the Sea of Reeds.

Jack collected his brood and ushered them into the kiddush. They snatched cookies and cakes unashamedly. Rhonda grabbed Little Joe and refused to release him from her grasp. She took the diaper bag and disappeared into the ladies' room, bringing back a sweet smelling, smiling baby. The small crowd roundly congratulated Matt, congratulated Isaac, and commiserated with Jack. People stood close together. They spoke face to face. Even Lee seemed to find a place where he could have his fill of sweets and solace.

Jack cautiously approached Sage and Lev. "You guys packing for Lithuania?"

"Nope," Sage began, "As soon as school's out we're headed to Costa Rica for the summer and then I've been admitted to Wesleyan University in the fall."

Lev was not to be left out. "I got admitted to Peabody Endicott Academy, it's a prep school out east. Really good. Can't wait to get there in the fall."

"Gonna miss you two. Gonna miss you."

Saturday night all were sated with take-out pizza - high fat, high sodium, high calorie takeout pizza. Jack ate all the left-over pieces with obvious relish and washed it down with Coke. Little Joe had his bath in the sink after the dishes were done. He laughed and all laughed with him. Jack fed him and rocked him until he fell asleep. He tucked him into his crib and summoned Simmy. "Can you keep an eye on things here for just a few minutes? I'm sorry to ask you to do this but I have to stop in on Isaac around the corner for a quick conversation. Can you manage?"

"Sure, Dad. If anything happens, I'll stay here and send Lee to get you."

Jack walked out the door without dogs. The night air was fresh and clear. He took the kind of slow, deep breath that acknowledges the end of the day. His pace toward the house on Crosscut was measured. There was not a hurry tonight. Somehow life would go on and he could manage it all.

The Chrysler hogged the drive, parked askew. It had the earmarks of a new driver. He mounted the stairs and knocked gently at the door. The sidelights shone bright from within and he could see Isaac peering out to determine who needed entry late on a Saturday night.

"Jack! Nice to see you. Come in and I'll get my coat on. We'll take a walk."

"No walk tonight, Isaac. Sorry. I left Simmy in command and it'd be unfair to leave for more than a couple of minutes."

Isaac stood in the entry to the dining room. Cardboard boxes were stacked about. Some already bore labels for shipment to Vilnius, Lithuania. Most were half-packed. In each of two corners were other stacks. One was marked, Levi Abrams, Peabody Endicott Academy and the other Sage Abrams, Wesleyan University. Spaces were carefully left for dormitory addresses. The evacuation was beginning.

"Did they fire you?"

"No. Not at all. They never had the votes on the board to fire me. It would have destroyed the congregation. Half the membership would have bolted, and the other half wouldn't have been able to find a rabbi to replace me after a fight like that. Congregations that fire rabbis get a reputation that lasts for a decade. They knew that."

"So why are you leaving?"

"I'm not leaving, Jack. I'm doing what I'm supposed to do. These people don't really need me. They'll get some young rabbi who's a better fit for them. But the Jews of Vilnius need me. I've handed over my life to other people, Jack. I sacrificed my life to the Nazis. I sacrificed my young manhood to the leather barons of Costa Rica. I sacrificed my adulthood to my boys and to this congregation. So, now my boys don't really need me anymore, the congregation doesn't need me, and I can become who I want to become. When I was twelve years old it was a dream to go to Vilna. After forty years of sacrificing every dream I had for myself, I'm going to Vilna. Only now, I'm not a yeshiva boy. I'm going to be the Chief Rabbi of Lithuania. God has a wonderful sense of humor. He's laughing at his little joke on me."

"I have a question for you."

"Yes?"

"Do you pray?"

"Jack, you always surprise me. Your ignorance knows no bounds. What the hell kind of a question is that? You see me up on the bimah. I lead services at least twice a week. I led the services at your shivah. Were you sleeping while I was doing all that? What kind of noodnik are you?"

"You missed it, you old goat. What you do in services is your damned job. You lead prayers because people pay you to do it. It's your profession. That's not praying, Isaac, that's work. You work for a living. You have all my sympathy. Now answer my question. Do you pray? Do you have a relationship with God? Do you talk to Him? Do you ask for answers? Do you demand explanations? Do you hold Him accountable for the injustices? Do you thank Him when things turn out right even when you didn't think they could? Do you beg Him to take away the pain and give you the strength to go on even when you'd rather die than take another breath? Do you pray to Him to heal you from the hurts that you know are never gonna go away? Do you beg Him to protect your children because you know that when they're out of your sight they're gonna get hurt and you can't protect them? Tell me. Do . . . you . . . pray?"

Isaac smiled. And then he laughed. And he doubled over in laughter.

"You really are a shtoonk. You know? I have a present for you. Don't ask. Just take it. Where I'm going, I can get another easily." He opened the door to the coat closet and reached up on the shelf. From there he took down his Persian lamb hat and placed it on Jack's head. "Now, my friend, you can take walks in Southmoor and taunt the police."

Jack laughed. "What'll I do without you? OK, old man. If you're ever in Chicago, look me up."

The two embraced. It was not the embrace of two bodies let at ease in one another's arms. It was the embrace of men who do not embrace. It was the touch of men who are afraid to touch. It was stiff and formal and there was no skin contact.

Jack straightened the Cossack hat on his head and headed out the door. As he walked, he bobbed from side to side, a pendulum in full swing. His hands exited his pockets to stab at the night in argument and animated disputation. He gestured aggressively to no one. He was in conversation. He was alone. His voice rose and fell, mumbled and mused more and more as words came faster and louder and hands jabbed and poked at no one in particular. He was audible. He was vocal. He was not to be idly dismissed. He spoke to no one visible.

AFTERWORD

They're real, of course. Isaac is real. Jack is real. Dunphy, Rae, Myron, Rhonda, Leyla, Simmy, Lee, Dinah, Joe, Levi, Sage, Phil Dorfman, Sasha, Cady - they're as real as you and me. Their lives are real. The incidents are real. The streets and the houses and the community - all real. These are their stories. Accurate in every detail? Of course not. There is no reality that's absolute, no story that's true. It's all interpretation, manipulation, emphasis, cadence. dIt's fiction. It's a story. And sometimes, all that we have to keep us sane in an insane world is our stories. So, we live in the stories.

ACKNOWLEDEMENTS

The Ethics of the Fathers [Pirke Avot] instruct "Provide for yourself a teacher and get yourself a friend; and judge every man towards merit." I am grateful to those from whom I have learned, to those who have been my friends, and to those who judge every person on their merit. Thanks to Isaac, my teacher and my friend of blessed memory. He judged every person on their merit. More thanks as well to Jessica Christie and to Joseph ben Ari McMahon from whom I have learned so much about telling a story to a reader. Even more to Henya bat Zvi Hersh v. Rivkah, the seventh-grade teacher who has earned a P.H.D, Proponent of Hebrew Discourse and my ever-present muse.

ABOUT THE AUTHOR

A thousand years ago the Emperor Charlemagne invited the Kalonymos dynasty to move from their home in Lucca, Italy, to Mainz in Germany. They arrived in Germany and founded houses of study where they taught lessons of ethics and piety to generations of scholars. Today the voice of the Kalonymides returns in story. Jeffrey Salloway, a descendant, lives in northern New England with his Newfoundland dog, between the forests and the sea. He has taught in universities for half a century. His stories continue to describe humankind's struggle to find mission and meaning in everyday life.